# LAST NIGHT WAS KILLER

A NOVEL

MARY PAULINE LOWRY

wm
WILLIAM MORROW
*An Imprint of* HarperCollins*Publishers*

HarperCollins books may be purchased for educational, business, or sales promotional use. For information, please email the Special Markets Department at SPsales@harpercollins.com.

hc.com

FIRST EDITION

Designed by Michele Cameron

Library of Congress Cataloging-in-Publication Data has been applied for.

ISBN 978-0-06-345111-7

26 27 28 29 30 LBC 5 4 3 2 1

For George

This is just as hard as anything I've ever learned.

*—Jennifer Lopez on learning to pole dance for her role in the movie* Hustlers

There is so much freedom in pole. The second my feet come off the ground, I'm in another world.

*—Jenyne Butterfly, pole artist*

# LAST NIGHT WAS KILLER

# ONE

*Monday, Presidents' Day*

A hangover is like childbirth. When it's happening, it's so miserable you think you'll never forget. But later, inevitably, you do. At least that was what I told myself as I took a long glug out of a bottle of OJ in the snack aisle of the Boise Co-op while my seven-year-old twins stared at me with wide, identical eyes.

"Grocery store snacking is usually not okay, but today it is," I said hoarsely, opening a bag of Pirate's Booty, hoping the distraction of food would erase their suspicions about my uncombed hair, the circles under my eyes. I handed the bag to Alice. She cradled it like a baby she was about to lay away in a manger, but Phoebe greedily plunged in a hand and started munching.

"Can we get a puppy?" Phoebe asked, sensing maternal weakness.

"A puppy would tip me over the edge," I said.

The truth: I had already tipped.

As a single mom, I always ended up paying for the rare night out—thus I hadn't even darkened the doors of a happy hour in months. But this level of grogginess and suffering seemed excessive. I steered toward checkout, swerving the cart to avoid the lane with the checker I recognized from my seventh-grade gym class. (I couldn't remember his name but could totally picture his pimply adolescent self in polyester volleyball shorts). For a split second I couldn't wait to tell my mom how I'd successfully avoided a Stop-and-Chat. And then, for the thousandth time, I had the gut-punch realization I'd never tell her anything again.

Now as I swiped my credit card, I noticed I'd somehow broken a fingernail. My eyes watery, head on the verge of imploding, I wondered: What the hell was in those drinks? They were a black hole that had swallowed hours of my life.

As Alice and Phoebe argued about what they'd name our new imaginary puppy, I silently swore I'd never again surrender to peer pressure from the members of my new pole dancing class. While I'd initially had a better time than expected, I couldn't go through *this* again.

The girls trailed behind as I pushed our cart through the parking lot. The sky, the snow, the leafless trees, all the color of concrete. The last nine months in Boise had been a blur of misery and grief. How I missed Los Angeles. The sunshine, my hilarious pals, the sense that I was at the center of the comedy world instead of stuck in some remote outpost of civilization.

With the twins buckled into their booster seats, I headed to the trunk to load groceries. That's when a familiar voice called out.

"Tilly! Tilly!"

When I turned, Layna had appeared beside me. "So good to see you!" she cried. "Last night was killer! Did you have so much fun?"

"Yeah," I admitted. "I mean, I feel like death now. But it was fun."

That's when I popped my trunk.

Layna and I screamed. She stumbled backward into my grocery cart. But I couldn't look away from the man crammed inside.

His skin was blueish gray with a waxy sheen. An egg-sized lump bulged from his forehead. Scratch marks raked his face. His belt hung unbuckled, pants undone. A tattooed string of numbers crawled across his neck. A pair of scissors lay beside him, yawning blades bloody.

But it was his frozen, gaping hole of a mouth that made clear—he'd never move again.

# TWO

*The Day Before*

Pole Kisses Aerial Arts Studio didn't look like much from the strip-mall parking lot. But inside, the bright space showcased aerial silks and gleaming hardwoods. The woman behind the front desk wore a faux college sweatshirt that said *KALE* instead of *YALE*. For an illogical moment, I felt embarrassed to tell her why I was there.

Maybe it wasn't too late to bail. I could zip over to the Flying M and experience the impossible luxury of drinking a latte, uninterrupted. Afterward, I'd go home and lie cheerfully to Emmylou, my seventy-four-year-old duplex neighbor, who'd gifted me this Intro to Pole Dancing series along with requisite free twin babysitting on Tuesday, Thursday, and Sunday nights. I hadn't had the heart to tell her I'd rather clean a litter box than try to pole dance. And I was expected to go three times a week!

But I couldn't even claim to be too busy. Because of a state budget crisis, I'd been furloughed for three weeks from my job as an assistant manager at the Capitol Grill, a windowless underground café attached to the state capitol building where doodoo state legislators went for soggy burgers between their efforts to permanently outlaw drag queens, reproductive rights, or books featuring either of the two.

Besides, Emmylou said, the owner of the pole dancing studio believed frequent classes were necessary to "create a transformation." But did I really *want* to be transformed by an establishment called Pole Kisses? I didn't worry the classes would be strip-club unsavory. I worried they'd be suburban-mom-feeling-her-strip-club-fantasy unsavory. Which was infinitely worse.

But if I went to a coffee shop, I'd end up watching clips of stand-up comedians on Instagram. Comedians who—unlike me—were still following their dreams in New York and LA.

Just thinking about it made me hate myself.

"I'm here for Intro to Pole?" I said.

"Pole Virgins."

"What?"

"We don't call the series Intro to Pole," the woman explained. "We call it Pole Virgins. After you complete the series, you'll be a Pole Kitten."

"Meow?" I managed.

"Don't worry. I'll explain all about pole names later. I'm Salma," she said. "Salma Hayek." Which was surreal given that an aughts Salma Hayek was her celebrity doppelgänger. She shepherded me into the "chill room," where students hung out until class started. As I stuffed my puffy coat into a cubby, a fellow Pole Virgin popped up beside me.

"Hi! I'm Layna!" she chirped. "My soon-to-be ex-husband is a douchebag. That's why I'm here. This is my first class!" Her face was candid and cheerful, her dark hair in a bouncy ponytail. She looked like she was in her late thirties and owned a label maker and a TJ Maxx/HomeGoods credit card.

"I'm Tilly," I said. "Tell me more."

"A couple months after our daughter left for college I found out the douchebag was cheating. Now I'm going through the Big D. Divorce. So I gotta do something just for me, you know?"

Since my mom died, I'd been trying to pretend I was fine. But this woman clearly had no such impulse.

"I'm so sorry you're going through it," I said. "But as my septuagenarian babysitter said right before I left for class, 'Hopefully you'll be body rolling up on a tasty young personal trainer in no time.'" Had I made a joke? How long had it been?

Layna plunked down on the couch and hugged a pillow that read: *Bitch, don't kill my vibe.* "Why'd you decide to come?" she asked, as if the decision to take a pole dancing class was as significant as getting a divorce, running for public office, or having a kid.

"I've been told I need a hobby," I said. "I tried scrapbooking, but it filled me with existential despair." It was true. All my scrapbooking stuff was in my trunk, waiting to be dumped at Goodwill.

"I used to scrapbook," Layna said. "Now I have fifteen perfectly crafted books full of photos of me and my husband and our daughter at Disney. Only now I don't want to look at them because the douchebag probably had a threesome with Moana and Jasmine. So don't give me that hobby stuff. This is a safe space."

Friendship begins the moment one person overshares and the other person responds in kind. But I had too much misfortune to unload in a soundbite.

"I'm here because I'm in a slump," I said. "I make my kids' lunches on Sunday night. Ten turkey sandwiches. And I freeze them. And I send them to lunch with blocks of ice that are probably only half-thawed by lunchtime." In truth, I'd only sent the twins to school with freezer sandwiches for a week, and as soon as they grumbled, I put money in the Therapy Jar. (I tossed a bill in anytime I had a major Mom Fail, so the twins would have a head start on paying for counseling.) But still, the sandwich anecdote gave a good snapshot of my mental state.

Layna made that little *mmmmh* sound people make in church or at poetry readings. "Packing school lunches," she said, "is a goddamn beatdown."

I realized I liked her. A lot.

"And on that note," Salma Hayek called from the doorway. She'd shucked her sweatpants to reveal what looked like leopard-print bikini bottoms. "It's time for class."

# THREE

*Monday, Presidents' Day*

Now my teeth chattered convulsively and my hands shook as I stared down at the man crammed into my trunk. Was he dead? He was still as a mannequin, his open mouth forever paused at the end of a death rattle. I reached out and touched the back of his hand. Ice cold. Time slowed to the pace of the numbers creeping across his neck in black ink. They read: *23/16*. I'd seen that tattoo before. I'd seen this man before. Last night.

"Jesus Christ," Layna said. "Jesus fucking Christ. What—? What the—?" She started making strange noises, like maybe she was hyperventilating.

"He's dead," I said. I must've been in shock because I'd picked up my scrapbooking scissors, the blood on their long sharp blades dried to a rusty maroon. My last name was on the handle in my mother's handwriting. She'd always been obsessive about labeling things, maybe because she couldn't afford to replace anything lost.

The sound of Layna slamming the trunk shut made me startle. The scissors clattered to the asphalt, skittering to the middle of the parking lot.

A Boise Co-op cashier with a severe black bob and huge hot-pink feather earrings appeared from behind the dumpster, where all the employees went for smoke breaks. While I watched, helpless and immobile except for my clattering teeth, she scooped up the scissors, using her green apron to hold the edge of the handles.

"The Satanists must've killed another goose out here," the cashier muttered. "Assholes."

The sliding glass doors of the co-op swallowed her up.

"Oh no! Oh no no!" I cried. "Those are my scrapbooking scissors! They have my fingerprints on them. And—" I couldn't squeeze out the words: *And the dead guy's blood. And my last name.*

My knees wobbled. I was a split second from collapsing onto the icy asphalt when the Impala's back door swung open. "Mom! Mom! What is it?" Phoebe called.

More adrenaline shot through me and I went into Mom Mode. "There's a spider in the trunk," I said. Spiders were my go-to for anything that scared me that I didn't want the twins to know about. Boise was absolutely made of spiders. "Close the door, honey. You'll let the cold in."

The car door clicked reluctantly shut, but the twins' round faces popped up in the back window.

Layna gasped. "They're straight out of *The Shining*."

"Smile and wave," I hissed. "They can't know there's something wrong."

Layna plastered on a smile and waved dutifully.

I couldn't make sense of it. Layna from my pole dancing class, here beside me in this parking lot. A dead man in my trunk. "What are you doing here?" I said.

"I was gonna grocery shop!" Layna said. "How. Did that guy. End up—?" She covered her face with her shaking hands, unable to go on.

"If I knew, you think I'd open it here? In the co-op parking lot?" My voice was coming out falsetto. Nothing made sense. "It's him. The creep. From . . . from Huckleberry's." My fingernails had made the scratch marks across his face.

"Tilly," she said, "this is in my no-fly zone."

"What do you mean, *your* no-fly zone? It's in everyone's no-fly zone," I cried. "It's a corpse!"

"But how did he *get* there?"

"I don't know!" I said. "I don't remember anything after like the third round of drinks." An unsettling stretch of time, wiped from memory. Could I have been—? I didn't want to let myself even think the terrible word. *Roofied.*

"Tilly," Layna said. "Tilly, my friend. This is not good."

"Do you think it could've been an accident?" I said.

"There's . . . there's blood. And bloody scissors. And it looks like someone maybe whacked him in the head," she said.

I felt like I was crawling around in a pitch-black cave, searching and searching for a dropped flashlight. "My car. My car was parked behind Huckleberry's. All night." Emmylou had driven me and the girls there this morning to retrieve it. Then I'd come straight to the co-op to restock my bare cupboards. "My keys. I left them at the strip club. Today I had to use my spare set."

"Keys?" Layna said. "Who cares about your keys?"

"Someone else could've opened my trunk. Stuffed him right in there." A niggling fear had lodged under my skin like a gangrenous splinter. But I had too much adrenaline to really feel it. The back doors of the Impala swung open in unison.

"Mom! Mom! Mom! We're booooored." That was Alice.

Phoebe chimed in. "Mom! Mom! Mom! Let's go!"

"Hang on!" I yelled. "I'm talking to my friend. Close those doors. You'll freeze!"

"Oh, hon," Layna said. "This is a lot. A lot. A lot. A lot. And with two little kids . . ." She looked at me with real pity. Something in her gaze reminded me of my mom, who'd always been there to provide solace and advice whenever life did me dirty. A tidal wave of sadness and overwhelm crashed over me.

"I was the one who chose to have kids on my own," I said. "I wanted it so badly. But I had my mom to help me. With my mom, I could get through anything." I took a hitching breath. "She died. Ten months ago."

Hot tears cut down my cheeks. The inside of my skull hurt so badly.

I would have given anything to climb back in bed, pull the covers over my head, and wake up yesterday morning. I wouldn't go to pole class and none of this would have ever happened.

Layna drummed purple Gel-X talons on the top of the trunk. When she spoke, I knew she'd decided to believe me. "So what do you do now?"

My mom always taught me that when overwhelmed, it's important to do the Next Right Thing, which is usually something small like taking a shower, making the bed, or chopping vegetables. Her theory was that if you take care of the little things, the big things will often take care of themselves. Suddenly I knew what my Next Right Thing was.

"That co-op cashier was carrying those scissors like a true crime fanatic," I said. "I need to go inside and get them back. Right. Now."

# FOUR

*The Day Before*

"Grab your pole up high with your inside arm, keeping your elbow straight. Now walk around the pole. You can point your toes and be sexy! You can stomp angrily. You can prance!" Salma Hayek cried.

I'd migrated to the pole studio with the others, staked out my bit of chrome, and participated in a series of warm-up exercises that'd reaffirmed my concerns about my basic lack of fitness. Now class had begun in earnest, and we were learning pole dancing's most fundamental move—the pole walk.

Salma Hayek hadn't gotten the memo that for most people, teaching a class half-naked would be a literal nightmare. Then again, if my buns looked like hers, I wouldn't ever wear pants. While I didn't have it in me to try to be sexy, I could definitely stomp angrily around my pole—which spun! Who knew poles spin?

I made eye contact with Layna, who pranced like a giggly reindeer. My usual friend type was "hipster artist from Westside LA who ferments her own pickles and has gallery shows." Layna definitely didn't fit that description. But we clearly had friend chemistry, which was more than I'd expected to find at pole dancing class.

"And remember," Salma Hayek said, "there's no need to compare yourself to anyone else in this room. Everyone is on their own pole journey."

*Give me a break*, I wanted to say. The journey was spinning around and around in a tiny circle, going nowhere. But at least pole walk time gave me a chance to survey the four other students.

Layna, of course, looking ripped in yoga shorts. She was somehow both stocky and lean, her ponytail bouncing jauntily with each exaggerated step.

A curvy girl in green velour pole undies and a cropped Wet Leg shirt, short hair dyed a silvery blue and shaved on one side, her face studded with colorful pimple stickers shaped like stars.

A slender woman in her fifties with thick black hair wearing a cherry-red two-piece with extra straps under her buns.

And a lone guy—tall, muscular, handsome as a young Idris Elba—with hair in long twists and a fade who clearly took his pole walk very seriously. His face was a mask of intense concentration, like a woman on a high-dose of SSRIs trying to orgasm.

When Salma Hayek had us pause for a water break, I stripped down to my T-shirt and a pair of running shorts. I caught a glimpse of myself in the side wall of mirrors and my brain did its usual critical rundown. My shoulder-length dirty-blond hair was three months past needing highlights and two days past needing a wash. Grief had drawn dark circles under my eyes and parentheses framed my mouth. But, I noted with satisfaction, my arms were strong from hauling groceries and I still had my mom's great legs.

When I turned back around, the slender woman with jet-black hair had shimmied up her pole, like a shapeshifter that transforms from nondescript middle-aged lady to weightless, comic-book assassin.

*I want to be able to do that!*

The hopeful thought surprised me. It was not the thought of a woman so depressed her main source of pleasure was staying up late to binge Chunky Monkey while watching a reality show about lone survivalists eating rancid seal fat in order to outlast each other in the Yukon.

"Get out of here! This is a Pole Virgins class," Salma Hayek called up. "Just kidding, y'all! Zhang Xiu is coming back from an injury, so she's retaking the intro series."

Zhang Xiu had a giant tattoo of a dragon covering her entire calf.

As she slid back down to the floor, the sound of her inner thighs against chrome echoed with a *squeeeeeak*.

"It's time for body rolls!" Salma Hayek cried. "Duck your head under an imaginary wire. Bring your face to the pole. Next your chest. Stomach! Hips! Knees! Now *pop* your booty back down."

Her body roll looked like a ribbon of silk.

My attempt was as jerky and spastic as a short-circuiting C-3PO.

"I'm giving more Chris Farley than Shakira," I said, louder than intended. Everyone in the class laughed. Hard. For the first time in a year, I'd made somebody (other than the twins) chortle.

After Salma taught us the L-sit, the class ended with a free dance to "Be My Baby" by the Ronettes. As I practiced my new moves, I let myself feel the fantasy. The pole sit required me to grab the chrome with both hands and *squeeze* it between my thighs while my legs stuck straight out in front of me, ankles crossed, hips tilted hard to one side. This was agony on my inner thighs, but I was doing it. I was flying around a chrome pole, hair streaming behind me as I belted out, "Be my baby now-ow-ow! A whoa oh oh oh oh!" And damn, it was fun. Life could be so cruel. So mean. But there could also be these unexpected glimmers of exhilaration, of joy.

During our cool-down stretches, we all did exuberant, sweaty downward dogs.

"Pretend your buttholes are flashlights and point them up to the sky!" Salma Hayek chirped.

There was something festive about the juxtaposition of the sexy moves with the intentionally unsexy metaphors of the body. And while I regularly carted my kids to art and gymnastics and violin lessons, it had been years since I learned something entirely new for no practical reason whatsoever.

"This week I want you all to decide on a pole name. Out there, I'm Lupe, stressed-out CPA. But in here? I'm Salma Hayek, inspiring pole instructor. I want each of you to have a pole persona that provides that escape. You get me?"

Out there, I was Tilly Turner. Forty-four years old. Motherless mother of twins. Failed comic who couldn't find it in herself to crack a joke. But here at Pole Kisses, I could be anyone.

"I'm heading to Huckleberry's for a drink after class," Salma Hayek continued. "Anyone want to come see how the pros do it?"

The Pole Virgins responded with a volley of "Hell yeah"s.

"I've got room if anyone needs a ride," Zhang Xiu said.

"Where's your motorcycle?" Salma Hayek asked.

"In the shop. My daughter loaned me her new Rivian."

"Baller!" Salma said.

"Girl knows how to spend that Allergan money," Zhang Xiu agreed. "She makes a fortune working at that place. Everyone wants a minimally invasive glow-up these days."

No way was I going to a strip club. So while the other students slowly wiped down their poles with a cloth and a spritz of alcohol, I gave mine a quick clean and scuttled to the waiting room where I prepared to slip out into the early evening. But a little sign over the shoe cubbies distracted me.

> Dearest Pole Hobbyists!
>
> Don't forget: The art of pole dancing was developed by strippers. Here at Pole Kisses Studio, many of us largely practice "pole sport." But we do not consider pole sport to be superior to—or necessarily separate from—stripper pole dancing! We count among our beloved instructors sex workers who bring their professionalism and knowledge to their classes. We respect and are grateful to them for creating this art form and for paving our way in pole!
>
> Love,
> Your Friends at Pole Kisses

This put the group trip to the strip club in context. It was like a bunch of Christians walking the Camino de Santiago to pay their respects to the apostle James.

"Come out with us," Layna cried, as she burst into the chill room. "Please!"

"I have needy kids to tend." Lately that'd involved letting the twins play endless games of "Dinosaurs versus Baby Dolls" while I hid in my office (aka the pantry) to cry in secret while eating Nutter Butters.

"Can't your husband watch them? Or better yet, do you have an Xbox? If you've got an Xbox, you've got a babysitter." Layna leaned in toward a little vanity mirror to apply lipstick so red Rihanna's pout now seemed understated.

"I don't have a husband. Or an Xbox." I pulled on my coat, a depressing L.L.Bean puffer I'd bought used at the Idaho Youth Ranch thrift store. Something about Layna's inappropriate disclosures made me feel comfortable being open with her. "My babies are from the sperm of an eighteen-year-old donor I've never met."

"Attagirl!" she said.

"I figured I needed to go young to counteract my dusty eggs."

"See? You're so funny! Just come have a drink with us."

The warm golden flutter in my stomach that said *This woman could be your actual friend* wouldn't let me say no.

My neighbor Emmylou answered on the first ring. When my mother was alive, Emmylou had been *her* bestie. I'd loved Emmylou's stories about her long-ago divorce in Mormon country, back when she'd bought a crossbow in the hopes she could turn her "no-good cheating husband" into a "man-sized Hollywood voodoo doll." But now my mom was gone. I'd never again sit next to her watching old George Carlin videos and eating popcorn dusted with nutritional yeast and Tapatío. Meanwhile, Emmylou was trying with all her bossy might to shove me out of my grief rut.

"I knew you'd love it!" Emmylou crowed when I asked if it was okay if I went out for a drink with people from my class. "The twins and I are baking lemon crinkle cookies. Go have fun with your new friends."

Phoebe shouted in the background, "Mommy, Emmylou said she's paying for classes so you can learn to grind up on a pool boy."

"We're getting a poooooool!" Alice shrieked.

"We're not getting a—" I started.

But Emmylou interrupted. "Stay out as late as you want—hopefully late enough to realize that even during hard times you can have some fun."

# FIVE

*Monday, Presidents' Day*

Trying to have a lighthearted night out during an epic rough patch had somehow resulted in this—me, disturbingly hungover, with a dead man in my trunk, dragging my daughters back into the Boise Co-op to reclaim my bloody scrapbooking scissors. I figured the twins would make me look less suspicious. The cashier with the hot-pink feather earrings stood behind the customer service desk.

"Hello!" I said, brightly.

"Twins!" She leaned over the counter toward my girls. "Does it freak you out to think you were once a single cluster of cells that split into two? Because it freaks me out!"

What was freaking the twins out was this line of questioning.

"It's all they know," I explained, as Phoebe and Alice hurried away to investigate bags of snowman noses (aka carrots) next to a towering display of Annie's Organic Green Goddess Salad Dressing.

"All bats know is sleeping upside down, but that doesn't make it less weird," the cashier insisted. "Twins have given me nightmares ever since—"

I interrupted. "Actually, I'm here because out in the parking lot, I dropped my—"

*CRASH!*

Phoebe lay sprawled in a pile of salad dressing bottles, glass fragments and oily green puddles all around her.

Once I finally had her upright and no longer crying and a clerk had arrived to mop up the mess, I spun back to the customer service desk—where the cashier with the hot-pink feather earrings was talking to a uniformed police officer with a Tom Selleck mustache. He held out a big clear evidence bag. The smug cashier dropped the scissors inside, a look of pure crime-fighting satisfaction on her face.

I hurried the twins to the nearby pastry case, too focused on eavesdropping to stop them from opening the glass doors and pawing the donuts.

"See the dried blood? And there's a name, right there on the handle," the cashier was saying with the eagerness of Elle Woods during her first week at Harvard Law. "*Turner.* Nobody ever said the Satanists were the sharpest crayons in the box. You can get forensics to dust for prints. See if they match with anyone in your database."

"Thanks for the advice. So helpful," the cop said dryly. He nestled the evidence bag in his shopping basket and headed toward the supplements.

"We're moving," I told the twins. But as I turned to follow the police officer, a woman stepped in front of me. Despite the changes rendered by twenty-five years (and plenty of tweakments), I recognized Miranda Carson instantly. She had the same icy blue eyes, but her hair was an even more fiery shade of red, and her skin looked poreless and smooth, like she'd been airbrushed (or, more likely, relentlessly lasered). She must've made a deal with the devil, or the best med spa in the Treasure Valley.

"Tilly! Tilly Turner!" she cried. "It's been too long."

No, no, no! I had to get those scissors back—I did not have time for a catch-up chat with my high school nemesis. Back when I was Mr. Potato Pants, the North Boise High School mascot, I'd suffered Miranda Carson's condescending presence as alpha cheerleader at pep rally practices our sophomore and junior years. She'd been Boise High royalty, while I'd been an oversized anonymous potato with googly eyes. But the truth was, I'd loved being Mr. Potato Pants.

Then, at cheerleading camp the summer before our senior year,

Miranda Carson and her drunk buddies triggered a cabin search. Coach Nichols discovered a mostly empty bottle of vodka in my duffel bag. Even though I was sober and everyone knew the vodka belonged to the girl our high school class had voted Most Likely to Get Her Way, I was defrocked of my Mr. Potato Pants costume while Miranda was promoted to head cheerleader.

"Miranda," I said now, watching the cop disappear down the aisle dedicated to supplements geared to support the flagging male libido.

"So good to see you!" Miranda cried. My mother—who'd held a grudge on my behalf—had reported karma had yet to come for Miranda. Not only did she still look thirty-two, she was married to a Micron exec, worked as a social worker for Child Protective Services, and lived in a mansion on Warm Springs Road. She'd never had kids, which made sense. Someone so selfish shouldn't procreate. Now Miranda bent down to be eye level with the twins. "And who are these perfect dumplings?"

Not only was Alice covered in dressing, both twins looked generally feral and ill-tended. They'd taken to heart my earlier edict that in-store snacking was okay—rainbow sprinkles coated Alice's face, while Phoebe was tucking into a maple bar.

"Any advice on how to tell you two apart?" Miranda cooed. I barely resisted the urge to kick her in her perfectly bleached teeth.

"I have a birthmark on my back," Phoebe said. "It's shaped like Florida."

"Mommy says it's an all-natural Florida tramp stamp," Alice added, helpfully.

"Haha! She's kidding," I said. "I don't really say that."

Miranda laughed gamely. "You have *always* been so funny." She batted the air with her hand to show off her pumpkin-colored manicure. "So many people said you'd never make it in Los Angeles," she continued. "But I always said, 'No, that Tilly Turner is so funny.'"

"Hmm," I managed. My abs tensed involuntarily for the gut punch I knew was coming.

"Such a shame how things turned out," Miranda continued. "Who would've guessed Mickey Larynx was an *actual* pervert?" There was the Miranda I remembered. Before I could interject, she was on to another sensitive subject. "And I'm so sorry about your mother. She was always so proud of you for making your way in LA, all on your own."

My eyes smarted and I vowed not to cry in front of Miranda. I could only imagine what she'd say if she knew I'd never been able to make ends meet on the Best Coast, not after the girls were born. No matter how many waitressing shifts I'd worked at Italian Kitchen on Ocean Park Boulevard, I'd never had enough money. Whenever I got a check in the mail from my mom, I'd always call her to say, "You didn't have to do that, we're fine." But I always cashed the checks. There is a particular shame in finding out after your favorite person dies that she was impoverishing herself to support you.

"I'm sure my mom will want to give you her condolences too—she's around here somewhere," Miranda said.

Back when Miranda and I were in high school, Mrs. Carson had a pet parrot with clipped wings that rode on her shoulder and squawked "You're so pretty!" into her ear all day. She'd seemed to enjoy negging me about not being "cheerleader material" and gave me copious "helpful" tips on how to "liven up" my Mr. Potato Pants dance.

"She called this morning to see if I'd take her shopping," Miranda explained. She leaned in to whisper, as if we really were old friends. "She can do it herself, but she likes the attention. Today I didn't think I had it in me." For a half second, I almost liked her.

Now, like a demon summoned by the sound of its own name, Miranda's mother appeared from behind a display of croutons. This could not get any worse. A glance to my left revealed the cop lining up at the register. I'd have to approach him in the parking lot.

"Mom, it's Tilly Turner," Miranda said. "She's back from California."

Mrs. Carson, who was probably in her late sixties, wore a fancy cashmere cape and blond hair upswept in a French twist.

"California!" she cried. "The land of fruits and nuts!"

"Mother!" Miranda stage-whispered. "You can't say fruits! Or nuts!"

"Nonsense!" Mrs. Carson said. "Next thing you'll tell me I can't say Merry Christmas!"

The cop was no longer in the checkout line.

"I just remembered I forgot to unplug my air fryer! Gotta go!" Waving goodbye at evil Miranda and her awful mother, I herded the twins out of the co-op in time to see the police cruiser rolling out onto Ninth Street.

When Layna spotted me empty-handed, sugar-coated twins trailing behind me, she raised her hands to the sky in a what-the-hell gesture. I mimed that we needed to stay quiet until the kids were in the car.

With the Impala doors finally closed, I said, "The cashier was already handing the scissors over. To a cop! He's taking them in as evidence."

"Yeesh," she said. "So what are you gonna do?" She sounded sympathetic and alert, and for a moment I let myself hope she was my very own Olivia Pope, ready to help me fix this shocking problem.

How was I supposed to know what to do? If only my mom was alive. She could have helped me figure this out. Right now nothing seemed real except the cold, which had my teeth chattering again. "Find a babysitter, drive up to Idaho City, dump the body in the woods, and hope for the best?" I said. It didn't sound great.

"That might work," Layna said. "I mean, Turner is a common name. Thank god you don't have a record."

"Well, I've never been *convicted* of anything. But I've sure been arrested and fingerprinted." When I was nineteen and home from college for spring break, the state legislature had voted on a bill to restrict abortion access. I may have thrown a couple eggplants. I may have squirted sunscreen from the balcony of the senate gallery while shouting: "Ejaculate responsibly!"

I've always believed comedy could change the world.

But the senators were not amused.

Charges were eventually dropped. But after that I'd kept my comedy out of the Idaho State Capitol.

"That is not good." Layna leaned against the trunk of my Impala as if there wasn't a corpse inside.

Freefalling down an elevator shaft would feel exactly like this. Could I be having the worst nightmare ever? A car drove past the dumpster, a little too fast. Layna barely sidestepped the spray, but the very real slush hit the calves of my jeans and soaked through to my skin. Nope. I was definitely awake.

"I need to go to the police," I said. "Like right now. Right? I can't remember anything after the bouncer threw that creep out of Huckleberry's."

"Hold tight. Let's think this through. You left with Shade. It was pretty early. Like maybe nine thirty."

"I left? With Shade?" The lone guy from our pole class with the sassy attitude and luminous skin. "That's amazing news! I need to talk to him! Did you get his number? I could call him. What's Shade's name anyway? His real name?" The cocktail of panic and hope had me talking too fast.

"I'm sorry, babe," Layna said. "I have no idea."

"Okay, okay," I said, trying hard to think clearly. What was my Next Right Thing? "I think before I call the cops, I ought to look in the dead guy's wallet, maybe even his phone. See if there are any clues." Hopefully the clues would point to a murderer who was definitively not me.

Layna gave a rapid-fire nod. "Yes, yes. Makes sense. You'll be in a way better position if there's another suspect."

"This is a nightmare," I groaned. "A literal waking nightmare. I'm never going to a strip club again."

# SIX

*The Day Before*

In the curtained entryway of the strip joint, a massive bearded bald man in a shiny lavender suit perched on a corner stool, immobile as a baseball bat and just as ready to be deployed in case of emergency. A woman in a microscopic minidress made of sequins the size of quarters handed out pads of paper and pencils. "Welcome to Huckleberry's Art Night," she cooed.

"Art night?" Layna said.

Salma explained Idaho state law forbids the sale of alcohol anywhere you could see nipples. However, Boise had passed a local ordinance that nudity with serious artistic merit was allowed. So "Art Night" was the workaround.

"You can practice drawing the female form," the hostess said with a wink. "Twenty bucks each, please."

I handed over the cash, guilty with the knowledge it should be spent on a jumbo box of Bagel Bites for my kids, not entrance to a low-budget nudie bar. Being furloughed meant everyday expenses would have to go on a credit card straining toward its limit.

Salma Hayek parted the velvet curtain, and we crossed the threshold from the plain, clothed world of Boise to the bare-bottomed, chintzy mise-en-scéne of booty floss and glittery platform shoes. The club was dark as sin with pops of purple LED strip lighting. As my eyes struggled to adjust, I stumbled on a carpeted step lost to the gloom.

Sunday nights probably usually weren't this packed, but tomorrow was Presidents' Day. Heavyset guys in trucker hats sat at the rails, ignoring their art pads. A gaggle of societal rejects—think waxed handlebar mustaches and paisley scarves—clustered at the end of the stage near a bunch of meatheads in *Unite the Right* T-shirts. The dancer onstage wore a silver thong and angel wings reminiscent of peak Victoria's Secret.

As we settled in at our little table, I made sure to sit with my back to the stage. I'm not a puritan. But I'd spotted my high school geometry teacher at the rail and would drown a kitten to avoid making eye contact.

The other Pole Virgins cheered at more advanced pole moves while Salma Hayek dropped wisdom like she was Mr. Miyagi and we were her five Karate Kids. I was relieved she was doing most of the talking—since I spent all my free time interacting with kiddos, my main conversational topic was whether or not My Little Ponies actually *liked* to swim in the toilet.

"Having a pole name helps you really lean into your sensual, strong side," Salma Hayek said. "The persona is a part of you that maybe you can't flaunt in the rest of your life. I want each of you to try a name on for size. See how it feels."

I sipped a Fly Line lager, because everything in Idaho is named after fly fishing. I wanted a cocktail, but at least with a beer, I'd be good to drive in an hour. Life as a single mom involves constant risk assessments. The plan, if I died tragically and unexpectedly, had been for my mom to take my kids. But it was my mom who had died tragically and unexpectedly of an aneurysm, and now there was no plan.

Zhang Xiu was explaining that while she'd first wanted her pole name to be Cupcake or Bubbles, she realized taking the name of a minor warlord of the Eastern Han dynasty would better suit her fierceness. Strands of silver streaked her jet-black hair. At first glance, I'd written her off as soft and uninteresting, the way I did sometimes with women in their fifties—probably because of internalized misogyny. But once she'd shot up the pole like a comic-book assassin, I knew better.

"I want my pole name to be I Don't Play I Slay," the lone guy said.

Did he slather himself in expensive serums every night or was that glowy skin a birthright? When assessing a twentysomething, it was tricky to tell nature from nurture.

"Is that a name?" I asked. "Or song lyrics by that one judge from *RuPaul's Drag Race*?"

"Throw shade for me. Shade for me, shade!" he sang, clearly pleased I'd gotten the old reference. He brought a finger to his lips. "I actually like that." He shifted to the enthusiastic demeanor of a trivia night emcee. "I. Am. Shade!"

Everyone cheered.

The girl with silvery-blue hair and bright star-shaped pimple stickers said her pole name would be Gucci. "First purse I'm buying when I'm no longer a broke grad student," she said.

I'd bet a Ben Franklin she was studying some obscure sub-branch of the humanities that would leave her with no real job prospects, but her hopefulness made me like her.

Salma Hayek offered to buy a round. "We'll have to come back some night when Cheyenne's dancing. She's a dream on the pole."

"Who's Cheyenne?" Shade said.

"The wifey bartender!" Salma said, pointing. "The real bartender is out sick. Cheyenne goes to noon open studio at Pole Kisses sometimes. Subs classes too! She just launched her own pole shoe company: Cheyenne's Sentient Strippers! I barely know her, but do you think it's too soon to propose?"

"Whoa, there, cowgirl!" Shade pulled on a set of pretend reins. "Maybe try talking to her first?"

Salma squared her shoulders and headed to the bar, the rest of us egging her on.

All I could see of Cheyenne was a pair of Maleficent-style horns perched atop bright pink hair and a slightly rodent-like face. It was hard to imagine what about her so dazzled the radiant Salma Hayek.

Gucci applauded wildly for a pole trick and hurried to the rail to tip the dancer. When she returned, she said, "I'm taking pole because I love strip clubs. You just have to bring your own Big Strip Club Energy with you. As soon as the dancers realize what I'm here for they start pulling out their best pole tricks."

A Miami ten in gold butt floss and matching thigh-high boots led the dorky guy with the paisley scarf into the VIP room.

"In the real world, that woman wouldn't give him a light," I said.

"What happens in the VIP room?" Layna asked.

Shade's eyes went wide. "What do you *think* happens in the VIP room?"

"Strip clubs do have a dark side, but there's light shining out of that darkness." Gucci had leaned in close so only I could hear her. She ran a hand through her blue hair, which looked purple under the LEDs. "That's the other reason I'm taking pole classes. To get in touch with my sexuality. In a positive way."

"Go on," I said. "I'm listening." My own grief had made me able to recognize it in others.

"My uncle. He was a bad guy. He did bad things. To me. When I was a kid."

"I'm so sorry," I said.

She shrugged. "He died of a heart attack. I was his next of kin. His only kin. So I donated him."

"Like to a medical school?" I imagined med students giggling over his corpse as it bobbed in a tank of formaldehyde. It seemed fitting.

"Better," Gucci said. "To forensics researchers. They left him out in a designated field and checked his decomp progress on the hour."

"Oh my god," I said, clapping my hand over my mouth. "You let him rot in a field?"

Gucci looked momentarily stricken. "I shouldn't have said anything. My boundaries are so porous."

"No. No, it's perfect. So rare. For someone to get exactly what they deserve. It's like you made your awful uncle do a selfless good deed. For science."

"Exactly!" Gucci said, her hand on my arm. "Thank you for not judging me."

"Judge you? You're incredible," I said.

"Honestly, learning about the decomp field, it's how I fell in love with—" Gucci didn't finish, because right then Salma Hayek rocked up to our table with a cluster of tequila shots and a pile of lime slices in the bend of her elbow.

"It's time to seal your bond as Pole Virgins," she said. "And to celebrate that I just got Cheyenne's number!"

Everyone grabbed a shot and lifted it to the heavens. "To Salma Hayek. Our fearless leader and a girl who has game!" Shade said. He paused, suddenly noticing one lonely shot still on the table.

Everyone looked at me.

"I hate tequila and I'm drinking mine," Zhang Xiu said.

"I've gotta drive home," I protested.

"You can Uber," Layna said.

"These shots are the equivalent of slicing our palms and mingling our blood," Shade said. "If you're sober—respect." He gestured at my beer. "But you're not sober."

"So much peer pressure!" I said. But it actually felt nice. When was the last time someone had wanted me to be a part of their group?

We downed the shots together, bit into lime slices, grimaced. My spirits lifted on the wings of alcohol. I'd forgotten how this worked. You had a shot, you felt better. You had another shot, you felt close to everyone around you. You became deeply convinced alcohol could never make you feel anything but more and more happy. More and more connected to others. More and more like your true self. Maybe alcohol *was* the solution to everything.

With a second tequila shot down my gullet, I couldn't understand why I didn't drink more often.

"You said you just moved here?" Layna asked.

Newly chatty, I told everyone I grew up in Boise, but had lived in Westside LA for twenty-five years. LA was my spiritual home, I said. Comedy my religion. "But as soon as I got my big break, my career imploded," I said. This was something I'd be loath to mention sober, but seemed imperative to share now.

"What do you mean?'" Layna said.

"You've heard of Mickey Larynx, right?" I said.

"Of course," Shade said. "He was one of my favorite comedians. With an emphasis on the *was*."

The others nodded solemnly.

"Who is he?" Layna demanded. "Sorry. Not a pop culture vulture."

It was rare to meet someone who hadn't heard the whole sordid story. "He is . . . well, he *was* a big deal in comedy. Asked me to open for him on a fifty-city tour." I'd heard the rumors about Mickey Larynx. But I'd waited so damn long for my time to shine, and I'd worked it all out. Me, my mom, the twins, we'd drive behind Mickey Larynx's giant tour van for three months while my mom homeschooled Phoebe and Alice. The first couple nights—Oakland, San Francisco—I had the audience rolling! On the third day of the tour, I got an email from a Netflix exec saying they were interested in having me do my own special—an unheard-of bit of good fortune for an unknown like me.

"Netflix!" Layna cried.

Shade heaved a great sigh. Gucci, Zhang Xiu, and Salma Hayek looked similarly mournful. Only Layna didn't know how this snakebit tale would end. I wanted so badly for it not to be my story.

"But then, the morning of the fourth day, I had all these alerts from *The New York Times*, the *Los Angeles Times*, *The Hollywood Reporter*. Mickey Larynx had been wanking it in hotel hot tubs full of unsuspecting people. The tour was canceled. Mickey Larynx was canceled. And I lost forty-seven cities' worth of pay."

I paused to take a fortifying gulp of beer.

"After he was busted?" I continued. "My manager never returned my calls. The Netflix execs definitely never returned my calls."

"Oh my god," Layna said. "What a disaster!"

I'd tried to bounce back professionally. But when I did my first show at Dynasty Typewriter, it seemed the whole audience had come to heckle me about being a Mickey Larynx enabler. Memes of the two girls in the front row with a handmade sign that read *WOMEN LIKE TILLY TURNER ARE THE REASON MEN LIKE MICKEY LARYNX GET AWAY WITH IT* haunted my nightmares—and all my social media pages—for months.

Then the worst thing ever happened: my mom died. Three weeks later, my appendix threatened to burst like a water balloon. Cue the emergency appendectomy to the tune of sixteen grand and a massive babysitting bill to boot. I'd assumed I could sell my mom's duplex to keep myself afloat. But an estate lawyer explained my mother had taken out three mortgages on the property. That's how she'd been able to send me all that cash over the years. The duplex was almost underwater. But paying those three mortgages every month would be way cheaper than my LA rent. That's when I just gave up. It was time to let go of my childish hopes and dreams. Time to finally grow the hell up.

"Then a duplex came available here in Boise," I said, skipping over the fact that it had belonged to my mom, because if I talked too much about her, I would cry.

Emmylou had known how desperate I was for health insurance. She'd helped me land a job as an assistant manager at the Capitol Grill, which provided a middling salary and amazing benefits. In a slow-motion collapse, I'd dragged everything that wouldn't fit into my minivan to the curb and drove the twins to Idaho.

Still, how to explain that being in Los Angeles had made me feel like

I was living my destiny? Los Angeles had blue skies, beaches, comedy clubs, and an understanding that if artists don't make their art, they are as good as dead in their souls. Back in my hometown, I felt diminished. In winter, an inversion capping the Treasure Valley kept the earth and sky the color of dirty snow, and my insides felt just as grayscale.

The whole table was staring at me with the sort of profound kindness that could make me burst into tears. Salma Hayek opened her mouth, but I held up my hand.

"Please, please don't say anything nice or I will lose it," I warned. I wiped my eyes on the sleeve of my sweatshirt and took another swig of beer. "Sorry to dump on y'all. I'm like: *Hi, I'm Tilly Turner. I'm dead inside.*"

"But your pole persona isn't dead," Salma insisted. "She's just being born. None of those bad things happened to her. She's all sassy and new. There's a fresh part of you, deep down, that can still enjoy things. That's what pole is all about."

I was just drunk enough to be swayed by the promise of a fresh start, even if it was just dancing badly around a pole with this bunch of friendly misfits.

"Ladies, I think pole is just what the doctor ordered for this cuckolded soon-to-be ex-wife." Layna thumped her chest. "I mean, there I was watching *The Real Housewives of Salt Lake City* on my iPad while I cooked the bastard beef stew. And guess what popped up on the screen? A very slutty text from my husband. To some other woman."

Shade made a horrified face and fanned himself. "What did you do?"

"The only thing I could do. I took all his clothes into the front yard. Suits. Ties. Designer sneakers. I doused it in his collection of rare scotch and set it all on fire."

Shade gave a low appreciative whistle. "Damn."

Layna's only daughter was off at college so she had room to go appropriately berserk. Moms with young kids at home could never really burn it all to the ground. There were always tears to be wiped, arguments to be brokered, lunches and Target runs to be made. But Layna would clearly rise from the ashes of a fire she set herself.

"Your pole name could be Phoenix," I said.

"You're a genius," Layna said. "I mean, really."

"Tilly, now you're the only one without a pole name," Salma Hayek said. It was stupid how seen this made me feel. Wonderfully, improbably, a Nina Simone song blasted from the speakers. It had undergone a techno remix, but miraculously had not been ruined by the refresh.

"*It's a new life for me*," Nina Simone sang. "*And I'm feeling good.*"

My tipsy mind skipped through associations. I'd first heard Simone's music when I'd watched *Point of No Return*. The main character, Maggie, was obsessed with Nina Simone. In the film, Maggie left her ruined life behind to become a female assassin. The movie was based on a French film, *La Femme Nikita*.

"Nikita," I said. "My pole name is Nikita."

I knew it with a certainty then—I was going to blow off some steam.

Up close, I could understand more of Cheyenne's appeal. The Maleficent horns suited her pointy little face and her fishnet top showed cleavage for days.

"Five vodka gimlets," I said, leaning against the bar.

Cheyenne slid the first drink my way. "You're with the Pole Virgins?"

I nodded and took a glug of the gimlet.

"When you're ready for pole shoes, you gotta buy some of mine. Cheyenne's Sentient Strippers."

"Okay," I said. "Will do."

"They're the best. I just gotta figure out the marketing piece."

"You will," I said. The alcohol made me believe it too.

"And in the club, don't be a woo girl," she said.

"What's a woo girl?" I asked.

"You know from that old episode? Of that sitcom? A woo girl takes up space at the rail yelling 'Woo' and not tipping for shit. When you ask if she wants a lap dance, she says, 'I respect what you do but I'm just here to drink.' Then she gets hammered and wants onstage to show off some shitty moves she just learned at her pole dancing class."

"I for sure am not going to do that," I said, and then, because I was tipsy, added, "Do you like it? Working here?"

"Being a Hucklebunny?" She seemed to consider it. "When I'm working the floor, I'm a therapist, a boundary setter, an athlete, a fantasy, a figment of my customers' imagination. It's hard." She shrugged. "But I keep a positive mindset. There's always money on the floor, and I know how to get it. But pole dancing? That's different. Emotional pain? It doesn't have a chance when I'm on the pole."

Cheyenne gestured toward a leggy dancer dangling upside down in full splits. The dancer made the impossible look effortless, her skin smooth and undimpled and gleaming in the purple LED lights.

Spinning in my beginner's L-sit, I had felt agonizing inner thigh pain, but also—for the first time in a year—elation. The oppressive despair of my everyday life floated to the floor. The grit and sadness had drifted away too, along with the overwhelm of being a single mom with not enough in the tank—or the bank.

"Other gals, at some other club, they might tell you different," Cheyenne said. "Consensual sex work ain't a monolith."

My brow furrowed at the thought of nonconsensual sex work.

"Don't look so surprised I know the word *monolith*," Cheyenne said, spinning away to grab a fresh bottle of Tito's.

"It's not that—" I called, but she was already out of hearing.

"I've never seen you here before."

I turned, half expecting someone from high school. But it was a stranger with a teal vest over his flannel—wiry, my height, weathered. Guys with neck tattoos who hung out in strip clubs were not usually my thing. But I was a little drunk and in a brutal dry spell, so what harm would it do to practice my flirting?

"This isn't my go-to watering hole," I said, stabbing at the ice in my drink with a tiny straw. Yikes. My conversational skills were not what they used to be.

Cheyenne set the second vodka gimlet down. She gave Mr. Neck Tattoo the side-eye instead of a hello. I dug around in my pocket, emptying out keys and lip gloss before finally laying cash on the bar.

"Can I tell you a secret?" Mr. Neck Tattoo said.

"I'm a literal vault," I replied.

"I come here to forget the one who got away. And her kid."

I tried to imagine stuffing dollar bills into a stranger's G-string to obliterate the memory of lost love. What even was the female equivalent? Eating a pint of cookie dough ice cream while watching *Normal People* for the eighth time? It hardly seemed comparable. "Everybody needs a cure for pain," I said.

"What's your sign?" he asked, looking me up and down. "If you give me a spin, I can figure it out."

I played along, turning in a slow circle.

"Capricorn," he said.

I made a sound like a game-show buzzer.

"Wait! I bet you're a sexy Scorpio," he said, hissing on the *S* sounds, as if overly proud of his alliteration. "Don't sting me, momma!"

It wasn't like I was looking for a boyfriend, or even a date. Not in Huckleberry's. Not with this guy. But it would've been nice to be able to banter for five minutes without experiencing this deflating feeling that whispered: *Forget about true love. You'll never again even find a man to have casual-yet-respectful sex with.*

Since I was trapped talking to him until Cheyenne finished the gimlets, I might as well have some fun. "Let me guess," I said, gesturing at his neck tattoo. "Your mother's birthday. So you don't forget."

He leaned in conspiratorially and pointed toward the table of Pole Virgins. "It means, why are you here with that group of—" He let loose a string of slurs insulting the sexual identities, ethnicities, and general whorishness of my new friends.

I tossed the second vodka gimlet in his face.

And I didn't feel like Tilly Turner.

I felt like Nikita.

A killer pole dancer.

A certified badass.

A female assassin.

Mr. Neck Tattoo let out an inhuman screech as the lime juice seared his eyes. He lunged, knocking me back onto a barstool.

Usually I would've run for cover. But white-hot fury flooded my every cell. And maybe I was mad at this guy for being a bigot. Or maybe I was furious that living in late capitalism meant Hucklebunnies had to grind up on men like him to make rent. Or perhaps I was enraged my creative dreams had been tanked by a pervert. Or maybe I was actually infuriated at how hard it is to be a mom in a country where childcare and healthcare are expensive luxuries instead of basic rights. Maybe I just needed a half-hour a day in a room alone where I could scream my head off and bash a piñata with a baseball bat until I could face my life again. But for whatever reason, I pushed off the stool and raked my nails across his face.

He grabbed me firmly by the shoulders. Time slowed. But before he could shake me, or headbutt me, or do whatever he was going to do next, the bouncer yanked him backward and shoved him out the front door.

For a moment, you could've heard a lipstick drop. Then a gossipy murmur rippled through the club. The bouncer returned, looming over me. A bear-sized mass of muscle encased in a lavender suit and cowboy boots.

"Whoa, whoa, whoa!" Cheyenne said, standing on tiptoes to lean over the bar. "That piece of trash pushed her. Can we eighty-six him from the club already? It wasn't her fault."

The bouncer glared at me, lifted a chin at Cheyenne, and stalked off.

"Thanks," I said.

"Let's be honest," she said. "This world would be better off without guys like him in it."

My new pole friends surrounded me. Never in my life had I tossed a drink, much less scratched the shit out of someone's face with my fingernails. For a second, I let myself consider there was something to this pole dancing alter ego nonsense. But I decided it was probably just good old-fashioned Mom Rage coming out sideways. The Pole Virgins hugged me, reassured me, asked me what had happened.

"He said something really awful," I said, not wanting to repeat the slurs. "And Nikita wasn't having it."

Everyone laughed, tension dispelling. My gimlet went down quick.

And after that? After that I don't remember a goddamn thing.

# SEVEN

*Monday, Presidents' Day*

My headache could cleave a boulder. My mouth filled with nausea water. I had the kind of hangxiety that can only be achieved after blacking out and finding a murdered man in your trunk. And my Next Right Thing was searching Mr. Neck Tattoo's phone and wallet for clues as to who might've wanted him dead. But luckily I hadn't forgotten the iPad. If there's one thing that could buy me a few precious minutes, it was plugging my kiddos into the Matrix. With *The Parent Trap* playing, Phoebe and Alice would happily sit alone in the back of the Impala until frostbite set in.

Layna and I stood by the trunk of my car. For a moment I hesitated to bring her further in on this, but since she'd seen the body, I figured I might as well. There were no passersby, no one watching, no nosey co-op cashiers having a smoke break behind the dumpster. I hit the key fob and the trunk unlatched. At the sight of the dead guy's contorted face, I shuddered and turned away. But then I forced myself to look again.

"It's him," I repeated. "For sure, it's him."

"That is not good," Layna said. She reached right in, wrenching a wallet and phone from his pocket. "It's creepy his pants are undone, right? He might've deserved it."

A bloodstain on the front of his checked flannel and another on his thigh had dried to a dark maroon. The purple egg on his forehead was nasty, but hardly looked lethal.

My stupefied brain tried to understand why this man was dead in my car. This guy and I. We'd fought in the club. He'd been thrown out. Then what? He could've waited for me in the alley behind the club. I wouldn't hurt anyone. Not under normal circumstances. But to fight him off? Maybe. And my pole dancing alter ego, Nikita? She wouldn't hesitate.

I couldn't confess this worry to Layna. To anyone. "Do you think someone really stabbed him to death with my scrapbooking scissors?" I asked. "There's not that much blood."

Layna shrugged. She glanced side to side to watch for passersby.

This was absolutely one time in my life where I could not misstep. I needed to pull it together and make good choices. As a solo mom, I'd spent the last seven years handling any disaster life threw my way. I forced myself to click into that competent-adulting mode now. Leaning forward, I pulled down his T-shirt to study his neck. "No strangulation marks. No obvious bullet wounds. Maybe someone smothered him."

"Without a forensic exam, who knows?" Layna said.

A forensic exam might prove I'd killed him. I mean, I didn't think I had. But before I acquired a pole alter ego, I would've sworn I'd never get in a bar fight with a strange man either. I held his phone up to his face to unlock it.

"Come on, baby," Layna said.

I glanced at the screen. "Bingo!"

Thankfully, it seemed All-Business Layna was back online too. She shut the trunk, and I followed her to her car. I hadn't imagined Layna as a purple Porsche kind of gal, but it suited her. She started the engine so we could run the heater. From the passenger seat I had a clear sightline to my Impala, and thus my kids.

"I'll look through my phone for clues about where the hell I was last night. You look through his. Okay?" I said. Layna nodded.

Emmylou had said I'd stumbled in at 4:30 a.m. and headed straight to my room, swearing I'd give her a full report in the morning. The "My Trips" tab of my Uber account revealed I'd been picked up from

Huckleberry's at 4:16 a.m. But according to Layna, I'd left Huckleberry's with Shade at 9:30. What had I been doing for almost seven hours?

Layna was equally absorbed in the dead guy's phone. "He deletes his text threads so there's not all that much in here."

"What kind of psycho doesn't have thirty-two thousand text messages on his phone?" I said.

"Well, here we have a chivalrous flirtation—your mansicle sent a contact called Baylee a picture of his junk. Wanna see it?"

Another wave of nausea hit. I fought back a tiny retch. "No thanks."

"And Baylee wrote back: 'Not tonight. He's home.' Sounds like somebody's getting cuckolded." Layna kept scrolling. "Sexting. Sexting."

A whimpering sound escaped me. If we couldn't find any clues, my situation was completely untenable. I could not have a corpse in my car and no alternate suspects. I could not.

"Here's a thread with a woman named Korielle," Layna said. "If I'm even pronouncing that right. But yeah, I'm going with Korielle rhymes with L'Oréal."

"My mom dyed her hair with L'Oréal," I said.

"Interesting, but not relevant," Layna said as she studied the phone. "The dead guy's all: 'I'm still thinking about you, baby. Please can we meet for a coffee.' And she's like: 'No. You know I'm not allowed to have you in my life.' And he's like: 'Don't listen to that stupid controlling—' He used the C-word! And not in a complimentary Gen Z way! What a charmer."

I was starting to suspect Layna was enjoying this. "At the bar, he told me he went to Huckleberry's to forget 'the one who got away.'"

"Sounds like Korielle's got good instincts," Layna said. "Run, girl, run." She turned her attention back to the phone. "Okay. Here's a text from someone called Natty Lite who's all: 'Let's meet up this week to discuss some plans.'"

"That sounds depressingly not that suspicious," I said. My headache blazed but I forced myself to look through the dead guy's wallet as Layna plugged in his phone so it wouldn't run out of juice. I found an

Idaho driver's license. A Visa debit card. A stack of ones. "His name was Connor Johnson. And I don't think he was a big tipper at the club. I might be sick."

Layna reached over to the glovebox and pulled out a piece of candied ginger. It was a tiny act of kindness. But still it felt wonderful to have someone taking care of me, even just a little bit.

"I don't want to lean in to the diabolical stripper trope," I said. "But Cheyenne—the bartender Salma Hayek is so hot for? She poured the drinks I had before I blacked out. She could've roofied me and stolen my car keys so she could murder him and pin it on me."

"Hmm. Do you have any evidence to support this theory?"

"She said the world would be better without guys like him in it. Do you think that's enough?"

"To take the suspicion off you?" Layna said. "No, hon. I don't think so."

"So what am I supposed to do?" I'd stayed calm when my appendix was about to rupture and I'd had to find emergency childcare for my kids and get myself to the ER. I could stay calm for this. "Maybe there's security camera footage from the alley behind Huckleberry's," I said.

"Yes!" Layna yelled. "If there's video of someone else stuffing this guy in your trunk, you'd be off the hook."

I started to cry. "I'm sorry," I said. "It's just—that would be amazing."

"Want me to follow you over there?"

"You don't mind?" I said, letting out another little sob of relief.

"I'll need to go to the police station with you after that anyway. They'll want my statement. Now pull yourself together. For your kids."

I nodded and wiped my tears. "Of course," I said. "It's what moms do."

# EIGHT

*Monday, Presidents' Day*

Did you kill him, Mommy?" Phoebe asked as I pulled the Impala out of the co-op parking lot. I almost hit a fire hydrant.

"Absolutely not!" I said. But did I know that for sure?

"So we still have a spider in the trunk?" Alice said, sounding terrified. "Is it poisonous?"

Relief gushed through me. "My new friend helped me get it out," I said. "Everything's fine."

Big white flakes had started coming down again. It'd snowed at least a couple inches overnight and the streets were in the ephemeral powdery state they achieved right before turning sloppy as a chili cheese dog. At the stoplight, Layna's purple Porsche idled behind my Impala. As the hangover nausea swelled again, the dead guy's waxy face appeared behind my eyes. I opened my door and heaved onto the snow.

"Mommy? Are you okay?" Alice asked. As I pulled myself upright, the twins' worried faces filled my rearview. Bags of groceries were crammed in around their booster seats. Was this the day they'd remember as the beginning of the end of their (relatively) happy childhoods?

A Jeep Cherokee cruised by on my right, Miranda Carson behind the wheel, her mother riding shotgun. Miranda stared at me, eyes wide with alarm. Could the dead guy's hair be hanging out of my trunk?

"It's the pretty lady you don't like," Alice said. "Why's she staring at us?"

"Maybe she's surprised I'm driving Grandma Lulu's old muscle car?"

I said, voice trembling. Blessedly, Miranda sailed through the yellow light. I stopped and Layna pulled up behind me. "Nothing scarier in this world than a CPS worker who thinks she's doing the right thing," I muttered.

"What's a CPS worker?" Alice said.

"They snatch people's children," I replied. "Sometimes for good reason. Sometimes not." This was perhaps my worst parental explanation ever, but it was the best I could do in my current state.

"Can we go to the YMCA?" Alice asked.

"We love it because it reminds us of Grandma Lulu," Phoebe said. No subtext with these two.

"Not today, love."

After my mom closed Cosmic Treasures, the vintage junk store she'd owned for thirty years, she worked the front desk at the downtown YMCA. I was a member there now, not to get fit or even because it reminded me of my mom, but because they offered one hour of free childcare daily. The catch? Parents had to remain in the building, ostensibly working out. But instead of using the hour for self-improvement, I'd drop the twins at the Kids' Club and hurry to the sauna, where I'd lie on my back in the boiling-hot, cedar-smelling room and let my silent tears run into my ears. But I was way too hungover today for the sauna.

The light turned green and I started driving, Layna still tailing me in the purple Porsche.

In the stark daylight, Huckleberry's looked like the sort of establishment where a horny grandpa might go to drink himself to death.

"This place is spooky," Alice murmured.

"Yeah," Phoebe chimed in. "Why are we here again?"

"When we picked up our car, there was no one here, so I couldn't get my keys. I left them here last night." I cruised around the alley behind the club, parked, and handed the kids their one-eyed babysitter. "Wait here," I said.

As Layna parked, I tromped through fresh snow to check the back of the Impala, which still sported my mom's LuvLife vanity plates. From the outside, there was no sign of a dead man.

That was the last of the good news.

Layna and I turned in futile circles, craning our necks for security cameras. But no dice. I marched up to the back alley door of Huckleberry's and knocked. A skinny man in a dirty dishwasher's apron and a backward ball cap answered.

"You again," he said.

I'd never seen him before in my life. "I think I left my keys on the bar last night. They have a My Little Pony keychain?"

"We're doing this again?" he said. He blew out a vape cloud that smelled like a piña colada car deodorizer. "I told you. Your keys aren't here."

"Wait. What?" I could feel myself rapid blinking, trying to understand.

"I told you. You're. Keys. Aren't. Here."

"Told me when?"

"At four this morning," the dishwasher said. "After you were pounding on this door."

"Any chance you saw me before then?"

He shook his head while sucking on his vape.

"Dammit," I said. "Are there any security cameras back here?"

The dishwasher gave an amused hoot. "As if the Orca's gonna splurge on something that doesn't make him money." He blew a vape ring, reached out with both hands, and spun it into two vape rings.

"The Orca?" I said.

"Yeah. The club owner. Can I ask? Like, how'd you get that asshole's ugly vest?"

"Wait. What?" I said again.

"How'd you get it off him? You let me take a pic, remember?" He held up his phone. Absolute dread gripped me as Layna and I leaned in to inspect it. In the damning photo, I stood alone in the same exact spot, my eyes lit up red like a possum's in the headlights—and I was wearing the dead guy's teal vest.

Shock rippled through me, of the sort you feel in the instant of a car wreck, when glass flies, metal crunches, and you can't yet fully assess the damage done. Because when Mr. Neck Tattoo sidled up to me at the bar, he'd been wearing that vest. The image of his dead body in my trunk was burned into my brain. I'd been able to see the bloodstain on his checked flannel shirt. Because the vest was gone.

I'd been keeping my suspicions at bay, but now they slammed into me like a pack of roller derby girls on a banked track. Maybe I did it. Maybe I killed him.

"I sent that pic to the whole staff," the dishwasher said. "Seriously, you're a legend."

I let out an agonized groan.

"Did you and that guy like kiss and make up? Or did you kick his ass and take the vest off him? You wouldn't say."

My queasiness worsened. "Was I with anyone?" I managed.

"I heard some woman yelling your Uber was here. You stumbled out of the alley. That's the last I saw of you." He repeated his one-vape-ring-into-two-vape-rings trick and paused to give us a chance to admire his talents.

"Jesus, kid. Get a real cigarette," Layna said.

His face fell. "Anyway, I gotta hit the dish pit." The alley door slammed in our faces.

"This is not good," Layna said, turning to face me.

"Not good" did not begin to cover it. I'd been trudging through life, miserable, depressed, grief-stricken. But I'd been with my kids, able to take care of them. I had actually been in heaven all along, and I hadn't even known it. But what I was facing now was literally hell. "I'm gonna have to go to the police, right? What else can I do?" The strip-club back alley with its dumpster, looming telephone poles, and gray sky held no answers.

Layna looked at me sadly. "So, the douchebag. He's the district attorney, right?"

The douchebag. Her soon-to-be ex-husband. I nodded.

"There were four unsolved murders in town last year," Layna said. "Before we split up, the douchebag was always saying Boise PD needs a good murder with a slam-dunk conviction. Something to make them look competent." She gestured at my trunk. "I'm not saying you're guilty. I'm saying that—unless you come up with a solid alibi—it looks like a slam-dunk case to me."

"But I'm a mom!" I shouted the words like an incantation.

Layna's shrug said that the justice system didn't give a shit.

I started pacing, the snow crunching below my feet. "Okay. Okay. I need a pro/con list."

Layna nodded furiously. "That's right."

"Going to the cops. Pro—they'll get the corpse out of my trunk." I couldn't make a Costco run with that body in there. "Pro—I'll look helpful. More innocent, right?"

"Maybe?" Layna said, her voice pitching high. "Cons?"

"Con—the police have a murder weapon with the dead guy's blood and my name and fingerprints on it."

"Major con," Layna agreed. "Con—the entire staff of this strip club now has a photo of you in this alley wearing the dead guy's vest at four a.m."

This pro/con list was not going well. "I have no idea where I was last night. And I'm a single mom. I get put in jail . . ." I trailed off. I couldn't even say the rest out loud.

How long would I be in jail? I didn't have bail money, not for a murder charge.

And who would take my kids?

And what if they ended up in foster care?

And what if I'd really killed this man?

"I can't go to the cops," I said. "At least not until I have more information."

Layna's big brown eyes brimmed with compassion. "I won't tell," she said. And even though I'd known her less than a day, I believed her. "High this week is thirty-seven degrees. It's not like the mansicle's gonna thaw."

"Can I get your number?" I handed her my phone.

She typed with her thumbs and handed it back. "Call if you need me. Don't text anything incriminating. To anyone. Tomorrow's Tuesday. I'll see you at pole class, right?"

"I'm not going back to pole!" I cried.

"You disappeared with Shade," she said. "You might've been with him all night."

If that was the case, I could prove—first to myself, then to the police—that I didn't kill anyone. The thought could hardly cheer me before another wave of anxiety kicked in. "But what if Shade roofied me?" I said. "I think somebody definitely roofied me."

Layna raised one eyebrow. "It'd be the first time in history a gay guy roofied a straight woman."

"Okay," I said, nodding. "Okay. Tomorrow night. Pole. I'll see you there."

# NINE

*Tuesday*

For a split second when I opened my eyes Tuesday morning, it felt like a normal day. Then I spotted the teal vest. Yesterday afternoon I'd found it crumpled under my sweats on the floor of my bedroom, gone through its empty pockets, and left it slung over my mom's old Eames dupe office chair in the hopes something about it would trigger my memory. But now it triggered a paralyzing surge of anxiety instead.

Still I dragged myself out of bed, shoved the vest into the back of my closet, and started the morning whirlwind of kid wakeup, teeth brushing, breakfast. Being furloughed might mean I was extra broke, but at least once I'd gotten the twins on the bus I could sit at my kitchen table, slumped over my phone and a cup of coffee, and have an uninterrupted panic attack. But my email contained a reminder from the twins' teacher, Mrs. Glidewell, that I was supposed to speak at eleven o'clock for Job Talk Tuesday.

When Mrs. Glidewell first hit me up, I'd suggested she ask a firefighter or garbage collector. My gig at the Capitol Grill wasn't the stuff of second-grade dream jobs. But she'd told me not to worry. "The kids are obsessed with the state capitol," she'd said. "Just tell them about the underground tunnels and they'll be all in."

I considered canceling for mental health reasons. But Phoebe and Alice were so excited about me speaking to their class. I didn't want to disappoint them. And once I went to the police, they might start scrutinizing my recent behavior. Right now, more than anything, I needed to act like everything in my world was normal.

I put my coffee cup in the kitchen sink. Like most horizontal surfaces in my mom's place, the window ledge above was lined with fake food. A plastic peach, a wooden crème brûlée, a rainbow of inedible patisserie. If my mom had had to name a religion, it would've been camp. She loved outrageous artificiality, bright colors, and anything so out-of-date as to be hilarious.

Her style definitely wasn't my style. But I couldn't bear to throw away a single slice of plastic quiche. Even the twins knew to return Grandma Lulu's fake food to its rightful place after playing with it. I picked up a plastic macaron, as if it might help me channel my mother's wisdom. No such luck.

Though driving with a dead guy in my trunk was a terrible idea, black ice coated the sidewalks and roads, so I couldn't bike. My friend Patzi—a witch who works at House of Intuition in West Hollywood—once told me that a powerful spiritual practice is thinking about things you have now that you once wanted. So to calm myself down as I headed toward the twins' school, I thought about how much I'd once longed to be a mom.

Comedy tends to attract sex addicts, alcoholics, people who are hogs for attention and like to put themselves first. So I was as surprised as anyone when I woke up one morning at thirty-six with a longing for a baby as powerful as hunger or thirst or the kind of horniness you only feel in your teen years.

I was waiting tables at a fancy sushi place near Abbot Kinney to make rent. My OB/GYN warned me I didn't have a lifetime left to find Mr. Mom. Any baby I carried would be at risk of a million unhappy scenarios merely because I was old enough to remember the release of Alanis Morissette's *Jagged Little Pill.* When I finally met the man of my dreams, I would probably yell, "What took you so long?! You've put our baby in danger!"

My mom was the one who said: "There are plenty of women who have babies on their own." She didn't have to remind me she was one of them. She offered to pay for my IVF. "I think of my savings as your inheritance anyway," she said. "You might as well spend it now." (At the time, I had no idea that my mom didn't have savings. It was a second mortgage on her duplex that paid for my fertility treatment! But maybe I should've known.) She promised once I had a baby, she'd come stay with me a week at Thanksgiving, two weeks at Christmas, a week at spring break, and I could come to Boise for a month in the summer. We would make it work. And in LA, I had two waitress friends I could nanny-share with and a host of pals who promised they'd babysit while I showered or ran to the grocery store, or even did an open mic night.

My mom had a pal from yoga who ran the sperm bank in Boise, so she managed to qualify me for a massive discount. I had a whole stand-up bit about that. ("You know how you should never buy chicken once it's been marked down? Food poisoning lasts twenty-four hours. Bad sperm lasts a lifetime.") But the joke was on me, because the sperm was super-powered—I got pregnant on the first round.

The wildest, most intense moment of my life happened when my OB first showed me two heartbeats. Twins! I'd never imagined such abundance. Sobs wracked me. Two babies! I was terrified, sure. But more than anything I felt like the Universe had seen my yearning and blessed me twice over. Twins are strange. Twins are a phenomenon. Twins are Nature herself whispering that life is full of mystery and magic.

No one tells you that if twins are magic, carrying twins is an ancient, fairy-tale-level curse. By the time I was eight months pregnant I was almost as big around (60 inches!) as I am tall (64 inches!). I was literally shaped like a beach ball. A bumpy purple-gray rash called "prurigo of pregnancy" made my skin resemble the hide of an elderly elephant.

When the doctor laid both babies on my chest, my mother was there with me. They were the most wrinkly, gunky, funny-looking creatures—perfectly identical except for Phoebe's Florida birthmark—and I loved them so much something inside me cracked open. I promised myself I'd be the best mom, always there for them. But I'd also show them a woman could be a mother and still pursue her creative dreams. And with the help of my own beloved mom and my misfit gaggle of artsy weirdo LA friends, I would raise them surrounded by love and community.

But sometimes life doesn't go according to plan.

Now as I slipped into the twins' second-grade classroom, Alice's wave was enthusiastic, Phoebe's too-cool-for-school. At their elementary school in LA, they'd been in different classes, the policy being to separate twins so they had a chance to develop their own identities. But in Boise, they'd been put in the same room, and I hadn't objected.

A bulletin board dedicated to the Heroes of the United States of America was decorated with kid drawings. Martin Luther King Jr. George Washington. Thomas Edison. Meanwhile, Phoebe had drawn Joan Rivers with a halo and real sequins glued all over her kaftan. Alice had sketched a stooped woman in a hat, clearly meant to represent comedic trailblazer Moms Mabley. Often my life felt like a long series of failures. But when I saw those drawings, I had the sense I was doing something right.

A dad stood at the front of the room wearing crisp jeans and a button-down shirt with the sleeves rolled up. A hot dad. Maybe Mrs. Glidewell had found a firefighter after all. School events like this made me worried for the day my kids would come home upset they didn't have a father. But if that happened, I'd tell them what I'd always told them. That I'd wanted babies so much. That I loved them so much. That our family was perfect and enough.

That last part was maybe a lie. Because while my mother had loved the girls as much as a second parent, without her our family was a wagon missing a wheel.

A kid in the row in front of me picked his nose and ate it. Hubert the Booger Eater. The twins had told me about him. I tried to focus on whatever Hot Dad was talking about. But his pecs were distracting. A glance at his left hand revealed a bare ring finger. Interesting.

"So basically, my main job is to take guns away from the bad guys who shouldn't have them," he was saying. "I don't go undercover myself. But I provide a lot of support to undercover agents. Any questions?"

Was he Boise PD? Or Ada County Sheriff's Department? Sitting up straighter, I tried to look like a woman who definitely did *not* have a dead guy in her trunk.

Alice's seatmate, Johnica, raised her hand.

"Why do the bad guys have guns?" Johnica asked.

Hot Dad considered the question. "Some of them want to sell the guns. A lot of them think they need to protect themselves from the government. Only a small percentage want to commit mass murders or actually *overthrow* the government. I definitely want to get guns and explosives away from *them*."

A glance around the room showed twenty-six horrified faces. Hot Dad obviously didn't spend much time with kids. Hot Absentee Dad, I should call him. Mrs. Glidewell must've pulled out all the stops to guilt him into speaking to the class. Which kid in the room was his? My bet was on a boy in the second row with big ears and adoring eyes. Poor kid. Lame, disappointing dads made me feel better about the fact that my kids had no dad at all.

Hubert shot his hand into the air. "How do I get that job? It thounds tho cool." The twins hadn't mentioned his endearing lisp.

"Basically you have to avoid doing anything illegal your whole life," Hot Absentee Dad said. "Like don't do things in Vegas expecting they'll stay in Vegas. Don't think weed's no big deal now just because three-fourths of Oregonians are stoned out of their minds on gummies at any given time. You're not in Oregon."

"Amen," I said.

Hot Dad smiled at me, and I could feel it in my toes. Mrs. Glidewell cleared her throat.

"You have to take a lie detector test when they hire you," Hot Dad continued. "So all illegal things are out."

"What would you lie about?" Johnica asked, looking concerned.

Mrs. Glidewell jumped in, clearly worried Hot Absentee Dad would start listing possible peccadillos. "Can we all give a big thank-you to Agent Duran for talking with us today?"

"Thank you, Agent Duran!" the kids intoned.

"Next up," Mrs. Glidewell said, "Alice and Phoebe's mom, Mrs. Turner."

"Ms. Turner," I corrected as I made my way to the front. Was I mistaken or did Agent Duran look interested?

But Mrs. Glidewell ignored me. "Mrs. Turner works at our state capitol, where lawmakers make the important laws we all need to follow if we ever want to work for the Bureau of Alcohol, Tobacco, Firearms and Explosives like Agent Duran."

Agent Duran was a fed! To my dismay, instead of returning to his cool and important job busting arms dealers, he settled into the tiny empty seat at the back of the room. Even with his knees up under his chin he was still smoking hot.

Twenty-six little faces stared up at me. I didn't want to embarrass the twins. I didn't want to mess up. "Hi, everyone. I'm Phoebe and Alice's mom, Ms. Turner, but you can call me Tilly. So I'm an assistant manager at the Capitol Grill. I help feed the people who work at the capitol—"

The eyes of every kid in the room were glazing over. Phoebe looked away, but Alice nodded encouragingly like, *Go on. You got this.*

"We make finger steaks," I was saying, "which were invented right here in Boise." At the Torch Lounge, back before it was a strip club, though now wasn't the time to mention all that. "Though lasagna is our most popular entrée."

It hurt to be bombing this badly. The tunnels. Mrs. Glidewell had promised if I talked about the tunnels, the kids would be all in.

"And did you know that the Capitol Grill is underground? It's in one of the tunnels under the capitol building," I said. "The senators and representatives can use the tunnels to get from place to place without going aboveground. It works well in case it's cold outside. Or if there's a security threat."

The kids seemed more bored than ever. Clearly Mrs. Glidewell was a liar. Several kids stared out the window. One yawned loudly. Another threw his pencil on the ground so he could crawl around pretending to look for it. I'd read once that in all human cultures, shame is considered the worst feeling, and I was basting in it now.

Phoebe stared down at the table, her face flushed.

Sweet Alice gave me a wan smile of encouragement.

The only way to avoid further humiliating them was to be more forthright, to be honest.

"Okay, let me explain something most adults won't tell you," I said. The kids perked up a little. "Some grown-ups have a job."

I wrote *JOB* on the dry-erase board in big capital letters.

"These grown-ups are happy with their work," I continued. "They're proud of what they do. They're like Agent Duran."

Agent Duran's eyes twinkled as he tipped an imaginary hat. Something zinged through me. Was it from a tiny bit of attention from Hot Absentee Dad? Or was it the feeling I got right before I really lit up a crowd?

"But other grown-ups, people like me, we don't have jobs. We have day jobs." I wrote *DAY* on the board in front of *JOB*. "The day job pays the bills. But it's not what day-job people really want to do. It's not what they're passionate about. They actually really want to do something else for a living. Ironically, a lot of day jobs—waiter, bartender, valet, escort—are mostly at night."

The kid I'd pegged as Agent Duran Junior raised his hand. "What's an escort?"

"Perhaps Mrs. Turner could stick to the subject of *her own* job?" Mrs. Glidewell said.

"You're gonna have to ask your dad," I told Agent Duran Junior. "So yeah, my day job is at the capitol. But my real job, my passion job, my job that doesn't pay the bills, is comedian. I mean, it was."

I paused. Should I go for it?

It had been so long.

I glanced toward the Heroes of the United States of America bulletin board where my kids had hung their drawings of Moms Mabley and Joan Rivers. Two women who knew the truth: We need comedy exactly because life is hard, often tragic, sometimes impossible. Laughter is a balm for the soul, sometimes the only thing that allows us to put one foot in front of the other during epically terrible, terrifying times. I hoped that was something Phoebe and Alice would be able to hold on to, no matter what happened to me, to us, in the days to come. It suddenly seemed urgent to remind them of that while I still had the chance.

"So I'm gonna tell y'all some jokes," I said.

Phoebe's head snapped up. Alice's smile transformed from the kind you give someone who just came back from the salon with a haircut so bad it makes your eyes water to an actual happy smile. "I don't have anything prepared for the under-third-grade set, so you might have heard some of these before. But go easy on me, okay? I'm rusty. All right. So two cookies are baking in an oven."

Hubert's hand shot into the air. How did Mrs. Glidewell deal with this kid all day?

"What kind of cookies?" he asked.

"White-chocolate macadamia nut. Obviously," I said. "So one of the cookies looks at the other one and says, 'Holy cow, it's getting hot in here!' The other looks back and says, 'Eeeek! It's a talking white-chocolate macadamia nut cookie!'"

Several kids laughed, which gave me the confidence to ad-lib. "Raise your hand if you've ever gone to the nurse's office for a lice check."

Every hand shot in the air.

"When I was your age, Bonnie Perrimeyer was the school nurse. She wore these purple gloves. I had to bend my head over and she'd part my hair with those long lice-check sticks." The kids nodded in recognition.

"Not to sound too strange, but I loved it. But you know what cured me of liking lice check?"

"What?" Johnica called out.

"Getting lice!" I said.

Most of the kids looked puzzled. But for some reason the "getting lice" joke really whacked Agent Duran's funny bone. He started giggling like a schoolboy. Which was gratifying, I have to say. Mrs. Glidewell, on the other hand, had a face of stone.

"See, my mom didn't believe in wasting money on lice shampoo," I continued. "So she covered all of my hair in—wait for it—Miracle Whip!" Agent Duran was literally doubled over, that's how hard he was laughing. "Next she wrapped my Miracle Whip–covered hair in Saran Wrap. She swore the lice and their eggs drowned in the Miracle Whip. I think it's more likely they were like, 'Can I get some chicken salad to go with this mayonnaise?' If I even see a jar of Miracle Whip in the store to this day, I'm all—" I grimaced and pretended to wipe dripping Miracle Whip off of my neck.

Some of the kids were giggling now, but more because Agent Duran's helpless chortles were contagious than because they liked my jokes. Still, it felt good to see Phoebe and Alice smiling at me. It felt good to be up there, giving it a go. I'd sound crazy if I tried to explain it to anyone, but when I was riffing in a way that made even one person really bust up, I felt like I was channeling something sacred. I was a hollow bone and the light of the divine dropped straight through me. It was the closest I ever came to feeling a part of the sacred energy of the world.

It was time to bring in the old guard of kid humor. "Knock, knock," I said.

"Who's there?" Phoebe and Alice called. They at least knew the drill.

"Ice cream."

"Ice cream who?" at least half the class said. The power of call-and-response lit up their brains like so many Christmas trees.

"ICE CREAM SO YOU CAN HEAR ME!" I yelled.

Agent Duran laughed so hard he was crying. Mrs. Glidewell gave me a dirty look. Phoebe and Alice beamed. No matter what happened in the coming days, they would remember this. Me up here, giving it my all, trying to help other people lose themselves for a moment in something akin to joy.

"Knock, knock," I said.

This time even more kids responded: "Who's there?"

"An interrupting cow." I was counting on the fact that most of them would know this one.

"An interrupt—"

Most of the kids joined me on the "Mooooo!" Agent Duran was wiping at tears. My heart glowed in my chest with the pure joy of returning—if only for a moment—to what I'd been put on this great earth to do. I waved goodbye to Phoebe and Alice—who actually looked proud of me—and thanked Mrs. Glidewell. And when I slipped out the door, Hubert was still mooing.

# TEN

Hey!" a voice called from down the hall. "Ms. Turner!"

It was Agent Duran. My heart triple gainer-ed, but I wasn't sure if it was because I had a dead guy in my trunk or because Agent Duran was a smokeshow. Either way, I needed to keep my panties on.

"I'm just reading about Midnight the Infinite Hamster," I said, trying to keep my voice even. I'd been pretending to study a bulletin board covered in fifth graders' poems. But I'd actually been savoring the feeling of having done an impromptu stand-up set that was not a total failure.

Agent Duran stopped next to me, our shoulders almost touching. I pointed to the drawing and he read the words out loud. "My hamster is named Midnight. After dark she flies to the moon. She whispers all the secrets of the universe in my ear and I get tingles. She is boundless." He paused. "Am I wrong or is this an extremely psychedelic poem?"

"What do you know about psychedelics? You're a federal agent."

"My dad listened to a lot of Jefferson Airplane," he said. "Also, I've seen *SpongeBob*."

I laughed. So he did see his kid, sometimes.

He looked over at me, his dark eyes kind and curious. "You killed it in there," he said.

"It was tough following up a dad who takes guns away from bad guys for a living."

"Are you kidding?" he said. "The guy who talked before me was a firefighter! I wanted to be like: 'Thanks for setting me up to fail, Mrs. Glidewell.'"

I giggled.

"Also," he said, "I'm not—I'm not a dad."

"So that little boy who was staring at you adoringly—?"

"Total rando," he said. "It's my niece that's in the class."

"Who's your niece?"

"Maricela."

"Don't know her and don't believe you," I joked. "Are you undercover right now? Is Mrs. Glidewell harboring a stockpile of weapons?"

"If so, she was definitely thinking about using them on you." Even in the middle of this endless winter, his skin was bronze (and weathered in a way I liked). Except for an adorably crooked spot below the bridge of his nose, he had the kind of facial symmetry usually only seen on movie stars. When he smiled, I saw his teeth were a little uneven too.

"It's not my fault she's bitter," I joked as we started walking toward the front exit. "Her life's dream is to teach sixth grade. But she can't because her last name is Glidewell."

"Seriously," he said. "With a name like that, it's third-grade-and-under only."

Agent Duran set off a strange inner turmoil in me. My romantic life was a desert, and he was a man-sized oasis. But it was more than that. Being near him, I had the strange, powerful sensation I'd known him for decades. Even though I'd absolutely never met him before.

We approached the front desk sign-out, which was manned by the principal's assistant, a sweet grandma named Tina.

"Can I ask the obvious question?" I said, taking the visitors' clipboard.

"Why I'm at Job Talk Tuesday when I don't have kids?" he replied. "Apparently, Mrs. Glidewell's class has a shortage of dads willing to spend an excruciating ten minutes trying to explain whatever they do for a living to a bunch of second graders. My sister made me fill the gap."

Tina smiled up at me. "He's the principal's *little* brother," she said.

Agent Duran nodded solemnly as he signed the visitor's sheet. Nathan. His first name was Nathan. "Guilty as charged."

"Nate! How'd it go?" Principal Cruz had appeared in her office doorway. If I'd seen her on the street, I would've guessed her profession as tarot reader or J.Lo's sister who has somehow been exiled to Idaho for bad behavior. Her black hair hung to the middle of her back and she had at least seven earrings in each ear.

"Not great since I was sandwiched between a firefighter and the world's funniest woman," Agent Nate Duran said.

My face flushed as Principal Cruz gave me an assessing glance. "Funnier than Maya Rudolph?" she said. "Funnier than Jean Smart?"

"Never," I said at the exact same time Nate said, "Absolutely."

"Thanks for coming, Nate," Principal Cruz said. "And you too, Ms. Turner."

"Anytime, sis. I always like it when you owe me one." Nate gently backed into the cross-bar of the school's front door, which he held open for me.

As we walked toward my car, our breath steamed. Nate was a fed, and there was a dead guy in my trunk. I couldn't tell if the feeling gripping me was pure panic—or panic mixed with a thrill that Nate clearly wanted to keep chatting. A hot guy who thought I was funny—now that was my kryptonite.

"Your sister seems cool," I said.

"Now?" he said. "Sure. But when we were kids, did she trick me into drinking toilet water? Sure did."

I could not stop laughing around this guy. I liked that he seemed a little bit unhinged, in the best possible way.

"My sister," he said, "she has a theory that straight single guys 'go off' by their mid-forties."

"What do you mean, 'go off'?" I said.

"Like milk turning bad. According to her, if you're a man, one day you're tasty and viable as a romantic partner. And the next you're spoiled, no longer fit for consumption by nice normal women."

"Sounds about right," I said. "Since I moved back to Idaho I've been on exactly two dates. One guy ate fried catfish with his hands and licked every single one of his fingers between bites. The other just wanted to show me instructional TikTok videos he'd made about how to detonate a grenade. 'Pull the pin! Throw! Duck below a bale of hay!'"

"Yikes!" Nate said. "Were they both mid-forties or older?"

"Can confirm," I said.

"My sister's other theory is that the going-off process might be sped up by repeat exposure to the kind of people who illegally stockpile weapons. Like maybe your grenade guy. Or the kind of folks I'm around for work. She thinks normal wholesome stuff is good for me." He leaned back against my trunk. A very attractive, very single, very child-free federal agent was literally inches from the corpse in my car.

"My niece is playing soccer on this team called the Saber-Toothed Turtles," he continued. "My brother-in-law is usually assistant coach, but he's taking some professional development classes at night until March. So I've been recruited."

"Wow! Any chance you want to sit in on PTA meetings for me too?"

"Not a chance."

"Does your sister think you might meet an eligible divorcée at Saber-Toothed Turtle practice?" I asked, edging toward the driver's side of my car. I normally would be doing internal cartwheels over this banter, but panic had a vice grip on my chest—I had to get him away from my trunk.

He shrugged and took another step toward me. "She probably thinks spending time around a nice single mom would slow down my 'going-off' process. Anyway, kids ages seven to nine are welcome." He paused and looked at the ground, then back up at me. "Any chance your girls want to play some soccer?"

In lady porn (aka contemporary romance novels), eligible men always go weak in the knees for disheveled moms in yoga pants. But in real life, super-hot employed guys do not trip all over themselves for a chance to see single mothers of twins again. But how to explain this sense Nate and I had been best friends or lovers in a previous life? Living in LA had made me woo-woo, but not woo-woo enough to believe that.

I shrugged. "I have to ask them. Phoebe is fierce. But Alice unfortunately inherited my utter lack of hand-eye coordination."

"You don't use your hands in soccer," he said. "So she's good."

I laughed. "I'll think about it. Can I ask you something? I mean, do I— Do we know each other from somewhere?"

"I probably just have one of those faces. Besides, I'd remember you." He paused. Was he blushing? "Soccer practice is Thursday at three thirty. At the indoor soccer fields over by Fort Boise."

"Okay," I said. "Maybe."

He looked right into my eyes. It was sexy and a little unnerving. "It was nice to meet you, *Ms.* Turner," he said. Even I could tell he was flirting.

"Nice to meet you, *Agent* Duran."

Flustered, probably by a whiff of his pheromones, I tried to hit the unlock button on my key fob, but heard the trunk pop open instead. I dove to slam it shut, blood rushing so hard into my head I felt like my eardrums might blow. Hurrying back around to the driver's side, I unlocked the door for real this time. But before I could climb in, Agent Duran said, "Knock, knock."

I suddenly got the kind of tingles that could usually only be achieved by having a hamster named Midnight murmur all the secrets of the universe in my ear. "Who's there?"

"Owl."

"Owl who?" I said.

"Owl be seeing you soon, right?"

I groaned. "Are you sure you aren't a dad?"

As I pulled the car out of the lot, his reflection waved, then did a quick little "Gangnam Style" dance move.

I was absolutely, positively not going to take my girls to join the Saber-Toothed Turtles soccer team. Nate Duran might be a manicorn—single, smoking hot, adorably goofy, and apparently heterosexual—but at this point, an ill-fated flirtation with a federal agent could land me in prison for the rest of my life.

So why was I still smiling?

# ELEVEN

Hopefully Shade could tell me where I'd been all Sunday night (and maybe how I'd ended up wearing the dead guy's vest). If not, my near miss with Agent Nate Duran had shown me I couldn't leave the corpse in the Impala. Countless murder mysteries had taught me a chest freezer would be the best option for hiding a body, but I didn't have one. Luckily, during a Boise winter, the whole damn town was a chest freezer. And so was my backyard shed.

This was what I was thinking about as I pulled the Impala into the snowy spot behind my duplex and spotted trash strewn around my garbage cans. I cursed under my breath. As I started picking up broccoli stalks and errant used tea bags, Oat Willimena appeared through her back gate wearing jeans, a brightly embroidered huipil, and no jacket. She was a libertarian potter in her early seventies who'd recently moved to Boise from Austin, claiming any town with double-digit billionaires was no longer a place for an artist.

"Raccoons in the garbage again!" she cried. "I'll help you clean up."

"You don't need to do that," I said. But Oat Willimena joined in anyway, grabbing empty cereal boxes and a deflated milk jug half covered in coffee grounds.

"Oh, raccoon, friendly neighborhood bandit!" she cried. "*Mija*, raccoons wash their produce more thoroughly than my second mother-in-law."

It did make me feel good when Oat Willimena called me *mija*. As if for that one moment I wasn't an adult with more grief and responsibility than I could bear.

"Come by my place anytime," she said as we threw the final bits of trash in the can. "I can give you a tour of my pottery studio. Bring your foxy neighbor too."

Did Oat Willimena have a crush on Emmylou? "I'm sure Emmylou would love to see your pottery studio," I said. "Anyway, thanks for your help. I gotta go make some calls."

"Sure, sure," she said, looking disappointed to see me go.

As I hurried through my back gate, my phone did actually ring. Miley O'Riley. We'd been friends in high school. Not besties, but we'd often sat with the same gaggle of misfit pals at lunchtime, forever debating whether Ani DiFranco's new album was more of a reflection of our souls than her last. Miley and I had lost touch once I moved to LA, but she was now the only person in town who didn't want to talk about how my career was DOA. She was obsessed with some stand-up reels I'd posted on Insta over a year ago, and she'd asked me to perform a set at Boise's Winter Will Never End Festival. I'd told her I wasn't up for it, but she kept trying to convince me. Fresh off making a hot fed laugh until he cried, I thought for a second it might actually be exciting. But I had no new material and more pressing things to deal with—like how to avoid being charged with murder. I sent the call to voicemail.

In the backyard, the storage shed hunkered alongside the privacy fence. Technically I shared it with Emmylou, but she only kept garden tools in there. A few boxes of my mom's things collected dust inside, but otherwise it was empty.

My key was hovering at the storage shed lock when Emmylou popped her head out of her back door. Now in her mid-seventies, she'd aged naturally and her beautiful skin was rosy pink and soft with wrinkles. She was solidly built and still strong. Even though it was thirty-five degrees out, she wore a silk kaftan splotched with giant scarlet roses, her silver hair upswept in a vintage turban à la Greta Garbo. Her philosophy was that hanging out around the house in winter wear was dressing to depress.

"Want to come in for tea? I need the skinny on Job Talk Tuesday," she called. "Were there any hot firefighters there? Or even a good-looking electrician?"

Instead of inspecting the shed, I headed into Emmylou's side of the duplex to tell her all about Agent Nate Duran.

After I picked Phoebe and Alice up at the bus stop, the twins and I played approximately seventy-six rounds of indoor cornhole as I counted down the hours until I could go to Pole Kisses and secure proof I hadn't killed anyone. (I won most of the rounds, with Phoebe coming in second. Alice was a distant third because she insisted on wearing her latex Betty White face mask, which has very small eye holes.)

Once we'd finished an uninspired dinner of frozen fish sticks, I put on *The Parent Trap* again to distract the girls. They looked so innocent snuggled up on the couch. I could imagine how their lives would soon be ruined by my absence and the ensuing media frenzy: MOTHER OF TWINS COMMITS BRUTAL STRIP CLUB MURDER.

Desperate to prevent this outcome, I popped open my laptop to cyber-sleuth. For starters, I googled the dead guy's neck tattoo—23/16—which led me to the online database of hate symbols. There I read that twenty-three stands for the twenty-third letter of the alphabet. Sixteen for the sixteenth letter. WP for White Power. At least the guy I might've murdered was a legitimately terrible person. That part at least was a relief.

I read on until Emmylou breezed in, arms loaded with ingredients for caramel brownies. The girls weren't allowed to go to Emmylou's side of the duplex much, on account of her crossbow. Mommy blogs had a lot to say about the dangers of keeping firearms in the house with kids, but much less guidance about weapons originating in the first millennium BC.

The twins squealed, rushing to hug her.

"Emmylou, I meant to tell you earlier," I said. "Oat Willimena wants to give you a tour of her pottery studio."

"Really?" Emmylou said, setting the baking ingredients on the kitchen counter. "Did she say that? How did she say it exactly?"

I studied her, surprised. "Do you have a thing for Oat Willimena?" I started to sing the song of childhood torment. "Emmylou and Oat Dub sitting in a tree. K-I-S-S—"

"I do not." Emmylou sniffed, turning away to put the eggs in the fridge. "Though I have seen enough flaccid man parts to last a lifetime."

"Ow!" Alice cried, her face contorted in pain.

"What is it?" I said.

"She bit me!" Alice held out her forearm for inspection. I didn't see any teeth marks.

"It was an accident!" Phoebe said.

I leaned down and looked Phoebe in the eye. "We do not bite other people. Those teeth are for chewing carrots, chicken nuggets, apples. Not for chomping your sister."

She nodded slowly, eyes huge and remorseful.

Emmylou cocked an eyebrow at me. "You want to nip that in the bud before it becomes a thing."

I swallowed my irritation. "We'll talk about it more later, okay, Phoebs? You all right, Alice?" They both nodded, and Phoebe tried to distract me from her bad behavior by shaking a maraca and singing a song she'd made up called "Sad Mother Goes to Sexy Dance Class."

Fifteen minutes later, I slid into the blessedly warm Porsche with its buttery leather seats. Layna's locks had grown seven inches overnight.

"Nice hair," I said.

"Thanks, babe. Five hours in the chair for this mane." She gunned the engine and the car shot forward like a Hot Wheel out of the racing gate. "I'm hoping I can get a man tangled up in it. Remember that co-op cashier, Magnus?"

"I do not," I said.

"Well, he's cute and he told me he has a yoga-coaching business. Next time he checks me out—pun intended—do you think it's too forward to hire him?"

"He'd be lucky to get to advise you on your downward dog."

"Thanks! I just want to learn how to line men up and knock them down like bowling pins, you know?"

"Are you even going to ask?" I said.

"About the mansicle?"

"Yes, about that," I said. Centrifugal force threw the back of my cranium into the head rest as she accelerated to pass a Bronco. I told her what the dead guy's neck tattoo signified.

"That's disgusting!" she cried.

"Yep. It's slang mostly used by a hate group called Imperial Dominion in Obliterating Tyranny."

"A white power group with the acronym IDIOT?" A derisive snort escaped her. "That's too rich."

"Exactly," I said. "But they call themselves either 'ID' or 'the Dominion.' According to the internet, they're a Pacific Northwest splinter gang that broke from the Aryan Brotherhood, because the AB prioritizes making money over racism. They're into dark shit. Arms trafficking, drug trafficking, extortion, murder for hire."

Layna's phone dinged and, as she braked hard for a stop sign, she glanced at it. "It's Gucci. She sent me Cheyenne's Insta handle. It's @cheyennethegoddess."

While I didn't expect Cheyenne to have posted any major clues about committing murder, I couldn't help feeling hopeful. "Looking it up now," I said. With her pink hair, Cheyenne's profile pic was unmistakable. "This is her!"

In Cheyenne's most recent post, from the day before, she was clustered with relatives in a hospital waiting room. I read the text caption out loud. "'When I found out my dear Grammy had a stroke, I left my shift early and raced to the hospital. I've been here with my fam since ten last night. We're praying Grammy pulls through.'"

"If she left Huckleberry's and went straight to the hospital, she wasn't hanging around murdering an IDIOT and stuffing him in your trunk," Layna said.

My stomach sank like my phone that time Alice dropped it in the deep end of the YMCA pool. "Oh my god," I said. "Was anyone even there when he died? What if everyone has an alibi but me?" Even coming out of my own mouth, the word *alibi* sounded official and terrifying. But I needed one.

"As soon as we get to Pole Kisses, you can talk to Shade," Layna said. "He'll know where you two went."

# TWELVE

Walking into Pole Kisses felt like an exhale. Gucci sat on the chill room couch with a laptop perched on her knees, arguing with Zhang Xiu about whether or not Megan Thee Stallion was the modern-day female equivalent of 50 Cent. Gucci had done a refresh on her hair color so it was an even brighter shade of blue, the right side shaved almost to the scalp. Her skin must've cleared up because she was down to one star-shaped yellow pimple sticker. I felt a surge of affection for her. She'd had a horrific upbringing and had somehow risen above.

But there was no sign of Shade.

Zhang Xiu spotted me. "You're alive!"

"Nikita!" Gucci said. "The girl who wields a vodka gimlet as a weapon."

"The girl who wields her fingernails as a weapon!" Zhang Xiu said. She fluttered her coffin-shaped nails at me. "Respect."

I winced. Luckily, Layna burst into the room behind me, giving Gucci and Zhang Xiu big, no-holds-barred hugs. The Bettie Page wall clock read 6:01. Still no Shade. But we seemed to be missing a teacher too. "Where's Salma Hayek?" I asked.

Everyone shrugged.

Gucci snapped her laptop shut. Standing up, she pressed her palms together overhead and bent her torso into a half-moon. "I'm so fried from studying."

"You at Boise State?" Layna asked.

"Yeah. But I'll be lucky if I get to do any real field work before I get my master's."

"How come?" Zhang Xiu said.

"My advisor has sidelined me because I don't flirt with him," Gucci replied.

"Ugh!" I said. After all she'd been through with her terrible uncle, she shouldn't have to deal with a vile professor wrecking her studies.

"Salma Hayek's out today," a voice said.

The substitute teacher stood in the doorway wearing a cropped T-shirt that said *Your Boyfriend Follows Me on Instagram.* A tattoo of a brontosaurus slithered up from undies I now knew were technically called pole shorts.

"Hey, Olympia!" Gucci said. "I love your cross-stitch." She gestured at a framed rectangle of needlework hanging on the wall over the couch that read *SEX WORK IS A VALID CAREER CHOICE.*

"Thanks," the substitute teacher said. "I made it while talking on the phone to some of my favorite clients." She spun and headed to the pole studio, revealing cheeky bottoms with garters that stretched right under her buns.

"I think I need to go," I said. The reminder that a whole bar full of people had seen me rake my nails across the dead guy's face made me feel sick. It was so unlike me it begged the question: What if I'd killed him too?

In the pole studio, Olympia idly grabbed onto the pole with her outside arm. "I have the biggest bruise in my armpit from doing teddy bears last night," she said. "They don't call them pole kisses for nothing."

"That's why I don't get rid of this." Shade sauntered in dramatically, lifting one arm to show off a thatch of armpit hair. A bluebird of hope landed on my shoulder.

Olympia laughed. "I wish I could get away with *that* at the club."

Luckily, Shade took the pole next to mine.

"Can I talk to you?" I whispered.

"After class!" Olympia boomed.

Shade shrugged apologetically. "The queen has spoken."

"Today we'll mostly be doing floorwork," Olympia decreed.

It didn't take me long to figure out *floorwork* was French for crawling around while trying to look sexy. I suspected it was a talent that couldn't be taught. Either you had it or you didn't. Olympia had it.

"First we're gonna learn the Vagina Monster," she said. Lying on her back, she propped herself up on her elbows and raised her legs into a giant V, so that her cookie—as Salma Hayek would've called it—was pointing right at us. When she waved her legs in the air, an optical illusion occurred. Her knees turned liquid, the entire length of her legs rubbery as octopus tentacles. "And if you get good, you can crawl it across the floor," she added. With each wave of her boneless legs, she scooched her hips from side to side, advancing across the floor, cookie first. She really did look like a giant Vagina Monster ready to devour us. "Easy-peasy. Now your turn."

My efforts made me look like a beached sea lion on epinephrine. Meanwhile, Layna appeared to be having a seizure while making the lewdest pass in the history of the world at an invisible paramour. But my inner comedian was beyond pleased with the absurdity. If I ever *was* going to work on a new set, this could be interesting.

As class ended, I snapped back to the fact that I was there for a *reason*. I hurried up to Shade, who was wiping down his pole.

"If it isn't Little Miss Houdini," he said. "You make it home okay Sunday night?"

"What do you mean, 'Miss Houdini'? Wasn't I with you?"

"We were outside waiting for my Uber. But I ran back in for my gloves. When I came back out, you were nowhere to be seen. I figured you grabbed a Lyft or something. You get home okay?"

"What can I say?" I managed weakly. "I'm a woman of mystery. Even to myself. What about you?"

"At the last minute I decided to meet friends for karaoke at the Neurolux. Did I do an impromptu version of 'River Deep, Mountain High' that Tina *and* Céline would've approved of? Yes, ma'am."

So Shade had been hitting high notes in front of hundreds of people. Meanwhile, I now had no hope of figuring out where I'd been from 9:30 p.m. to 4:16 a.m. the night in question.

Shade nattered on, oblivious to my distress. "I swear on my granny's grave it's almost time for me to debut my drag queen persona, Ida Hoe. But I don't want to lip-synch! I want to SING!" He belted out the last word like Lady Gaga at her Vegas residency.

But I wasn't listening. Pinpricks of sweat had broken out all over my body. I excused myself and stumbled into the chill room. After yanking my coat and shoes out of their cubby, I burst out into the cool night air, my breath coming short and fast. My one chance at answers about Sunday night was shot. A frozen, rigor mortis-ed dead guy was still crammed into my trunk and heaps of evidence pointed to me as the killer. This was a disaster, a nightmare of epic proportions. The sort of thing that would give you a delicious thrill of horror to watch on-screen because you knew deep down it could happen to sad desperate fictional movie characters but never ever to you. But now it had happened to me. I was deeply and truly screwed.

Layna followed me out a moment later. "So?" she asked.

"A total bust," I managed.

"Oh, hon," she said. "I'm sorry." She unlocked her car.

As I sank into the ridiculously luxe leather seat, an idea came to me. A flimsy, improbable idea. But it was something. "Do you think it's weird Salma Hayek didn't show up to teach?"

"Not that weird." Behind the wheel, Layna snapped down the mirrored visor to admire her cascading pigtails.

"Salma Hayek did bring the first shots to the table," I said.

"You seriously think Salma Hayek roofied you while she was proselytizing about how pole would give you a chance to reclaim your zest for life?"

As Layna gunned the engine, I gripped the door handle in anticipatory terror. “For all we know she had a long-standing vendetta against that jerk,” I said.

“I suspect lots of people might’ve,” Layna agreed.

“So say she murdered him and stuffed him in my trunk. She could’ve left the country by now. She might plan to lay low until the whole thing blows over. Or until after I’m convicted.”

“That is dark,” Layna said. But she didn’t say it was unlikely.

“Yeah, well, this whole thing is dark,” I muttered.

We spent the remainder of the drive in gloomy silence. I directed Layna to pull into the alley behind my house. As she cut the lights and the night enveloped us, a phone dinged inside my coat. The dead guy’s phone. After charging it last night, I’d kept it in my pocket on the irrational pipe dream a clue might come in. (Like what? A text from someone apologizing to the dead guy for murdering him?)

I whipped out the phone before the alert disappeared.

“It’s a voice memo,” I said. “From someone called Ralphie the Lizard.”

# THIRTEEN

Even in the dark of the parked car, I had no trouble sensing Layna's disdain when I asked her to unlock the dead guy's phone again. "So you just want me to dive back into the trunk with the mansicle?" she said.

"I feel like you're rising to the level of your incredible competence here," I replied. "Puh-leeeese? Otherwise we can't play the voice memo."

"Oh my god, fine! But you are a serious wuss."

Outside the warmth of the Porsche, our feet crunched crusty snow as we walked a few feet down the alley to my Impala. Maybe it'd all been some sort of joint hallucination. Maybe the dead guy would be gone. But the trunk light revealed his cramped figure and shadowy, contorted face.

"Shine your phone flashlight in here to brighten him up," Layna said as she reached in.

"I'd rather not," I said. But I did it, breath held, hands shaking. Scratch marks from my nails raked the corpse's waxy cheek. "Do you think he could've stolen my keys, climbed in my trunk, and suffocated himself by accident?" This sounded immensely preferable to the alternative—that I'd killed him myself.

"Oh, babe," Layna said. "We've been over this before. Somebody clearly hit him over the head and stabbed him with your scissors. So no, I don't think he suffocated himself." She handed me his unlocked phone and slammed the trunk shut.

"I'll turn off auto lock so you don't have to do that again." With trembling hands, I went into the phone's settings. "It's not working!"

"Give it here." Layna stabbed at the phone with her index finger.

"Glitchy piece of crap. Auto lock won't turn off. But I changed it from 'thirty seconds' to 'five minutes.' That's something."

I grabbed the phone and hit play on the voice memo.

"Hey, buddy." Whoever had left the memo sounded like he smoked two packs a day and ate gravel for breakfast. "Your payment arrived. I haven't been able to get ahold of Errol for a few days. Confirm you can meet his girlfriend, Baylee, at Burgdorf on Saturday at one for the hand-off. She'll have the potato mashers and plans for Day of the Rope. A full layout of the capitol building with targets. We're twenty-one days out."

"Saturday at one," Layna echoed. "A potato masher is a hand grenade."

"Jesus! Seriously?"

"One of the many things I learned from being a DA's wife. And Day of the Rope—that's an attack on the capitol."

"An attack? On the capitol? I work at the capitol!" I wailed. It was one thing to know, vaguely, that political violence had been on the rise for years. Another to know people were actively planning some kind of dystopian assault on the state house. "Also, how could anyone possibly think the politics here aren't right-wing *enough*? Insane!"

"I kept saying I was sick of being bored. I need to be careful what I ask for." Layna rubbed her hands together to keep them warm. "The only Burgdorf is the hot springs, right?"

"Yup," I said. When I was a kid, Burgdorf Hot Springs was my summertime happy place. My mom would take me there for the weekend and we'd stay in one of the historic cabins surrounding the warm soaking pools. "And a woman named Baylee will be there? The dead guy sent Baylee a picture of his junk."

"So maybe Baylee's been cheating on her boyfriend with the man-sicle," Layna said.

Miserable with cold, I stomped my feet, wishing for warmer socks. "I mean, white supremacist gangs? A plan for a domestic terror attack on the capitol? This is bigger than just this one dead guy."

I thought of my coworkers at the Capitol Grill. Wendy the cashier, who had big square glasses, a necklace of giant moles, and a dream of going to cosmetology school. Fry cook Sammy, who was saving up to buy an amplifier for his boyfriend's birthday. Nancy, a server who made the best meatloaf and had seventeen grandchildren. "I think I need to go to the authorities about all this."

"But Tilly," Layna said, "what if you did it?" The words lingered in the air before she rushed to fill the silence. "I mean, not you. But your pole alter ego, Nikita."

Not that the cops would get the distinction. "No," I said, shaking my head. "No. I couldn't have done it." I needed to convince us both. But how the hell had I ended up wearing the dead guy's hideous teal vest?

"Not to be a total downer," Layna said, "but the cops could charge you with murder, set your bail at half a million, send your kids to foster care."

I'd been thinking the same. "Even if I'm not convicted in the end, my kids would be traumatized. Maybe for life."

"The voice memo's gone," Layna said. "And one thing we know, if we tell the cops, they'll already have a prime suspect." She gestured at me.

I moaned. "But what if we tell them about this handoff at Burgdorf?"

"Cops are not going to remote hot springs accessible only by snowmobile with zero evidence other than the word of a woman trying to wiggle out of a murder charge," Layna said, running her hands down her hair extensions, as if still getting used to them. "Besides, Burgdorf is in Valley County. They don't even have a PD. They have a sheriff's department that may or may not be full of white supremacist sympathizers. Boise PD calls them up and asks them to go to Burgdorf? They'll bust a gut laughing."

My innards seized. In the interest of the public good, I should go to the police and tell them about the IDIOTs and their possible plans for an attack on the capitol. In three weeks! But I needed to be selfish right now. For my kids' sake. Turning over the body would be like handing the authorities a murder conviction—against me! There had to be a better option. “How do you know all this?” I asked. Layna’s husband was the DA. But that didn’t explain just how much she seemed to understand about this stuff.

“When I was in my twenties,” Layna said, “I wanted to be an investigator. But I would’ve had to start as a beat cop. Too dangerous, the douchebag said. A good mother would stay home full-time. I didn’t need to work, he said. He’d take care of me. What he really wanted was for me to run his life. And I did. But I lived vicariously through his work too. Studied the details of every criminal case he prosecuted.”

So I had an armchair expert on my side. It wasn’t nothing. “Okay, so what’s my plan B?” I said. Connor’s phone buzzed in my hand. Layna huddled near me as we bent over the glowing rectangle.

This is Baylee from a burner. Sorry I went dark.

“It’s Baylee!” I cried, as the three gray dots reappeared.

**Baylee:** Errol found out about us Sunday. he was pissed. texted me saying he was gonna kill u. LMK ur ok. I can’t wait to wank ur noodle on Sat at Burdorf.

“We’ve got a cuckolded hothead threatening to kill Connor. That’s good!” Layna said. “Keep her texting.”

My heart fluttered and my thumbs flew across the screen. I spoke the words out loud as I typed. “That asshole! can’t wait on the noodle wank.” I hit send.

“Now ask her about Errol!” Layna said.

what about errol? I typed.

Layna and I leaned in toward the phone, breath mingling in a cloud over the little pool of light until the next text came in.

**Baylee:** ralphie is taking errol to lake cascade. on saturday.

I let my thumbs outrun my anxious brain. So sunday errol threatened to kill me?

"Ooh, that's good," Layna said as the gray dots appeared again.

**Baylee:** oh yeah he sent abt 50 texts telling
me he was gonna rip yr lil connor off

"Ew!" Layna cried.

The phone buzzed again.

**Baylee:** He came by yesterday and smashed
my phone. scary as hell. so pissed.

"Maybe after Errol murdered the dead guy, he was worried because he'd sent his girlfriend fifty incriminating texts about it," I said.

"So he smashed her phone," Layna said.

"This is a lead!" I yelled, my legs wobbly with newfound hope. "A real lead! We need Baylee's phone!"

"Screenshots?" Layna said. "Ask for screenshots."

"can u send me screenshots?" I hit send.

**Baylee:** can't. I told u. errol smashed my phone.

"Dammit!" I yelled.

"SIM card," Layna said. "We need that SIM card."

"You're a genius!" I cried. Connor's address was on his driver's license.

I wrote: can u mail me yr old phone? with the SIM?

As the gray dots appeared, I held my breath. I didn't think Layna was breathing either. Could it be that easy? A package would arrive at Connor's house. A smashed phone containing a SIM full of texted threats from Errol on the very day Connor was killed. I'd swing by and scoop it off his front steps.

**Baylee:** haha no way. i'll give it to you at burgdorf.

I swore as I paced a big circle between the Impala and the Porsche, gnawing on my thumbnail. It felt like Layna and I had been out here in the cold darkness of the alley for ages. On the other side of the privacy fence, across the yard, my children slept in their bunk bed. Hopefully Emmylou was dozing on the living room couch. It would feel so good to plunk down next to her. But I couldn't. Not yet.

"Clues are coming in faster than green grass through a Boise goose," Layna said.

"We just need time," I agreed.

"We could stash the mansicle nearby while we're figuring this out." Layna pulled a rubber band off one of her pigtails, wrapped her hair in a low side bun, and secured it. The fact that she said *we* made me feel slightly less panicked.

The thought of trying to move the corpse was beyond unsavory, even horrifying. But I certainly couldn't keep zipping around town with a dead guy in my trunk. Stowing the body might be necessary to buy me a couple days.

"That's what I was thinking," I said. "If people start looking for him, I could text from his phone, make sure no one thinks he's missing. Maybe there's evidence at Connor's house." It made me squeamish to say the dead guy's name out loud, but sending missives from his phone somehow made it real that he had one. "And . . . and . . . this is going to sound insane, but if there isn't more evidence, I need that SIM card."

Those threatening texts from Errol to Baylee would link Errol to Connor's murder. It was the first evidence that didn't point squarely at me. Baylee would be at Burgdorf Hot Springs with her smashed phone, and grenades, and plans for an attack on the capitol. Would it be possible to go there and convince her to give them to me? No, I told myself. Absolutely not. I couldn't leave my kids to go off to the snowbound woods to wrest evidence from a strange woman romantically involved with an arms dealer and a domestic-terrorist-turned-corpse! It was too dangerous. Still, I hearted Baylee's last text, then pulled up Ralphie's contact and typed a thumbs-up emoji.

"What are you doing?" Layna said.

"Making Ralphie the Lizard think Connor is alive, well, and planning to meet Baylee at Burgdorf," I said, hitting send. We stared at the phone as if *it* was a grenade. A moment later, it buzzed with another voice memo.

"Hey there."

The words came not from the phone, but from the darkness of the alley behind us. Layna and I both screamed. For a split second, I thought it was a phantom. But it was only Oat Willimena wearing a straw hat that gave her the silhouette of the Flying Dutchman from *SpongeBob.*

"Oat Willimena!" I said. "You scared the bejeezus out of me."

"I noticed earlier you didn't put your recycling out," she said. "Want me to grab it?"

"I'll get it," I said, my voice strained.

"All right," Oat Willimena said. "Back to the garage. I'm going to listen to *Women Who Run with the Wolves* on audiobook while I throw a few more Basque mugs. My bestsellers. You and the girls really should come see them."

"We'll do that," I said, knowing we wouldn't. "Night, Willimena."

"Oat Willimena," she corrected. "It's a play on Oat Willie, a cult comic book character from Austin. He was mashing oats when—" She must've sensed my impatience. "Oh, never mind." She disappeared through her gate, her walk defeated.

"Jesus, that old lady scared the shit out of me," Layna whispered. "Do you think she heard anything?"

"I don't think so. But I do think she has a crush on my babysitter-slash-duplex neighbor."

"You should set them up," Layna said.

"Do you think I have time for matchmaking right now?" I said.

"Maybe your pole name should be Buzzkill." Layna snatched the dead guy's phone from my hand and tapped at the screen to keep it from locking. "You ready?"

I nodded. We leaned together, our breath joining in one steaming cloud. She hit play.

"Let me hear *your voice*, my brother," Ralphie the Lizard said.

Layna let out a string of expletives that would've made Ali Wong blush. "They must only communicate in voice memos so they know it's not a cop." She got to work transforming her other pigtail into a side bun. As she finished the task, she said, "But you know, I actually think we can figure out who did this."

What was this slightly unbalanced almost-divorcée doing in this alley with me anyway?

"Why are you helping me?" I asked. "Being bored is not a reason. Not for this."

"I spent twenty years keeping my husband's life in order. Maybe I want off the sidelines. My own chance to finally be an investigator—even if just an amateur one! And I don't want you to take the fall for murdering this POS. Being married to a DA for so long, I've seen how this kind of thing can go. I like you. I don't want it to go wrong for you."

"Aren't you worried if you help me it'll go wrong for *you*?"

Layna shrugged. "The douchebag hasn't just been cheating. He's been doing all kinds of shady shit. I've got dirt on him—serious dirt! Not just the usual DA party tricks. He turned a blind eye on some criminally shoddy construction work on some multimillion-dollar downtown condos. If I go down, he goes down with me, and he knows it. He's the Ada County district attorney. I'd say that gives me a fair amount of wiggle room. Besides"—she shrugged—"everything I read about divorce is all: Self-care! Self-care! Self-care! But I don't need self-care. I need an adventure."

I nodded as I let this information soak in. "All right, then. How would you feel about helping me stash a mansicle?"

# FOURTEEN

When I opened the door to the storage shed, I found it packed tighter than a box of Thin Mints. I cursed, remembering I'd agreed Emmylou's granddaughter could store her furniture and clothes there while studying abroad.

A quick scan of the yard revealed the twins' Victorian playhouse, an extravagant present from my mom. I couldn't pry the girls out of it in the summer, but during this never-ending Boise winter they hadn't set foot in the backyard, much less gone near the playhouse.

I kicked snow away from the wide faux French doors, dragged them open, and peered inside. A grown man certainly couldn't lie flat in it. But it might be the exact right size for a crumpled corpse.

The twins' large plastic sled leaned against the house. I carried it back out to the Impala, where Layna stood shivering, breath coming out in cartoon thought bubbles.

"I've got a spot for him," I said, popping the trunk. "My kids' playhouse."

"Not the first place someone would look," Layna agreed.

Now that it was time to actually move the body, I was having reservations. "I'm not sure we'll be able to lift him."

"Not a problem," she said. "I deadlift 220. I only started pole because I need to get in touch with my feminine side." She slipped her hands under the mansicle's shoulders.

When I wrenched his legs, the body slid and lifted. But one of his feet snagged on something. A few more grunting yanks and the frozen body crashed down onto the plastic sled. A beat-up sneaker fell off, revealing a socked foot with the big toe pushing through a hole. Something clattered onto the ground. I moaned in disgust.

"I *really* don't think you killed him," Layna said.

"Of course I didn't," I hissed. "That is not up for debate." Even as I said it, I rubbed at my broken fingernail with the pad of my thumb. I knew there was a chance I was wrong.

The ice and snow bit into my shins as I dropped to all fours, on the hunt for whatever had fallen out of his pocket. My fingers closed on a pill bottle. My phone flashlight illuminated the label. The name of whoever the pills had been prescribed to had been scratched off.

"Ambien," I said. "Do you think that's what I was roofied with?"

"And he died with his pants unbuckled," Layna said. "The bastard!" She gave the corpse a swift kick before stepping into the big loop on the front of the sled.

I followed behind as Layna pulled like a Clydesdale headed to the barn. I propelled the Flexible Flyer forward with hard shoves, trying not to touch the stiff legs clad in denim. "Say the dead guy drugged my gimlet, then grabbed me when I was standing outside waiting for Shade and dragged me around to the alley. But then what?" Had I killed him, put on his vest, and then passed out in my car for seven hours? I shoved hard on the sled, as if to push away the thought. "I honestly don't think I murdered him and stuffed him in my trunk while zoinked out on Ambien. Maybe I got away from Connor and this Errol showed up and offed him."

"Possible," Layna concurred.

"But it still doesn't explain where the hell I was for seven hours." I'd woken up in my own bed, which somehow only added to the mystery. "Maybe I should've gone to the police. Ambien would've shown up in my system the day after, right?"

"Life can only be understood backward," Layna said.

"Did you see that on a sign at TJ Maxx/HomeGoods?" I said.

"That's pure Etsy, baby."

As we passed through the fence gate, I stood up straight to close it as Layna leaned forward, straining against the rope loop. When it snapped, she fell face forward, hitting the ground with a hard thump.

"William Shatner!" she said.

"Shhhhh!" I said. "My babysitter will hear. Also, you okay?"

She crawled up onto her hands and knees. "TBD."

"I got it," I said. Squatting all the way down, I pushed on the sled with all the power of my haunches. It didn't budge.

"Move it," Layna said. With one powerful shove, the sled slid forward until the front tip pressed up against the open double doors of the playhouse. She deadlifted the back end. "Come on, wussy. Buck up!" she whispered.

Holding my breath, I leaned in and pushed the rigor mortis-ed butt cheeks. The scrunched-up corpse slid into the playhouse and out of sight as the back porch light came on.

A silhouetted figure stepped through my sliding glass door and raised the stock of a crossbow to her shoulder. "Who's there?" Emmylou cried.

I stepped out of the blackness. "Emmylou, it's me—Tilly! Put that thing down."

"You scared me!" Emmylou said. "What in the heck are you doing in the backyard?"

A sigh of relief escaped me. She hadn't seen anything. "I'm loaning a sled to my friend from pole." I hadn't lied to a maternal figure since my teenage years, but apparently it was like riding a bike.

Layna popped up from behind the playhouse, holding the sled. "Just giving it a test push around the yard," she said.

"I'm Emmylou!"

"Emmylou! The fabulous neighbor!" Layna said, sounding like she'd never been so pleased to meet someone. "The fact that you look after the kids so this one can get out of the house—" She hooked a thumb in my direction. "Incredible!"

"I knew Tilly would meet some fun ladies at pole!" Emmylou cried.

"Thanks for the loan, Tilly!" Layna lifted the sled aloft with both hands, which was either a nice touch or too much. I really couldn't tell.

"Sorry to scare you," I told Emmylou. "Be right in."

"It might be a minute," Layna said, conspiratorially. "I'm going through a divorce and I need a little more advice from this one."

"I've been there!" Emmylou said. "Why don't you two go grab a drink and talk it out? I just started that movie. You know, the one where Emma Thompson hires a hot young prostitute to help her experience her sexual fantasies, but they actually *connect*?"

"We don't say *prostitute* anymore," I muttered.

"Tomato, to-mah-toe. I'm not budging off your sofa until this movie is over. Seriously, you two! Get!"

As Emmylou disappeared back into my side of the duplex, I closed the doors of the playhouse.

"I've told her a million times I don't want that crossbow around my kids," I grumbled.

"You ought to be thanking your lucky stars she babysits your horror-movie twins for free," Layna said. "And at least it's supposed to dump snow tonight."

Six inches of snow would bury our tracks. But that could only buy me so much time. It's like my mom used to tell my girls anytime we visited from LA and they complained of the cold: "Winter seems like it will last forever, but that spring thaw is coming, girls." And I needed to figure out who killed the mansicle long before it did.

# FIFTEEN

After hiding a dead body and finding myself in the sights of a loaded crossbow, I was as wired as a tween after her first Frappuccino. So when Layna said Zhang Xiu had texted to see if we wanted to meet her and the other Pole Virgins for a drink in Garden City, I agreed. Shade had been no help, and Salma Hayek was MIA, but maybe Gucci or Zhang Xiu had seen something at Huckleberry's, and it would be easy enough to ask over a beer.

When I was a kid, locals called it Garden Shitty, but now people dressed for a night out thronged the riverfront area. I groaned when I saw who was working the door at Barbarian Brewing. Landry Arnold. We'd bagged groceries together at Albertsons when I was a sophomore in high school and once had a regrettable make-out session at a keg party.

"If it isn't Tilly Turner!" he said warmly. "Back from Hollywood."

"Hey, Landry." It was unsettling to see glimmers of the skinny teenaged boy inside this hairy middle-aged man with bulky forearms.

"What was it like? Opening for Mickey Larynx? I love that guy so much."

"Still?" I said.

"Of course. He's not afraid of his urges." He lifted his eyebrows suggestively.

I rolled my eyes.

"Cover's ten bucks each," he said. "Feminazi fundraiser."

I started to protest, but Layna handed Landry a twenty and hurried me into the warehouse-style building. A Tribe Called Quest blared from the speakers. A metal second-floor balcony dangled a massive, hand-painted sign that said *SMASH THE PATRIARCHY* (with the first *S* in *SMASH* fully crossed out). In the middle of the room, hipsters dumped pots of clumpy white stuff into a huge kiddie pool. Artsy weirdos drank, chatted, and watched the proceedings. The whole scene was cooler than anything I'd expected to find.

Zhang Xiu waved from a long tall table where the Pole Virgins sipped craft beer.

"What's up with the kiddie pool?" I asked.

"It's this mashed-potato wrestling competition called Mash the Patriarchy," Zhang Xiu said.

"Ah, those are mashed potatoes! I get it now," Layna said.

"Why does everything in Idaho have to be about potatoes?" Shade mused. "You just missed the Potatohole competition. It's like cornhole, but the bean bags were hand-sewn to look like Yukon Golds. I took third." He blew on his nails and rubbed them on his shirt.

"Dammit!" I said. "I'm actually really good at cornhole. My twins are obsessed."

As Layna headed to the beer line, Zhang Xiu explained the event was being put on by a feminist performance art collective called She Burns Bright. "I'm on the board," she said. "We're raising money for the National Sexual Assault Hotline."

"Feminist performance art!" I said. "I've never felt so at home in my own hometown. How'd you get involved?" I always told myself once my life calmed down, I'd do more to give back. But right now my life was calm as a Category 5 hurricane.

"Worst thing that can happen to a mother is to not be able to protect her own child," Zhang Xiu said. The tears in her eyes surprised me.

"You have a grown daughter, right?" I said.

As Zhang Xiu nodded a tear slipped out. "She's better now."

"Is there a creep I need to hunt down?" I said.

She gave a sad laugh. "Guys like that get theirs. Eventually. That's what I have to tell myself. Anyway." She batted at the air. "How do you like Pole Kisses so far?"

"I wasn't expecting it to be so . . . life-changing." I leaned in. "Weird question. Last Sunday, after I left Huckleberry's with Shade. Did you see me again?"

"Nope," Zhang Xiu said.

"What about that asshole who got chucked out of the bar?"

Zhang Xiu took a long gulp of beer before responding. "Salma Hayek went for a quick smoke out front and that same guy grabbed her butt. She hit him in the head with an old beer bottle that was lying in the parking lot. Least that's what she said." Zhang Xiu shrugged. "I was inside."

That would explain the giant goose egg on Connor's forehead. Could Salma have then stabbed him to death and hidden his body in my trunk? "Where is she?" I tried to sound casual, but my heart was about to burst out of my chest.

Zhang Xiu shrugged. "No idea."

Before I could figure out how to continue this line of questioning, Gucci appeared, eyes red and face streaked with tears.

"What's wrong?" Zhang Xiu asked.

"I just got an email that my grad school funding has been cut—in half," Gucci wailed. "I know it's because my skeevy advisor only funds students who stroke his ego. I suspect he makes the female students stroke other things too."

"Ugh! Can't you file a Title IX complaint?" I said.

A bitter laugh burbled out through Gucci's tears. "Please. That guy has racked up more complaints than Beyoncé has Grammys. The Title IX office means well, but they have no teeth."

"She's right," Zhang Xiu said. "Tenured male faculty in this town still think #MeToo meant: 'You sleep with your students and suffer no consequences? Hashtag me tooooo!'"

I felt the old anger boiling against men who didn't care whose lives they ruined as long as they could get their saggy rocks off. Men like Mickey Larynx.

"I can't quit grad school, no matter how bad my advisor sucks," Gucci said. "I'm that weirdo that loves DNA phenotyping more than anything. But I am gonna have to quit pole." She sniffled. "I can't afford it now."

"DNA say what?" Shade said.

"DNA phenotyping. It's a forensics technique," Gucci said.

"Forensics?" I said. "You're studying forensics?"

"Yeah," Gucci said. She gave me a meaningful look. "Remember what I told you, about my uncle?" She'd donated his body to rot in a field where forensics experts could check the progress of his decomp on the hour. A win for science—and righteous revenge. I nodded slowly. "Well, meeting those experts—hearing about how they use their research to solve crimes. That's how I got into forensics. It's all I've wanted to do since."

Gucci's skills might come in handy, if I got desperate enough. Though I couldn't assume everyone in my pole class would be as eager to try to help me solve a murder as Layna.

"But you already paid for the Pole Virgins series, right?" Shade said.

Gucci shook her head. "The owner's letting me pay by the class because I'm a broke grad student."

The music stopped and a microphone-wielding emcee stepped into the spotlight. They were an adorable enby with high cheekbones and a bowtie. "In ten minutes, we'll start our Mash the Patriarchy wrestling match," the emcee said. "It's a performance-art event exploring the dangers of domesticity, performance as living sculpture, and how hard it is for women to act with agency while being objectified. Winners of each round will receive four hundred dollars. First up is the women's match." A gazelle in a tight silver dress hurried up to the emcee and whispered in their ear. The emcee frowned and looked worried. "We have an unfortunate development," they said. "One of our women's teams is out due to a bad breakup coupled with a bad batch of finger steaks. Would any pair who identifies as female like to volunteer to wrestle in their place?"

"Four hundred bucks would pay for the rest of your pole classes," Zhang Xiu told Gucci.

Gucci's eyes lit up. "Two hundred would cover it. My teammate could have the other half of the prize money. Who's with me? I wrestled in high school."

"Sorry. I'm one hundred percent, grade-A gay man," Shade said. "You need a gal."

"Wrestling would mess up my back again. Guaranteed," Zhang Xiu said.

Layna rocked up with two beers. I couldn't wait to tell her all I'd learned.

Gucci grabbed Layna by the arm. "You know how now that you're getting divorced, you want to go wild and try everything life has to offer?"

"That's right!" Layna said.

"Will you wrestle with me?" Gucci gestured toward the massive kiddie pool.

"I seized the day today by getting keratin-fusion hair extensions that took five hours," Layna said. "The one person in this world I'm actually afraid of? My extensionist. I show up tomorrow with half my extensions pulled out and the rest caked with mashed potato? She might lit-er-ally kill me."

Four pairs of searching eyes turned to me, the last possible option.

"Nikita, you've got a rage inside," Shade said. "We've seen it."

"Is wrestling really about rage?" I asked.

"Absolutely not. It's about technique," Gucci said. "Still, I need this." She dropped to one knee as if proposing marriage. "Won't you please go out there with me and mash the patriarchy?"

I liked Gucci and didn't want her pole dreams crushed by a skeeve. Still, more than anything, I wanted to say no. But Gucci had forensics expertise. I couldn't pass up having her owe me a favor. Just in case. And also, I'd never been proposed to. I gave a tiny, almost imperceptible nod.

"We're in!" Gucci yelled, leaping to her feet. She grabbed my hand and raised it high in the air. "We're in!"

"It's now time for the wrestling to begin!" the emcee cried. Gucci and I had stripped down to our pole clothes, which we still had on under our sweats. I felt exposed in my exercise bra and running shorts, though I looked positively matronly next to Gucci's velour pole undies. "The winning team takes home bragging rights and four hundred big ones! Now remember the rules: no eye poking, no choking, no drowning your opponent in the taters. Each team has to pin their opponents for five seconds. Now let's see what these women have to dish out!"

An excited energy hummed through the gathered crowd. Across the way, the two women on the opposing team prepared to enter the pool. One of them had short, bleached-blond hair and a build like a WWE wrestler. She sported bikini bottoms and the kind of jog bra built to lock down even the largest ta-tas. Our other opponent was more petite, but still intimidating. She'd donned a skintight catsuit leotard ending in booty shorts, her black hair wrapped in a tight bun. Out of context, it took me a beat to place her.

"Principal Cruz!" I gasped.

"Phoebe and Alice's mom!" she said, waving as if we were meeting for a mimosa brunch.

"You know her? You take her," Gucci whispered. "Besides, I want the thick one."

"I don't think that's a good—" I started, but was cut off by a barbaric yawp coming from the WWE lookalike. "Okay, you might be right."

"On three, our four powerful ladies will step into the pool and start mashing the patriarchy," the emcee cried.

The crowd chanted with the emcee. "One! Two! Three!"

Tentatively, I stepped into the kiddie pool. Ankle deep in mounds of mashed potato, Principal Cruz and I circled each other while Gucci charged Ms. WWE and hooked a leg behind one of her knees. The two women crashed into the white slop, which caused me and Principal Cruz to shield our eyes from the creamy splash.

"Come on, Ms. Turner," she taunted. "Aren't you gonna take me?"

I tried to tap into my inner rage, but nothing about my twins' cool principal triggered it. Still, I was gearing up to make a move when I spotted Agent Nate Duran, beer in hand, mouth hanging open.

Our eyes caught. Time froze. As the split second stretched on, the rest of the crowd dropped away. I no longer saw Gucci and her opponent grappling in the white gloop. All I saw was Nate.

But Principal Cruz hadn't actually vanished—she rammed me in the gut with her shoulder and I landed on my back in the potato mash. Gucci had Ms. WWE on her stomach and was pulling her head up by the shoulders, both to pin her and keep her from inhaling spuds. "I've got mine!" Gucci screamed. "Now pin yours!"

Struggling and thrashing in four inches of slippery potatoes as the full weight of my kids' elementary school principal pressed down on me was an incredibly visceral experience, and not one I would recommend. Since Gucci was still firmly atop Ms. WWE, the audience howled for me to wriggle out from under Principal Cruz and pin her. Or maybe they were cheering for Principal Cruz to crush me?

As she fought to grab my arms, I thrashed like a greased pig at the Ada County Fair. She caught one of my wrists.

"I think my brother likes you," she said.

"Really?" I managed as I tried to scissor-kick out from under her. One of my ears filled with sludge and I could feel potato squelching in my butt crack.

"He only told me about five times how hilarious you are," she said. She stretched out the word *hilarious* in the singsong of sibling torment.

"He did?" I panted, so dumbfounded she had a chance to grab my other wrist and pin it. I struggled hard but couldn't twist free.

"One!" the emcee cried. "Two!"

I yanked hard in a futile attempt to free myself.

"Three! Four! Five!" the crowd screamed.

"And the match ends in a TIE!" the emcee said. "Looks like we'll have to split the prize money between the two teams!"

The crowd bayed its approval.

Principal Cruz staggered to her feet as I rolled over onto my hands and knees. She patted my back. "Good effort!"

"Sorry," I said to Gucci when I'd climbed out.

"Are you kidding? Nobody else would've done that for me," Gucci said.

"You won your fight, and I lost mine, so you should get all the money," I said, using a finger to scoop tater from my ear. When Gucci started to protest, I raised my palm. "No. I insist. Two hundred dollars will cover the rest of your pole classes." It would also buy groceries for my kids, but I didn't say that. I wished so hard I hadn't taken all that money from my mom. This somehow felt like a tiny (if indirect) amends.

"You sure?" Gucci asked. When I nodded, she thumped her chest. "You are my ride-or-die. Whatever you need, I'm here for you." She threw both arms around me. My mom used to say, "The Universe gives you what you need when you need it." And it wasn't lost on me that the person hugging me right now while declaring she owed me a favor had forensics expertise.

Instead I asked if she'd seen Salma Hayek smashing the "dirtbag that got thrown out of Huckleberry's" over the head with a beer bottle. But Gucci reported she hadn't spotted anything noteworthy at the club after I left, except for Layna climbing on-stage to show off her (very amateur) body rolls.

Disappointed, I was heading to the bathroom to change—holding my sweatsuit at arm's length to keep it from getting covered in mashed potatoes—when Agent Nate Duran stepped out in front of me.

"Job Talk Tuesday and now this?" he said. "Please tell me this is not a normal weekday for you."

*I also learned a floorwork move called the Vagina Monster and hid a dead body in my kids' playhouse.* But what I said was: "I wouldn't say *normal.* But the real question is: Why was your sister wrestling *me*? Or anyone, for that matter?"

"She lives to get rowdy," he said. "Also, I dared her. The woman will not pass up a dare. It's how she ended up an elementary school principal, but that's a story for another time."

Layna rocked up and introduced herself to Nate, tossing one of her fake ponytails over her shoulder and holding out a hand for him to kiss. Which was as awkward as it sounds.

"She has no game," I explained.

She looked at me. "I love you, but you are not riding home in my Porsche like that."

"I can Uber. I'll just find a trash bag to sit on."

"I'm already gonna have one mashed-potato-covered woman in my car," Nate said. "Why not two?"

"No game, my ass," Layna said, shooting me a sassy look. "I just got you a ride home from a hottie."

Nate blushed scarlet and let out an unrestrained laugh. I already loved that sound.

As I sat on an emergency blanket Nate had pulled from his trunk, I tried not to get any potato sludge on his backseat. I'd stripped off my undies, shorts, and jog bra in the bathroom and pulled on my sweatsuit. Now my gloopy underclothes were in a plastic grocery bag.

"You really should have sat shotgun," Principal Cruz said.

"Shotgun goes to the wrestling victor, not the vanquished," I replied. "Your brother said you mashed the patriarchy because he dared you to. True or false, Principal Cruz?"

"Call me Lucia!" she said. "Half true. I have a lot of adrenaline to burn off after work. And you should know: If there's anyone in this world wilder than an elementary school teacher, it's an elementary school principal." She wiggled in her seat. "I have to say, it's gonna be interesting getting mashed potato out of my private bits."

Commenting on the current sloppy state of my own orifices seemed inappropriate. "Mrs. Glidewell doesn't seem wild."

"Mrs. Glidewell has a stripper pole in her bedroom," Lucia said.

"She doesn't!" I cried.

"Sure does. But if you quote me on that I will deny," she said.

"I'll put it in the vault," I said. Then to Nate, "You're quiet."

"It's because he likes listening to you," Principal Cruz teased. "Because you're 'hi-lar-i-ous.'"

"Stop that," Nate said.

"Normally, I can't shut him up," Lucia continued. "But around you he's too twitterpated to speak."

"You need to stop right now," Nate said. But he sounded more embarrassed than mad.

As my face flamed, I felt grateful it was dark in the car. "This is me right here," I said, gesturing at my duplex, which looked cozy through the falling snow.

"It was fun to get to know you a little better," Lucia said, her voice sparkling. I had the sense I could hang out with these two forever and never get tired of them.

"It was. Thanks for the ride," I said, barely remembering to grab my bag of starchy underclothes.

Once I'd told Emmylou about my wild night, I listened to her (somewhat irritating) concerns that Alice's Betty White face mask was an "odd toy for a little girl" and that Phoebe's biting was a sign of a deeper emotional ill. After I bid her good night, I took a hot shower to blast potato out of my nooks and crannies, then went to work on laundry mountain.

As I completed the mindless task of going through pockets before tossing clothes in the machine, I let the words *Day of the Rope* and all they implied sink in for the first time since I'd heard the voice memo from Ralphie the Lizard. In three weeks, my furlough would be done and I'd be back at work. But even if I quit my job altogether, my coworkers would be there at the Capitol Grill serving sloppy joes to crusty old legislators and idealistic young staffers. I was currently tortured by the thought I might've had something to do with the murder of one slimeball who probably deserved to die. I certainly couldn't live with the blood of countless innocents on my conscience.

I'd fished a purple marker out of Phoebe's jeans and a tin of Crazy Aaron's Thinking Putty from Alice's hoodie. Now inside the pocket of my L.L.Bean puffer, my fingers closed around something with sharp edges.

A bottle cap. It had a tiny hole drilled through the middle and *BuckSnort Root Beer* stamped on it. I'd always thought BuckSnort only came in cans. I turned it over, studying it. Had this bit of flotsam been in my jacket pocket for months? Or could it be a clue to my whereabouts during my blackout Sunday night?

With the washing machine running and the BuckSnort cap tucked into my purse, I put on my jammies and crept to the twins' room. They lay conked out in Alice's bottom bunk, *Paddington 2* still running on the iPad propped up against a pillow. The Brown kids huddled in a London phone booth where they played Joanna Lumley's recorded voice into the phone receiver to trick Hugh Grant.

Gently lifting the tablet, I hit pause and studied my girls. Phoebe wore a red Little Mermaid wig and slept with one arm flung out as if trying to grab something just out of reach. Alice's pajamas were on inside out, and she had her beloved Betty White face mask tucked into her elbow, as if she'd had an attack of narcolepsy right after robbing an armored car. Seeing them sleeping, so perfectly rumpled, always made me remember that sometimes life is joyful and beautiful. Sometimes even our wildest dreams come true (times two)! But the twins' soft breathing also terrified me. It was my job to stay alive and well and out of prison so they'd have a shot at a reasonably trauma-free childhood. I wanted to give them that, more than I'd even wanted to have them in the first place. To that end—as soon as I'd gotten my twins onto the school bus tomorrow—I'd head to Connor's house to see what I could discover.

# SIXTEEN

*Wednesday*

The dead guy lived in a part of Boise called the Bench, because it sits on a plateau north of downtown. The Bench is being rapidly gentrified, but his street still could've been the establishing shot of a 1970s sitcom about a down-on-its-luck working-class family. After parking a few houses down, I slouched behind the wheel to stuff my hair under a beanie. Next I pulled on thin gloves to avoid leaving prints. I was on a three-pronged mission:

1. Nab any packages so they wouldn't blare to the neighbors that Connor had gone missing.
2. Break into his house.
3. Find further clues (or better yet, proof!) as to who killed him and why.

Bonus points if I could find evidence re: a plan to attack the capitol.

I carefully avoided patches of black ice on the sidewalk. The last thing I needed was to have an ambulance on record rescuing me from Connor Johnson's doorstep.

Connor's house was so small it seemed impossible he'd have a roommate, but his sidewalk had been shoveled—hopefully a Good Samaritan neighbor had done it. His mailbox was a drop-through slot, but a couple UPS boxes sat stacked at the door. If anyone asked, I'd say I lived three streets over and my packages had been delivered here by accident.

As I scooped up the parcels, a dog's panicked barking erupted. Someone was inside! With a dog! A 1990s John Travolta might as well have slammed a syringe full of adrenaline into my heart. I was bolting toward my car, stumbling on black ice, when a lightning bolt of understanding struck.

If Connor was dead—

And had no roommates—

Maybe the dog inside belonged to Connor. If so, it'd been alone for three days. I couldn't in good conscience leave a hungry, thirsty, abandoned animal trapped all alone.

And maybe I could search the place after all. I dumped the packages in my trunk and headed back to the house.

To be safe, I knocked on the front door. The dog barked desperately but no one answered.

Despite the piled-up snow, a hard shove opened the back gate. After a couple of short yaps, the dog started whining pitifully. I couldn't find a key under the mat or the snow-filled ceramic pot. But when I turned the knob, the back door swung right open. A sleek gray pit bull, barely out of puppyhood and smelling of potting soil, jumped on me.

"Hey there, buddy," I said, squatting down to pet him. "What happened to your ear?"

His torn ear had been neatly stitched together. Something rumbled—a neighbor rolling a garbage can to the street. Hurriedly, I yanked the blinds closed.

"Hello?" I ventured.

Nothing.

Scooping up the water bowl, I filled it at the sink. The dog danced and whined at my feet as if to say: *I have plenty of toilet water, you beautiful idiot. I need food!*

As soon as I poured dog food into his plastic bowl, the ravenous pit bull started scarfing. My Mom Instincts forced me to sweep the drying piles of dog doo into a dust pan and fling them into the backyard. Next

I dropped tea towels on the pee puddles to soak them up. Only then did I begin to scan the house for clues.

The fridge hosted a bottle of ketchup and some moldy leftovers from Panda Express. My hopes the box of Tillamook ice cream sandwiches in the freezer would be full of cash, illicit drugs, or bars of gold were dashed. But the sandwiches were salted caramel, my favorite.

I peeled off a glove, unwrapped a sandwich, and nibbled as I walked the house. A couch and giant flat-screen dominated the living room. A poster for the movie *Face/Off* hung from a shiplap wall alongside a life-sized cutout of comedian-turned-podcaster Joe Rogan. Go figure.

Soap and a disposable razor sat on the bathroom counter. A cracked leather belt dangled from the shower rod. The cabinet drawers housed tweezers, aspirin, Q-tips, and not much else.

In the bedroom, an open laptop with a sticky-looking screen made me willing to bet the whole thing was radioactive with porn. I didn't have the slightest idea how to open it without a passcode.

In the lone framed photo on the desk, Connor stood with his arm around a smiling woman with bleached hair. Was this Baylee? A little boy, maybe four years old, stood beside her. Connor wore a happy smile. The woman smiled too, but her eyes were melancholy. The little boy looked worried. Anxiety sank its talons into my guts. I suddenly remembered Connor saying he went to Huckleberry's to stop thinking about "the one who got away. And her kid."

This must be them. I set the ice cream sandwich on the desk and used my phone to snap a photo of the framed picture.

The dog trotted into the room, looking at me with big wet eyes.

"Don't try to make me love you," I said.

*Bam! Bam! Bam!* A fist pounded the front door. The dog raced toward it, barking wildly.

Dropping to the hardwood, I army-crawled to the window and lifted the corner of the blinds. A muscular man with a crooked nose stood on the front stoop. His thin T-shirt defied the breath-clouding cold. Squinting,

I could make out the smiling face of a golden retriever and the plain black outline of a dachshund inked on his arms. Part of me wanted to throw open the front door and ask if he wanted to take this puppy home with him. But then, to my horror, the front door actually clicked opened.

"Aw, hey there, sweet boy." The intruder's voice reached me from the living room. What did the dead guy have against locking his doors?

Looking around in a panic from my vantage on the floor, I saw my fatal mistake: the uneaten half of the ice cream sandwich lay in plain view on the desk. The bedroom door was open—the intruder would see me if I made a grab for my pilfered snack. I had only one option. Using a floorwork pole dancing move called the cobra wiggle, I shimmied through the quarter-inch thick dust under the bed until I was entirely hidden from view.

"Connor! You home?" the intruder called. "Looks like your ear's healing up nice," he said to the dog. "Now tell me, buddy—where is that shit-heel owner of yours?"

As he headed to the kitchen, I prayed he wouldn't glance out into the backyard and see my lone set of footprints. Next, I heard him rustling through the bathroom cabinet. The dust was making my brain tickle. I pinched my nose to fight back a sneeze as the footsteps headed my way. Any second now he'd come into the bedroom, spot what was left of my ice cream sandwich, and realize he wasn't alone.

Dog nails clicked into the bedroom. Paws hit the desk and I heard a happy gobble as the dog wolfed down my ice cream.

A blink later, the interloper strode into the bedroom. I didn't dare breathe. As desk drawers opened and closed, the dog trotted over and sniffed at my feet. I desperately tried to telegraph to the pup that, despite having just saved me, it now needed to stay the hell away.

"What are you doing over there?" the man asked. The dog continued to sniff at my ankles. I sweated it out in the dust as a pen scratched paper. "You'll tell Connor I'm looking for him, won't you, boy?"

Blessedly, dog nails clacked after the intruder as he tromped from the room. The front door opened and closed; I let out the longest breath of my life. Only when the truck motor faded did I dare wriggle out of my hiding place.

The dog galloped back into the bedroom and licked my face.

"Thank you," I said, giving him a grateful pat. I'd climbed to my feet and was trying to brush dust off my clothes when I spotted a handwritten note laying where my ice cream sandwich had been.

*Connor,*

*Give me back the meds you stole. I'm serious, bruv.*

*—Harlan*

Maybe the Ambien that'd rolled out of Connor's pocket belonged to this Harlan guy. If so, I didn't blame him for being pissed. I'd had two bad night's sleep in a row and already I felt borderline psychotic. Harlan's note slid into my back pocket.

After taking one last look around, I scooped up the mail from under the mail slot and grabbed a leash from a nail in the kitchen. The dog wiggled so much it was hard to hook the leash to its collar. It looked up at me with warm, shining eyes.

"Technically I owe you," I said. "But I cannot handle a dog right now. You understand. I'm sure someone will adopt you from the shelter very soon. All I know for sure is: You are *not* coming home with me."

# SEVENTEEN

"Don't get attached because we're not keeping it," I said, as the twins dropped to their knees and threw their arms around the dog's neck.

"Oh, Mommy," Alice began. Phoebe finished her sentence, "We love her so much."

"Don't start! We are *not* keeping it," I repeated, feeling like an ogre, but an ogre without the bandwidth to care for a high-maintenance pet.

The dog thumped its tail in delight as Phoebe draped herself over its back. "Everyone at school has big families," Phoebe said. "Can't we at least have one dog?"

"Johnica has seventy-two cousins!" Alice said.

"And her mom has like three sister wives," I added, under my breath.

"Only two," Phoebe said. "And they live across the street."

Alice looked concerned our conversation was veering off-track. "What we're trying to say is we miss Grandma Lulu. So much. No one else in the whole world can do a Kermit voice like she could."

"I miss her too," I said, my voice catching.

"And we think having a dog could help," Alice said.

Clearly, the girls were yearning for things I hadn't been able to provide—a big extended family, or at the very least more friends around. A dog did not seem like too much to ask. Yet all I could think about was how if we kept the dog, it might run away or get hit by a car. I didn't want my girls to go through that sort of loss. I didn't think I could take it myself.

With the twins busy throwing a blanket over the dog and pretending it was a ghost, I opened Connor's packages and letters in the kitchen, hoping for an Ipsy box full of clues instead of makeup. Instead I found payday loan offers, a round blanket that looked like a giant tortilla, and a T-shirt that said *ASK ME ABOUT MY COCK*. Trial and error revealed that if the wearer pulled the hem over his head, it looked like he was a rooster. And he got to show off his abs. A nifty optical illusion for the strip club.

Connor's phone dinged. Another voice memo from Ralphie the Lizard—which I couldn't listen to unless I used Connor's face to unlock his cell. The last thing I wanted to do was climb into a playhouse with a corpse. But having kids on my own had taught me how to do things that terrified me.

First, I went to my bedroom closet and stuffed Connor's teal vest into a Hefty Cinch Sak. I'd give anything to be able to remember how I ended up wearing that vest! The twins didn't even look up when I told them I was taking out the garbage. Instead I trudged through the fresh snow of the backyard, dragged the playhouse doors open, and crawled inside. Now that I'd been in Connor's house and had eaten one of his ice cream sandwiches, it was even harder to see his stiff, cold, crumpled body. I pushed the trash bag into the far corner of the cramped space and leaned in to examine the lump on Connor's forehead—likely caused by Salma Hayek whacking him with a beer bottle. A decent egg, but it hardly looked fatal. I couldn't bring myself to yank his pants further down to check out the stab wound on his thigh, but the relatively small bloodstain told me all I needed to know there. Next, I unbuttoned his shirt to examine the stab wound on his chest. It was partially obscured by dried blood, but didn't look deep enough to have killed him either. Clearly I was missing something.

I crawled out and headed toward the house, then stood shivering by the sliding glass door with Connor's unlocked phone. I hit play on the voice memo. "Confirm you can meet Baylee at Burgdorf Saturday at one for the handoff. If I don't hear your voice, she's not going."

There was no chance Connor would be at Burgdorf, but I couldn't exactly send Ralphie a voice memo from Connor telling him that. Hurriedly, I checked to see if any other messages had come in.

**Natty Lite:** Let me know when we can meet up. It's urgent.

I texted back: sorry, man. out of town.

In the living room, Alice and Phoebe were wrestling the dog's hind legs into a tutu. Instead of being annoyed, the pit bull beamed.

"Her name is Little Sister!" Phoebe and Alice yelled in unison. It was spooky to see them actually agreeing on something.

A rooster crowed and the dog barked. My mom had been pretty tickled when she'd installed that rooster doorbell. I threw open the door, ready to tell the person on the other side I needed organized religion like a bear needs a prom dress.

But it was Miranda Carson, looking stylish in a fur-trimmed coat. The blood in my veins turned to Slushee. Had she come to investigate my unfit parenting for CPS? A loud thunk sounded behind me, followed by a wail. Alice had tripped over the dog.

"Is now a bad time?" Miranda asked, but she was already sailing into my living room. You have to welcome in a vampire, but former-high-school-cheerleaders-turned-CPS-case-workers are apparently a type of creature who can cross the threshold into your home with no invitation whatsoever.

The dog barreled at Miranda. Everything went into slow motion as I experienced the sort of terror you can only feel when your foster pit bull is about to attack a Child Protective Services worker.

But Little Sister stopped short at Miranda's feet, spun in a circle, let out a joyful bark, and looked up at her with adoring eyes. Jesus, Mary, and Joan Rivers, if I had a Xanax, I'd take it.

Miranda stared at the dog.

“Her name is Little Sister,” Phoebe said, running over and hugging Little Sister’s midsection territorially. “If you think she’s your dog, you’re wrong. She’s ours.”

“That’s not my dog,” Miranda said, staring at the pup as if trying to place it. “But I’ve met a dog before that looked exactly like that one.”

The twins beamed. The fact that Miranda was not here to reclaim Little Sister was clearly enough to win them over.

“When we saw you before, we didn’t like you,” Phoebe said. “But you seem nicer today. Even though you snatch people’s children.”

“Phoebe!” I said. “That’s not polite.” I made a mental note to talk to her about how it was sometimes important not to tell annoying people how annoying they are.

“I help keep children safe,” Miranda said, but she didn’t seem ruffled. She’d likely heard worse. She glanced around the living room, taking in my mom’s odd decor. The disco ball dangling from the ceiling; the window ledges lined with fake food; the avocado tree my mom had named Frank Sinatra; the couch draped with her DIY tie-dye slipcover; the walls hung with David Hockney prints she’d bought at a gallery show in LA.

“This was your mom’s place, right?” Miranda said.

I nodded, and tried to push down my grief. Seeing Miranda made time collapse. I was a junior in high school again, complaining, “Why couldn’t I have been born a Miranda Carson?” But my mom said I was perfect. In reality I was funny, awkward, weird, dancing and sweating fiercely in my Mr. Potato Pants mascot suit, just to make my fellow students laugh—until I was defrocked because Miranda hid her vodka in my duffel bag.

“Your mom was always so cool and quirky,” this middle-aged Miranda said, and for a second I thought I detected an unexpected note of jealousy in her voice.

“She sure was,” I said.

“I remember one time both our moms were around to pick us up at the end of practice. My mom was starting in on me for not being crisp enough on some stupid cheerleading move and your mom said, 'Miranda, honey, I thought you looked just great out there.'" Miranda's eyes gleamed and for a second I thought she'd start to cry. Instead, she set her purse down on my couch, and said, "Any chance you'd like to offer me a cup of tea?" She didn't look like she was here to document my parenting fails for CPS, but perhaps it was a sneak attack.

*Absolutely not*, I wanted to say. But instead I went to turn the kettle on.

# EIGHTEEN

There's nothing like serving tea to the former queen bee of your high school to make you feel like you've never actually grown up. Add the irrational fear that said queen bee was there to snatch your children or expose the murdered corpse in your yard and you'd have my mental state.

"Low-stress chamomile," I said, casually scooping up Connor's mail and dropping it in the recycling bin with a prayer to sundry pagan goddesses that Miranda hadn't noticed his name on the envelopes. Miranda did not know, could not know, I had a mansicle on the property. But why was she here? My only hope was she'd joined a twelve-step program and wanted to make her ninth-step amends for letting me take the fall for her teenage misdeeds.

"Is it that obvious I'm stressed?" Miranda said. She actually did look tired and anxious. "After this I'm headed to one of my mom's scented-candle parties where she'll neg me about my looks and all my life choices."

"Your mom's still that hard on you?"

"She could have a side hustle training abusive Marine Corps sergeants."

"Ugh! I'm sorry," I said. "My mom told me your mom complained you wouldn't carry a handgun. Your mom said the taser she gave you as a stocking stuffer wasn't going to cut it."

What I didn't say was that, according to my mother, Mrs. Carson's television had gotten stuck on Newsmax, turning her into a full-fledged right-wing extremist. It had made me feel a tiny bit sorry for Miranda. But right now I needed to feel sorry for her from a distance.

As if she could read my mind, Miranda walked to the sliding glass door. She gazed in the direction of the playhouse; I grabbed for my phone and typed an SOS.

"My mom worries about me because of my job," Miranda said. "When it's necessary, I remove kids. So plenty of people in this town aren't happy with me." She paused. "It's kind of nice talking to you about my mom. You've known her since forever so you get it."

"I've hardly seen her in twenty-five years, but I remember how she was," I admitted.

"If I tell you something about her, promise you'll take it to the grave?" she said.

*Don't confide in me, Miranda. I don't like you.* "Pinky promise," I said, eyes on my phone. Send. Phone down.

"She's started making deepfake candle labels with her Cricut Joy Xtra."

"Her what?" Maybe I'd been on the Best Coast so long I no longer understood the basic vocab of your average Boisean.

"It's a design and cutting machine for making labels, tickets, stickers, you name it. Even the founder of D.S. & Durga wouldn't be able to tell my mom's Big Sur After Rain label from an original. My mom sells them at her candle parties at a 'deep discount.' For sixty bucks each!"

"Damn!" I said. "Does her Big Sur After Rain candle really smell like Big Sur after rain?"

"It actually does."

"So it's *almost* a victimless crime?"

Miranda shrugged. "These guys she hires to haul her candles around, you would not believe how dodgy they are." She turned and spotted the Pole Kisses studio brochure Emmylou had stuck on my fridge with a magnet. "Pole Kisses?"

"Wait, do you do pole?" I asked, hoping she'd say no. The last thing I needed was Miranda horning in on my forced hobby.

But she crinkled her face as if I'd suggested she lick my garbage can.

"No way. Like, don't strippers teach some of their classes? That's what I heard."

*Heaven forbid a professional pole dancer should teach people trying to learn how to dance on a pole*, I wanted to say. But I couldn't afford to get on the bad side of a CPS worker. So instead I said, "Miranda, it's interesting to catch up. But can I ask why you stopped by?"

She glanced at me nervously—maybe she *was* here to make a ninth-step amends! Little Sister let out a happy bark from the living room, which was followed by a rush of whispers and giggles.

"What happened to your dog's ear?" Miranda said, clearly stalling.

*Well, Miranda, the thing is: I have a dead white supremacist in my kids' playhouse, and I went to his house to find clues as to who actually murdered him. When I was there, I stole his dog.* "I'm not sure. He belonged to a friend of a friend of a friend who couldn't keep him." I leaned in and whispered, "We're not keeping him either."

Phoebe and Alice and the dog collapsed into a pile in the kitchen doorway, all of them panting and smiling from exertion and the comfort of being part of a pack.

Miranda glanced from them to me. "Good luck with that."

"Can we let Little Sister out into the backyard, Mommy?" Alice asked.

"No!" I said. Visions of the dog dragging the corpse out of the playhouse danced through my head. "The fence isn't secure enough. We can't have the dog in the backyard. At all!"

Disappointed, the twins wandered back to the living room, trailing the dog.

"What I need to say is," Miranda began, "people make mistakes."

The rooster doorbell crowed.

The sight of Emmylou on my doorstep brought a wave of intense relief. Little Sister stared at her curiously, sniffing and backing slowly away. The dog didn't have an instant crush on her, like it had with Miranda. But at least Little Sister wasn't jumping on a senior citizen.

"Whose adorable puppy is this?" Emmylou demanded, bending down to pet the dog.

"Long story," I said, suddenly worried Emmylou was going to lose track of the assignment.

"I'm having an emergency!" she cried, sounding so convincing for a moment I believed her. "Can you and the girls take me to Rite Aid? I'm out of insulin and not feeling so great." She spotted Miranda. "I'm sorry. I didn't realize you had company. I'll go home and slip into a diabetic coma alone."

"That's okay," I said. "Miranda was just leaving." I felt the slightest twinge. If Miranda had come to apologize for her twenty-five-year-old misdeeds, I was almost sorry to miss it.

But Emmylou was already handing Miranda her purse and hustling her toward the door. "My blood sugar. It's a mess," she said. "You understand, dear."

With the front door shut tightly behind Miranda, I collapsed onto the couch, feeling unsettled. "Thanks so much for saving my life," I said. "Again."

"I saw your text and came right over," Emmylou said. "Who was that anyway?"

"A mean girl I went to high school with."

"She's got that look." Emmylou waved her hand around her head to indicate Miranda's flawless hair and makeup.

The dog flipped onto its back in hopes of a tummy rub and Emmylou obliged.

"Her name is Little Sister," Phoebe said.

"Should be called Little Brother by the looks of it," Emmylou said.

"We hope Mom lets us keep her," Alice said.

"Otherwise, our hearts will break," Phoebe chimed in.

"No one can emotionally blackmail like a child can emotionally blackmail," I murmured.

"Having a dog would be good for these girls," Emmylou said.

This input was annoying, given that Emmylou wouldn't be the one caring for the dog. "Last thing I need is to be responsible for another creature," I managed, trying to keep my tone light. "Mind hanging with the kids for a few? I'm desperate for a shower."

"Sure thing, toots."

Behind the locked bathroom door, hot water blasting, I sobbed silently as I rubbed my skin raw with lavender salt scrub, my favorite witchy remedy for clearing energy. Normal single motherhood was hard. But this . . . all this was too hard.

Back in the living room, my hair wrapped in a towel, undereye masks slapped on to hide the fact that I'd been crying, I sank down next to Emmylou on the couch. She was still talking with the twins about the dog.

"You should definitely take him to the dog park." Emmylou said. "Single men galore! And in ten days, it'll feel almost like spring!"

A sense of foreboding descended, and not just because Emmylou was being bossy. "What do you mean, 'it'll feel like spring?'"

"I just saw the extended forecast," Emmylou said. "A week from Saturday, highs will be nearly seventy! And it'll stay warm for days!" The clock was now officially ticking. I had ten days to get the corpse out of my yard, before it started to rot.

# NINETEEN

Phoebe always insisted on having the top bunk, but she now wanted Alice's bottom bunk so she could be closer to Little Sister. This caused a normally docile Alice to lose her ever-loving mind. Phoebe retaliated by biting Alice again—and this time I could see teeth marks! After a half hour of calming Alice down and talking to Phoebe about the importance of respecting other people's bodies (by not chomping on them), I had the girls snuggled on the floor in sleeping bags with Little Sister between them. Suddenly Alice pulled on her Betty White face mask.

"What is it?" I asked.

"Nothing," Alice said, sniffling audibly.

"I can hear you crying," I said.

"Don't tell her," Phoebe hissed.

"I can hear you, Phoebe," I said.

"We did something really bad," Alice confessed, letting out another sad, wet snuffle and pulling off the mask.

The twins talked over each other as the story tumbled out. When Miranda and I were in the kitchen, Little Sister had grabbed Miranda's purse strap with his teeth and pulled the whole thing off the couch. Lipstick and hand sanitizer and Kleenex and keys and an unzipped wallet spilling credit cards had all fallen out onto the rug. Not wanting to get Little Sister in trouble, the twins had shoved everything back into the purse and set it on the couch. But after Miranda left, Phoebe had noticed Miranda's driver's license under the coffee table. Instead of telling me about it right away, they'd hidden it.

"And the pretty lady—she's really bad at sex!" Alice reported.

I'd given the twins the-birds-and-the-bees talk, but clearly something had been misconstrued. "What do you mean?" I asked.

"She got an F!" Alice and Phoebe shouted in unison.

"I really thought she'd get an A," Phoebe said. "Or at least a B."

"I'm so confused," I said.

Alice pulled Miranda's driver's license from between the pages of her current favorite book, *Hamster Princess: Harriet the Invincible*. "See!" she said, pointing.

Under Miranda's name and address, the license read:

> Hgt: 5' 05"
> Sex: F
> Eyes: Blue

I laughed, relieved. After explaining to the girls that "Sex: F" meant that Miranda was female, not a bad lay, I assured them I wasn't mad at them and encouraged them to share discoveries such as Miranda's lost-and-found license with me as soon as possible. Then I rubbed their backs until they fell asleep and retreated to my room, carrying the Betty White mask with me. (I'd told Alice plenty of times it wasn't safe to sleep with it on, but still I worried.) Wanting to avoid giving Miranda the impression that my kids were thieving mini-delinquents, I decided to drop her license in her mailbox when she wasn't home. For now, I'd slip it into my own wallet for safekeeping. As I reached into the side pocket of my purse, my fingers brushed against the BuckSnort bottle cap and I wondered again if it was a random bit of trash or a clue to where I'd been Sunday night.

Grateful for the quiet, I plunked down in my mom's Eames chair dupe and spun Connor's phone in my fingers, trying to think. Layna had said there was no way we could get the Valley County Sheriff's Department all the way out to Burgdorf. Which was a moot point because Ralphie the Lizard wouldn't let Baylee go to Burgdorf unless he heard Connor say *in his own voice* that he'd be there.

Which was impossible, of course.

Feeling frustrated, I decided to do the thing I always did when I needed answers. I opened my laptop and hit up Dr. Google. My first search was for "Connor Johnson Boise." It didn't turn up much at first—just social media pages with a couple hundred followers each and not many posts. Connor didn't follow anyone named Ralphie, Errol, or Harlan, either. Next I searched "Connor Johnson Idaho." Lo and behold, up popped a YouTube channel called *Idaho Connor the Patriot* with a head-shot that was definitely the dead guy. There were only nine videos. All posted a year ago, in January. Connor must have made a short-lived New Year's Resolution to become an influential YouTuber.

I hit play on the first video. Connor stood in front of a Confederate flag, which made no sense because Idaho wasn't even a state during the Civil War. Though maybe he should've declared war on whoever had given him that haircut.

"Hey, guys. What's up? It's Idaho Connor the Patriot here," he said. He shifted from foot to foot, a clear tell he had on-camera nerves. "I'm coming to you from the greatest state in America. Where we have majestic mountains, beautiful hot springs, and some of the most dedicated patriots in this great country."

Hot springs. He'd said hot springs. My eyes fell on my kids' tablet. I tapped the screen, and suddenly there was *Paddington 2* still on pause, the Brown kids huddled in the iconic London phone booth. A recording of Joanna Lumley's voice had been enough for them to fool Hugh Grant. Maybe it could work for me.

After downloading an MP3 recorder app, I started the YouTube video over from the beginning, listening for any phrase I might need now, or for future phone communications. "Hey, guys," Idaho Connor said, by way of salutation. I skipped back a few seconds and recorded the phrase on my phone, labeling the MP3 file "Hey, guys." The second file was called: "What's up?"

Much of Idaho Connor's rambling was useless. But I listened for the short little phrases. "When you hear about rallies at the capitol of your state, rallies to protect our freedom to control women's bodies," he said about a quarter of the way through the first video, "I want you to say: 'Yes! I'll be there.' I don't want to hear: 'I can't make it.'" I rewound and hit record right before he said: "Yes! I'll be there." I recorded him saying "I can't make it" as another file.

For tonight at least, I had what I needed.

No solo mom has the bandwidth to crawl around with a corpse every time she has to check messages. So I hit up YouTube to find tricks for overriding iPhone setting glitches. Armed with techy wisdom straight from some generous nerd's basement—"Try restarting the phone"—I tiptoed down to the kitchen, grabbed a flashlight from the cupboard, and headed out toward the playhouse. When the twins were babies and I was dealing with blocked nipple ducts and double diaper blowouts on the regular, I marveled at the sort of horrors a person could get used to. But this was taking things to a whole new level.

Back at my mom's desk, I was able to set the lock setting on Idaho Connor's freshly restarted phone to "Never." What did it say about my life that this felt like a major accomplishment? No calls had come in to Connor's phone, but Natty Lite had responded to the text I'd sent.

**Natty Lite:** This is not cool, man. When will you be back in town? We have work to do.

I typed quickly, not letting myself think too much about who this Natty Lite might be or why he wanted to meet with the dead guy.

**Connor:** i'm still out of town. and im sick. it's gonna be a few

I added a green-faced emoji and hit send.

Baylee had texted too.

**Baylee:** i'm still safe at Ralphie's. can't wait to c u saturday. I miss lil connor. can't wait to give him a kiss.

"Ew!" I said out loud. What I typed was: any way u can meet me in boise?

**Baylee:** no way. u know how controlling ralphie is.

I shuddered. Thank goodness Baylee didn't want to talk to Connor on the phone. Probably she didn't want Ralphie the Lizard to know about her burner.

**Connor:** Okay. see u at Burgdorf. bring yr old phone please, sweetums

**Baylee:** u bet. cabin 9. I'll hang my red swimsuit on the line

**Connor:** right on

I added a heart emoji for good measure and hit send. Now it was time to deal with Ralphie.

Carefully, so carefully, I held down the voice memo record button on Connor's phone as I played the MP3 from mine. "Yes!" Connor's voice said. "I'll be there." If Errol *had* murdered Idaho Connor, and he happened to be around when Ralphie the Lizard listened to this voice memo, it would give him quite a shock.

A moment later, Connor's phone dinged. "Watch out Idaho State Capitol building," Ralphie growled. "Here we come."

As a responsible citizen (and an employee of the capitol) I needed to report this impending attack to law enforcement. Day of the Rope was in less than three weeks! I promised myself I'd tell the police—as soon as I had evidence pointing to Errol as a murder suspect. I didn't trust the cops not to pin Connor's murder on me. I needed to be absolutely sure there was someone else to take the rap.

After plugging in Connor's phone, I crawled into bed, hoping my dreams would not be haunted by his slightly blue, slightly contorted, very dead face. But before I even closed my eyes, the phone sounded. I lunged to grab it, knocking a slice of plastic opera cake to the floor. This new voice memo was from a contact called "the Receiver." Even distorted by a filter, the voice sounded very authoritative.

"Confirm once you've picked up the potato mashers," the voice said, "and we can set a meeting time to trade mashed potato recipes."

Idaho Connor must be the middleman, slated to pick up the hand grenades and plans for Day of the Rope and deliver them to this mystery person called the Receiver. Obviously Connor wasn't going to be able to fulfill either of those obligations. But I needed the Receiver—and everyone else—to believe Connor was going about his business as usual. At least for as long as possible.

After a few minutes of pondering my next move, I sent back a voice memo of Connor saying, "Will do, my red, white, and blue."

Deciding whether Connor should cancel the meeting at the last minute or stand up the Receiver altogether would be a problem for another day.

# TWENTY

*Thursday*

Needing advice, I got Phoebe and Alice on the school bus in the morning and walked down to meet Layna for coffee at Dawson Taylor. In Los Angeles, my go-to coffee shop was Intelligentsia on Abbot Kinney, which was always packed with stylish, relevant people. In contrast, Dawson Taylor had zero people in line to order and a gaggle of grandpas having a coffee klatch under a painting that looked like a Louis L'Amour novel cover. As I waited for Layna, I checked the ten-day weather forecast, hoping there'd been a change. But the gods had not been so benevolent. In nine days, temps were still expected to shoot up to almost seventy.

Layna's outfit—a flouncy red skirt with tights and a black beret—distracted me from my panic. With her newly long hair, muscular calves, and bright red fingernails and lipstick, she was pulling it off.

"I'm in my French era," she said. "These extensions have given me a new lease on life!"

"*Oui, oui,*" I said.

The gaggle of grandpas sitting nearby were clearly eavesdropping.

"*Bonjour, jolie demoiselle,*" one of them called out.

"*Bonjour,*" Layna said, gamely. But as soon as we settled in at a table out of earshot of the men's hearing aids, she moaned, "Oh my god, I'm grandpa bait!"

"He was very into you," I agreed.

"I don't know if I should be flattered or depressed. I want a sexual adventure! But with someone who doesn't need Viagra!"

"If you were wearing that beret and nothing else, that grandpa wouldn't need Big Pharma."

"Please," she said, waving away the suggestion. "At that age they're looking for a nurse or a purse. But I matched with a hottie on Hinge! He's old, but not grandpa old." She held out her phone to display the Wikipedia page of a smiling man in a puffy orange astronaut suit holding a helmet under one arm. "He's been DMing me—from the space station!"

"Kendrick B. Johnson is an American engineer and retired NASA astronaut," I read. But I had to stop because I was laughing so hard.

"What?" Layna said.

Tears streamed from my eyes. "That guy's retired. He is definitely not DMing you from outer space. You, my friend, are being catfished."

Layna dropped her head down into her arms. "Noooooo!"

"Don't feel bad. It's not your fault people are despicable." I reached out and patted her hand. "This conversation does not pass the Bechdel test, by the way."

"What's the Bechdel test?" she said, looking up at me.

Internal sigh. In my LA social circles, the Bechdel test had been a given for fifteen years. "For a movie—or in this case a conversation—to pass the Bechdel test it has to have two women who talk to each other about something other than a man."

She looked thoughtful. "If you give me an update on the mansicle, would that pass the Bechdel test? I mean, we're still two women talking about a man—but does it count if the man's dead?"

I laughed and gave her the rundown on my trip to Idaho Connor's house, how I'd gained a (temporary) dog, and the ingenious way I'd figured out how to send voice memos that sounded like they were from Idaho Connor himself.

"I think you might have a knack for this shit," Layna said.

"Someone with a knack wouldn't've brought the dog home." The twins had taken it upon themselves to feed Little Sister a can of chili when I was in the laundry room, which had caused a bout of violent doggie diarrhea. When I'd wailed we weren't keeping the dog, I'd upset the twins so much I threw ten dollars in the Therapy Jar. "But I was thinking . . ." I paused. "Isn't my only real option to go meet with Errol's girlfriend, Baylee, and get her smashed phone?"

"But you know that in winter Burgdorf Hot Springs is only accessible by snowmobile, right?" Layna said.

I nodded. Of course I knew it. I'd always begged my mom to take me when the whole place was snowbound, but she'd tell me she couldn't blow our weekly grocery budget on a snowmobile rental. "Since Baylee is bringing"—I lowered my voice to a whisper—"hand grenades, maybe I could get the ATF to go out there."

"You just want to see that hot ATF agent again," Layna said.

I exhaled a "Puh!" of denial, accidentally blowing sugary donut dust all over the table. "I know about an impending attack on the capitol! In nineteen days! Telling the authorities seems like the only right thing to do!"

Layna lifted one eyebrow. "How do you think that's going to turn out for you?"

"Fair," I said. "I need some evidence first—against someone that isn't me. I think I might need to go out there. To Burgdorf. On a snowmobile. To get that SIM card from Baylee. And maybe the plans for Day of the Rope. Maybe I could see what Baylee knows. Errol's clearly been abusive. She's probably ready to talk."

"Maybe! And either way, the SIM card, the plans—that's hard evidence." Layna took a pensive sip of her latte. "You don't need that agent to save you, Bechdel babe. You can clear this up yourself. You know, I always wanted to be a badass Bond girl. This snowmobiling trip could fit the bill."

My eyes pricked with tears. "You'd go with me?"

Layna smiled and gave the tiniest of nods.

"Well, hopefully it won't come to that," I said.

The flirty grandpa passed us on his way out, pausing to give a little bow to Layna. "*Au revoir, mademoiselle.*"

"*Au revoir, mon prince,*" Layna said.

I gave her a look as the beaming grandpa exited the coffee shop.

"What? I have to practice my game on someone," Layna said. "So say we pop Baylee's SIM into a working phone and see what Errol actually texted her. It might be incriminating enough to hand over to the police. Especially if we have grenades and plans for Day of the Rope too."

"I don't want to mess with grenades," I said.

"Fine, we'll leave the grenades."

"Baylee won't be happy to see us instead of Connor," I said.

"We can tell her Connor's scared of Errol. He got cold feet. He was too ashamed to tell her himself. Blah blah blah." Layna considered. "I think it could work."

Burgdorf had always been such a safe happy place for me when I was a kid. Still, I sure as hell wouldn't go out there to meet some guy named Ralphie the Lizard. But if Layna and I were together, there couldn't be much harm in meeting with one woman. I took another bite of donut. "I really don't want to go to the cops. Not unless it's clear someone else killed Connor."

"If we've got solid evidence Errol probably did it, I think you could get immunity for stashing a body in a residential neighborhood," Layna said. "The police won't like that you went citizen rogue, but they'll have to help you out if you've thwarted an attempt by the IDIOTs to blow up the Idaho State Legislature. And you wouldn't have to spend your life worrying you're about to"—she leaned in and whispered—"go to prison for killing someone who's better off dead."

I shook my head to clear it of Layna's convincing argument. "I still think I better ask Agent Duran to help me. Maybe I should have the girls join his soccer team."

"Do not believe for one second that just because you want to bone a man, he'll rescue you and make all your problems go away!" she cried, so loudly the remaining grandpas turned to look. Her tone softened. "I may not know whether or not I'm being DMed from the moon, but even I know better than that."

But Layna's bossiness couldn't change the fact I still hoped the ATF might go to Burgdorf and seize the evidence and explosives. Which meant it was time for the twins to learn how to bend it like Beckham.

# TWENTY-ONE

With its fake turf, fluorescent lights, and screaming kids, indoor soccer practice was the fifth circle of hell. The sole bright spot was an unfettered chance to ogle Agent Nate Duran from afar. I wasn't the only one admiring him—when he bent down to scoop up an errant ball, the moms sitting in the bleachers stared like a gaggle of hungry pigeons watching a loosely attended basket of fries.

"Is it just me or is the new assistant coach hotter than a two-dollar pistol?" one mom said. She was naturally beautiful in a way that made me want to go home and exfoliate.

Instead of plunking down near the other moms, I'd settled in a little ways away. I didn't have the energy to make friends. But I always had energy for eavesdropping.

"I heard that two-dollar pistol works for the ATF," another mom said. She rocked a messy mom bun and eyelash extensions that gave her the look of a minor Kardashian. "I'd like him to take me on a stakeout. It's been a minute since I've gotten busy in a car, but I've been going to yoga. I think I'm ready."

The other moms busted up. Clearly these ladies were more fun than I'd expected.

To occupy myself, I texted Layna a photo of Matt Damon from *The Martian*.

**Tilly:** Do you think it's possible this guy is texting me from Mars? I just matched with him on Tinder.

**Layna:** HAHA I hate you.

As I slipped my phone back into my purse, my fingers brushed the BuckSnort bottlecap again. If that bit of detritus was a clue to where I'd been Sunday night, I still couldn't decipher it.

When Agent Nate Duran spotted me, his bright smile made me feel like a stick of butter floating on the surface of a warm pan. The other moms shot me assessing glances.

*I get it, ladies,* I wanted to say. *He seems too good to be true. But we all know that means he probably is.*

When the head coach blew his whistle for a break, the minor Kardashian mom took a tray of sliced oranges out to share with the team. Alice was busy chasing around a towering girl with waist-length black hair I recognized from the twins' class and who I'd secretly dubbed the Beautiful Giant. Phoebe grabbed an orange slice, forcing the rind under her lips to create an orange smile.

As Agent Duran jogged toward the stands, the moms' chatter faded and they held a hopeful collective breath. He stopped right in front of me, flashing such a high-wattage smile that it shielded me from the rays of jealousy coming from the other women.

I hadn't had sex since before my mom died. It was obviously getting to me, because relatively close-range eye contact with Agent Duran was making me feel that in a past life we'd made love at the base of a waterfall while the spray misting our skin sparkled like diamonds in the sun.

"Ms. Turner, the mashed-potato-wrestling comedian with a day job," he said.

"Agent Nate Duran, the federal agent who runs an Uber service exclusively for women covered in carbs," I said, feeling the other moms staring like I was a Bridgerton who'd captured a duke's fancy.

"The twins have been telling everyone they have a brand-new little sister?" He raised an eyebrow.

"We got a dog," I said. "At least temporarily. They named her Little Sister. I think so I'll feel like a monster if I try to find her a new forever home. Well, him. It's definitely a boy dog."

He laughed. "Sounds like they know how to get what they want." He glanced back at the twins. Phoebe was chewing a second orange slice, while Alice hung on to the Beautiful Giant's shirttail. "My niece needs to watch out."

"The Beautiful Giant is your niece?" I said. I was hot for him. His sister was a blast. My kids adored his niece. But I couldn't allow myself to hope.

"That's what you call Maricela? I think she'd be honored. But honestly, it looks like Alice might take her down."

"You can tell my kids apart?" I said, flabbergasted. It had taken Mrs. Glidewell a month.

"On the soccer field, anyone could tell them apart," he said. "Phoebe knows where the ball is at every second. Meanwhile Alice is busy playing with her Baby Yoda Band-Aid."

It was nice to talk to someone who saw my kids as separate entities. *I like you*, I wanted to say. *I'm not just here because I've stumbled onto a terrorist plot and need an ATF agent to bail me out.*

"How's work?" I asked. "I'm so curious about your job. So many questions."

"ATF questions? Fire away," he said.

"You sure do have those dad jokes locked and loaded." The joke I'd just made was criminally bad. "Oh my god! Your horrible gun puns are contagious. This is unforgivable."

He did a funny little victory dance, as if he'd scored an NFL touchdown, not just teed me up for a terrible wisecrack.

My plan A, to ask him about ATF raids and immunity, suddenly seemed both tonally off and way too forward for soccer practice.

A whistle blew. Nate glanced back at the field. The Beautiful Giant was crawling on hands and knees, the twins draped over her back like wiener dog puppies on an Irish wolfhound.

"Would you want to—" he started at the exact same time I said, "I guess you'd better—"

"What were you gonna say?" I asked.

"Getting a dog. Even temporarily. It's a big deal! Any chance I could take you and the girls to The STIL after practice to celebrate?"

The STIL was the one local place that could beat out any ice cream from an Abbot Kinney creamery. My mom used to take me and the twins there on a splurge, but it was definitely out of my price range. Especially while I was furloughed.

"The thing is—" I started.

"I'm buying," he said. "They have a patio. With heaters. And it's dog-friendly. I want to meet Little Sister."

Maybe this was a sign from the Universe that I needed to hand some of this burden over to Agent Nate Duran. I wouldn't tell him everything. Just enough to get the ATF to Burgdorf. Talking to him with the twins around wasn't ideal, but at least I wouldn't have to worry about things turning romantic. If he was interested in me now, he wouldn't be after he had ice cream with me and all my adorable baggage. He seemed to interact with the twins nicely here at soccer, but he'd never seen them all hopped up on sugar and lurching around with their shoulders pressed together, trying to convince strangers they were conjoined.

"We'd love to," I said. "But we'll have to swing by my place for the dog. And we can't stay too long. I've got a class tonight." Pole dancing class. But it sounded too flirty to say it out loud.

"I can meet you over there. Wanna swap numbers, just in case?" He handed me his phone. I put my number in his contacts and gave it back. "I'll call you so you have mine."

My phone dinged as he turned and jogged back to the team. Was I mistaken or did he have an extra pep in his step?

Some of the other soccer moms were giving me looks of baffled admiration, probably wondering how a woman like me could get the number of a guy like him. Frankly, I didn't know either, but I planned to enjoy it while I could.

When the twins and I arrived at The STIL, the patio lights imparted a feeling of good cheer to the cold and dark. Nate stood waiting in fitted jeans and a gray puffy coat. He dropped to one knee and rubbed Little Sister's ears while the twins looked on approvingly.

"Do you think you could teach her to play soccer?" Alice asked. Her eyes were bright again.

Nate laughed. "I could definitely teach her to play poker."

"Dogs don't play cards!" Phoebe cried.

True to his word, Nate bought us all ice cream and a cup of whipped cream for Little Sister. Phoebe thanked him by showing off her double-jointed elbows. Alice followed suit.

"Girls! Stop it!" I said. "He's eating."

Nate grinned and overextended his own elbows.

"You can do it too!" Alice said. "Mom can't."

"Billie Eilish and Taylor Swift. Also double-jointed!" he said.

"Seriously?" Alice asked, clearly in awe.

Not to be outdone, Phoebe made her tongue into that weird cloverleaf shape. Nate copied her. "Only the Irish can turn their tongues into the leaf of a clover," he said, with a fake brogue.

"You're not Irish," Alice said.

"Say something else like that!" Phoebe insisted.

"My grandpappy on my mother's side was born in Belfast," Nate said, not dropping the accent. He let out his signature unhinged laugh, which got me to giggling.

Phoebe wasn't as easy to impress as Alice, but even she seemed swayed by Nate's odd abilities. "Mom can't do that thing with her tongue either!"

"What can I say?" Nate met my eye, suddenly serious. "I'm a man of many talents."

A tingle spread through me, and I reminded myself I was not there for romance.

As the twins stomped around the patio eating their ice cream, Nate and I huddled on a bench. I pulled up the hood on my L.L.Bean coat, hoping it would make me look like Gisele in a Moncler puffer. As if understanding my need for a mammalian foot warmer, Little Sister lay down on top of my shoes.

I needed to bring up the difficult subject of an illegal backcountry arms deal. But I wanted to know more about this handsome fed who was taking me and my kids out for ice cream.

"How'd you end up in Boise?" I asked.

"Long version or short?" he said.

"I like a man who has a long version."

He raised an eyebrow at me and grinned. "I grew up in Seattle and did my freshman year at Boise State. But I felt like I'd been relegated to Bumpkinville, so I fled to Portland State." He held his ice cream in my direction. "Want to try?"

"What'd you get again?" I asked, digging in my spoon.

"Coffee with Baileys. And no offense about this being Bumpkinville?" he said, looking worried.

"None taken," I said. The bite of his ice cream made me moan—it was that good. "You can only stare at sagebrush for so long before you think there's got to be more to life." Now would be the perfect time to segue the conversation to what I'd "overheard" at Huckleberry's. But instead I found myself saying, "So you went to Portland State. Then what?"

"I'll hit the high notes because I want to hear about you," he said.

"A man who asks questions! A rare breed," I replied. "But go on. You first."

"Okay, I graduated," he said. "Went to culinary school. Loved it. Became a chef at a fancy Portland restaurant. Burnt out on restaurant culture."

"I've seen *The Bear*, so I get it."

"Exactly. I know chefs who couldn't even watch that show because it retraumatized them." He ate a bite of my ice cream. "Damn, that's good."

"Salted caramel. The best."

"So then, I became an air marshal. After a few years, I applied for the ATF. Don't tell, but most flights go pretty smoothly. I was ready for more action."

"Like raiding bad guys with caches of weapons?"

"Exactly," Nate said. "Though the ATF's a uniquely unpopular branch. Liberals don't like us because we're law enforcement. Conservatives don't like us because we take people's guns."

Now was definitely my chance to segue the conversation. But it had been so long since I'd had fun on a date. I didn't want to spoil things yet. "So why'd you come back to Bumpkinville?"

"When the ATF accepted me, they had me pick and rate seven cities. Boise was my seventh pick, only because my sister and her fam are here. The ATF offered me a job. They gave me twenty-four hours to decide whether or not to take it. My dream job. But in Boise—where I never wanted to live again." He shrugged. "Here I am."

"While we're on the subject of the ATF—" I began.

"Oh no," he said. "Fair's fair. You have to tell me about you." He patted my thigh as if to say, *Your turn*. Even through my jeans his touch made a warmth spread up into my groin.

"I'm from here but I lived in LA for twenty-five years. Swore I'd never move back."

"Never, ever, ever, ever," he said. "I get it."

It was nice to talk to someone who understood what it was like to be forced by purely practical reasons to leave a place that really spoke to your soul. And Nate had a grounded, calm way about him that gave me the sense that, as long as I was with him, nothing really bad could happen to me. The fact that we were hitting it off might make him more likely to believe me. To help me. I was *not* a damsel in distress, but maybe he could fix this one giant mess I'd stumbled into.

"Little Sisssssster!" Phoebe called. The dog bounded to his feet and ran to the girls, trailing the leash.

"I had a sperm donor," I said. People always wondered, so I figured it was better to just tell him. "I know that's maybe more like third-date talk, but there it is."

"Good for you," he said, and didn't chime in with any stupid questions. "Well, if we're doing third-date confessions about sperm donation," he said, looking suddenly nervous. "You know how I told you I don't have kids?"

"Were you lying?" I joked.

But he didn't laugh. "I donated sperm once when I was in college. I told my sister and she almost killed me—made me swear I'd never do it again no matter how much I needed beer money. So you should know, I might open my email inbox at any time to a message from a twenty-five-year-old writing to tell me they're my biological kid."

*If you and I got married, your adult donor-baby would be shocked to find out they have such a hot bio-stepmom*, I almost joked. What was wrong with me? But there was something eerie about this whole conversation. Because I could imagine the twins' sperm donor. Off somewhere on a date, making this same confession to some other woman. Only the twins' donor would be mid-twenties by now, likely still too young to drop such a full disclosure on a date. The impulse to not misrepresent oneself, to immediately share the very facts that would most likely scare off a potential partner—it was the impulse of middle age, not youth. On a first date, a twentysomething guy would never say, "I have herpes and 80K in student loans." But a fortysomething man—a good man, who was serious about a woman—was likely to lay it all out there right away. Did this mean Nate, who I'd just met but felt I'd known all my life, was serious about me?

"Wow, and I worried I was going to scare you off with all *my* baggage," I said, which made him laugh with relief.

"Do you have anything else you need to confess?" he said.

This was it. Now was the time to tell Nate the IDIOTs were planning an attack on the capitol in nineteen days. Surely he'd want to know a woman would be at Burgdorf the day after tomorrow with grenades and plans for the attack. "Not a confession exactly." I paused, gulped, forced out the words. "But like does the ATF take tips from civilians?"

"Every day," he said. "Though most of them are about Dua Lipa being held hostage at the Treasure Valley skating rink."

"As if she'd darken the doors of that place."

"Exactly. Charli XCX? Maybe. But not Dua Lipa. She's too fancy."

"You really know your pop divas," I said.

"Don't judge. I like a bop."

I held up my palms. "Not judging, sir." I paused. "But the civilians who give you real tips? Like, what happens to them? Do they get immunity if they're involved in the crime somehow? Like . . . accidentally?"

His eyes looked concerned, but he kept his tone light. "You asking for a friend?"

"Haha, no," I said, suddenly feeling overheated despite the cold. "I'm reading this murder mystery—*Dial AD for Arms Dealer*—and it seems totally unrealistic. So I was just wondering how things work in real life."

He looked relieved. "So what's the situation?"

"The protagonist is trying to prove she didn't murder this lowlife so she's gathering evidence against his gang of . . . of arms traffickers. She's hoping to get immunity by being helpful to law enforcement and prosecutors and everything."

His brow furrowed. "Well, if she did murder him she'd likely still get prison time."

"It's more like she *didn't* murder him but in the process of trying to find out who *did* she committed some smaller crimes," I said.

"Whether or not to grant immunity is up to the individual judge," he said. "But I've never seen a judge deny immunity for someone with evidence implicating a bigger fish. Especially if it was an arms-trafficking ring."

A heady mix of relief and sexual attraction flooded me. "How come?"

"Even judges who are hardcore pro-gun hate weapons traffickers."

As Nate delivered this fantastic news, I stared into his dark eyes, which were flecked with gold. I wanted to stare into them for the rest of this lifetime—what was *wrong with me*! My headspace was like a Hallmark Valentine movie.

"Oh good. Because I was worried. About my protagonist," I managed.

"This sounds like some book you're reading."

"It's pretty harrowing," I agreed.

"You know, I could see liking it here," he said. "In Boise. If I knew the right people."

By *right people* I could tell he meant me. I don't know if I leaned in or he did. But our lips were about to touch when the twins and Little Sister trotted up to us, laughing and breathing hard from chasing each other.

Nate and I pulled back. What in the holy hell was I doing? I was supposed to be convincing him the ATF needed to go to Burgdorf Hot Springs to thwart an attack on the capitol and nab a SIM card with evidence that might help exonerate me in the case of a murder trial!

"Were you two about to kiss?" Phoebe asked. The girls had never seen me with a date, but they seemed more delighted than fazed.

Nate smiled at me, his eyes warm, as if to say, *Your kids are pretty cool.*

"How about you say something more polite to Coach Duran?" I said, pointedly.

"Thank you for the ice cream," Alice and Phoebe said in a singsong unison that was meant to be charming, but actually had horror-movie vibes.

Nate scratched Little Sister's ears. "Sure thing," he said, and for a split second, I could picture what it would be like to have a Hollywood-movie, picture-perfect nuclear family.

I needed a minute after that near-kiss to pull myself together. "That salted caramel made me thirsty," I said. "Anyone else want some water?"

As I filled a plastic cup at the cooler inside, I kept an eye on the patio. Phoebe was pretending to ride the dog like a horse, with Alice holding the "reins." Nate watched them, smiling. But then he pulled out his phone and started texting.

Suddenly, Idaho Connor's phone vibrated in my coat. I pulled it out to read the text, as Nate slipped his phone into his back pocket.

**Natty Lite:** Where the hell are you? We have work to do.

Natty Lite. Nate. A shiver went through me.

Outside, Nate had taken the dog's leash so both twins could pretend to ride Little Sister at the same time. This sweet, goofy man who seemed to have endless patience could not possibly be "Natty Lite." There was no way Nate had just texted Idaho Connor about work they needed to do together.

I must be imagining things. Stress had turned me paranoid. But I needed to be sure. I yanked on the bathroom door but it was locked. I knocked, knocked again, pounded until a mom came out holding the hand of a little girl. "Geez," she said. "We tried to hurry."

Not even apologizing, I brushed past her, locked the door behind me, and laid my cell next to Idaho Connor's phone on the edge of the sink. A speaker near the ceiling blared an old song about a hot-blooded guy with a fever of a hundred-and-three.

My hands shook so badly I nearly dropped my phone while opening Nate's contact. I compared the numbers for "Nate" in my phone and "Natty Lite" in Idaho Connor's phone.

THEY. WERE. THE. SAME. NUMBER.

Bending over the sink, I splashed freezing water into my face. Belatedly realizing there wasn't a paper towel dispenser, I stuck my face under the hot blast of the hand dryer. After a quick glance in the mirror, I shoved a phone in each coat pocket and headed back out into The STIL. Through the window, I could see Nate helping the twins teach the dog to sit.

How could it be that Nate almost kissed me and then went straight to texting the corpse I'd found in my trunk! Who was this man out there on the patio with my kids? He definitely might not be the person I thought he was. Was he a criminal? A dirty fed, working with white supremacist gang members? Was he a secret arms trafficker? Did he suspect I knew where Connor was? This was what I got for thinking there was a hot eligible man dying to take me and my kids out for fancy ice cream. I tried to think clearly.

"I don't go undercover myself," Nate had said as he stood in front of a classroom of second graders. "But I provide a lot of support to undercover agents."

The dead guy could've been one of Nate's colleagues—a federal agent, deep undercover as a white supremacist named Connor Johnson. In which case, he probably hadn't deserved to die. What kind of prison time would I face for stashing the remains of a federal operative? And—infinitely worse—what if I'd killed him? Federal agent or no, Connor drugged me. He could've hustled me around to the back alley behind Huckleberry's. If he'd tried to assault me, I very well might've stabbed him with my scrapbooking scissors, shoved him into my trunk somehow. Locked him in. He could have suffocated! I pushed the thoughts away. Told myself it had to have been Errol. It was something I needed to believe right now or else I'd be paralyzed with fear. And that wouldn't do because—now more than ever—I needed Baylee's SIM card. I could not become the prime suspect in the murder of an undercover federal agent!

But first I needed to keep my cool, fake my way through the last few minutes of this date, and get my kids home and in bed. Then I could try to make a plan. I exited the bathroom, pasted what I hoped was a chipper look on my face, and headed toward the door to the patio.

Through the front window I saw Nate and Phoebe and Alice all petting Little Sister, probably heaping the dog with praise. My girls looked so happy. They were drinking in the positive attention. A feeling like one of Emmylou's crossbow bolts lanced my heart. Because despite what was going on out there, Layna was right. I'd been a fool to think I could ask Nate to come to my rescue. I was going to have to handle this myself.

# TWENTY-TWO

*Friday*

Phoebe cried Friday morning because Alice had come down with a fever after we got home from The STIL and Phoebe wanted to be sick too. Somehow I managed to get Phoebe off to school on the bus. By midmorning, I'd read Alice nine chapters of a seemingly endless middle-grade book series about warring clans of wild cats. By eleven I was stir crazy—and uneasy. Being stuck in my duplex fretting about the fact that Nate had somehow been in cahoots with the dead guy in my playhouse was making me beyond anxious. Plus Baylee would be at Burgdorf to meet Connor tomorrow! And now I could hardly ask Nate to send the ATF.

If I was going to avoid going to Burgdorf myself to get that SIM card from Baylee, I'd need more information about what happened to Connor. I had to talk to Salma Hayek. While Errol had sent texts to Baylee threatening to kill Connor, Salma Hayek had actually hit Connor in the head with a beer bottle in the Huckleberry's parking lot. Other than the killer, she was likely the last person to have seen him alive, and she might have the answers I needed.

With Alice feverish, I'd missed Thursday night pole dancing class. Layna texted me that Olympia had subbed again. But I hoped Salma Hayek would be at the open pole studio at noon. Luckily, Emmylou saved my bacon *again* by saying she'd watch Alice while I went to Pole Kisses.

"Moms need their self-care," Emmylou said, which would've been incredibly sweet, but she followed it with, "It's really hard on the twins when you're stressed. I think that's why Phoebe's been biting."

Inside the pole studio, I didn't see Salma Hayek. But the sight of Cheyenne's pink hair glowing like a halo of cotton candy made my heart vault nearly out of my chest. Before I could approach she'd twisted into a spinning helix. Even if she stopped for a moment, I had no idea how to pump her for information about Salma Hayek. Normally I'd open a convo with a compliment about her outfit. But she wore a strappy metallic bra with the tiniest of deep-purple G-strings. What could I say? *I like your butt floss? Your buns are like hard plastic?* No and no. So instead of approaching her directly, I headed to a nearby pole and practiced my awkward pole walk.

*BAM!* A noise like someone had tossed a microwave off a ladder made me flinch. A girl in yellow patent-leather thigh-high boots had dropped from her pole into front splits. And from quite a height, by the sound of it. I kind of loved this place.

I grabbed my pole with both hands and pinched it between my knees. But I spun too fast, like SpongeBob about to fly off a merry-go-round. Meanwhile, Cheyenne was doing an airwalk with the grace of an Olympic gymnast in an antigravity chamber. At Huckleberry's, I couldn't quite figure out what about her held Salma Hayek so in thrall. But now, as she shifted easily to fly her body from the pole like a flag, I understood.

I'd always thought of strip clubs as sad places where dancers endured the grotesqueries of rando male desire to rake in much-needed cash. Or where a few transgressive, anthropologically curious gals with other options (cue Diablo Cody's memoir) went to walk the wild side or fund their art projects. You could consent and be exploited, all at the same time. Wasn't that true? But watching Cheyenne's prowess on the pole helped me see things another way. Given her talents, of course she'd want to be a well-paid, *professional* athlete.

As she executed an elegant pole combo, I wondered if she might have another motive for her work. I knew from my LA social scene that many forms of sex work allowed artists both a flexible schedule and financial freedom. Stripping had, after all, funded Lizzie Borden's films, Chris Kraus's novel writing, Kathleen Hanna's seminal work in Bikini Kill, Cardi B's life before her rise to hip-hop superstardom. The list could go on forever. But for Cheyenne, my guess was that pole dancing didn't *support* her art form—it *was* her art form.

Impervious to my deep thoughts, Cheyenne inverted, her legs flipping up and overhead until she was in an upside-down straddle known as a helicopter.

"Vagina to Jesus!" the girl in yellow thigh-highs called, clearly teasing.

"F off," Cheyenne said. "It's perfect." But she hoisted her hips higher.

"Dolly Parton always said the higher the hair, the closer to God," I called. "So why shouldn't that apply to your landing strip?"

Cheyenne giggled and slid down the pole, thighs giving off a faint squeak. "Vodka gimlet girl," she said, looking up at me from her crash mat.

"My name's Nikita," I said. "I heard about your grandma. Is she okay?"

"She had a stroke but it's like a miracle—a little weak in her right hand, but otherwise, totally fine," Cheyenne said. "We'll be playing *Mortal Kombat* together again in no time." She pointed at me. "You got Connor good the other night. Cat scratch fever." She waggled her rhinestone-encrusted nails at me, causing my armpits to prickle with nervous sweat.

"You know Salma Hayek, right?"

Cheyenne nodded, climbing to her feet and stretching an arm across her torso. "Sure do." I probably had two minutes max before she ran out of patience with me.

"I haven't seen her since Huckleberry's," I said. "She missed class on Tuesday. Last night too."

"I actually saw her Monday night." Cheyenne's cheeks flushed a pretty pink. "She told me she was headed out of town."

I tried to sound casual. "Oh, fun. Where to?"

"You're more likely to get water from a stone than a secret out of a dancer," Cheyenne said, giving me a wink.

"I heard she got into it with that creep that got thrown out of the club," I blurted.

"She smashed him upside the head with a bottle of Dos Equis," Cheyenne said. "Wish I could've seen it, but I was behind the bar."

"You know what happened to him after?"

She gave a delicate shrug. "By the time I got the text from my fam and rushed off to the hospital, he was long gone."

"Do you have Salma's number?"

"Yeah, I don't give out other people's numbers."

"I lost my car keys that night," I said. "They had a My Little Pony keychain?"

"I think I saw them, actually! On the bar when you were talking to Connor."

So he did steal my keys! "Speaking of keys, someone keyed my Impala," I fibbed. "It was parked behind the club. Any chance you saw anything going on back there before you left?" I studied her face for any flicker of unease but it was smooth and blank as a professional poker player's.

"When I was getting in my car to leave for the hospital, I did see Pumpkin Spice heading down the back alley. Though Daniel Radcliffe would be more likely to key a car."

"Who's Pumpkin Spice?" I said.

"She took a few classes here a while back. No idea what her real name is, but I never forget a pole name." Cheyenne flicked her pink locks over one shoulder. "Look, I gotta work on this combo I'm hoping to try out at the club tonight, okay?"

"Wait! One more thing! Salma Hayek's real name? Lupe something?"

"You'll have to ask her when you see her, hon." Cheyenne grabbed her pole, inverted, and began a series of moves that would confound Nadia Comăneci. Our conversation was over.

As I headed back to my own pole, fresh anxiety rippled through me. Because now it was clear: I had just one option. The only way to prove to myself—and the police—that I didn't kill Connor was to prove that someone else did. I needed to go to Burgdorf to meet Baylee and get that SIM card.

My cell phone rang. The woman in the thigh-high boots speared me with a blistering glance. I shrugged apologetically and answered in a whisper. It was the nurse at the twins' school, calling to tell me Phoebe had a stomachache and needed to be picked up as soon as possible.

# TWENTY-THREE

*Saturday*

During an Idaho summer, there are two kinds of folks: mountain bike people and ATV people. The mountain bike people are generally lean, college-educated liberals who feel superior about it. The all-terrain vehicle people are often thickset high school grads with a libertarian conservative lean who love the sound of an engine gunning in open air. During an Idaho winter, these same groups transform into ski people and snowmobile people (aka sladnecks).

Before heading into Cheap Thrills Rentals for a snowmobile in McCall, I'd donned Phoebe's red Little Mermaid wig, while Layna wore a platinum-blond number that had once been part of a *Kill Bill* costume. A grumpy clerk with hair bottle-dyed the exact color my mom always used—L'Oréal Paris Light Amber Brown—fitted us with suits, boots, and helmets and gave us a map to the snowmobile pickup site. But when she asked for an ID, I panicked. I'd emptied out the Therapy Jar to pay for the rental in cash, but hadn't considered I'd need to show identification. I'd meant to drop Miranda's driver's license in her mailbox, but with everything going on I'd forgotten. Now I slid it across the counter. The guilt pang only lasted a moment. Miranda did me dirty in high school. Some would say she had this one coming.

Though I'd never ridden a Ski-Doo, as Layna and I walked across the snowy parking lot in our black snowmobile suits, I felt we were doing a decent approximation of slednecks.

"I'm having second thoughts about this probably terrible plan," I confessed.

"What choice do you have?" Layna said, tossing platinum strands over one shoulder. "You've got to get some proof Errol murdered the mansicle."

"By five thirty," I reminded her.

Last night after I'd put the twins to bed, I'd found Emmylou sipping Malibu rum and Diet Coke on her purple velvet couch while watching a comedic lesbian murder mystery set in Tasmania. Instead of confessing everything, I rattled off a white lie about getting an evite reminder for a baby shower in McCall I'd totally forgotten about. She agreed to loan me her all-wheel-drive Subaru to make the two-hour-and-fifteen-minute snowy trek up ID-55. All I had to do in return was swear on *The Comedy Bible* I'd be back by five thirty so she could make it to her date with Oat Willimena.

"I wasn't sure Oat Willimena would be your type," I'd said. Nate was my type. Just last night we'd nearly kissed and now he was completely and permanently out of reach.

"Oat Willimena is from a huge Catholic family," Emmylou said. "It's not the same as being raised Mormon like me, of course. But the guilt parallels are there. And she pulls a tarot card every day! Do you know how hard it is to find a man in this town who doesn't think the King of Cups is a brewpub?"

"I'm excited for you! Oat Willimena seems really—" I searched for words to describe my interactions with the potter. "Artsy and . . . and knowledgeable about raccoons. Is she really into animals? Maybe she'd want to adopt Little Sister."

Emmylou made a face. "This is about my date, not your desire to dump that dog. Just promise me again you won't be late."

"I promise," I said.

Now the neon-yellow snowmobile wrapped with the Cheap Thrills logo sat waiting for me and Layna at the end of the parking lot. A bulky guy wearing a worn fleece and well-fitting jeans waved us over. His baseball cap said *The Man Behind the Bump*. There was perhaps nothing more irritating than a man trying to take all the credit for the hard work a woman does growing, carrying, and giving birth to a baby.

"Where are you two coming in from?" the Man Behind the Bump asked.

"Boise," I said.

"Twin Falls," Layna said at the same time. She shot me a look.

"I mean, I'm from Boise, but we both live in Twin," I said.

"The sleds are pretty simple." He showed us how to turn the snowmobile on, hit the gas, brake, and change gears. "Eco mode will get you up to forty-five or so."

"Miles an hour?" I said. Jesus, Mary, and Joan Rivers, these things could fly.

"Yep. But if you really want to rip, you can switch it into Sport mode."

"I'm sure Eco mode will be fine," I said primly. I didn't intend to go wild.

For a second, I worried I wouldn't be able to get my helmet on without dislodging my wig, but I managed. Once I'd swung my leg over the beast, Layna climbed on behind me. When I squeezed the throttle gingerly, the snow machine jolted forward and Layna let out a happy shriek.

Soon we were flying along Warren Wagon Road under blue skies, surrounded by the vast expanse of Payette National Forest. I'd only been on the road in the summer, when my mom would drive us to Burgdorf. Unplowed in winter, the thoroughfare transformed into a snowmobile highway. Fresh powder piled high on every branch and needle of every ponderosa pine and Douglas fir. In Boise, I longed for LA—warm weather, relentless sunshine, palm trees, the sense of being in the middle of everything that mattered. But even I had to admit there was nothing in SoCal quite like this.

"Faster, pussycat, faster!" Layna yelled in my ear. I pushed on the gas and the speedometer needle crept up to thirty-five. Forty. Forty-five. "Take it out of Eco mode!"

"No way!" I shouted. We were on track to get to the hot springs early. We did *not* need to go that fast.

After an hour, I spotted the gate up ahead, beyond which a snow-packed lane led to the cluster of historic log cabins built around a rising cloud of steam. I'd never witnessed this lonely, snowbound version of Burgdorf. I felt sad my mom never had a chance to see it like this.

A tight U-turn had the snowmobile parked with its nose facing back toward Warren Wagon Road. Layna and I tucked our wallets and phones into the console, not wanting anything on us by which Baylee might discern our true identities. Layna grabbed her bear spray.

When I pulled off my helmet, my wig came off with it, but Layna helped me wrench it back on. We both donned oversized sunglasses to hide as much of our faces as possible.

"It's not too late for us to hightail it out of here," I said.

"No way," Layna said. "You need that SIM card. Besides, I'm not leaving here without a soak."

I glanced at my watch—it was twelve thirty, and we were supposed to knock on the door of Baylee's cabin at one. We crunched past two battered old snowmobiles parked front to end like cars on a train. The front office attendant waved us on in to the hot springs.

The fifteen log cabins, built in a haphazard semicircle in the late 1800s, didn't have running water or electricity and could be rented for a couple of days at a time. Cabin Nine sat about a hundred yards from the pool edge. The red bathing suit hanging on the line made it easy to spot. In a wooden hut marked *Dressing Room*, Layna and I stripped out of our snowmobile suits next to a wood-burning stove. We'd both worn bikinis underneath. Layna yelped as we made our way across freezing stepping stones to the steaming rectangular pool. A relaxed-looking old guy floated on his back and a couple kissed in one aqueous corner. Otherwise the pool was all ours.

"I wish I could have you take my photo for the Gram," Layna said. "This place would inspire FOMO in anyone."

As I lowered my freezing body into the steaming-hot water, I groaned. I'd forgotten how amazing this place was. It really did beat anything I'd ever done on a Saturday in LA. "If we weren't here to secure evidence proving I didn't commit murder, I would feel so relaxed."

"Except I kind of like that that's why we're here," Layna admitted. "You know, all those years when I was playing supportive wifey to the douchebag, I didn't realize it, but I think this was the woman I wanted to become. I mean, I'm finally doing it. I'm finally investigating a murder."

"I get it," I said. How to explain it, even to myself? Being out here in the wilderness somehow felt better than just being a grief-stricken wreck. "Should we practice what we're going to say to Baylee?"

"We'll say Connor sent us," Layna said. "He was embarrassed to tell her, but he's too scared of Errol to come. He wants her to send her smashed phone and plans for Day of the Rope with us."

"What about the grenades?" I said.

"We take them and maybe ditch them later?" Layna said. "We can play that by ear."

We were quiet for what felt like a long time. The steam rising around us, clouds rolling in, no kids around, the tips of our wig hair trailing in the water. I couldn't even find it in me to be nervous anymore. I was in a snow-capped world of warm water. For once I was living in this very moment as it happened.

Layna looked down at her watch. "Looks like it's go-time," she said.

# TWENTY-FOUR

After the steaming waters, the frigid air felt good as we climbed the creaky steps of Cabin Nine in our bare feet. We figured we'd look less suspicious and entirely unthreatening in our wet swimsuits. Layna gestured I should knock, so I rapped my knuckles on the ancient wooden door.

"Baylee?" I called. "Are you in there?"

The door swung open and a stocky, big-eared guy grabbed us each by an arm and yanked. We stumbled inside and the door slammed behind us, lock clicking into place.

A tall, broad-shouldered man with iron-gray curls pooling at the base of his neck stood with his back to us, warming his hands at the wood-burning stove. He turned slowly to reveal a craggy face with acne scars and brows like overgrown cliffs. "Baylee's not here," he said.

"Ralphie?" Layna said.

"That's right," he replied. "Ralphie the Lizard."

My mind hadn't caught up to the true danger we were in—I was still panicking that Baylee wasn't here. Which meant her smashed phone with its SIM card full of evidence wasn't here either.

But shock slowed down time enough for some part of my brain to take in the cabin. It was more rustic than I remembered, probably because these guys didn't have my mom's penchant for battery-operated fairy lights and cozy blankets. A sleeping bag lay on top of each twin bed, and tins of sardines, a loaf of white bread, and a canister of instant coffee perched on a little ledge along the back wall. A pan of water on the stove struggled to reach a boil. My internal alarm bells clanged even louder at the sight of a rifle leaning in a far corner.

"Where's Connor?" Ralphie demanded.

"He sent us. I'm Nikita," I said, before I could think.

"Fucking chickenshit Connor," Ralphie said.

"Where's Baylee?" I said.

The stocky man spoke in a girlish falsetto. "'*This is Baylee from a burner. Errol smashed my phone.*'" He snapped back into his normal voice. "Tell dipshit Connor it wasn't Baylee. It was me. Errol. Making sure she deserved what she had coming."

Something inside me collapsed in on itself like a building imploding, because Errol clearly thought Connor was still alive. Which meant he hadn't killed Connor. Which meant Layna and I had made this dangerous trip for nothing.

Ralphie looked me and Layna up and down in a way that was clearly not avuncular. "At least Connor sent us a tip," he said.

"I'm gonna stick in more than the tip," Errol said. "That piece of shit banged my girl. Was planning to do it again. Right here."

"And I was looking forward to giving that rat what he deserved," Ralphie said. "But these girls'll have to do. For now."

Layna looked at me, eyes wild. I jerked my head toward the door. I spotted a large backpack slumped against the wall nearest me. The top wasn't cinched. I could see a large ammo tin inside. If it held grenades, we might have a fighting chance.

"Yeah," Errol said. "We're gonna have fun with these two."

Layna fumbled for the bear spray tucked into her bikini top, but before she could aim it, Ralphie grabbed her wrist, twisting it until the spray clattered to the sloped pine floor and rolled away. Layna let out a pitiful yelp.

"We've got a present for you to send Connor," Ralphie was saying. "For trying to rat us out to the feds." He dragged Layna toward a small red cooler, popped the lid, reached inside, and pressed whatever he'd extracted into Layna's hand.

"Connor fucked my girl," Errol said. "So we took her finger." As the scream ripped out of Layna, something dropped to the floor. A fingernail with flaking orange polish. Waxy skin. A bloody stumped end. It took me a shocked instant to understand it was a severed pinkie. Ralphie clamped a hand over Layna's mouth and growled into her ear.

My own ears rang as shockwaves of terror rippled through me. I dove for the cabin's lone door, but Errol had blocked my escape. He grabbed my arm, yanking it behind my back. A sharp pain ripped through my shoulder socket.

"Let go of me!" I yelled, but he slapped a hand over my mouth, yanking me against him so I could feel the redneck boner swelling in his pants. My mind fragmented, pieces flying in shards to every corner of the room. The only intelligible thought was: *This is going to be very, very bad.*

Ralphie grunted with pain and Layna wrenched herself from his grasp. As he shook out his bitten hand, he backed her toward the cabin's far corner. She lunged to grab the pot off the wood-burning stove. Boiling water arched, splashing onto Ralphie, who let out a bloodcurdling yowl. The sickening thud of the scalding pan hitting him upside the head was followed instantly by the wafting smell of burning skin and hair.

As Ralphie slumped to the ground, I reached back like I was doing a reverse pole grab, but instead of grasping chrome, I jammed my thumb into Errol's eye, then brought my elbow down, ramming it into his solar plexus.

"Aarggh! You fucking bitch!" Errol yelped. He released me to leap for Layna, who'd hauled her pot-wielding arm back for another swing. I did a one-legged fan kick and caught him in the side. He held up an arm to block the searing metal, the pan branding his fingers and palm like an iron. He let out a shriek. On Layna's next swing, hot metal connected with his head. He hit the floor with a thud.

Layna was already headed for the door. But even if we made it to our snowmobile, we probably couldn't outrun Errol or Ralphie if they gave chase on their own sleds. We needed a deterrent. So I grabbed the backpack and swung it onto my back. The ammo tins inside bit into my spine.

Layna and I burst out into the cold, slamming the door behind us.

After the dim cabin, the sun shining off the pristine snow blinded me. I stumbled down the stairs behind Layna, my center of gravity thrown off by the heavy backpack. We hurried barefoot down the icy paving stones. But before we could veer toward the dressing rooms for our snowmobile suits, helmets, and boots, the door of the cabin clicked open. I looked over my shoulder to see Errol lurching out, clutching the rifle, one eye squeezed shut. He lifted the rifle to his shoulder but yelped in pain and abandoned it on the porch—clearly between his burned right hand and gouged eye, he wasn't up for trigger duty.

"Somebody stop those skanks!" he shouted, staggering down the stairs.

Barefoot and weighed down by the backpack, it'd be easy for me to lose my head start. "Get the snowmobile turned on," I shouted to Layna.

"But—" Layna said.

"Just do it!" I yelled.

She started to run. Following behind, I passed the two battered old snowmobiles parked end-to-front like railroad cars. In clear relief, I saw a big sticker of a lizard slapped onto the side of the front snowmobile. I gave another burst of speed before halting in my tracks. I spun halfway so I could see Errol advancing. The backpack hit the white ground. Behind me, Layna fired up the Ski-Doo as my fingers fumbled at the latch of the rectangular ammo box. Errol veered toward the two snowmobiles as if knowing he'd need aid to give further chase.

Snow seared my feet and the grenade felt round and solid in my hand. When I raised it overhead, Errol froze and his mouth dropped open, an O of shock.

"I'd back up if I were you," I cried.

"Bitch, you wouldn't," he said. But he was already scrambling backward.

"That's Boss Bitch to you!" I yelled. Or was it Nikita talking?

The pin slid out easily. Muscle memory allowed for the perfect underhand toss. The grenade rose, rose, rose, and fell in a great arc, landing smack dab between Ralphie and Errol's snowmobiles. I hadn't played a thousand games of cornhole with my kids for nothing.

Swinging the backpack onto my back, I sprinted barefoot toward Layna, who straddled our snowmobile in her Barbie-pink bikini. I leapt on behind her. Layna flipped it into Sport mode and hit the gas as the world exploded behind us.

# TWENTY-FIVE

You've never been cold until you've ridden a snowmobile on a freezing Idaho day wearing nothing but a wet bikini. Clutching both wigs in my fist, I pressed my front to Layna's back for warmth as she gunned down the snowy highway. She was heading the opposite way from which we'd come—a good instinct. If we'd gone straight back down Warren Wagon Road, we surely would've run into law enforcement coming from McCall with instructions to nab two women in bikinis on a neon-yellow sled.

Once we were out of sight of the hot springs, Layna turned off the road toward the ridge, zigzagging to avoid trees and stick to patches of powder already churned up by other slednecks. Big flakes had started to fall, as if the sky itself conspired to cover our tracks.

But once we'd crested the ridge and ridden half a mile or so down the other side, the snowmobile sank into a snowdrift and refused to budge. When Layna revved the accelerator, the sled dug itself deeper. She cut the engine. Quiet descended. Acres of snow-laden forest surrounded us, the white drifts eager to swallow us whole. The backpack straps cut into my shoulders. Feeling had already left my bare feet.

"We are so fucked," Layna said, her teeth clacking like a frightened Scooby-Doo's.

We sat with that truth for a long terrible moment. My mind felt foggy. I couldn't process all that had just happened, the horror of it. The near miss. Baylee's severed finger. I was too cold to consider it now. Our crisis was too immediate. We pulled our phones from the console, but neither of us could get service. I didn't think I had the requisite strength to posthole over the ridge and wave for help—which would come in the form of an arrest. But I wasn't afraid anymore. Just very sleepy. As a kid, I'd heard about people who'd taken wrong turns on snowy hikes. Suddenly the lost person desperately needed a little snooze in a snowbank. Then that old thief, hypothermia, would sneak up and rob them, first of their good sense, then of their life.

"Are you thinking what I'm thinking?" I asked.

"I need five minutes. Lie down. Get my strength up. Figure out our next move," Layna said.

"Yes," I concurred. "That sounds so good. Just five minutes."

Layna was already climbing off the Ski-Doo and searching the snow for the perfect place to nest. Soon I'd ditched the backpack and was fetal in my own white dent. The snow burned my skin at first, then as I drifted toward sleep, I felt nothing at all.

A half-dream, half-vision arrived. The twins laying blankets over a recumbent Little Sister.

"She's still cold," Alice said, piling on another chenille throw.

"Still freezing," Phoebe concurred, draping a tattered blanket over me. Because I was Little Sister.

Alice started poking one of my closed doggy eyelids. "Wake up," she said.

"Seriously," Phoebe added, poking the other eyelid. "Waaaaake up."

My eyes snapped open. "Wake up!" I shouted, staggering to my bare feet. Layna sat up with a snort. I climbed to stand on the seat of the snowmobile and gazed in every direction. The white sky dropped white flakes to the white ground. There was nothing else to see but snow-frosted trees. But then, through a thick stand of ponderosa pines, I spotted something rising between pointy tree tops. A trail of smoke.

We left the backpack of grenades leaning against the snowmobile. Taking only our wigs, wallets, and phones, we postholed through snow drifts, the slowest form of earthly transportation. Though we only traveled fifty yards or so, it took what felt like hours. My skin had turned bright red, my legs and feet wet and angry, my mind thickening like flour and water stirred endlessly over low heat. A mountain cabin appeared, its windows radiating light and warmth, its chimney releasing a happy stream of smoke. Layna argued for knocking on the front door and begging for help.

"I'm so cowald too," I managed to slur. "But explosives! That's federal charges, missy. Narthing the douchebag can do to proterct us from the feds." I definitely had hypothermia.

"Then let's cherk the barn," she said, gesturing at the hulking building behind the cabin. "But sshhhhhhhhh! Out here, they shoooot firs' and arsk questions later."

With a heave we lifted the sliding security bar and opened the barn door. The inside glowed like the briefcase in *Pulp Fiction*. An ancient black snowmobile sat with its nose pointed toward the door. Snowmobile suits and helmets hung on hooks. Best of all, two pairs of boots leaned into each other below.

While I stepped into a suit, Layna inspected the snowmobile. "Goddammit," she said. "There's no key!"

I wandered the barn, phone held high, searching for service. When two bars appeared, I typed furiously. Our golden ticket appeared in the form of a three-minute video by YouTube personality MonkeyNuts96 called "How to Start a Snowbobile Without a Key."

MonkeyNuts96 may not have mastered the art of proofreading, but he sure knew how to fire up a Ski-Doo.

# TWENTY-SIX

The Subaru's heater blasted hot enough to roast a weenie. Still, my hands shook badly enough to make the steering wheel wobble. I drank a slug of gas station coffee to warm myself up from the inside.

As Layna and I had blazed along Warren Wagon Road on the stolen black Ski-Doo, four Valley County Sheriff's Department snowmobiles roared by, lights flashing. But they didn't even glance our way. Of course they didn't—the officers were looking for two women in bikinis on a neon-yellow snowmobile.

Now darkness cloaked the canyon and the Subaru's headlights cut through the spitting snowflakes as we drove along the Payette River. "What a mess," I said. "Errol didn't kill Connor. And I didn't get Baylee's SIM card. Poor Baylee. That finger. Jesus Christ."

Layna didn't respond so I snapped on the radio to drown out our still-chattering teeth. A local deejay let loose a relentless patter: "By next Saturday, get ready to leave your coats at home because it'll be fifty-eight degrees in McCall! Sixty-eight in Boise! Those high temps should hold for several days."

If I didn't take drastic action, Connor's corpse would be thawed out and rotting in my backyard in a week. "You heard what they said, right? That Connor is a rat. A narc. Not a federal agent. That's good news." But Layna said nothing. How long had it been since she'd spoken? "You okay?" I asked.

"Those guys—" she said. "That almost went so sideways."

I risked a glance in her direction—she was shivering violently and staring straight ahead, glassy-eyed. "Except you saved us," I said, desperate to bring her back to the present. "Swinging that hot pan like a *Lemonade*-era Beyoncé with a baseball bat." I was a solo mom. And I'd chosen to do something I thought was low risk. But it hadn't been. Not at all.

"That was a woman's finger," Layna said. "I'm out. I can't. No more of this for me." For an instant, the Subaru's back tires lost their hold and we skidded toward the river. But rubber gripped pavement again before we flew off the road and into the icy water.

"Jesus," I said. I'd been the one texting Baylee from Connor's phone. Or at least I thought I was texting Baylee. Actually I'd just confirmed her affair with Connor to Errol, who'd chopped off her finger in retribution. A lump of guilt sat in the pit of my stomach like a petrified double cheeseburger.

"That was too close," Layna said, and she didn't mean the Subaru's veer toward the Payette. "And . . . and I can't go through something like that again. I've got to tap out. This isn't an adventure or me playing detective with no consequences. It's real people getting hurt." She scrabbled in her backpack, pulled out a spare bear spray, and stuck it in my glovebox, as if to do what she could to protect me. As if to rid herself of the whole situation.

"I understand," I said. "I appreciate everything you've done for me." I tried to sound brave. But I was terrified. Because Layna's meaning was agonizingly clear. When it came to managing the nitty-gritty of corpses and white supremacists, and staying out of prison, I was on my own.

# TWENTY-SEVEN

When I finally stepped into my kitchen, I felt a tsunami of relief to have made it home alive. But as soon as I saw Emmylou, I realized my mistake. She wore a purple silk top with jeans, her hair upswept, lips painted red. A date outfit.

"Are you okay?" she cried. "You didn't answer your phone."

"I'm fine!" I said. "Totally fine."

In real time, I watched her worry transform to molten rage. "You. Are. Two. And a half. Hours. Late. And. I missed. My date," she fumed.

During my struggle to survive the afternoon, Emmylou's plans to see *Funny Girl* at the Egyptian Theatre with Oat Willimena had not been top of mind.

"You didn't even text!" Emmylou said. "And that g-damn dog!" She pointed an accusing finger toward her favorite faux-fur-lined snow boots, which lay by the door. Little Sister had chewed the left one into a slobbery lump.

"I'm sorry," I said. "I really messed up. I didn't mean to ruin your night."

"And where the hell have you been?" She gestured at my stolen snowmobile suit. "Obviously not at a baby shower!"

"I'm doing the very best I can to handle a really, really stressful time," I said, my voice cracking with exhaustion. "I can't tell you what I needed to do in McCall. But please, please believe it was important. I messed up. Big time. And I apologize. Truly. I know you have your own life. I know you have your own things you need to do."

The cloud of anger around Emmylou dropped like a curtain, revealing raw, aching disappointment.

"It's okay, toots," she said. "I was just worried. And so excited to go on a real date."

Somehow this made me feel even worse. "You know what? It's only eight. What if you texted Oat Willimena? Tell her I finally made it home. Ask her if she'd want to go to the Modern with you for a drink. You could maybe even get some dinner?"

"It's too late. She probably already ate."

"But you could ask? Maybe split a piece of cake or something?"

"I do like their chocolate torte," Emmylou conceded.

Blessedly, Oat Willimena texted back almost instantly that the Modern had the best old fashioneds she'd ever had and she'd be ready in five. Once Emmylou was out the door (wearing a cute pair of white Sorel boots I gifted her from my mom's closet), I peeked in at the twins, who slept on the floor in an improvised fort, Little Sister between them. They were alive. I was alive. I'd made it back home to them unharmed. But barely. That was all too close.

A text notice had come in to Connor's phone: A quick Cricket reminder! Your month of Cricket service is up in less than forty-eight hours. To continue your service, please make your payment of $40 before 4 PM Mountain Time Monday.

If I couldn't use Connor's phone, people would realize he'd gone missing. I'd been dumb enough to bring it to my house, so if the police started looking for him in earnest, they might access his phone's location data and see it'd been here. I was going to be so screwed.

The horror of the day bore down on me. I barely managed to turn the shower on full blast to hide the sounds before I started sobbing uncontrollably. I collapsed onto the bathroom floor. I'd never cried like that in my life, hysterical, like an animal, plumes of snot and slobber dripping from my face. I kept seeing the severed finger, with its chipped orange polish. Baylee must've painted her nails the way all women do—in a burst of optimism and self-improvement. Never imagining what would soon occur. It was my fault.

Once I'd cried myself into a puddle, I crawled into the shower. The warm water brought me back to life, though it took twenty minutes for my teeth to stop clacking. As I toweled myself off, my exhaustion lifted, leaving me anxious as an eighties club kid riding the back half of a cheap 8-Ball. Dr. Google informed me this was a hypothermia side effect. I decided to ride the jittery wave and get to work.

I sat at my mother's old desk, wolfing down a Hot Pocket while ordering a high-end fake pistol via overnight shipping. My general philosophy about firearms was that the best way to get shot was to own a gun, but if I ever encountered Ralphie and Errol again, I wanted to appear to have one on me. I worried my credit card would be declined but the payment went through.

Next I checked Connor's phone again. A new voice memo from the Receiver had arrived while I was in the shower. The now-familiar, slightly distorted voice said, "Did you get the potato mashers and the *mashed potato recipe*? You're supposed to keep me posted. Let me know."

Because I didn't have voice recordings from Connor explaining the nuances of the situation, I sent one of him saying: "Success." In the YouTube video he'd actually been saying: "Success—for white men—means keeping our trad wives at home and taking our power back." Which was nonsense because Idaho Connor didn't have a trad wife—or any wife!

With Errol—and Ralphie—out of the running, who did I have left by way of murder suspects? The anxiety humming through my veins whispered it could've been just me. Nobody else.

There must be someone who could explain what happened in the alley behind Huckleberry's that night. Other than Salma Hayek, who seemed to not want to be found, there was only one person I hadn't spoken to who might have seen how Connor ended up in my trunk—the mysterious former Pole Kisses student named Pumpkin Spice. And that was just great, because I had no idea who Pumpkin Spice could possibly be.

Connor's phone buzzed. The mere sight of Ralphie's name made my mind feel like it was flying off into fragments again. Hello, trauma, my new friend.

"Your skanks went off script," Ralphie growled. "They didn't take the special present we brought for you. But hopefully they told you we know you're a rat. And we exterminate rats. We find your skanks, we'll exterminate them too."

I slid Connor's phone into my purse, my shaking fingers brushing against the BuckSnort bottle cap. I pulled it out and spun it in my fingers. I could not for the life of me remember drinking BuckSnort out of a bottle. But I wanted so badly to have an alibi, to know where I'd been for those lost seven hours. I wanted to know how I'd ended up in the alley behind Huckleberry's wearing Connor's fashion-faux-pas vest.

My hypothermia-induced anxiety insisted I do something, anything, to fix this mess, to figure it out. So the next thing I knew, I'd pulled on jeans and a sweater, woken up the twins, helped them put winter coats over their pajamas, and loaded them—sleepy but compliant—into the Impala.

We blazed west on State Street, the charms of central Boise soon replaced by anonymous strip malls. Up ahead, the twins spotted the sign for Caffeina.

"Mommy, we went there once! Remember the hotty choc?" Phoebe cried.

"It had whipped cream!" Alice chimed in.

"And chocolate sprinkles!" Phoebe said. "Can we go there now?"

"Not tonight," I murmured. The purists at Caffeina only sold espresso drinks, tea, and hot chocolate, that much I knew. I wrenched the wheel to roll into the parking lot of the strip mall across the street from Huckleberry's. Caffeina. Library! (All Boise library signs have a charming exclamation point.) Spin Laundry. The Idahoan Diner, a sign advertising BuckSnort root beer in the front window. Bingo! When I'd left Huckleberry's that night, I must've stumbled across the street to the Idahoan—the only place around that served BuckSnort.

"Mommy!" Alice whined as I hustled the girls into the cozy warmth of the diner. "Phoebe says I'm not pretty."

*You know you're identical, right?* "You're both very pretty," I said.

When the hostess with the crusty lip piercing offered to seat us, I asked if they sold BuckSnort.

"Sure do!" She gestured at a soda dispenser.

"In bottles. Do you sell BuckSnort in bottles?" I demanded.

"It's real good outta the dispenser," she insisted. "We get the mix right. And we got an ice cream sundae looks like a loaded baked potato. It's not as good as the one at the West Side Diner, but it's still pretty good. We close in thirty minutes. You got time."

I dropped into a mirror-lined booth, too deflated to refuse the twins a sundae. If the diner closed at ten o'clock, I hadn't been hanging out there until four in the morning the night Connor was murdered. As the twins argued about which came first, God or dinosaurs, I pulled the BuckSnort bottle cap out of my purse and examined the tiny, baffling hole drilled through the middle.

Across the booth, the twins leaned together toward the mirror.

"I don't know what people are always talking about," Phoebe was saying.

"Me either. It makes no sense. Why are they always sayin' it?" Alice mused.

"We don't look alike *at all*," Phoebe said.

"Not even a little bit," Alice concurred.

I started laughing—how was this the one thing they could agree on?

The sundae arrived, a true optical illusion. Vanilla ice cream shaped like a baked potato, rolled in cocoa powder and split down the middle, loaded with whipped cream (for sour cream), shredded coconut dyed yellow (for cheese), and green sprinkles (for chives). As the three of us stuffed our faces, an unexpected shimmer of gratitude rippled through me. Sugar molecules danced through my bloodstream, suffusing me with the gentle pleasure of being alive, in a warm room, with my girls. For a moment, I felt better, hopeful, even if I still had no idea how to get out of this mess.

# TWENTY-EIGHT

*Sunday*

A lifelong Johnny Cash fan, my mom taught me from an early age there's nothing half as lonesome as a Sunday. But this one was worse than usual. I was too bone-tired from the previous day's terror, hypothermia, and guilt to do anything but lie on the couch and nap through *Encanto* and *Inside Out 2*. When the FedEx delivery man arrived with the fake pistol, I unwrapped it in the bathroom and ripped off the orange tip. It wouldn't pass close inspection, but from a distance or in a chaotic situation, it might do the trick. I put it in my purse alongside the spare bear spray from Layna.

By the time Emmylou arrived to babysit, I'd barely managed to don my clothes for pole class. As tired as I was, I couldn't miss a chance to see if anyone at Pole Kisses knew the true identity of a pole student named Pumpkin Spice. Besides, if Salma Hayek showed up, I needed to be there to grill her.

Before I could leave for class, I listened to Emmylou's tale of drinks with Oat Willimena, which apparently had ended with a walkthrough of Oat Dub's pottery studio.

"So she did actually give you a tour of her hot dark kiln?" I said, doing my best to make my usual jokes.

"She's very talented," Emmylou said primly.

"You should get her to give you a lesson," I said, raising an eyebrow. "Maybe reenact the pottery scene from *Ghost*?"

"Stop it!" Emmylou swatted me. But she was smiling.

It actually felt good to walk into Pole Kisses. Despite everything, this had become a safe place for me, full of familiar faces. But more even than I needed the release of a good pole class, I needed information.

Cheyenne sat behind the front desk, absolutely rocking an orange one-shoulder bra with matching booty shorts. Behind her, I spotted stacked boxes of shoes with her name on the label.

"Are you ready to buy your pair of Cheyenne's Sentient Strippers?" she asked. "I think pink patent leather six-inchers might be your speed."

"Currently furloughed," I said. "But I promise I will, as soon as I'm getting paid again. Question for you. Any chance there's a master list of Pole Kisses students? You know, with like their real names and pole names?" I put my folded hands under my chin and batted my lashes.

"Still trying to track down Pumpkin Spice?" Cheyenne said. Clearly this was not her first rodeo. She stood, grabbed her ankle, and casually lifted her leg so high in the air she was basically doing standing splits. For a second I thought she'd tuck her ankle behind her head. "I only taught her a couple times, but I promise you, she's not the type to key your car."

"But she might've seen who did," I lied. *Or she might have seen me kill someone.*

Through the door to the chill room I spotted Layna talking to Shade and Gucci. She'd texted to say she was running late and couldn't give me a ride. Yet I clung to the hope that after a good night's sleep she'd realized she was still up for being my criminal sidekick. I desperately needed help moving the corpse out of my yard before the weather warmed up in six short days.

As the other Pole Virgins headed toward the studio, I hurried to catch up to the only student who'd been around Pole Kisses longer than I had. From behind, I could see the dragon tattoo on her calf in all its glory.

"Zhang Xiu, wait up," I called. "I love your tat. Are you a fan of *The Girl with the Dragon Tattoo*?"

"It's an homage to that book!" she cried. "I love that you get that."

I raised my hands to the roof. "Totally random question: When you were taking Pole Virgins the first time, did you meet a woman with the pole name Pumpkin Spice?"

Zhang Xiu shook her head. "Sorry, Nikita."

"You sure?" I pressed.

"I'm always counting the days till the pumpkin spice latte drops. So, yeah, I'd remember."

During our warmup, my mind raged against investigative dead ends as my cold muscles protested against jumping jacks. It wasn't until Cheyenne taught us a pole move called the martini spin that I finally dropped out of my overthinking head and into my body. The spin involved flying around the pole with one leg bent and the other pointed up at a sixty-degree angle. My attempts made me look less like a martini glass than an out-of-shape suburban mom suffering from the delusion she's a Hollywood stunt double. But damn, it was fun.

My mood lifted with every spin around the chrome. Gucci swore pole reconnected her to her sexuality, but using pole to try to tap into my eroticism felt like buying what patriarchal capitalism was peddling instead of what actually made me, Tilly Turner, feel sexy. In class, I was more giggling dork than gyrating sexpot. What pole dancing reconnected me to was my sense of humor.

After class, Gucci came up and said, "I owe you to the moon for mashed potato wrestling with me. I paid off my whole Pole Virgin series—I don't know what I'd do without this class for my stress relief."

"Sure thing," I said. "I was glad to do it."

"Now I'm off to study," Gucci trilled. "Big drug toxicity exam tomorrow!"

Once everyone else had trickled out, Layna and I convened on the sidewalk.

"You feeling better?" I asked. "You look better."

"Mentally, better. But I was so tired today. Like Taylor-Swift-after-an-entire-Eras-tour-concert tired. Are you so tired?"

"Exhausted," I concurred.

"I'm so sorry to bail on you," Layna said. She let out a shuddering breath. "I just can't help with anything else. Not after yesterday. Not with anything criminal. Not with anything remotely to do with guys like that. That was just too close." That glassy-eyed look again. Like part of her was somewhere else.

I didn't blame Layna. But I didn't have the luxury to tap out. And facing this alone felt monumental, overwhelming.

"It's okay," I said. "I get it." And I did. But as I watched Layna climb into her Porsche and drive away, I felt more alone than I'd ever been in my whole life.

Back inside the Impala, I needed to cry again, but no tears came. I was empty, numb, hollowed out. I wracked my brain for someone, anyone who could help me move the mansicle. Emmylou was an obvious no-go. She didn't have the requisite brute strength or tight lips—I didn't need her entire Silver Sneakers aerobics class knowing where I'd dumped a murdered corpse.

A phone vibrated. Idaho Connor's, not mine.

**Natty Lite:** Any chance you know about some recent happenings at Burgdorf Hot Springs?

My heart squeezed like Phoebe's fist around the last Jolly Rancher. The phone rattled again with even more unwelcome news.

A quick Cricket reminder! Your month of Cricket service is up in less than twenty-four hours. To continue your service, please make your payment of $40 before 4 PM Mountain Time tomorrow.

Once Cricket turned off Idaho Connor's phone, surely people would notice he'd gone dark. My crimes—and culpability—were adding up.

I couldn't deal with this madness on my own. And I needed to find out how much the ATF knew about the explosion at Burgdorf. So in a moment of weakness or clarity, I pulled out my phone and invited over a federal agent.

Perhaps staring down the barrel of a prison sentence had spiked my libido because as I carried tumblers of whiskey to the living room, I couldn't help but notice Agent Nate Duran looked distractingly sexy in jeans and a scotch plaid flannel. Now that he was actually sitting on my couch, it was hard to know whether I'd invited him over to pick his brain about the law-enforcement investigation at Burgdorf, warn him I'd heard rumors of an attack on the state capitol in sixteen days, or merely experience adult companionship and a whiff of his pheromones. I suddenly suspected it was the latter.

I'd closed the blinds against the darkness, the cold, and Emmylou's prying eyes. The twins and Little Sister slept in their room. Nate's arrival hadn't woken them, which confirmed my suspicions Little Sister might not be a natural watchdog.

Nate thanked me for the whiskey. "After the day I've had I could use a drink."

"Stressful?" I asked, sitting next to him. Every ounce of my attention went to the square inch where our knees touched. That was the thing about pure attraction. It could blot out every trying thing in this world—at least for a little while. And I was desperately in need of a break from darker realities.

"Very."

"Like busting-down-doors stressful?" The whiskey was going down too easy.

"More like interviewing-an-outraged-suburban-lady-about-possible-federal-crimes stressful."

"Yikes," I said. "Sounds worse."

"For me? Definitely worse."

I wondered if I could get Nate to reveal how close law enforcement was to identifying me and Layna as the women who were at Burgdorf. But I hadn't found my in yet. "Tell me more," I said.

"I was following up a lead about this woman who maybe blew up a couple of snowmobiles yesterday with a hand grenade," he said.

My heart rate spiked to the heavens. "What?" I said. "People are crazy!" That was another of my go-tos. Like "Boise is made of spiders." I downed another slug of whiskey. "What's the lead?"

Nate picked up a piece of the Doggyland affirmations jigsaw puzzle off the coffee table. "She paid cash to rent a snowmobile up in McCall, but used her real driver's license at the rental place."

I'd forgotten about using Miranda's license! Even though she may have karmically deserved it, I didn't actually want to get Miranda in trouble. She was a CPS worker. If she found out I'd implicated her in a crime, she could take my kids!

Nate leaned over a partially assembled section of puzzle that so far read: *My Feelings*. "She said she lost her ID a few days ago. But she doesn't have an alibi. Said she was snowshoeing alone on some trails up by Bogus Basin to clear her head."

"So what'll you do next?"

"If she has the grenades, she'll likely try to sell them. I'm gonna tail her to see if it might lead to bigger fish." He snapped the puzzle piece into place with a satisfying click. *My Feelings Matter.*

Relief that the ATF wasn't onto me swirled with guilt that I'd made Miranda a suspect in a federal crime. Those were my feelings. But Nate and his ATF buddies could tail Miranda Carson for a year and all they'd see her do was drink rosé at her mom's fake designer candle parties.

"What would some suburban lady be doing blowing up snowmobiles?" I said.

"You know how radicalized so many people have become," Nate

said. "But that's enough about my work." He set down his whiskey and turned to face me. I couldn't tell if my every cell was electric with lust or confession nerves. "How about you? What'd you get up to today?"

I couldn't bring myself to say I'd been trying to recover from hypothermia incurred after blowing up the aforementioned snowmobiles. So I told him about pole class and my comic attempt to master the martini spin.

A lesser man would've made a salacious comment, but Nate just listened. When I was done, he said he'd read an interview with Seinfeld once where Seinfeld said he knew lots of rich people, and you'd think they'd be happy, but they're all miserable. According to Seinfeld, the key to happiness isn't money. The key to happiness is trying to master a skill. "That's why he's always working on his jokes," Nate said. "Even though he's insanely successful and—at this point—kind of old."

"But I haven't written any jokes for months," I said.

"No, no. I meant you're learning an entirely new skill. Pole dancing."

"A month ago I would've laughed in your face if you said I'd be learning pole."

"Why?" he said.

Looking into his eyes was disconcerting. "Because it's ridiculous!" I said.

"I think I might like ridiculous," he said.

There was a gravitational pull to this gorgeous, smart, sexy man who seemed to really see me. An elemental chemistry bubbling between us. And if I failed to figure out who murdered Idaho Connor (or worse, if I discovered I was the culprit), this might be my last opportunity for an evening like this. At least for a long, long time.

That's when I leaned in and kissed Nate. And, oh! That first kiss! It was like eating gelato in the sun after a lifetime of only ever having Froyo under gray skies. Suddenly I was ravenous for him, this lover from a past life. I peeled his flannel from his muscular arms. My hands ran over his strong bare shoulders. He was saying, "Are you sure?" And I was saying, *yes, yes, yes.*

# TWENTY-NINE

Five orgasms later (Tilly: three, Nate: two—those were my kind of stats!), I was in a postcoital love fog, floating on a mattress cloud, anxieties annihilated by the cocktail of dopamine, serotonin, and oxytocin sloshing in my brain. With my head on Nate's chest, his fingers twirling a lock of my hair, my loved-up hormones told me the ultimate lie—nothing bad could happen if I trusted him.

"I have something to tell you," I said. I'd begin at the beginning, only leaving out Layna's assistance. He would take care of me. He would get me out of this disastrous mess.

"All ears," he said. "But hang tight." He threw back the covers and sat up. That's when I saw it, glowing in the moonlight. A birthmark on his lower back. An all-natural Florida tramp stamp. A perfect copy of Phoebe's. Or hers was the copy.

It was like being slapped across the face with a dirty dish towel.

Because I suddenly understood why I'd felt such an instant connection.

As if I'd known Nate forever.

He'd donated sperm in Boise.

I'd received donor sperm in Boise.

Now I knew why his every gesture seemed familiar! When we'd gotten ice cream, the girls had shown Nate their double-jointed elbows, their ability to fold their tongues into that weird cloverleaf shape. Only he could bend his elbows back and fold up his tongue like origami too—because those were genetic anomalies they'd inherited from him!

As Nate padded—clueless and happy—to the bathroom, I curled up into a literal ball of shock. The sperm I'd gotten had been from an eighteen-year-old donor. That was eight years ago, so I'd assumed the donor would now be twenty-six. Nate was at least forty-five. That math didn't add up. But he'd been a freshman at Boise State when he sold his sperm. It could have sat in a freezer for twenty-something years before being released to me.

A gargling moan escaped me.

"You okay?" Nate called from the bathroom. The toilet flushed.

*No biggie. Just realizing you're probably the father of my children.* "Fine!" I squeaked.

I'd been fifteen when I stared across the syrup-sticky Kansas City diner booth at my bio dad for the first time. A year before, I'd developed an overpowering urge to meet him. It didn't come from a dissatisfaction with my mother—even during my resentful teenage years, I still deep down knew she was the greatest. It was more of a pressing need to solve the mystery of who I was and why. I had my mother's sense of humor and limp hair, but I wanted to meet the man who'd bequeathed me my flat feet and strange cravings for Sun Chips with cottage cheese.

In that diner booth, I'd studied my father's graying hair and puffy neck. The red veins that crisscrossed his nose and cheeks, alarming as cracking glass. What had I expected? That he'd be handsome and fascinated by me. That he'd ask me about my friends and interests. That he'd want me to explain how Alanis Morissette's music was actually more important than grunge, but when looked at critically, could also be considered an attempt to cash in on the riot grrrl movement's revolutionary sentiments. That he would gaze at me admiringly and say, "You are so hip and smart—just like I imagined."

But after a perfunctory, "You're pretty like your mother," he'd ordered the meat lover's breakfast plate for both of us—not even bothering to learn I was in my vegetarian phase—and proceeded to natter on about an import business scheme he was trying to get off the ground.

"You probably haven't heard about it yet because you live in Boise, but button-up shirts worn backwards are about to be big," he'd said, using his toast as a sponge for his revoltingly runny egg yolk. "My company'll sell men's dress shirts designed to fit perfectly when you wear 'em backwards." He leaned forward as if to impart an insider trading secret. "It's a style that's gonna be huge."

The year before, a hip-hop duo had had one irresistible top-of-the-charts banger. They'd done it while wearing their dads' dress shirts backward. For about a month, tween boys across the land had copied them. Like a defective firework, the fad had never fully popped off. Yet my biological father was pontificating on this "future" trend as if he was Sir Mix-a-Lot predicting the comeback of the big booty.

By the time he'd paid the check, my dad had asked me exactly two questions about myself. "You freeze your ass off up in Boise?" and "You get along with your mother?" When we left the restaurant, he didn't even offer to walk me to the motel where my mother waited to console me.

When I burst into our motel room, I wailed, "How could you let a man like that get you pregnant?"

She'd hugged me, her familiar smell of menthol Virginia Slims a comfort. "Oh honey," she said. "Hot young men with swagger sometimes turn into middle-aged blowhards."

Now a gush of water hit the bathroom sink. Nate. If he was the twins' sperm donor, they would never suffer the disillusionment I'd felt when I encountered my bio dad in the flesh. They already adored him.

My thoughts picked up speed like a skateboarder bombing down Fuller Avenue toward Hollywood Boulevard. Was it possible Nate knew he was the twins' dad? I dismissed the idea instantly. He wasn't a psycho—if he was their father and knew it, he wouldn't keep it a secret from me.

If I told Nate what I suspected, he might react badly. And if he discovered I'd committed multiple felonies, he could actually want to have some say in Phoebe and Alice's lives. Then again, what self-respecting bachelor would want custody of seven-year-old twins? But if Lucia (aka Principal Cruz) found out what I'd been up to of late, *she* might want to take the kids.

Ever since I first saw those two heartbeats on the sonogram monitor, I'd called every shot with regards to the twins. Breastfeeding or formula? Co-sleeping or no? How much screen time was too much screen time? My own mother had provided input, but ultimately every choice had been mine alone. Every time I heard a nightmarish co-parenting story from a divorced friend, I'd felt grateful not to have to compromise. I was an imperfect parent, but I knew what was best for my girls. I wasn't about to give that up—no matter what else I had to relinquish.

Nate stepped out of the bathroom, naked and painfully beautiful in the dim light. He was smiling, hair tousled, eyes dreamy. "Now," he said, "what did you want to tell me?"

I sat up, grabbing frantically for his clothes. "You have to leave," I said.

His face fell as I tossed him his jeans. "I thought we were—?"

I scrambled to explain my sudden vibe shift. "I don't want the twins to see you when they get up."

"Could we talk for a minute?" he said. "Before I go?"

His bewildered expression ripped my heart from my chest. I wanted to tell him being with him was better than rollerblading on the Venice Beach Boardwalk, or laughing on a patio in the sun with friends, or even crushing a stand-up set. But sometimes the hardest thing is the necessary thing. To protect my kids, I could lift a car. I could move to my hometown and work a job I absolutely hated. I could push away the sexiest, sweetest man I'd ever been with.

"Alice wakes up at two every morning from a nightmare where SpongeBob is stranded on land and is drying out. So I need you out of here," I said. "You understand."

# THIRTY

*Monday*

I woke up with a profound feeling of sadness and dread. Little Sister seemed to sense my mood, staring at me with woeful eyes until I'd locked him in his makeshift crate (aka the bathroom). Next I hurried the twins to the bus stop before embarking on a few overdue errands.

As I waited in line at the post office to mail back two pairs of too-small Velcro low-tops I'd bought for the twins, I dove headfirst into Google to read about sperm donor rights (or hopefully lack thereof). Of course I'd heard the spiel at the donor clinic eight years ago, but back then I'd been distracted by visions of babies dancing in my head. Now all pertinent state statutes I found online reassured me I had full parental authority and autonomy. Thank God.

My phone vibrated in my hands.

**Nate:** I had a great time with you last night. Like really great. But it felt kind of weird at the end. Want to talk?

A pipe bomb of heartsickness went off inside me. But I slid my phone into my pocket without texting him back.

As I walked through my front door an hour later, Little Sister frisked joyfully at my feet, but all I saw was carnage. The faux delicacies my mother had lovingly collected over the years were now in masticated tatters all over the carpet. Plastic fried eggs with fake browned edges, a packet of wooden French fries, and a slice of quiche Lorraine with lifelike bacon bits had all been gnawed to pieces.

The grief I normally kept at bay crashed in, and I felt with a piercing clarity that my mom was never, ever coming back. I floated outside my body and up to a corner of the ceiling, where I watched myself sobbing and yelling, "What have you done!" at the dog, who stared up at me with his head tilted as if concerned for my well-being.

A knock sounded on the door and Emmylou sailed in wearing her favorite shimmery green silk robe. "You okay?" One look at me and she could see I was not okay at all. "The dog was barking and barking while you were gone so I let him out of the bathroom."

"Why would you do that?" I said. "Why would you come in here without asking?"

"You told me where you keep the spare key. I was trying to help."

"That wasn't helpful! He chewed up my mom's stuff!"

"Oh, toots," Emmylou began, but she paused. "You know, this might be the Universe sending you a sign. It's time for you to stop living in a museum."

"A what?" Surely I had not heard her right.

"I know you miss your mother. But staying in a shrine isn't helping you and the girls move on. Why don't you throw some of this junk out? Make this place your own. It's time. Past time."

A shrine? I couldn't help it. I snapped. "I'm getting tired of you trying to boss me around."

"Boss you around?" Emmylou said. Clearly I'd hit a nerve. "I'm getting tired of you taking me for granted! And somebody needs to boss you! You want help. You *need* help. But you don't trust anyone. And you won't give Idaho a chance. You won't wake up to the fact that you live here now. You spend your time thinking about how great LA is and how terrible it is here. But you're in limbo. One foot in the past, one foot in an imaginary future. Meanwhile, you're just pissing on the present."

"I'm not pissing on anything," I fumed. But I was a little taken aback. Emmylou didn't usually swear. "And I have a right to miss Los Angeles."

"There are things you can do here to make your life better, is all I'm saying. You think it's good for your girls to see you moping around all the time? That's why Phoebe's been biting. That's why Alice is always hiding in that smelly old lady mask."

"Betty White was not any old lady!" I said. Nothing got my dander up like an attack on my parenting—or an iconic comedian. "And *I'm* not in the wrong here. This isn't a moratorium on how I raise my kids. You came into my house without my permission!" I gestured at a tattered plastic slice of pepperoni pizza. "This is your fault! You're always meddling!"

Emmylou's face turned steely. She'd been furious when I came home late from McCall, but that was mostly because she was worried about me. This was different. I'd never seen her possessed by this calm, cold wrath.

"You know what? I knew your mother well, and at some point, she'd want you to pull yourself out of the self-pity bog you've been wallowing in. She didn't practically bankrupt herself to give you the life and career of your dreams only to have you give up on it all the second she died. She wouldn't want you to use grieving as an excuse to quit comedy. She wouldn't want you holed up here, isolated, and not even trying for anything better for yourself or your girls. I'm tired of helping you when you won't even help yourself."

Emmylou and I had never spoken of all the money my mother had sent me—the fact that she knew about it made me feel like someone had dumped a bucket of shame over my head. Shame . . . and fury. "Why don't you mind your own damn business! And. Butt. Out. Of my. Life!" I yelled, suddenly irate as a teenager.

But my brutal outburst only seemed to further calm Emmylou. "Certainly," she said, stiff and dignified as a royal at Queen Camilla's birthday. "I'll miss the twins. But the free time will be nice, now that I'm officially dating Oat Willimena. Not that you asked."

She glided to the front door, silk robe fluttering around her ankles as she went. It closed behind her with a gentle accusatory click.

What just happened? My knees hit the carpet. I curled up into a fetal ball—it had been less than forty-eight hours since I cried hysterically on the bathroom floor. But this time my sadness and desperation found no release in tears. The dog sniffed at my face as if to say, *I did a great job chewing up this delicious kitsch. What are you so upset about?* But still I lay there unable to move, pinned down by grief and the desperate impossibility of my situation. My mother was dead and my career ruined and I was embroiled in a possible murder and had committed federal crimes. My fight with Emmylou meant now if I went to prison there would be no one to take my kids. And I really, really liked Nate, and even my kids liked him, and sex with him had been incredible, and yet I needed to shut him out for fear of what he might do if he found out any number of truths about my situation.

It was all too much to face. So I stayed curled up on the floor like a child longing desperately for her mother.

In an effort to avoid upsetting the twins, when I met them at the bus stop I told them I'd put some of Grandma Lulu's fake food in storage. They'd taken this lame explanation in stride and had hardly commented on the changes in the duplex. (As it turned out, Little Sister had only shredded the fake food in the living room. The plastic delicacies in my bedroom, the kitchen, and the twins' room were largely intact.) Now my girls sat at the kitchen table, Little Sister lying at their feet as they played a game they called Mirror, in which Alice had to mimic Phoebe's every movement. The game was unsettling, but today I let them do their thing without parental intercession as I stared out the back kitchen window, feeling numb and overburdened.

Idaho Connor's phone buzzed twice in my pocket. I hurried to the bathroom where I ran the tap to cover the sound of the voice memo.

"Meet me at Bar Gernika tomorrow, Tuesday, at one thirty for the handoff," the Receiver said. While my brain chewed on this new dilemma like Little Sister gnawing a plastic slice of key lime pie, I read the new texts that had come in for Connor.

**Natty Lite:** LMK you're okay, man.

**Tony Jerkoff Neighbor:** I've shoveled your sidewalk a few times but no sign of you. you out of town?

**Ralphie the Lizard:** u dirty fucking rat u need to call me asap i'm serious

**Cricket:** Your phone has been cut off for nonpayment. To reactivate your phone, call 888-458-9000 with your credit card number.

I swore like Sarah Silverman getting a Brazilian. I'd been worried about the temperature spiking in five days. But now it seemed like something would give even before Connor started to rot. My breathing grew shallow and my heart felt like a pecan in a nutcracker.

"Mooommmmmy!" Alice wailed from the kitchen. "It's Phoebe's turn to be the mirror and my turn to be the giiiiirrrrrlllll!"

"It's not my turn," Phoebe said, as I hurried in to manage the dispute, "because I'm tired of this game. Can we ask Emmylou to come over?"

"Will she make brownies with us again?" Alice chimed in.

Too distracted and panicky to sugarcoat the situation, I said, "We won't be seeing much of Emmylou for a while."

Both their faces fell. Alice started to cry.

"It's okay, honey," I said. "Sometimes we need a little break from people, even if they are people we love very much." But that only seemed to make her cry harder.

The inside of my head was as chaotic as a summer camp shaving cream fight and my chest pain had reached an eight out of ten. "I need to go to the bathroom again," I managed. On the toilet, head between my knees, I battled a sudden certainty I was dying. I told myself if expiring on the john was good enough for Elvis, it was good enough for me. But I was not convinced.

I took calming breaths and tried to make myself think. If I got caught for any or all of my crimes, I'd need information to trade for immunity. So far all I had were descriptions of Errol and Ralphie the Lizard, which definitely wouldn't cut it. But if I had the ability to hand over the exact location of an arms trafficker named the Receiver—now that might do the trick.

# THIRTY-ONE

*Tuesday*

Imagine this. In a brand-new *Ocean's Eleven* spin-off, Margot Robbie prepares to go to Bar Gernika to locate an illegal arms dealer, then flirt with him, buy him a drink, and generally charm him long enough to plant a tiny GPS device on his person or vehicle so she can share his location with law enforcement as needed. The stakes are high, but as she's headed out the door to Best Buy to procure the tracking device, her phone rings with a call from her daughter's school. Does she ignore it? Or pick up?

"Hello," I said.

"Tilly," a familiar voice replied.

I cursed silently. "Principal Cruz." If she was calling to ask why I'd blown off her darling brother after we had great sex, I might burst into flames.

"I'm going to need you to come pick up Phoebe. She's bitten another child."

Oh, no! Emmylou was right, dammit! My kids were struggling and it was likely my fault. And this was an escalation—Phoebe'd never chomped anyone before who didn't share her exact DNA. And while I *wanted* school to provide my kids an education, I *needed* it to provide childcare. "Lucia, I take this very seriously. But please can she stay at school? I have a meeting I can't miss."

It was Tuesday and almost noon. The Receiver would be at Bar Gernika waiting for Connor at one thirty.

"We need our students to understand we can't tolerate biting here at

Roosevelt," Lucia said. "Otherwise we could end up with mayhem. And a Hep B outbreak."

"Not to be that kind of mom, but why'd Phoebe bite this kid? What'd the other kid do?"

"Phoebe claimed she mistook the girl's arm for a Pop-Tart," Lucia said dryly. "Is anything going on at home?"

I understood the unspoken transaction being offered. If I told her how my mother's death was affecting me and the twins, she wouldn't make me come get Phoebe. I was desperate, but not desperate enough to perform Grief Porn.

"Look, Lucia," I said. "I'm a single mom with no backup childcare today and I literally can't tell you how important this meeting is."

I heard Principal Cruz sigh. And then in a firm but kind voice she said, "I need you here to pick Phoebe up within the hour."

"From your wrestling moves, I thought you'd be a lot cooler than this," I said, but she'd already hung up.

My impending lack of childcare made me panicky again, my anxiety latching on to the fact that I still had Idaho Connor's now-defunct phone. I'd never been a tech goddess and wasn't entirely sure if law enforcement could ping it now that it was turned off. But if they could, I didn't want them seeing it at my house. I needed to feel in control. I needed to DO SOMETHING. So on my way to Roosevelt Elementary, I took an impulsive detour, parking in a random lot. Crusty remnants of snow crunched underfoot as I walked out onto the Ninth Street Bridge. Cars whizzed by and I leaned over the rail to watch the icy river below. I pulled Connor's phone out of my pocket, dangled it over the edge, and let go. It landed with a satisfying splash. Soon someone was bound to notice Connor wasn't responding to messages and report him missing. It might even be Nate. But at least Connor's phone wasn't at my house anymore.

When I got back in the car, still feeling pleased to have taken some positive action, however small, my own cell was bleating like a drunken sheep.

"Layna!" I said.

"I have my tantric yoga coaching session with Magnus at four o'clock," Layna said, "and I'm trying to decide between black tights and pink booty shorts."

"Black tights," I replied. "Any chance you can babysit Phoebe for an hour starting like an hour from now?"

"I've got divorce mediation till three," she said. "Then Magnus. But I could cancel that."

Three o'clock was too late. "That's okay. I'm just frazzled. You-know-who's phone got cut off for nonpayment." I was barreling over her boundary, but I couldn't help it—I was freaking out.

"Did you turn it back on?"

"I can't use my credit card! It would be so traceable."

"Buy a Visa gift card at CVS," she said. "Duh."

"Too late for that," I moaned, staring toward the river. "I really *don't* have a knack for this shit."

There's nothing more distressing than looking in the rearview to see your ashamed little kid twisting and untwisting the hem of her T-shirt.

"Phoebe, why?" I asked as gently as possible. "Why would you bite Johnica?" I glanced at the clock. Twelve thirty p.m. I had one hour before I needed to arrive at Bar Gernika with a GPS tracker.

Phoebe sniffled. "I don't know," she said. "I didn't do it on porpoise. My teeth felt mad." She paused. "Since I can't go to school, can I stay home with Emmylou?" She looked at me, sad and hopeful.

"Did you bite Johnica because Emmylou and I aren't getting along?" I said.

Phoebe shrugged a helpless shrug. "My angry teeth bit her," she insisted. "Not me." But the look in her eyes told me all I needed to know.

After I made Phoebe a snack, I asked her to stay in her room for a few minutes to think about ways to express feelings of sadness that didn't involve sinking her teeth into another kid's flesh. Twelve forty p.m. Fifty minutes. I shut myself into the pantry and pondered babysitting options as I stress-ate potato chips. My pants wouldn't fit soon if I didn't stop eating like this. At the very least I needed to start going to the gym.

The gym! That was it! My emergency babysitting solution.

The price to pay for entering the Boise downtown YMCA was a Stop-and-Chat with the front desk attendant, Wendy Lou, my mom's former coworker and frenemy, who wanted to ooh-and-ahh over Phoebe, and perhaps compare her unfavorably to her own progeny. ("To hear Wendy Lou tell it," my mom would say, "one of her grandkids is Simone Biles, the other Greta Thunberg.")

After waving a cheery goodbye to Phoebe—who was already starting a round of *Just Dance* with the YMCA Kids' Club attendant—I ducked into the women's locker room, where I stripped off my workout gear and pulled on tights and a sexy little black dress. I topped it all off with the Little Mermaid wig and managed to sneak out the front door without being recognized by Wendy Lou.

Behind the wheel of the Impala, I yanked off the red wig. One p.m. I had thirty minutes to rush to Best Buy on Franklin, buy a GPS tracking device, zip downtown, park, and hustle to Bar Gernika to meet the Receiver. He'd be waiting for Idaho Connor. But hopefully I could spot him, chat him up, get him to buy me a beer, and slip the GPS tracking device into his pocket. A tall order but not impossible.

The icy wind nipped my flesh as I hustled down the Basque Block at 1:39 p.m. in my short black dress, so it felt good to slip through the side door into the warmth of Bar Gernika.

The place hadn't changed—the Basque dive was still dishing up croquetas and lamb grinders greasy enough to stop a triathlete's heart. A group of university professors shared a boozy lunch while making eyes at a gaggle of co-eds obliviously giggling into midday beers. But at the long bar, two rough-looking guys sartorially inspired by lumberjacks perched on stools. One had a stern face dominated by a massive unibrow that would put Frida Kahlo to shame. The other sported a raised scar along his temple, shiny and pink as a newborn hamster. One of them must be the Receiver, the other his muscle.

They studied me like a juicy pork chop in a meat case, and I flashed a smile I hoped was dazzling. I hadn't expected to have to try to charm two men, but that also gave me more options for where to slip the quarter-sized GPS (ostensibly designed to track errant suitcases).

That's when I spotted Miranda's awful mother, Mrs. Carson, sitting alone at a table in the corner, looking prim and mean as ever, if a little frail. Shit! I absolutely could not stand a Stop-and-Chat with Belinda Carson. Not after I'd accidentally framed Miranda for blowing up two snowmobiles with a hand grenade!

A woman hustled out the front door, head ducked, as if to avoid being recognized. Under her unzipped navy peacoat, she wore one of those front-facing dog slings, so popular in LA. But with her red hair, she was unmistakable. Miranda Carson! Why in the hell was she rushing out of here without her mom? Nate told me he'd be tailing Miranda. Last thing I needed was him seeing me bellied up to the bar with a couple of arms dealers. Mrs. Carson glanced my way and, panicked, I rushed out the side door.

Heart pumping with adrenaline, I ran full tilt down the Basque Block, darting across Sixth and cutting down an alley to the side street where I'd parked the Impala.

One hour and nine minutes after I'd dropped Phoebe off, I raced into the YMCA dressing room. My half-baked mission to plant the GPS on the Receiver had been a total failure and now I was late to pick up my kid. After stripping off my disguise and yanking my workout clothes back on, I hustled to the Kids' Club to find Phoebe shaking it to RuPaul's "Sissy That Walk."

"Workout went long?" the Kids' Club attendee said, pursing her lips.

"I'm so sorry," I said, wiping actual nervous sweat from my forehead. "I was on the treadmill and got into the zone."

# THIRTY-TWO

Late that afternoon, the twins huddled on the couch with Little Sister, watching *The Parent Trap* again while I curled up in the recliner. Darkness had fallen outside and we were a cozy unit of four. How many more sweet quiet times like this would the girls and I have together before something finally gave? The corpse couldn't stay in the playhouse forever—a big thaw was coming in four days!

I needed some relief from this sense of impending doom. Before the Mickey Larynx debacle, taking notes on joke ideas had been my most reliable form of escapism—better than booze, or ice cream, or even online shopping. Even though my comedy ambitions were both ferocious and stymied, actually working on comedy had always been my happy place, my flow state, my communion with the divine. Nuns prayed the rosary. Buddhist monks chanted and meditated and swept floors. I wrote raunchy jokes.

But once my fledgling career imploded and my mom died, I'd stopped jotting down ideas. I'd always believed we need comedy precisely because life can be so cruel. But sorrow had turned off my creative tap. Now pole dancing class—of all things!—seemed to have twisted it back on. It had jarred loose the stuck part of my brain that used to notice humor everywhere.

Before I could think twice, I flipped open my laptop and started typing up some of my funniest bits about being a Pole Virgin. I told myself it was just a way to think about something, anything, other than the mess I was in. I didn't let myself admit I might be writing a stand-up set. It was better to squint and look away, to pretend what was happening wasn't happening, so as to not scare off the Muse.

But the climax of *The Parent Trap* interrupted my flow. A fully clothed Dennis Quaid climbed out of the Stafford Hotel pool to find himself reunited with the identical twin daughter he'd raised, the identical twin daughter he hadn't seen since she was a baby, and their mother. My own twins' lips moved along with Lindsay Lohan as she said: "Well, I'm quite grown up now, and quite without a father."

"Life," I bellowed, "is not a Nancy Meyers movie!"

Before I could snatch up the remote and turn off the television, the rooster crowed. A peek through the blinds revealed Layna stomping her snow-booted feet in the circle of porch light. I threw open the door and the twins crowded around as Little Sister approached Layna, sniffing warily.

"My divorce mediation sucked and my yoga session with Magnus was a total disaster," Layna said. "I need advice. Can I come in to talk now, before pole?"

"Pole!" While writing jokes about pole, I'd forgotten all about my actual class. "I can't go! I'm down a babysitter."

"Little Sister seems shy," Phoebe informed Layna. "But he liked the other lady."

"Which lady?" I said, distracted.

"The pretty one," Phoebe said. "From the grocery store." The last thing I wanted to hear was Phoebe carrying on about how beautiful Miranda was. Freaking Miranda Carson! Thanks to her and her horrid mother, my mission to plant a GPS on the Receiver had been a total bust.

"Little Sister liked her because they already knew each other," Alice said.

"Miranda said she met a dog that looked like Little Sister, it wasn't actually—" I began.

Layna interrupted, reaching into her bag for stuffed animals. "Forget that other rando. *This* pretty lady brought you presents!"

Instead of giving Layna my undivided attention, I headed into the kitchen and started unloading the dishwasher. The sudden impulse to resent her was childish, but I couldn't help it. My afternoon escapade had taken its toll on my emotional maturity. And Layna seemed to have forgotten the horrible mess I was in—she'd already launched into her anecdote of romantic dejection without even asking how I was doing.

"I'm so mortified. There are no words for how mortified," she said as she sat down at the kitchen table. "There I was in downward dog. When Magnus started adjusting me from behind, I thought he was being suggestive!"

I paused with a coffee mug outstretched toward the open cabinet. "Oh no—you didn't."

"Crabwalk right back into his crotch? I did! Only he was horrified instead of turned on. And then the session was over and I paid him a hundred and fifty bucks." She moaned and dropped her face into her hands. "It was awful. How do men in strip clubs do it?"

"I think it makes the men feel baller to pay. Like they own their very own sexy girl, even just for a song or two."

"I did not feel like I owned Magnus! I felt like he was pitying me for being desperate when he really just wanted to help me improve my mountain pose! How did I get this so wrong?" She started to sniffle. "And the mediation. It was awful. I'm gonna have to go to Portland and put our vacation home in Lake Oswego on the market. I want to be divorced from the douchebag. I really do. But it's like I'm so angry and my feelings are so hurt that he didn't think I was sexy or desirable. He just wanted me to be his chaste personal assistant while he had sex with his *actual* personal assistant, like at work!"

"Oh, Layna," I said, abandoning the half-empty dishwasher to sit across from her.

My phone rang. Miley O'Riley.

"Not again." I swore, sending it to voicemail.

"Who's that?" Layna asked, seeming glad to be distracted from her woes.

"This girl I went to high school with. She's trying to get me to do a stand-up set at the Winter Will Never End Festival on Saturday."

Layna smacked both palms so hard on the table my long-abandoned coffee jumped in its mug. "You should do it!"

"You think I don't have enough on my plate?" I said. But if things weren't going so terribly, maybe I'd want to. My new jokes about pole dancing were pretty funny. It would feel good to try them out, even in front of a dinky hometown crowd.

"Fair," Layna said. "Maybe Shade could perform instead."

"Stand-up?"

"No! Drag! Send me that woman's info. I'll ask her if she'd be interested."

It wasn't a bad idea. While I was forwarding Miley's contact info to Layna, my phone dinged.

**Nate:** Tilly! Me again. Want to chat?

Inside me, hankering and lust muddled with sadness for what might've been. It was quite the feelings cocktail. I flipped my phone face down.

"Everything okay?" Layna asked.

If I shared my suspicions about the twins' paternity with Layna and she insisted I tell Nate, it would make me furious at her. Then I'd be more alone than I could bear. Before I could decide whether to give her an edited version of my hookup or not mention it at all, a scrabbling clatter sounded behind me.

Little Sister's rump was sticking out of the open dishwasher—the rest of the dog had vanished inside. He thrashed and flailed and yelped pitifully, stymied by the dish rack.

By the time I was on my feet, full-scale pandemonium had erupted.

As the dog's nails scrabbled against clean dishes, the twins stampeded into the kitchen to investigate the hullabaloo. I grabbed onto Little Sister's hind end and yanked as a foul-smelling fluid reeking of rotten fish sprayed out of the dog—and all over me. I cursed and stumbled backward, dragging the dog with me. We landed in a fetid heap.

"I think his anal glands expressed," Layna said, pinching her nose.

"We are not keeping this animal!" I shouted, and the twins burst into tears.

Layna saved the day, entertaining the kids in the living room while I cleaned the kitchen. An anxious Little Sister stuck close by while I mopped. The repetitive motion calmed and distracted me, giving my brain free range to linger on my petty annoyance that the twins thought Miranda was pretty. I leaned the mop against the wall, and grabbed for my phone, searching Instagram for Miranda's profile, which was public. Her grid featured carefully curated shots of her interior decor sprinkled between outdoor selfies with her handsome husband. In each photo she seemed to be saying:

*Look at how good my hair looks when I'm snowshoeing!*

*Don't you wish you had a hot husband who would chop down your Christmas tree by hand?*

*Don't you wish you could be me?*

Then, in a photo of Miranda in workout gear, I spotted it: a tote bag slung over her shoulder, printed with the Pole Kisses logo.

That liar! Miranda had told me to my face—in this very kitchen—she didn't go to pole classes!

Even further back on her grid, a smiling Miranda held up a giant Starbucks cup. The caption read: "The pumpkin spice latte has dropped! My favorite day of the year!"

And just like that I'd found her: Pumpkin Spice.

Cheyenne had seen Miranda Carson heading down the alley behind Huckleberry's the night Connor was killed. Which meant Miranda might've been the last person to see him alive.

# THIRTY-THREE

*Wednesday*

Miranda's redbrick Queen Anne, with its wraparound front porch, multiple chimneys, and big bay windows, was basically one big ornate flourish. An incongruously rusty GMC Jimmy blocked in Miranda's white Jeep Cherokee, so I parked on a side street. The twins were at school, so Little Sister and I were on our own. When I opened my passenger door, the dog leapt out with Alice's Betty White latex mask hanging from his teeth.

"Gimme that!" I said, but when I lunged for it, the dog danced away. As I made another grab, a flash of movement inside Miranda's big bay window caught my eye. A large figure shoving someone with flaming red hair. Miranda. My heart contracted.

Little Sister slunk toward the house, teeth bared, a low growl thundering in his throat while I made a grab for my handbag. After tucking the fake pistol down the front of my pants and the bear spray in my bra, I scooped the Betty White mask from the ground and hurried after the dog.

Through a side living room window, I could make out a man pressing Miranda against the living room wall, his forearm to her throat. Ralphie. And standing to the side like a fireplug, Errol. Dark spots swirled in my vision. I could see it again. Baylee's severed finger with its chipped orange polish. I didn't like Miranda. But I couldn't leave her alone and undefended with two men who shared a kink for women's terror. Little Sister was already barreling through the cracked side door, snarling and barking. Before I could think, I yanked on the Betty White mask, pulled out the bear spray, and followed behind. (Maybe the fake gun would've been more effective, but I wanted something with the potential to inflict actual pain.) As I stumbled through Miranda's kitchen to her living room, the eyeholes of the latex mask were so criminally small I clipped my hip on the edge of the kitchen counter.

"Where's Nikita?" Ralphie was shouting. "Tell me!"

"I don't know what you're talking about," Miranda sobbed. "Leave me alone."

"What in the actual fuck?" Errol said as he spotted me. That's when Little Sister sank his teeth into Errol's calf meat, his pit bull jaw locking tighter than a pickle jar. As I headed toward an astonished Ralphie, my foot caught on a coffee table and I went down hard, hitting the floral rug with a *WHUMP*! Realizing I'd need to rely on chaos rather than fighting precision, I rolled onto my back and screamed like an Irish banshee bringing an omen of death as I pointed the bear spray at Ralphie and squeezed.

Ralphie's yowls of pain eclipsed my own shrieks. When he clutched his hands over his eyes, Miranda grabbed his shoulders and executed the classic fight move known as "knee to nuts."

Amidst the general pandemonium, I climbed to my feet, yanked the gun from my pants, and pointed it at Ralphie while shouting, "The ATF is on its way! The ATF is on its way!"

In a panic, Ralphie staggered out the front door, tumbling down the steps. From what I could make out through the mask's eye holes, Errol was trying to follow him, but the forty pounds of pit bull clinging to his leg hampered his progress.

"Little Sister!" I shouted. "Let go."

The dog unclenched his jaws. At the bottom of the steps, Errol pulled Ralphie to his feet and the two staggered through the snow to the GMC Jimmy, shouting off-color expletives as they went.

"Tell Nikita we'll find her!" was the last thing Ralphie yelled before he slammed the car door. The Jimmy caught on some slush, its wheels spinning impotently before it skidded out of the driveway.

Little Sister frisked worriedly as Miranda limped to the couch. The adrenaline in my bloodstream told me to beeline out of there before Miranda could call the cops. But as I made for the door, she said, "Tilly? Even with that ridiculous mask on, I know it's you. Besides, I recognize your dog."

Sheepishly, I tugged off the mask, happy to take a gulp of air that didn't smell like a plastics factory.

"You saved my life," Miranda said, collapsing on the couch. "I think I sprained my ankle."

"Shoot," I said. "Again?" I could picture high-school-cheerleader Miranda doing back handsprings across the football field until her ankle gave out and she went down like a sack of potatoes.

She waved a hand at my pistol. "Can you put that thing away? You're making me nervous."

"It's fake." I slumped into a yellow gingham chair as I waited for my heart to stop jackhammering. A lamp and coffee table had been knocked over in the scuffle, but otherwise the only sign of violence was a cacophony of floral patterns slugging it out for dominance. The place seriously looked like the Lilly Pulitzer catalogue had thrown up all over it. To stall, I said, "You really nailed that guy's nuts."

"I took self-defense classes at the Krav Maga studio one time. Thank god I have an alarm system. Maybe I should borrow a real gun from my mom? In case they come back? No, that's crazy. Wait. Tilly, why are you even here?"

"Who were those guys?" I said. Better to find out how she knew Ralphie and Errol before I started asking questions. Little Sister whined and nuzzled my hand. That's when I noticed the blood. The stitches in his ear had ripped during the kerfuffle.

"God knows. As far as I can tell somebody stole my license and used it to rent a snowmobile and then blew up those guys' snowmobiles? It's so trashy it makes me dizzy." Wincing, she swung both legs up onto the couch. "Could you grab me a bag of peas out of the freezer?"

I needed a minute to think so I headed to the kitchen. Miranda's freezer was clearly the purview of a child-free couple. There was nary a chicken nugget, fish stick, corn dog, or waffle to be found. I grabbed the frozen peas and a daisy-printed dish towel.

"Here you go, *Pumpkin Spice*," I said, tossing her the frozen peas a little too hard. I wanted her off-balance.

Despite her shock, she managed to catch the projectile. "Why'd you call me that?" She was blinking fast, trying to put the pieces together.

"Because it's your pole name."

"Yeah, but how'd you know?"

"You said you'd never been to Pole Kisses," I said. "Why lie about taking a pole dancing class?" Without asking, I used her tea towel to catch blood dripping from Little Sister's ear.

She made a face as she set the bag of frozen peas on her swelling ankle. "Because pole is kind of low rent, right? Like for strippers."

"Then why go at all?" I pressed.

"When I started taking classes, I really liked it. But my mom went ballistic when I told her. Said she didn't raise me to be a stripper-whore. So I quit going."

Miranda was clearly rattled enough by Ralphie and Errol to tell me anything, if I was smart about it. There was a chance she'd seen me kill Connor. She might've stopped by my house the other day to confront me, then chickened out. But whatever happened, I needed to know.

Being a mom had taught me sometimes the best way to get information out of a reluctant witness is to feign omniscience. So I bluffed. "Miranda, I know what happened in the alley behind Huckleberry's the other night."

All color seeped from her face. "Tilly, I'm so sorry. I had no idea it was your car."

Relief flooded every cell in my body. Followed by rage. How dare this woman frame me *again* for crimes she committed. First she hid her empty vodka bottle in my duffel bag. Now she'd stuffed a dead body in my trunk! I couldn't wait to tell the police what she'd done.

But that's when the thing happened that ruined my tidy plan to turn in Miranda.

A familiar sound came from a monitor tucked behind an end-table lamp.

A baby's wailing.

# THIRTY-FOUR

It's common knowledge nothing brings a sense of calm like the smell of an infant. So when I found the perfect, black-haired little girl with a strawberry birthmark on her neck lying in a white crib in the office down the hall, I scooped her up and started sniffing the top of her head like a wayward teen huffing gas.

Once I'd returned to the living room and handed the precious cargo to Miranda, she snuggled the babe to her chest and sighed. I recognized it. The relief and wonder at finally having a baby (or in my case, babies, plural) after knowing for so long it might never happen. The infant made a happy gurgling noise. Glancing around the room, I spotted a baby swing tucked alongside the couch. I hadn't noticed it in the scuffle. I was starting to feel whiplashed.

"Miranda," I said, "whose baby is this?"

As I went to work stanching the fresh bleeding from Little Sister's ear, a story of longing I knew too well flooded out of Miranda. After what she'd done to me, I didn't want to listen or sympathize. But I was curious about where this baby had come from. And I needed a minute to think, to figure out my next steps, so I listened. More than anything in this world, Miranda said, she'd wanted to be a mother. I remembered that yearning, the soul ache for a child. Even had I truly known how much cleaning up of vomit and poo, maternal anxiety, financial insecurity, and eventual twin bickering motherhood would entail, I still would've wanted it.

But like me, Miranda had fertility issues. Round after round of heart-breaking, expensive IVF treatments, complete with hormone injections that would've turned even a young Emma Watson into an unhinged weeping crazy lady, had walloped Miranda's body, spirit, and bank account. For once in her life, her mother had actually been supportive, saying the right things, being there for her. "I literally couldn't have done it without her!" Miranda said. Belinda Carson was unwavering in her support, an actual dream mother, right up until Miranda and her husband decided to adopt, at which point Miranda's mother turned mean again, ranting about the insanity of raising a child from an unknown bloodline. Miranda had soldiered on, wading through mountains of red tape and expenses. Then, ten days ago, a beautiful baby girl was discovered on the doorstep of an Airbnb shaped like an oversized potato off Highway 84. The twenty-eight-foot fake spud had had a first life as a promotional tool for the Idaho Potato Commission. The origins of the three-day-old baby—whom CPS workers had nicknamed Tater Tot—were more mysterious.

The infant was placed into emergency foster care, but Miranda had immediately petitioned to foster and adopt the baby.

"Did you ever read that Shel Silverstein book about the circle that was missing a piece and went around looking for it?" Miranda said. "As soon as I held Tater Tot, I knew I'd found my missing piece, that we were meant to be together. I felt like I was born to take care of her."

"You don't have to get all trad wife about it," I said. But my volcanic anger had started to cool. The appearance of Tater Tot had turned my rage into something more complicated. "So tell me why you murdered that creep and tried to pin it on me."

I thought she might backpedal, but new motherhood had clearly left her raw as a skinless, boneless chicken thigh. Her face crumpled and she told me everything. On that notorious Sunday, she'd gotten the call that she could pick Tater Tot up in a few days. She spent the evening hunched over her laptop at Caffeina, furiously trying to get ahead on her casework.

"I'd parked behind Huckleberry's because Caffeina's lot was full.

When I headed back to my car, I saw this guy," Miranda said. "He was—well, he had his pants down a little and his butt backed up to the open trunk of a blue muscle car." She paused and looked sick. "Your muscle car. But I didn't know that then."

"Ah-ha!" I said. "So he did steal my keys!" I paused. "But what do you mean he had his butt backed up to my car?"

"I think," she said, wrinkling her nose in distaste. "I think maybe he was trying to take a dump in the trunk?"

"Ugh!" I cried. But it made sense. I explained Connor had probably spiked my drink with Ambien and nabbed my keys. When his plan to lure me out of the club failed, he must've decided to take a revenge dookie in my trunk instead.

"As soon as I walked under a motion light, we recognized each other," Miranda said. "From this CPS case I investigated a few months ago."

"Wait! You'd already met Connor? And this dog?" I hadn't believed Alice when she said Miranda and Little Sister were previously acquainted. But maybe she'd been right.

"That's actually Connor's pit bull?" Miranda said. "Tilly, why do you have his dog?"

"I went to his house looking for clues. The dog was stuck there. Alone. Starving. Come on now. Tell me about this CPS case."

"Okay, okay. So Connor had a girlfriend named Korielle."

Where had I heard that name? There was too much coming at me.

"Korielle's son told his preschool teacher his mom's boyfriend beat her up," Miranda continued. "That's why CPS was called. I met Connor and the dog on a visit to Korielle's. Later, she admitted Connor was physically abusive. Controlling. A total loser. CPS policy is to take kids out of violent homes." Tater Tot let out a little cry and Miranda jostled and soothed her.

"So a mom has a bad boyfriend she can't get rid of and CPS yanks her kids?" I said, suddenly angry again.

"CPS policies are beyond terrible," Miranda agreed. "I realize that.

Korielle was a really good mom. And she wanted to break up with Connor. So I told her to use me as an excuse."

Then I remembered. Korielle rhymes with L'Oréal. "Connor was texting with a woman named Korielle!" I said. "That's where I've heard the name." I pulled out my phone and showed Miranda the picture I'd snapped of the framed photo on Connor's desk. A smiling Connor had his arm slung around a woman with bleached hair. A sad-looking little boy stood beside her. I'd thought the woman was Baylee.

"That's her," Miranda said. "That's Korielle."

"So Connor thought of you as the meddling caseworker who made his girlfriend break up with him," I mused. And he thought of Korielle as the one who got away.

Little Sister was trying to wriggle away from me, but I kept two fingers under his collar and the tea towel below his torn ear. Not that I cared if the dog bled on Miranda's floral rug. I wouldn't be surprised if a 1980s Laura Ashley called wanting that rug back.

"You got it," Miranda said. "In the alley that night, Connor had a big goose egg on his forehead. And he seemed like, kind of out of it? When he saw me in the alley, he staggered at me. Making this wheezing sound. And his face—it was like a monster."

"Jesus," I said. If Idaho Connor had attacked me in a dark alley, I'd think he looked like a monster too. "What do you mean, though?"

"He was like this!" Miranda contorted her face, mouth wide open and twisted, one eye squinted shut. "Then he was making these horrible rasping noises and trying to push me into the trunk of his car. Head first. At least I thought it was his car. There were scissors. Like right in front of my face. In the trunk, right? So I grabbed them and managed to get him in the leg. I spun around and got him again before he knocked the scissors out of my hand. Somehow I pulled my taser out of my purse. I always thought it was so insane my mom made me carry it." She laughed, a little hysterically, and took a big sniff of the top of Tater Tot's head, as if to ground herself. "Tasing him—" She shuddered, and I knew she wouldn't say more. "He toppled forward and I ran to my car. But when I looked back. He was . . . he was . . . His top half was in the trunk, his legs hanging out. I could tell he wasn't moving. I went back and he was . . . he was dead."

"Dead," I said flatly. "You think the taser really killed him?"

"Oh, he was dead, all right," Miranda said.

"Tasers *can* kill people," I said. A social worker had been tased to death by the cops at a routine traffic stop in Culver City a few years back. Still, I didn't think people died of being tased that often. "But you said he was wheezing?"

"It was weird," Miranda agreed.

Having just discovered Connor's killer, I wasn't eager to convince her she hadn't actually done the deed. Still, I wondered if there was more to the story than Miranda knew. After all, I still didn't know where I was for seven hours or how I ended up in the alley of Huckleberry's at four in the morning wearing Connor's vest. "Any chance you saw a teal vest lying around?" I asked.

She shook her head. "Why?"

"No reason. Never mind. So you lifted up his legs and stuffed him in my trunk."

She nodded, weepy and trembling. "I wiped the keys and tossed them in the dumpster. But I promise: I had no idea it was your car. I would have never. Can I ask?" she said with real trepidation. "Is he . . . is he still there?"

"No," I said sharply. The corpse was in my backyard. Where he was my problem, when he should've been Miranda's. "But for god's sake, why didn't you call the police?"

"I'm in the process of trying to adopt a baby!" Miranda said. "And then suddenly my file says I tased a guy to death behind a strip club? Even if I don't get charged with manslaughter, I lose my chance at keeping Tater Tot. One baby. Is that too much to ask? When every piece of trash on this earth has at least two without trying."

"Are you seriously calling me *trash*?"

"Sorry," she said. "I didn't mean you."

I sucked my teeth. But it was starting to sink in that Miranda hadn't intended to do me harm.

Miranda explained that when she drove by me the next day, after seeing me in the co-op, she'd recognized my LuvLife plates and realized what she'd done. "That's why I came by your house last Wednesday!" she said. "I was going to tell you everything. But then your neighbor showed up and you hustled me out of there."

"You could've come back," I said. "But of course it was easier for you to let me deal with it."

"I got Tater Tot on Sunday," Miranda said. "And then some ATF agents came around questioning me because someone stole my license. I've been terrified and overwhelmed. And you're right. Honestly I wanted to pretend that nightmare didn't really happen."

A tiny flame of guilt had sprung up at the mention of Miranda's stolen license, but I tamped it out. "Yeah, I want to be sympathetic, Miranda. But it's a little hard because you put a dead body in the trunk of my car! I have kids, Miranda! Two! I could go to prison!"

"I'm so sorry, Tilly. I'm so sorry." She let out a sob. "And this is going to sound silly. You probably don't even remember this. But I'm also really sorry I hid my vodka in your duffel bag at cheerleading camp. It was so stupid. I was drunk and I didn't think you'd get caught. I should have come forward. I've always felt bad about it."

"It was really shitty," I said. The old bitterness and grief rose in my throat. "I actually loved being Mr. Potato Pants." But it felt cathartic and good to actually hear her apologize.

"Your Rump Shaker dance was the best," Miranda said, sympathetically. "In the alley, I was panicked, I was desperate, and I thought it was his car. Please believe me. I never in a million years would've put you in this terrible position on purpose. I didn't mean to screw you over again."

And in spite of myself, I believed her.

Miranda could sense I was softening. She expertly swung Tater Tot onto her shoulder and gently patted her back. “I want to help you. We can fix this somehow—together.”

“Fix it by going to the police,” I said, but I didn’t sound convincing. Miranda was a mother now too. I could not make my heart unfeeling enough. Even though I didn’t fully trust her, if we were both going to stay out of prison, we’d need to work together. “If we’re doing apologies—” I pulled my wallet out of my coat pocket and handed over her driver’s license. “The dog pulled your purse off my couch and your license fell out.”

She stared at me, baffled. “You stole my license and used it to rent a snowmobile?” she asked.

“Because *someone* put a dead man. In. My. Trunk,” I said. “Another long story but I was trying to get proof I didn’t kill him.” I gave her the *Reader’s Digest* version of my trip to Burgdorf, leaving out the fact that Layna had accompanied me.

When I got to the part about lobbing the grenade, Tater started to cry. Miranda snuggled and bounced the baby.

“I think she’s hungry,” Miranda said. “Could you—?”

Under Miranda’s direction, I made a bottle. The process of heating the formula and tamping a splash from the nipple onto my wrist to make sure it wasn’t too hot was soothing. As soon as Miranda gave it to Tater Tot, the baby quieted and began drinking happily.

I told Miranda about my unsuccessful trip to Bar Gernika to try and plant a GPS on the Receiver. “I saw you and your mom there. It spooked me and I took off.”

“My mom was craving a lamb grinder so I dropped her for lunch. I had to hurry because I was taking Tater Tot to her pediatrician appointment.”

“That wasn’t a dog sling you were wearing,” I said. “It was a baby sling!”

Miranda laughed. “I promise I wouldn’t wear a dog!” She paused, her eyes suddenly glassy. "I was also trying to get out of there before I committed matricide—my mom had been baiting me about how I shouldn't get too attached to Tater because she's not actually mine."

"Brutal," I said.

Little Sister whined and scratched at her head. The tattered ear was clearly bugging her. As if I didn't have enough to deal with already, I was going to have to tack on a trip to the vet.

Miranda paused as if deciding whether or not to make a confession. "I was always so jealous of you."

"Of me?" I said, flabbergasted. "Why?"

"Your mom was so mellow and cool and loving. I wanted a mom like that."

"She was the best," I said, my eyes filling. When the Great Goddess had been handing out mothers, I'd been at the front of the line. Losing her still felt sharp and fresh.

"Then I ran into you in the co-op and you had not one kid but two," Miranda continued. "Twins! That's why I was throwing barbs about your career. I don't care about your career. No offense."

"None taken." I cared so much about my vocation that I was always assuming other people were sizing up my failures. It was a relief to know Miranda didn't care at all. Suddenly I could see my life the way Miranda saw it. Sure, there had been heartache and setbacks. But I'd been raised by a kind, funny, loving woman who always thought I'd hung the moon. And then there was the fundamental fact of my own motherhood. I had identical twins who were amazing—in totally different ways. If Phoebe moved into a sorority house tomorrow, she'd be president in a week, no matter that she was only seven. Meanwhile, Alice had enough empathy and compassion to run an international aid organization. Motherhood was such a wild adventure. I might lose sight of it sometimes in the daily grind, but it was still a blessing of epic good fortune.

"You know what kills me?" Miranda asked. "My mom's right. I don't have a legal right to keep this baby yet. I'm just fostering. We've been together less than a week. But I know we're meant for each other." She examined the bottle. "I think she's done. Are you done, sweet girl?"

"I have all the legal right to my kids in the world," I said. "But if law enforcement finds the corpse of the guy you murdered, I'll lose them."

"Like I said, we can fix this somehow," Miranda vowed. "Together."

"I'll need your help moving the body," I said. "Before Saturday. It'll be hot then. The body will start to decomp—and stink."

She looked alarmed. "Where is it now?"

"I'm not telling," I said, in case Miranda decided to frame me after all. "Not yet."

"Where do you want to move it to?"

"It's kind of ironic you expect *me* to have a plan for this. How about *you* come up with some great ideas?"

"We can't bury it," she said. "Even with the warm snap, the ground'll be frozen until April."

"We could toss it in Lucky Peak?"

"That reservoir gets dragged three times a year! At least!" She patted the baby's back again, trying to coax out a burp. "Could we just go out to the Boise National Forest and do a dump-and-drive?"

I explained about the bloody scissors and how they were currently in the Boise PD's possession. Since Miranda used them to stab Connor, they probably had her fingerprints on them too. Boise PD had likely been unmotivated to run prints on scissors not connected to an actual crime. But if a body with wounds matching those scissors turned up, they'd surely find the motivation.

"Aaaargh!" Miranda said. "I can't believe I'm saying this, but I have a chest freezer in the garage that could work until the ground thaws."

"Now you're talking." Better to keep Connor at her house than mine.

"How about Friday night? I could get my husband to take Tater to visit his mom. If I elevate my ankle and ice it like crazy, hopefully it'll be okay to limp on by then. I'll just have to find somewhere to put forty pounds of elk meat."

"Does your husband look in the freezer?"

"Please! He thinks cooked food drops from the sky every night at six."

The warm snap should start Saturday. Friday would be cutting it close. But what choice did I have? "In high school, you never would've been voted Most Likely to Help Tilly Turner Hide a Corpse."

"As long as at our thirtieth reunion I'm not voted Least Likely to be Paroled by Our Fiftieth."

"So it's a plan?" I asked.

As if in agreement, Tater Tot let out a giant baby belch.

# THIRTY-FIVE

With Ralphie and Errol possibly cruising the streets of Boise looking for me because I'd stolen their grenades and blown up two of their snowmobiles, I kept my head down as I hustled Little Sister into the vet clinic. All the animals in the waiting room were blessedly calm except for a healthy-looking parakeet that kept screeching, "I've been shot!" I checked in with the bouffanted receptionist, then sat in a chair holding Little Sister by the collar. His ear didn't look good, but I needed to get this show on the road. I had to meet my kids at the bus stop at three thirty. (Normally I could ask Emmylou to meet them for me, but not anymore. The thought gave me a pang—and not just because I needed the childcare assistance. Life was lonelier without Emmylou.)

"I've been shot!" shrieked the parakeet.

"I don't know about you, but that bird's wreaking havoc on my nervous system," the receptionist said, to no one in particular.

A moment later, a muscular guy in scrubs appeared behind the doggy gate. "Little Sister?" he called.

My whole body prickled with the sort of sensation you get when you walk into a coffee shop and see your ex behind the counter, because I recognized the vet tech. The leash slipped from my fingers. Little Sister bounded toward the muscular man with arms inked in tattoos of Labradors and wiener dogs, stopped short, spun in a circle, and barked.

"Snowflake?" Harlan said. "Where's your pop?"

I had the urge to flee from the man I'd crawled under Connor's bed to avoid. But when Harlan leveled me with a questioning gaze, instead of sprinting for the door, I followed Little Sister through the doggy gate. I hated to admit it, but I might have become a little bit attached to that dog.

Alone in the exam room, door closed, Harlan got to work taking Little Sister's vitals. He leaned over to press his stethoscope to the dog's chest.

"Why do you have Snowflake?" he asked, not looking up.

"His owner was a friend of a friend who wasn't up for dog ownership," I lied. "Heard he was kind of a jerk."

"*Jerk* about sums it up," Harlan said, warming to me. "Not even Connor Johnson's own dog likes him. Isn't that right, Snowflake?" He typed information about the dog's vitals into a computer on a rolling cart.

Little Sister wagged his tail in agreement.

"Was Snowflake already a patient here?" I asked, my heart thrumming in my chest.

"Nah. Connor called me a while back and said the dog tore his ear on an old nail."

"When was that exactly?"

"Maybe like Sunday before last," he said, rolling a scrub tray over and beginning to clean Little Sister's ear. "If I tell you something, you won't tell my boss?"

"Never," I promised. Because Sunday before last was the day Connor died.

"I did these stitches. Off the clock. As a favor. To the dog, not Connor. Otherwise Connor wouldn't have had Snowflake stitched up at all."

"That was kind of you."

"Like I said, I did it for the dog. I can't stand to think of an animal suffering. I had just enough lidocaine. Vets don't part with that stuff lightly—you could stop someone's heart with it."

My eyes widened, but I said nothing.

"Legally, I could sew up my own dog. But someone else's dog, it's practicing without a license," Harlan continued.

"That makes sense," I said. This guy should not be telling me any of this. My diagnosis: sweet, good-looking, dumb as a bag of hair.

"So when Dr. Jehangir asks, you'll tell her someone else did the first stitches?" he said, suddenly nervous he'd overshared.

"Totally. The dog tore his ear on a fence nail in Portland. And I got it stitched up there. I can't remember the vet's name."

He looked relieved.

"So you and Connor were . . . I mean, *are* friends?" I ventured.

Harlan shrugged. "I know him from our four-wheeling club. Saw him try to run over a bobcat once. So I wouldn't say close friends."

"After that you bumped him down to acquaintance?"

Harlan laughed. "Pretty much." He had a nice smile to go with his tattooed biceps. Maybe I could set him up with Layna. But he seemed too naïve for this world. *Focus, Tilly.* "But I'm never doing him a favor again."

"Because . . ." I prompted

"He stole my Ambien *while* I was sewing up his dog's ear."

Here we go. "What a special person," I said, and then, off his blank look, continued, "I'm a mom so I try not to swear. 'Special person' is French for 'asshole.' Did Connor steal anything else? Like your lidocaine?"

"I didn't have any more lidocaine," he said. Dammit. "But he stole a bottle of pentazocine from me too. Not as big a deal to me since I don't use it, but still."

"Penta—pentaz— What's that again?"

"Pentazocine. An injectable opioid," he said. Off my look, he added, "It's not like that. I have a bulging disc. When I have to pick up a bigger animal, it flares up. My girlfriend gave me the pentazocine. Well, my ex-girlfriend."

I shivered. "Are injectable opioids generally prescribed for bulging discs these days?"

"My ex, she read on the internet that it's fine if I don't use that much," he said. "I work here. I know better. But she insisted." He'd be easy to railroad, too sweet to refuse.

The door opened, effectively ending our conversation. A bespectacled

Dr. Jehangir breezed in. I gave her my canned story about the fence nail in Portland, then topped it off with more lies about how Little Sister had torn his stitches at the dog park. While Dr. Jehangir set to work sewing up the dog's ear, I considered what I'd learned from Harlan.

I wasn't entirely convinced Connor had died of being tased. Maybe he'd shot up with the injectable opioid after the bouncer chucked him out of the club. One thing I knew for certain: He'd been wheezing when he came at Miranda. Could there've been OD levels of pentazocine in his system? I'd need a toxicology report to know for sure.

I knew someone who'd likely just aced her drug toxicity exam. Surely Gucci would be unsympathetic to a murdered sleaze like Connor—after all, she'd left her own abusive uncle to rot in a field. And I had a feeling she'd be excited to do some real forensics. Telling her I had a dead man in my playhouse was a calculated risk. But the time had come to take it.

"All done," Dr. Jehangir said. "Little Sister is going to be absolutely fine. Aren't you, boy?"

I thanked her, shot Harlan a grateful look, and headed out to the waiting room. After I set up a payment plan with the bouffanted receptionist—who smiled amenably and said, "I get it, girl. My bank accounts on E too"—I hightailed it out of there with Little Sister trailing behind me. I'd have to hurry to make it to the bus stop in time to meet the twins. And if things went as I hoped, I'd have a long night ahead of me.

# THIRTY-SIX

*Thursday*

Inside Pole Kisses, I was relieved to spot Gucci stripping off her sweats in the chill room. As Layna and Zhang Xiu gushed over Phoebe and Alice, a figure emerged from the pole studio. Salma Hayek in a cropped sweatshirt and cheeky pink pole shorts! I was unsure if I should ask her what happened after she smashed Connor in the head with a bottle of Dos Equis or beg forgiveness for showing up to class with kiddos in tow.

Gucci gave Salma a giant hug. "Olympia and Cheyenne were great subs, but they weren't you!" she said. "We missed our fearless leader. Where ya been, girl?"

Salma gave a sly smile. "Let's just say I did something hard, but necessary." Before I could drill deeper, she spotted the twins. "Tilly, your girls are adorbs, but Pole Kisses is an adult space."

I switched instantly out of detective mode to throw myself on her mercy, giving her a (very true) line about the impossibilities of solo parenting and my need to continue my pole journey despite obstacles such as lack of childcare.

Phoebe and Alice, sensing they'd infiltrated a grown-up haven for bad bitches, were on the charm offensive too. They stared up at Salma adoringly.

"You are prettier than my Barbie," Alice said.

"And you have better legs," Phoebe chimed in.

"All right," Salma said, softening. "They can stay."

The twins cheered, and I hurried to install them on the couch under the embroidered sign that read: *SEX WORK IS A VALID CAREER CHOICE.*

As all the Pole Virgins headed toward the studio, I rushed to catch up to Gucci. She'd shaved off the other side of her twilight-blue bob and was rocking a floppy mohawk. Until now, seeking her forensics help had seemed unwise, too risky, especially because—after Layna and I moved the body—any DNA evidence might point to one of us. But asking her to run a toxicology report to see if Connor had lethal levels of pentazocine in his system was more straightforward. And now I knew Gucci well enough to feel certain that even if she declined to help, she wouldn't narc.

"What's up, my ride or die?" she said.

"About that," I said, leaning in to whisper. "Any chance you might be able to help me with some rogue forensics?"

"I mean, I'm definitely gonna need more information?" She held up both palms, then pressed them to her heart. "But the term *rogue forensics* absolutely thrills me."

Two hours later, Gucci's heart-shaped rump stuck out of the playhouse, which incongruously reminded me of Little Sister in the dishwasher. Unlike the dog, Gucci put it effortlessly into reverse, crawling backward until her torso and head reappeared. She sat back on her heels.

"He definitely has two red taser marks on his chest," she said. "But also, his forearms look like a constellation chart. Major track marks."

Layna and I hadn't even thought to check his forearms. "Track marks! Amazing news!"

"It could've been fentanyl. That shit is in everything on the street these days."

I never thought the word *fentanyl* would make my heart sing with joy. Yet here we were. After pole class, I'd given Gucci a shorthand account of how the skeeve from Huckleberry's had turned up dead in my trunk. I told her I suspected he'd died from being tased by a woman he assaulted in the alley, but that he might've ODed on pentazocine.

"I thought Salma hit him with a bottle of Dos Equis?" Gucci asked.

"No, after that," I'd clarified. "He assaulted a different woman in the alley."

"And she tased him and he *died*? Instant karma!" Gucci said.

"But I don't want that woman to have this on her conscience. I'm hoping something else killed him," I said.

Gucci had literally jumped up and down clapping—that's how excited she was to help. She'd gone straight from Pole Kisses to her lab on campus to liberate supplies while I put the twins to bed and set Layna up with Netflix and popcorn. Now Gucci crawled back into the playhouse. The sounds from within were the sort I'd make trying to solve the *Los Angeles Times* Sunday crossword. "Hmm. What about— Shoot, that doesn't work."

When she reappeared, I asked, "Can you do it?"

"Like I told you," Gucci said, "I've never done an unsupervised percutaneous liver biopsy before. Much less on a frozen guy in the dark. Since he's rigor mortis-ed and nearly fetal, there's the possibility of bowel juxtaposition along the biopsy tract."

"Is that a yes?" I asked.

"I'll give it the old grad school try," Gucci said. "What's in the garbage bag?"

"The what?"

"The garbage bag? In there." She gestured at the playhouse.

His teal vest was in the garbage bag. "Clothes," I said.

Gucci seemed happy enough with that explanation. "Lucky for you, even though freezing can alter the histologic appearance of tissue, if we can get a liver sample, it should still biopsy fine. I'm gonna need you to light his midsection. These camping lanterns are dim as an inbred cocker spaniel." She rooted around in her backpack and handed me a flashlight and a footlong needle attached to a gigantic syringe.

"Jesus, Mary, and Joan Rivers," I said.

"Professor Bidelspach thinks he can keep me from doing actual fieldwork. Well, he can suck a big bag of—" The last word was lost as Gucci crawled back inside. "Sharp!" she called with the sudden seriousness of a leftist surgeon tasked with performing an emergency tracheotomy on Bernie Sanders. "Light!"

Reaching in with the hefty flashlight, I could see Gucci had already further peeled back Connor's shirt. A liver biopsy needed to be performed from the front. It'd be just my luck to end up with a biopsy of Connor's colon.

"Feels like I'm shoving the needle into a gallon of sorbet," Gucci effused. "This is fire!"

"You are definitely in the right line of work," I said, barely managing not to faint.

# THIRTY-SEVEN

Sneaking across the Boise State campus in the frost-bitten darkness with Gucci by my side, I felt hopeful, terrified, and very much alive. With a swipe of Gucci's keycard, the side door to the forensics building clicked open. We slipped inside just as plump snowflakes began to fall.

"Anyone shows up," she said, unlocking the door to her lab, "we pretend you're my auntie visiting from LA." She switched on the fluorescent lights.

"Wouldn't it be more realistic to say I'm your hot big sister?" I grumbled. I had twenty years on her, but "auntie" was still a bitter pill.

Beige machines ranging in size from a toaster to an industrial dryer filled the lab. Gucci wasted no time opening a tiny metal portal on the front of a contraption that was straight out of an eighties sci-fi movie. She inserted the syringe and squirted some of the corpse sorbet inside. "Not to brag, but I left no crumbs on that liver extraction." She snapped the portal shut and pushed a few buttons.

"What does this thing do?" I asked.

"It's a gas spectrometer," she said. "In three minutes it'll test for narcotics, amphetamines, aspirin. Also fentanyl and its two metabolites—norfentanyl and despropionylfentanyl—in case he got a bad batch of street drugs."

"Any kind of OD would make my life so much easier. You're absolutely glowing, by the way." It was true. Gucci looked radiant as a British baking show contestant who'd managed to pull off a perfect Bakewell tart.

"I can't tell you how good it feels to do actual fieldwork," Gucci said.

"Having my research sidelined by a skeeve has been the worst. Academia will break your heart."

"Not just academia," I said, thinking of Mickey Larynx.

A series of peaks and valleys appeared in an electronic window on the side of the gas chromatograph machine. Gucci studied them intently.

"Well?" I said.

"He's got narcotics in his blood—"

I punched the air with my fist. "Woo-hoo!"

"—but not at anywhere near lethal levels," she said. "He did not die of a pentazocine or fentanyl overdose."

"Dammit!" The media and criminal court system would paint Miranda as a violent murderess. And I likely wouldn't fare much better.

"I'm so sorry, Tilly," Gucci said.

"Before he died, the woman he attacked said he was wheezing," I said. "And . . . and he looked like a monster."

"Monster how?"

I shrugged. "Like this, maybe?" I made the face Miranda had shown me—mouth open and twisted, one eye squinted shut.

Her brow furrowed. "You didn't tell me that. That doesn't sound like opioids. But it might be— Wait. No. You know what?" she said, perking up. "I could run a test in the mass spectrometer."

"Assume I know as much about forensics as the average boomer dad knows about child-rearing."

"Sorry. The mass spectrometer can test for drugs that won't show up on a gas spectrometer. But it'll take an hour."

"Layna said she'll babysit all night if I need her to," I said.

In the adjacent lab room, the mass spectrometer loomed like an oversized copy machine with a robot head and arms. Gucci placed a single drop of liver sample into a tube and inserted it via an airlock. With the machine running, Gucci switched off the lights. "I don't want to draw attention to the fact that we're—" She stopped mid-sentence. "Do you hear that?"

Footsteps. The rattle of a doorknob.

Gucci's eyes went wide and she gestured for me to hide. So much for introducing me as her hot aunt.

We crouched behind a lab bench as the intruders entered the next room. A man who clearly had a chub for the sound of his own voice was saying, "You're a talented girl, Chloe. I don't think you know how talented."

Next to me Gucci mimed a gagging motion.

"Thank you," Chloe said. She sounded young, but was definitely a full-grown woman—*not* a girl.

"I'm excited to write your recommendation for the PhD program at Penn State," the blowhard continued. "I even have a friend there on the scholarship committee. I can give him a call."

"Do you think I'll be ready, Professor Bidelspach?" Chloe said. Her lack of confidence made me want to add watching *Alien*, *Moana*, and *Mad Max: Fury Road* to her homework for the semester.

"I think I can get you there," Professor Bidelspach said.

"I haven't even mastered bacterial oral decomposition," she said.

"Oh, I can help you master oral, all right," Professor Bidelspach said.

There is no grosser sound than a slurping, predatory kiss. Gucci and I stared at each other in horror. An eternal second passed. For the sake of my future and my children's future, I needed to stay silent during this grotesque abuse of power. But one day Phoebe and Alice might be grad students too. I needed to do this for them.

Enough streetlamp light came in through the window for Gucci to see me wrap my hand around the base of a wheeled lab cart. I asked permission with my eyes. She gave a little nod.

The cart sailed through the door and slammed against a lab bench. Professor Bidelspach let out a high-pitched shriek.

As fluorescents flooded the room, Professor Bidelspach skuttled away from Chloe like a cockroach in a midnight kitchen. In his younger years, he might've been handsome, but now his blooming nose and sizeable paunch suggested a liver the size of a watermelon. Meanwhile, Chloe looked as mortified as a teen whose parents have arrived at a keg party wearing matching sweatshirts that read: *We love our chess champion daughter!*

I stood up. "Professor Bidelspach," I said sternly.

"We were just— I was just giving Chloe a tour of—" As he took in my puffy coat, sweatpants, and messy topknot, he seemed to regain his confidence. "Who are you and why are you in my lab?"

"I'm the new acting provost of the graduate college," I said in the most regal voice I could muster. "Here to do an after-hours tour of campus with my assistant."

From the other room, Gucci cleared her throat and rattled a lab stand to underline the fact of an additional witness. Professor Bidelspach wilted.

"Chloe?" I said, gently. "If an older man with power over your career tells you that you're special and then tries to get in your pants, he doesn't care about you. But that doesn't mean you aren't special. He's right about that part, even if he doesn't know it. Why don't you go on home?"

Chloe gave a teary nod and fled, the lab door slamming in her wake.

I glowered at the squirming professor. I'd heard of support groups where strangers act out the role of your family members to allow you to heal old traumas. Right now, as far as my psyche was concerned, Professor Bidelskeeze was a stand-in for Mickey Larynx.

"Professor Bidelspach," I continued, "I expect you to turn in a write-up of what happened here to the dean. Tomorrow at eight a.m. Two copies, please, because I'll be reading it too. No obfuscations. No lies. I saw it. My assistant saw and heard it. And I want Chloe's name redacted from the matter. Do you understand? Just a history of these encounters and your part. You can call her 'my master's student Jane Doe.'"

He looked sick.

"Unless? Chloe is an—"

"Undergrad," he replied miserably. But then the swagger of an untouchable tenured professor returned. "I don't think you understand. That girl seduced me. I'm the victim here."

I puffed up like an offended dragon queen. "Don't bullshit me, Professor Bidelspach," I said. "I recorded an MP3 of your promises and flattery followed by your advances." I pulled my phone from my pocket and pretended to type away on it. "There! Emailed to the dean, who'll be quite interested to hear you're offering rec letters and special tutoring in exchange for oral sex. So I expect your honest account in the dean's mailbox by eight a.m. tomorrow." I pointed at the door of the lab with a trembling finger. "Now go!"

Professor Bidelspach let out a sad little muffled sound and scurried out the door. I held my breath as his trundling steps dissolved down the hallway.

"He's gone!" I said, hurrying into the next room.

"That was some Wonder Woman shit!" Gucci gushed.

"Thank you! Thank you!" I said, taking a tiny bow. "Stand-up was my game, but I always thought I would've been decent at micro-impersonations and—"

The beep of the mass spectrometer interrupted me. The test results were in.

"This guy's blood shows near-lethal levels of botulism toxin," Gucci said. She'd plunked into a wheelie office chair to study a graph on the computer screen.

"What does that mean?" I demanded.

"Either he ate a bunch of spoiled canned food or—"

"We had Mormon neighbors when I was a kid," I interrupted. "They were always rotating the canned goods out of their pantry on account of botulism risk. The mom used to say a teaspoon of canned peaches gone bad could take out the whole town of Nampa."

"Does the dead guy seem like he would've been eating spoiled Mormon canned goods?"

"Good point. So what's the *or*?'"

"He could've been injected with a massive dose of Botox."

"Botox!" I leaned against the nearest lab bench as my mind rippled and stretched to take in this new information—like that long-ago day I found out Martha Stewart and Snoop Dogg are friends.

"That would explain the wheezing," Gucci said. "And it could've caused some facial paralysis, which would make him look—"

"Like a monster!" I cried.

# THIRTY-EIGHT

After we made a Pole Virgins' promise to never speak of the night again, Gucci dropped me at the end of my alley so I could roll the garbage out for morning pickup. A fresh inch of snow had fallen, but the alley stank like someone had tossed a well-fed squirrel into their backyard firepit. As I pinched my nose to block out notes of burnt flesh and incinerated hair, Oat Willimena dragged her own can through her back gate.

"Are you getting that smell?" I asked.

"I fired my kiln, not knowing there was a raccoon inside. Poor little guy." She sounded truly mournful. "All that was left was a few teeth and a little bit of tail. And his penis bone, of course. Also known as a Texas toothpick." Oat Willimena illuminated a charred, hooked bit of bone with a flashlight.

I stepped back, horrified.

"Raccoon penis bones are considered magical talismans," Oat Willimena continued. "Jerry Hall—the supermodel?—she told me once that when she was growing up in Mesquite, Texas, boys gave girls they liked racoon penis bones, you know, as a simple love spell. Maybe I should give this one to Emmylou?"

"Woo away," I managed, feeling a pang at how fun it would have been to tell Emmylou about this conversation.

"Friday, I'm taking her for a tour of the women's ward of the Old Idaho Penitentiary. It'll be romantic. How many illicit love affairs took place between those walls?"

"So many?" I said. If Emmylou and Oat Willimena went out Friday night, it would be much easier for me and Miranda to move Connor's body undetected. "What a great date idea!"

I excused myself and hurried through the back gate. Snow had covered all my muddy tracks. I decided to take a quick peek at Connor's track marks and taser burns—I felt dumb for having missed them. But as I approached the playhouse Emmylou appeared on the back deck looking radiant in an ankle-length blue silk kaftan.

"Hi, Emmylou," I said, feeling sad and regretful.

"Evening," she said.

But before I could make an attempt at reconciliation (or warn her about the amorous penis bone coming her way), she disappeared back into her side of the duplex.

My own television blared the nineties gem *Striptease*. Layna sat up from where she'd been sprawled on my mom's old tie-dyed couch.

"I have amateur sleuthing FOMO so bad right now," she said.

"Do you want an update?" I asked.

"No. Don't," she said with a shudder, as if remembering the severed finger pressed into her hand. "The douchebag was right about one thing. I wasn't cut out to be an investigator."

"You'll find your post-divorce thing," I said. "And it will be amazing. Thank you for tonight. For everything."

Layna tossed the bag of popcorn onto the coffee table and rose to her feet. "Not to be weird, but I just put a listing for a new best friend on Facebook Marketplace. Any chance you wanna apply?"

"Expect my application by morning," I said.

Layna gave me a hug and slipped out into the night.

I checked on the twins, who were both conked out. Next, knowing I wouldn't be able to sleep myself, I went to the kitchen to call Miranda Carson, who'd given me her number before I left her place. "Did I wake you up?" I said, putting on the kettle.

"I'm feeding Tater Tot," she whispered.

"Is your husband there?" I sniffed the air of the kitchen, but luckily could pick up no lingering Eau de Anal Glands or Bouquet of Burnt Racoon.

"Chauncey's downstairs."

"What kind of name is Chauncey?" I said.

"East Coast. Old money. He can't help it. Don't judge."

"Oh, I'm judging," I said.

"He's watching *Alone: Frozen*."

"I love that show! Did the hot girl eat all that seal fat yet?" I tossed a chamomile tea bag into my mom's vintage Boynton mug that read: *Don't Let the Turkeys Get You Down*.

"Tilly, those creeps. They keep driving by my house. Like slowly. My home security alarm's on, but I'm totally freaked."

"Does Chauncey know?"

"I haven't told him anything," she hissed. "About any of this! This whole thing, it's like a nuclear leak. I need to keep it contained. I can't let it contaminate the groundwater of my life."

"Okay, okay. Good," I said. But I was freaking out too. If Ralphie and Errol were still cruising by Miranda's, they were still in Boise, still looking for me.

"If those guys grab me, I'm giving you up," Miranda said. "I'll tell them your name, where you live, everything."

"Jesus, Miranda," I said.

"I'm sorry. I'm not made to endure torture. And I have to protect Tater."

"That's fair," I said. "But what about protecting my kids?"

"I'm really, really scared, Tilly."

"Me too," I said. I took a deep breath. Tried to sound strong. "But I do have some good news. You didn't kill him."

I heard something clatter to the floor. "What?"

"Connor. He died of a massive Botox overdose. You didn't kill him."

A gasp sounded, followed by a little whump.

"Are you okay?" I said.

"I'm . . . I'm on the floor," Miranda said. "Literally. How do you know? Are you sure?"

"I'm sure," I said. "I got a friend to run a toxicology report. He must've been starting to OD on Botox when you saw him. That's why he was wheezing."

Miranda let out a sob. "Thank god, thank god, thank god," she said.

"How do you think he ended up full of Botox?" I said. "I've never heard of that kind of an OD before."

"Who cares?" Miranda said. "As long as it's clear it wasn't us."

But I did care. I wanted all the pieces to fit. "Hopefully it'll be clear to the cops," I said. "Connor was a junkie so maybe he made a lethal mistake." I didn't exactly have vials of Botox and syringes in my possession, so I felt confident about my innocence. Mostly. But the nagging mystery of how I'd ended up wearing his vest kept me from feeling entirely in the clear.

"Since you know what killed him," Miranda said, "can't you go to the police? Like maybe now?"

Just the thought of sitting in a police station for hours made me feel exhausted beyond all reason. "You mean *we*," I said.

"It won't be that bad for you. You're probably more used to that kind of thing anyway."

"What kind of thing?"

"I don't know," she said. "Being around lowlifes, talking to cops, all that. You've been arrested before. I remember."

"If we're gonna do this, you're gonna have to quit with the mean girl shit," I said.

"Sorry. Old habits and all that."

"I still need *you* to explain to the police how the body ended up in *my* car in the first place," I said.

Miranda groaned. "I'll do it if I have to. I will. I just don't want to. It puts everything with Tater at risk."

"Let's think this through," I said. We were both moms. We needed to fully consider possible repercussions of getting tangled up in the criminal legal system. I paced to my office (aka the pantry) to do some brainstorming (aka stuffing shortbread cookies into my face). "My mom always used to say: 'When in doubt, don't.' She'd meant it like: 'When in doubt about whether or not you should get a pixie cut, don't.' But I think the saying could still apply to this more dire situation."

"Agreed. We still need to predict the outcomes," Miranda said. "Maybe we should talk to a lawyer first?"

"Oh no!" I said. "You are not lawyering up and throwing me under the bus!" Miranda would preemptively have the best attorney in the state, while I'd have to roll the dice on a public defender once I was charged with something.

She made a noncommittal noise. "Maybe just one little lawyer."

"I'm serious," I said. "It'll be hot by Saturday. If we want to try to figure out how he ended up full of Botox before we go to the police, we need to put him in your freezer tomorrow. But wait—how's your ankle?"

"Still sprained, my dear." She paused, then admitted, "But it's not a bad sprain."

I started to laugh. "If someone told me when I ran into you and your mom in the co-op the other day that you'd be calling me 'my dear' during a late-night phone call, I wouldn't've believed it." I stuffed in another cookie.

"True. Why are you chewing soooo loudly," she complained.

"I do my best thinking when scarfing processed food."

"I've got a feeling right now your brain is a bad neighborhood. Don't go there alone."

"It's been a bad neighborhood for a while now," I admitted. "And I'm so tired. I'm not thinking straight. How about we sleep on it?"

"Okay," she said. "Tomorrow morning, we'll decide."

Turn the body over to the cops. Or stick it in Miranda's chest freezer. Personally I liked the thought of the corpse being on Miranda's property instead of mine. "I'll call you once I get my kids to school," I said. "And then we'll make a plan."

I hung up and shoveled in one last shortbread cookie before trundling toward bed.

# THIRTY-NINE

*Friday*

When a masculine rap sounded on the front door while I was trying to get the twins ready for school, I sensed in my cytoplasm it was bad news. Little Sister did too, because he barreled toward the front door, barking savagely.

I was hunched over holding the dog by his collar when I opened the door to a bulky man in a black ATF vest looming on the doorstep, legs wide. He had a face like a ball of mozzarella. A few feet behind him, Agent Nate Duran stood looking like he wanted to teleport to somewhere more fun, like Hell.

"Good morning, ma'am," Agent Mozzarella said.

"Top of the morning to you," I said in an Irish accent. That's how nervous I was. Little Sister whined and pulled, desperate to jump on the visitors. I wished I'd had a chance to brush my hair. I wished I wasn't hunched over like a fairy-tale crone in order to hang on to the dog's collar. I wished I'd replied to Nate's texts and calls. Why had I been such a coward? "I mean, can I help you? Hi, Nate." At least I managed that in a normal voice.

Nate gave a pained nod.

"We're looking for a man named Connor Johnson," Agent Mozzarella said.

"Connor?" I said. If Miranda had turned me in to the feds, I would literally kill her. "No Connor here. Just me and my kids." Little Sister lunged, which threw me off-balance. "And my badly behaved dog."

"We spoke with a couple people at Huckleberry's who said you were seen talking with Connor Johnson the Sunday before last," Agent Mozzarella said. "Reports were that you two got into a lover's spat."

"Lover's spat!" I protested. "I don't have a lover!" I looked at Nate. "I mean, not that guy. I mean, I remember that guy now!" I slapped my forehead with the palm of my free hand. "I didn't catch his name. We weren't flirting. Or fighting. Not hardly. I'd never met him before."

"He's missing and his phone pinged here."

"Missing?" I echoed, my voice about three octaves higher than normal.

"A witness took a picture of you in the alley behind Huckleberry's wearing Connor Johnson's vest at about four on Monday morning. And his phone pinged here," Agent Mozzarella repeated, clearly happy to be busting me in a lie. "How long have you two been seeing each other? And is he staying here?"

"That rando from Huckleberry's? Here?" My laugh sounded deranged. If the ATF thought I was dating Connor, how could I expect them to solve an actual homicide—or even an accidental overdose?

"We have a warrant to search the property," Agent Mozzarella said.

"A warrant? For what?" I stammered, but stood aside as he trooped into my living room.

Nate followed, averting his gaze. Was he remembering the hot sex we'd had last time he was here? I blushed at the thought. Or maybe he felt ashamed he hadn't given me a heads-up about this warrant business.

"What's going on, Mommy?" a small voice said. The twins stood in the doorway of their bedroom, looking frightened. But then Alice spotted Nate. "Coach Duran!" she squealed. The twins galloped toward him.

"Phoebe! Alice!" he said. The twins had Nate's chin. I could see it so clearly now. Regret I hadn't told Nate he might be the twins' bio dad rushed through me. At least then they'd have someone to take them after Nate and his fellow agent found Connor's corpse in the playhouse and hauled me to prison.

Little Sister's collar slipped from my grip and he beelined for Agent Mozzarella, shoving his nose into the agent's crotch.

"Little Sister! No!" I dove for the dog. "Girls, go to your room and get ready for school!" My voice was so strangled the twins actually obeyed. I shoved Little Sister into their bedroom behind them and closed the door.

"We'll need to search in there too," Agent Mozzarella said, clearly put out about the invasion of his privates.

"We'll be respectful of your things," Nate said, glancing sternly at his colleague.

"Thank you," I said, but I couldn't bear to look at him.

Nate walked glumly into the kitchen as the other agent disappeared into my bedroom. Collapsing onto the couch, I dropped my head in my hands. My only hope was that they wouldn't search the yard.

But when Agent Mozzarella emerged from my room, he said, "We're going to need to take a look in your outdoor structures."

I trailed after him to the kitchen where Nate was already sliding the glass door open. Outside, only the spindly branches of a leafless maple sheltered me from the cold gray sky.

I suddenly understood something essential about myself, my life. I was fundamentally unlucky, born under a bad sign. Nothing I'd tried ever would or could go right.

"Do you have a key to the outdoor shed?" Nate said, his words forming a cloud in the air as Agent Mozzarella tromped toward the playhouse.

The twins' identical faces pressed against their bedroom window. I'd done one perfect thing—I'd had those two girls. And now, for all practical purposes, they'd be orphans.

I leaned in close to Nate. "I don't want the twins to see me handcuffed," I whispered. "Promise, promise me, you'll let me put them on the school bus first."

Nate looked stricken, but he gave a tiny nod.

For the twins' sake, I needed to start cooperating with the feds before they found the corpse. "The playhouse. Look in the playhouse!" I shouted. I needed them to see me as an asset.

"I'm about to," Agent Mozzarella huffed.

"I want to cooperate," I said. "I'll tell you everything. See, Botox is one of the world's most powerful toxins. People don't seem to realize, but it's deadly."

Nate gazed at me, as if trying to solve the puzzle of my bizarre behavior. Meanwhile, Agent Mozzarella put his hand to the gun on his hip, concerned my manic babbling might take a violent turn. Nate stepped forward and pulled open the playhouse doors.

The only male figure sprawled inside was a twelve-inch Ken doll.

Idaho Connor had vanished.

# FORTY

Nate and Agent Mozzarella stared at me, waiting for me to explain my outburst. But all I could think was: *Where in God's green acres is the corpse?* Even the Hefty Cinch Sak containing Connor's teal vest had disappeared.

"Sorry," I stammered. "I got Botox. For the first time. Yesterday." I pointed at my forehead, which had enough lines to make my story unconvincing. "And it's a toxin. A neurotoxin. And I think it's affecting me." This ridiculous excuse was the best I could manage. "I wanted you to . . . to look in my kids' playhouse and . . . and see that Ken doll because basically that's what I feel like. Plastic fantastic." The men looked baffled. "You'll wanna search the shed, right? I have the key. Let me grab it."

Nate followed me inside, ostensibly to make sure I wasn't going to flush a pound of cocaine down the toilet. But as soon as we were in the kitchen, he said, "Tilly, what's going on?"

We faced each other, no more than two feet between us. There were gold flecks of concern in his eyes. If I stood on my tiptoes, I could've kissed him. But of course I didn't. Not now.

"Going on?" I squeaked.

"Why'd you think we were going to arrest you?" he said.

I opened and closed my mouth, as if I'd *Freaky Friday*-ed with a goldfish. Now was the time to say: *Some creepy white supremacists are planning to attack the capitol in eleven days.* But no sound came out.

"You know, if you need anything, you can let me know," Nate said, his face creased with worry, confusion, and—could it be?—longing. It'd only been five days since we'd pressed every possible square inch of our naked flesh together. Surely he was wondering why I'd ghosted him, and why I seemed so off my nut now.

But instead of trusting the first man I could actually see myself with for the long haul, I said, "I need you and your work buddy to finish up and get out of here so I can get my kids to school."

Hurt flashed in his eyes, even as he nodded. "Okay. If that's what you want."

By the time Nate and his fellow agent had searched our whole side of the duplex, the twins had missed the bus, so I drove them to school.

"Why did Coach Duran and that other man want to look through all our things, Mommy?" Phoebe asked.

"They're trying to find a bad guy," I said, meeting her eye in the rearview mirror.

"There's a bad guy hiding at our house?" Alice said, sounding worried.

"No, no. Everything there is safe and sound," I said. "They were just making sure."

"Is Coach Duran going to be your boyfriend?" Phoebe asked.

"We like him," Alice said.

"I don't need a boyfriend," I said, as I pulled up to the front entrance of Roosevelt Elementary. "I'm too busy being a mom."

"You don't seem that busy," Phoebe added, helpfully. "Maybe you could find the time."

When Gucci sashayed in to meet me at Guru Donuts in her ankle-length fuzzy black coat printed with green alien faces, I wanted to jump up and hug her for making me feel a sliver less alone. Since I figured Ralphie and Errol wouldn't darken the doors of a donut shop offering hipster-berry donuts for $40 a dozen, I'd already taken off my scarf, hoodie, and sunglasses and now offered to buy Gucci's donut and coffee even though it was fifty-fifty whether or not my credit card would be declined.

"What do you mean, the body's gone?" she said in a shocked whisper as we tucked into our sprinkle donuts. (By the time this mystery was solved or I went to jail, I might be three-quarters sugar.)

"Gone. Vanished. Disappeared. Two inches of snow covering any possible tracks. Did you, by any chance, move it? You got a pink sprinkle. Right here."

"Of course I didn't *move* it," she said, wiping at her nose. "Got it?"

"Got it," I said.

"Who else knew it was there?"

"Layna," we said in unison.

"I called her the second I dropped my kids at school," I said. "She didn't pick it up." That was when I'd texted Gucci an SOS.

"She's flying to Portland," Gucci said.

"To sell that house!" I said. "I spaced it."

"Did anybody, *anybody* else know it was there?"

"Nope." But one person might've been able to figure it out. "I think I know who could've done this," I said. I gave Gucci a powdered-sugar-dusted kiss on the cheek and headed toward the door at a trot.

When Miranda threw open her front door, she had a crutch under one arm and wore gold-rimmed aviator reading glasses and an ombre sweater that looked like a struck match. She seemed slightly less happy to see me than if I'd been a member of a religious order hell-bent on convincing her to renounce her favorite holidays.

"What are you wearing?" she said, as I hustled inside.

"Ralphie and Errol might be out looking for me." The floral curtains were drawn so I took off my sunglasses, pulled down the hood of my coat, and unwrapped the scarf from around the bottom half of my face. "Look, I know you have Tater Tot. But I have a question for you." I didn't want to talk about corpses anymore over the phone. And also I thought that in person, I'd be better able to glean whether or not Miranda was telling the truth.

Tater was fast asleep on the couch in a jelly bean onesie.

"She is definitely the cutest baby in the world," I said.

"I'm glad to see you, but why are you here, Tilly?" Miranda said.

I turned to face her. "Did you move Connor's body?"

"Did I *what*?"

"Move it. You know, without me?"

"How could I move his body?" she said. "I don't even know where it is."

"But did you?" I pressed.

She waved her crutch as if to say: *Earth to Tilly*. "Do I look like I could move a body by myself? What is this about? Wait, wait, wait. So he's . . . it's . . . gone?"

"Into thin air," I admitted.

"Where to?" Her voice had turned shrill.

"I have no idea, but I'll tell you when I figure it out," I said, wrapping the scarf back around my head and donning sunglasses as I turned to leave.

"Not so fast," Miranda said. "You know the proverb 'It takes a village to raise a child'?"

"Um, yeah?" I said.

"I have a baby and a sprained ankle. So how about being my village?"

Oddly, taking out Miranda's trash and loading her dishwasher made me feel less like her lowly house girl and more like a beneficent auntie with goddess vibes. It was good to be part of something.

I was behind the wheel and sweating in my scarf, beanie, hooded coat, and sunglasses when my phone rang. I put it on speaker as I drove past three jaunty Canada geese marching regally down the sidewalk.

"You okay?" Layna asked. "I just landed and saw your test frenzy. Text frenzy." I could hear another woman's voice in the background.

"Did you move the *package*?" I demanded.

"Package?" she said. "Whatta I want wif jour packages?"

"Wait! Are you drunk?"

"Do drinks drunk at forty thousand feet even count? They're like calories eaten standing up."

"You know, the *package* we stashed in my yard the night you *borrowed my sled*? Did. You. Move. It?"

"Oh, *the package*!" she said. "I don't want to eat Indian for dinner. I'll be farting all night. Sorry. Talking to my friend, Elaine. We're in an Uber. I brought her to be my emotional support animal since you're busy."

"Layna! Focus! Did. You. Move. The. Package?"

"No, I didn't move him."

"Not *him*," I insisted. "*It*."

I slammed on my brakes to avoid hitting a goose. My car skidded, then blessedly stopped without plowing into anything. The guy behind me laid on his horn. I rolled down the window and leaned halfway out. I might have screamed a couple choice obscenities at the driver—and the goose.

"Tilly, wash goin' on?" Layna said. "Are's you okay?"

"It's nothing. A goose in the road."

"You can't swing a dead cat in Boise without hitting a freaking goose. No sushi! You know wasabi burns my sinuses. Wait. Is he—the package—is he gone? Like *Gone Baby Gone*?"

Longing for my mother sliced me like a hot knife through cheesecake. And I missed Emmylou too. Layna might want to be my new bestie, but right now she was hammered in an Uber with someone named Elaine who had a craving for sashimi. I forced myself to push my grief down, to focus.

"I can't talk about it now. Not on the phone," I said. "But don't worry about me. Good luck listing your house."

"Burt, Tilly!" she was still shouting as I hung up.

# FORTY-ONE

Outside Roosevelt Elementary, bundled to the gills in my winter camouflage, I avoided the other moms as I shivered under a sky so gray it was hard to believe it would ever be blue again. Where the hell was Connor's body? If law enforcement somehow came across it, they'd surely pair it with my scrapbooking scissors, in which case Miranda and I would both be in deep shit. The police might come for me at any moment. Or worse, Ralphie and Errol might find me. I needed to spend some quality time with my girls while I still could.

When the twins came out the school's front entrance and spotted me, they ran toward me, arms outstretched to give me a giant double hug.

"Why are you wearing sunglasses, Mommy? The sun is never out in Boise," Alice asked.

"You look weird in that scarf," Phoebe added. "I can't even see your face."

"Since it's Friday, I thought we could go to Caffeina for hot chocolate," I said.

They jumped up and down, clapping and cheering, my odd outfit forgotten.

As I drove, I told myself the rest of the day would be fun and festive because I'd make it fun and festive. But the twins and I had only tramped halfway across Caffeina's parking lot when I slipped on an icy patch and landed right on my butt in a dirty pile of slush.

I was still brushing bits of snow from my soggy jeans when Phoebe yelled, "Look, Mommy!" and pointed toward the entrance of the Library!

*No*, I thought. *No, no, no*. Because Agent Nate Duran, Principal Cruz, and Maricela were emerging, laughing and joking, each of them carrying a stack of books. They looked like that impossible thing: a happy extended family.

"Maricela from soccer! And Coach Duran!" Alice said, like an LA tourist spotting Timothée Chalamet and Zendaya in the wild.

"And Principal Cruz!" Phoebe said. "Mommy, let's hurry so we can say hi!"

"No!" I hissed, pulling the twins behind a parked Sprinter van. No one would recognize me under the bundle of my scarf, sunglasses, and hooded coat, but the twins were unmistakable. I peeked quickly around the edge of the van to see Nate and his family climbing into his road-worn Land Cruiser.

"What's wrong?" Phoebe asked.

"Why are we hiding?" That was Alice.

"I can't handle a Stop-and-Chat right now," I said. Not after Nate had searched my house with his ATF bro that morning, both of them thinking I was hiding my white supremacist paramour in a nook or closet.

"Why can't we talk to them?" Phoebe demanded. "We like them. We need frieeeeeeends."

"We get lonely," Alice chimed in, looking mournful.

Ugh! I hated to admit it to myself, but Emmylou had been right. The twins were clearly craving more connection and community than I'd been able to provide since we moved to Boise. Without Emmylou on our side, our little household felt so small and sad, so broken. Perhaps I was denying my kids their actual family! After all, if Nate was their biological father, then technically, Principal Cruz was their aunt and Maricela was their cousin.

Blessedly the Land Cruiser pulled out of the parking lot and receded down State Street.

"Now who's ready for some hot chocolate?" I said, forcing cheer into my voice.

"Me!" both twins said, but they sounded melancholy.

With all the joie de vivre knocked out of me, the depictions of local landmarks gracing the walls of Caffeina seemed aggressively ugly, especially the Idaho State Capitol cut from a potato sack and the Lucky Peak Reservoir made of soda can pop-tops. But the twins seemed to be cheered by the warm cozy space. I took off my scarf and sunglasses, confident Ralphie and Errol wouldn't venture into a place on the far north side of town that sold seven-dollar oat milk matcha lattes.

While I waited for our drinks—sweater tied around my waist to hide my soggy rump—I spotted an abandoned *New York Times* splayed across a nearby table. The leering face plastered across the front of the Arts section gave me an electric shock. Mickey Larynx. As if in a trance, I picked up the paper and started to read.

> **Totally Depraved Comic Mickey Larynx Finds His Voice**
> Mickey Larynx believes in second acts and second chances.
>
> "Should anyone tug their tug boat in a hotel hot tub?" Larynx asked as I sat across from him at a booth in famed Santa Monica hamburger stand Father's Office. "Probably not. But find me a person who hasn't made a mistake and I'll never pick up a microphone again."
>
> After complaints last January that Larynx had committed lewd acts in the hot tubs at the Four Seasons San Francisco at Embarcadero and the Fort Sutter Hotel Sacramento, his fifty-city comedy tour was canceled. But less than a year later, he seems to have cracked the comeback code. For his sold-out Totally Depraved tour, he's renting out arenas himself instead of going through bookers.

"Tilly!" the barista called.

In a daze, I shuttled our drinks to the twins, who sat engrossed in a game of Connect Four. Once I joined them at the table, I tried to scan the rest of the article but I'd basically blacked out, as if my unconscious mind wouldn't let me absorb any more information about Mickey Larynx's happiness and success.

Why should Mickey Larynx be allowed a comeback so soon after endangering public health? What he did was beyond disgusting, potentially traumatizing—and unsanitary! While he'd ruined my prospects with his public perversions, he'd totally recovered his own footing. Meanwhile, I was stuck at rock bottom in Boise, Idaho, with no career, no boyfriend, no babysitter, and a couple of sadistic bigots trying to hunt me down.

"Mommy!" Alice wailed, snapping me out of my mud bog of self-pity. "Phoebe is cheating."

"Her *face* is cheating!" Phoebe snapped. "And I have to go to the bathroom!"

As I guarded the bathroom door, I studied the craft abomination hanging on the opposite wall. Hopefully no one would call the bunch of bottle caps strung together in the shape of Idaho "art." It wasn't a perfect rendering of the state either—the bottom southeast corner was missing, a few loose threads hanging down. As I mentally critiqued the piece, it finally soaked in that the bottlecaps were stamped with the word *BuckSnort*.

Hands shaking, I reached into my purse and pulled out the BuckSnort bottle cap I'd found in my jacket pocket soon after I discovered Connor's body.

The hole drilled in my bottle cap was a perfect match for the ones on the wall.

When the twins emerged from the bathroom, I hurried them to the front counter where a bored barista with algae-colored hair and a glistening silver beauty mark gazed off into the middle distance.

"Have you by any chance seen me in here before?" I demanded.

"People from your generation all look alike to me," she said with a shrug.

"Were you working two Sundays ago, like at night?" I insisted.

"Nope."

My heart flattened like an indecisive squirrel under a sixteen-wheeler as the barista spun on her heels and disappeared through the swinging door to the kitchen. But then she reappeared with a gangly blond wearing a jean jacket.

The gangly blond stared at me. "Ugh. You again."

"You recognize me?" I said.

"You owe Ellen DiMarco eighty bucks for damages."

"Ellen who?"

"The artist." She gestured at a rendition of the Boise Depot woven out of shredded grocery bags.

Hope was the most dangerous emotion, but I couldn't guard against it now. I turned to the twins. "Hey, will you two go see which T-shirts they have in a medium?"

As Phoebe and Alice scampered off to investigate the T-shirt rack, I leaned in toward the gangly blond. "So you were here?" I asked. "Two Sundays ago?"

"Unfortunately."

Adrenaline shot through me. "Somebody Ambiened my drink before I came in here."

"Ambien!" she said. "That makes sense. You passed out on that couch at about nine thirty." She pointed to a purple velour couch that'd seen better days. "It was slow in here so I just let you sleep. You woke up at like four."

"I didn't go anywhere? From nine thirty to four? I was right there?" Though I'd been at an all-time nadir five minutes ago, sunshine shot through me now.

"In plain sight."

"Thank you, sweet St. Lucille Ball." My knees felt like they might buckle. I'd been sleeping here all night, in plain view. I had an alibi! An alibi! It was a joyful mantra. It wasn't like I went around with vials of Botox and a syringe in my purse. Still, without knowing where I'd been all night, I hadn't been able to chase away the niggling worry I'd been involved. But now that worry dissolved. I had an alibi!

"You were making me anxious," the barista continued. "I kept thinking like, what if you were my mom, you know?"

"I'm way too young and fresh to be your mom," I said.

"She's forty-three," the barista said. "How old are you?"

"Never mind."

"Once you woke up, you were staggering around. When I followed you to the bathroom, I saw you rip a chunk off of *BuckSnort, Idaho.*"

It made sense. Even sober, I was always appalled by truly bad coffee shop art. "Did you see where I went?" I said. "When I left?"

The twins had pressed their shoulders together so they looked conjoined and sidled up to an old woman eating an oversized blueberry muffin. Ten bucks they were asking for a handout. Normally I would've intervened, but I was grateful they were distracted.

"I made you call an Uber," the barista was saying. "You were so messed up I waited outside with you—because I'm an *altruist.* But I had to run in to help a customer. When I came out you were heading down the alley behind Huckleberry's. I kept thinking: If my mom was in such a bad state, I'd want someone to look out for her, you know?"

*Oh my god, enough about your mom.*

"So I went to the end of the alley and yelled that your Uber was here," the barista continued. "The weirdest thing was, when you staggered back out you were wearing a vest you hadn't had on before."

"A teal vest?"

"Yep."

"Hot damn!" I said, my heart exploding into a hundred cavorting Jack Russell puppies. "How long? How long was I in the alley?"

"I don't know? Two minutes? Three minutes?"

A drugged-up Connor had probably stripped off his vest before deciding to take an ill-fated dump in the trunk of my car. Only after Connor was dead in that same trunk and Miranda long gone had I wandered down the alley in my drunken and Ambiened state, picked up his abandoned vest, put it on, banged on the back alley door of Huckleberry's, and talked to the dishwasher. (I hadn't been in the alley nearly long enough to do all that *and* murder Idaho Connor *and* stuff him in my trunk). My alibi now made total sense! Which didn't change the fact that hiding the (now-missing!) body in my yard might come back to bite me in the ass. And I couldn't exactly confess all to the police without leaving Miranda and poor Tater Tot out to dry. Still, relief—that I had an alibi, that my conscience was clear—bathed every single cell in my body.

"Amazing!" I said. "Seriously, you've saved my life."

I happily handed over my last eighty bucks from the Therapy Jar to pay for damages to the ugly bottle cap art. In exchange, I requested the gangly blond's full name and number.

"That night got crazy," I explained. "And there is a teeny-tiny chance law enforcement will need to talk to you."

# FORTY-TWO

To celebrate the joyful news that I for sure wasn't a murderer, I herded the twins to the Library! to pick out a few books. As Phoebe sank into a bean bag chair to giggle over *Narwhal and Jelly* and Alice lay on the kid's rug devouring *Amelia Bedelia*, I collapsed into an adult-sized chair nearby and took a moment to consider all I'd learned in the last hour.

The low-low of reading about Mickey Larynx's comeback followed by the high-high of discovering an alibi for the night Connor died had been twin electrical shocks to my system. They'd caused the record needle of my brain to bounce out of its familiar groove. I could suddenly see beyond my recent predicament to a more bird's-eye view of my life. If Mickey Larynx could rise from the ashes, why couldn't I? Was my career really over? Or had I taken myself out of the game? If I'd had a thicker skin and a more resilient creative well, I might not have let getting dumped by my manager—and deeply heckled by one crowd—stop me.

After that audience had treated me like a Mickey Larynx apologist, I could've gone the DIY route, filming myself doing micro-impersonations and posting them on social media. And if that felt too overwhelming, I could've kept writing down every funny thing the twins ever did or said, just to keep my creative muscles strong. Just to tell my inner artist child I hadn't given up. After all, success wasn't just doing stand-up to a packed theater of adoring fans. Success was continuing to tend to the little fire of my creativity, no matter what.

Taking downtime to recalibrate after my mom died made sense—the rawness of my grief demanded a fallow period. But that time of composting didn't have to be the end of my creative life. I could see that now!

Even if the gatekeepers of comedy never allowed me to have a stand-up special, I could still make my art. I could still write jokes. And if jokes weren't available to me, I could watch great comedy. I could pay attention to the funny grandpa cliques at Dawson Taylor or hilarious kids at the roller rink. I could go to pole dancing class. I could fill the well.

And it wasn't just that I'd let my career go. When I moved to Boise, I dug into isolation. But did my parenting life have to be so solitary? I could check in with my LA friends—who'd called for months before finally giving up on me. And if I ran into someone I knew, I could say hello instead of hiding. Maybe the first Stop-and-Chat after I hadn't seen someone in years would involve questions about Mickey Larynx and my tanked career, but the second one certainly wouldn't. Hell, I could even chat with other moms at soccer practice.

During my big fight with Emmylou, she said my mom wouldn't've wanted me to use grieving as an excuse to quit comedy. That had made me volcanically furious because Emmylou was right. I'd felt so guilty since my mom died because I'd taken all that money she'd sent me. Money she'd needed for herself! But she sent it because she believed in me and my dreams. Continuing to follow those dreams was a way to honor her.

Grief was like a Boise winter. A grayscale, seemingly endless time when the earth and sky looked like concrete. But suddenly I could hear my mother's voice saying, "Winter seems like it will last forever, but that spring thaw is coming, girls."

There would be risks with thawing out, trying again, being vulnerable. But Emmylou was right: It was time. I'd loved my mom—God, how I loved her. Losing her sucked beyond all imagining. But it didn't mean I had to lay down in the snowbank and die. I had to keep slogging toward happiness. The only way to be the sort of woman and mother I wanted to be was to keep reaching for my creative potential and for the life my kids deserved.

Making things right wouldn't happen overnight. But I'd start by taking the tiniest, most obvious step. I'd make my first attempt at a comedy comeback. It didn't matter if it was at an event that wouldn't register a blip on the coastal comedy scenes. I had to start somewhere.

But I couldn't start afresh as an extrovert and public performer with Ralphie and Errol cruising the streets of Boise hoping to dismember me—or worse. Boise was a small enough town that they'd find me eventually. Or, more likely, they'd grab Miranda on her way out for a grocery run and she'd tell them everything. I had to move fast—and control how and when they came for me. Ralphie and Errol needed to go to prison for all they'd done. They still had the plans for Day of the Rope and probably more explosives. They had to be stopped before they and their IDIOT buddies attacked the capitol—in eleven days. I'd never met Baylee, but I was partially responsible for Errol chopping off her finger—where was she now? She might still need help.

It was time to put this dark chapter of my life behind me. But I couldn't do it alone. I needed help too. Now that I knew I was innocent, it might be time to open up to Nate, at least a little bit.

"Hold tight," I told the girls as I rose to my feet. "I'll be right back."

I stood outside the Library!, watching the twins through the glass front window, breath fogging as I dialed. But I wasn't calling Nate. Not yet.

"Tilly! My friend!" Miley O'Riley answered, sounding genuinely happy to hear from me.

"Hey, Miley. You know that comedy set you've been trying to get me to do?"

"At the festival tomorrow! Of course. I talked to your girl Layna. We've got your friend Shade on the books to do a quick number for us."

"Oh, awesome!" I said. I'd forgotten all about that. "Is it too late for me to join the lineup?" I was talking fast. "I'd have to perform as my alter ego, Nikita. I don't want my real name on the advertising. I'm trying out some new material."

"We can squeeze you in! This is going to be more epic than your talent show."

"Don't remind me." I laughed. Junior year, I'd done a skit dressed up as Pat from *Saturday Night Live*. "Though I'm glad Pat's been reclaimed as an icon. But I have one other request." Through the window, I could see Alice's lips moving to *Amelia Bedelia*. Meanwhile, Phoebe was rubbing the page as if trying to actually pat the Narwhal. *Screw the iPad*, I thought.

"For you? Anything," Miley said.

"Could you make a flyer? One with my photo and stage name on it? One I could blow up to poster size?"

"Tilly, the festival is tomorrow."

"It's important. I'd do it myself but I do not have the requisite design skills."

"Okay. Okay. I've got a bored intern here," Miley said. "I'll get him right on it. Send me your headshot and stage name now, okay? He'll turn it around quick."

"Thank you! Thank you so much. And not to be pushy, but are there other ways to get the word out this late in the game?"

"I'll put it on all our socials," Miley said. "It'll be tight but I can probably push for my pals at *Boise Weekly* and the *Statesman* to add your stage name to morning announcements on their websites too."

"You're a rock star," I gushed. "An MVP. A total she-beast!"

Now I had less than twenty-four hours to get the ATF on board, make sure Ralphie and Errol would know where to find me, and put together a comeback-worthy comedy set.

# FORTY-THREE

Holding each twin by a hand, I marched to the entrance of Huckleberry's. Inside the foyer, a bouncer I didn't recognize gave us the once-over.

"Aren't they a little young to be auditioning?" he asked. He looked at Phoebe. "It's gonna be real sad to see you on the pole." To Alice, who was sporting her Betty White face mask, he said, "Hey, why don't you and me go rob a bank?"

"Very funny," I said. "I just need to duck in for a minute and talk to Cheyenne."

"These two got ID? We're twenty-one and over."

"I'm down a babysitter," I explained. This was definitely a parenting low.

"You don't say," the bouncer said.

"Ugh! Fine!"

The sun wouldn't go down for another hour and a half. After locking the twins in the backseat of the Impala with their stacks of library books and stern instructions not to unlock the car door for *anyone*, I headed back to the club. After I'd hung up with Miley O'Riley in front of the Library!, I'd called Miranda. With a shaking voice, she whispered she'd already seen Ralphie and Errol cruise by her house twice since I left. "What if they throw a grenade through the front window?" she said. "I have to tell Chauncey. I have to tell the cops."

This was an option. Miranda could tell the cops everything. I had an alibi. The cops could stake out in front of Miranda's house and maybe catch Ralphie and Errol as they drove by. But I wasn't a total rube. No one was going to let Miranda foster a baby, much less adopt, if law enforcement found out a bunch of white supremacists were after her for tasing an ODing man and stuffing him in a trunk.

And we couldn't let Errol and Ralphie go free. They'd keep harassing Miranda. They'd find me. They'd get their revenge. I told myself I could survive having a finger chopped off. But I knew deep down whatever they did to me would be worse. Much worse.

I wasn't a murderer. I didn't have that worry and guilt hanging over me anymore. And the dead body in my backyard was gone too—hopefully for good. I was ready to move on from all of that, but also from my grief. I was ready to live a full life. Ralphie and Errol were the last remaining block. The truth was, writing jokes again had woken me up to the fact that to be truly alive, I needed to do my art. But I'd never be able to perform comedy publicly unless Ralphie and Errol were caught. And I really wanted to do my set at the Winter Will Never End Festival. Standing at the mic again would scare me almost as much as trying to lure out Ralphie and Errol. But it was time to do something really brave. To perform again. To clear all this up. To make sure Ralphie and Errol didn't hurt me or anyone else.

On the phone outside the Library!, I'd told Miranda all of this and outlined my alternative idea for next steps. She was all for it.

Now, as I stepped into Huckleberry's, it took a moment for my eyes to adjust to the strip club's seedy lighting, the sequins and glitter, the men with lonely ravenous eyes, the women towering on their hollow plastic shoes. It was only five o'clock, but the place was already filling up with the Friday happy hour crowd. In a corner, a dancer in a thong and clear eight-inch pole shoes had her hands on the floor and her legs backed up wheelbarrow-style on either side of a wide-eyed man in a chair, who feasted his peepers on her bare rump.

A halo of cotton-candy-pink hair beckoned from the bar. Cheyenne's microscopic mermaid-scales bikini and glittery skin made her mythic as she batted her eyelash extensions at a man with skin so pale it bordered on translucent. He looked like a mouse that had been dropped into an aquarium with a five-foot rat snake, the rat snake being Cheyenne.

She looked less than pleased to see me. "You here for a private show?" she said. "Because this guy is."

"Actually I'm not," he said and fled.

She sighed and gave a slow blink of her massive lashes. "He was finally ready to be in close proximity to a woman for the first time in three years. But you ruined it for him."

"I'll be quick," I said.

She pointed at the cash machine. "Great. I'll be waiting. It's twenty a song in the VIP room."

"Each song lasts about a minute," a grandpa on a nearby stool warned.

"And don't forget, Woo Girl. I feel most respected when tipped well," Cheyenne added.

The ATM confirmed I had eighty-five dollars in my bank account, but the machine refused to give me eighty, citing the twelve-dollar fee. On a second try, it spit out three twenties. So much for tipping well.

Cheyenne took the Jacksons and my hand and guided me through some chintzy silver curtains into a little room with cheap LED light strips, a fuzzy bench seat, a pole, and way too many mirrors. The VIP room next door emanated Eminem and a man's soft sobs.

"It's okay, baby," a woman murmured until the speakers in the corner of our little slice of strip-club heaven drowned her out.

Cheyenne was a mercenary in eight-inch heels and I had three minutes to convince her to do me a major favor. "Take off your shoes and sit," I said, with as much authority as I could muster.

"That's right. Hot-girl shit," Cheyenne said. Now that I was a paying customer, her demeanor had changed entirely. She unstrapped her Sentient Strippers and sat on the bench.

After a scared glance at the floor (is there anything in this world more disgusting than strip-club carpet?), I sat down cross-legged and started rubbing one of her feet.

"You're an angel." Cheyenne groaned in surprise as I dug into her arch with my thumb.

I kept working, hoping to soften her up. "I'm wondering if you and a friend would be up for pole dancing behind me at the Winter Will Never End Festival tomorrow afternoon?" I said. "I'm doing a ten-minute comedy set about taking pole classes and I need two incredible pole dancers behind me to highlight my own incompetence."

She opened one eye wide enough to shoot me a skeptical look as Dua Lipa and Megan Thee Stallion sang about giving someone a bite of their sweetest pie. "You doing comedy about being a woo girl?"

"Kind of. It's more about how hard pole dancing is," I said, putting extra pressure on her big toe mound. "And how strippers invented it. I want to talk about how women manage to survive and thrive in a capitalistic patriarchy hellbent on objectifying them."

"Interesting," she murmured.

"But it's also about how surprised I am. That pole dancing makes me feel so much joy."

"Sweetest Pie" had already ended, clearly trimmed to a thumbnail of its full glory. Now two women rapped about it being time for the Twerkulator.

I started in on Cheyenne's other foot. "I do have to warn you," I said. "A couple white supremacists might try to come after me during the performance."

"Half the time I carry a knife at work." Cheyenne moaned as I hit a sore spot. "I'm not scared of a couple Proud Boys."

"So you'll do it?" I asked, so astonished I stopped rubbing.

She opened one eye and I started up again. "Oooh! That's better. Sure thing. I'll come tomorrow. I'll bring a friend too. No problem. Just don't stop."

"Are you serious?" Her generosity blew me away. Maybe I'd imagined the divide between newbie pole hobbyists like myself and professional stripper pole dancers.

"—For a major discount," Cheyenne said. "Fifteen hundred, each."

"Three thousand dollars!"

Cheyenne shrugged. "When my friend and I danced as twin bitches at a Travis Scott concert, we charged 6K for both of us."

My third and last song had begun. I was going to fail at convincing Cheyenne to help me with my dinky comeback, just as I'd failed at most everything in my professional life. I kept rubbing Cheyenne's tootsie absentmindedly as the salty sting of defeat soaked all my wounds.

Lil Nas X was singing about how ignorant people thought his career was over. Once he was back on top, they'd remember he didn't run from anything. *I don't want to run anymore either, Lil Nas X.* If Mickey Larynx could use the media as a tool to make his comeback possible, why couldn't I?

*Get your soldiers, tell'em that the break is over,* Lil Nas X sang.

I massaged the arch of Cheyenne's second foot. "What if I could get you great press for Cheyenne's Sentient Strippers?"

Both of Cheyenne's eyes snapped open. "What kind of press?"

# FORTY-FOUR

When I opened the bathroom door, Little Sister barreled out at me and the twins, clearly delighted we'd arrived back home. "We're keeping the dog," I announced. After the twins had finished screaming with joy and hugging me and Little Sister, I ducked into the pantry, but instead of crying while stuffing my face with Hint of Lime Tostitos, I took out my phone. I couldn't do everything alone. Not anymore. I needed to let other people in.

> **Tilly:** Hey Nate! I want to apologize for being so standoffish and weird. Would you be up for coming over after my kids go to bed tonight so I can explain some things?

Too nervous to stare at the phone and wait, I cued up George Michael's *Faith* album.

"Grandma Lulu used to say it's impossible to listen to this album and not be cheered up," I told the twins. "So we're going to play it while we pack up the rest of her fake food. You can take it out anytime you miss her."

Sure enough, George Michael's voice released some much-needed chemicals in my brain. With a trash bag in hand and the twins looking on, I started going through the duplex, tossing in fake quiche and ice cream while shaking my ass and singing, "I got to have faith, faith, faith!" I didn't have time for this, but it felt necessary. The twins couldn't resist George Michael either. They started dancing along with me. Even Little Sister wagged his rump.

With the twins' counsel, I left a few favorites out to honor my mom—a tray of nachos in the twins' room, a cluster of grapes on a high shelf in my bathroom. The rest I dumped in a toy tub in the hall closet. Next I pulled off the tie-dyed couch cover and put it in the twins' costume box. With a couple holes cut in it for eyes, it would make a great hippie ghost costume. The actual couch sported a couple of stains, but I could cover them up with thrift-store throw pillows. Otherwise, I liked the sunny yellow fabric. Inspired, I stood on a chair to take down the disco ball. "We can hang this back up for dance parties," I said.

"It is a little much for every day," Phoebe agreed.

"But that was Grandma Lulu," Alice said, fondly.

Everything felt better, brighter, less cluttered. The duplex looked less like a museum showcasing my beloved mother's quirky tastes. The duplex looked more like me.

While the twins settled in to color their *Groundbreaking Female Comedians* coloring books, I called Miley O'Riley.

"Me again!" I said. "Things are shaping up for my set tomorrow, but I've got a question for you." I explained about Cheyenne and her new line of pole shoes and asked if any of Miley's pals in the local press might want to write a feature about her.

"Do you remember Evelyn Pellegrino?" Miley said. "She was a grade ahead of us?"

"Glasses? Obsessed with Sheryl Crow—like weirdly obsessed?"

"That's her. She writes for the *Idaho Statesman* and she's been doing a series about women entrepreneurs. I'll call her now."

"That would be incredible, Miley. I really appreciate it." I hung up, wondering why I hadn't ever asked Miley O'Riley to hang out before.

Still nothing from Nate. A watched phone never buzzes, so I started work on my comedy set. When a text arrived twenty minutes later, I lunged for it. But it was Miley.

**Miley:** Evelyn says hi! And she'd love to do a feature on yr friend and her pole shoe company!

Maybe there were perks to being in my hometown after all.

**Tilly:** THANK YOU! Hey, wanna get a coffee sometime?

**Miley:** Sure! And we could do a kid date too? My daughter Bam-Bam shows an early aptitude for social drama. A potential friend triangle with twins would def be her jam.

As I laughed out loud, my phone rattled again. This time it was Nate.

# FORTY-FIVE

For the second time that day, I opened the door to find Agent Nate Duran outside. But instead of lurking behind his ATF colleague, he now stood alone in jeans and a puffy coat. I ushered him inside, my heart flapping like a decapitated chicken.

He paused to take in the living room. "It looks great in here! Don't get me wrong, I have nothing against tie-dye and disco balls. But it's calmer now. I like it."

This time I offered tea instead of whiskey. We sat across from each other at the kitchen table to avoid our thighs accidentally touching. It should've felt even more awkward than it did, all things considered.

"I have a lot to explain," I said.

"I'm a good listener."

I took a deep breath. New Tilly trusted people. New Tilly let people in. I could do this. I wanted to be open and honest with Nate. To be able to tell him everything. But I'd only known him for a week and a half. If he had to choose between his loyalty to the ATF and a rando who'd slept with him once and then ghosted him, he wouldn't pick me. And if I had to choose between being honest with him and staying out of a prison cell, I'd choose my own freedom. So I looked deep into his gold-flecked eyes and started spouting half-truths and lies.

I'd been acting so weird partly because I was under a lot of stress, I said. I'd met a creepy guy named Connor at Huckleberry's. He'd drunkenly told me all about an attack he was planning on the capitol in three weeks. That was almost two weeks ago now. His friends—Ralphie and Errol—had been threatening me ever since. They told me they'd chopped off a woman's finger and mine was next. I hadn't confessed any of this to Nate and the other agents that morning because I was too afraid. But it was time for me to be brave now.

I left Layna, and Gucci, and Miranda out of my story entirely. Though I knew at that very moment Gucci was likely staking a giant poster advertising "Nikita's" stand-up set at the Winter Will Never End Festival into the ground of Miranda's front yard. Hopefully Ralphie and Errol would drive by and see my smiling mug on the poster before my set tomorrow afternoon and think it was a message from Miranda, giving me up. They'd stop harassing her. They'd know where to find me.

Nate took in everything I told him calmly, only interrupting to ask clarifying questions. I kept my answers short, concise, the better not to trip myself up.

"Why did you think we were going to arrest you?" Nate asked.

"Two federal agents show up at my house? I'm a solo mom. Maybe sometimes I get paranoid that something will happen and I won't be able to care for my kids."

When Nate spoke next, it was calmly, slowly, as if he was sorry to ask me a question it wouldn't be in my best interest to answer. "Why do you think Connor Johnson's phone pinged here? At your house?"

I shrugged, my heart slamming into my ribs like the time I got busted shoplifting lipstick in junior high. "I'm a left-leaning feminist from Westside LA," I finally said. "I promise I am not in cahoots with a proto-Nazi I met at the strip club."

Nate's look said he knew there were things I wasn't telling him. But after an eternity, he gave a small, almost imperceptible nod, then leaned toward me, elbows on the table. I feared he was about to demand the full and unfiltered truth. Instead he said, "Connor Johnson is a federal informant. We have reason to suspect he might have gotten crossways with other members of the Imperial Dominion. That he might be dead."

"Oh my god," I managed.

"Ralphie 'the Lizard' Wheeler and his nephew—Errol Wheeler. They're major illegal arms suppliers," Nate said. "Practically on our Most Wanted list. We've had Day of the Rope on our radar. Our sources tell us the attempt will be in eleven days. Catching them could help us stop it. Especially if we could get them to talk."

"Well, here's our chance!" I said, so nervous I made jazz hands. I told Nate about my stand-up set at the festival, how it was being advertised with my photo and my pole dancing name, Nikita. Ralphie and Errol would likely be there, looking for me.

"Your pole name is Nikita?" Nate grinned. "Like *La Femme Nikita*?"

"You've seen *La Femme Nikita*?" I said.

"Watching Anne Parillaud assemble that Steyr AUG A1 rifle in her underwear is probably why I got into the ATF." He grinned at me. "Nikita. Nice."

"Yeah, except I'm not an assassin," I said. "But I'm still kind of a badass. Like a Bond girl, but one who survives." I tried to keep my voice steady. "Basically, you can use me as bait."

"I don't want to use you as bait!" he said.

I needed to sound calm and strong. To not let on how scared I was. "If those two are wandering free, I'm gonna be living in fear—for myself and my kids. Better to draw them out and catch them than live in terror they'll find me." This was the truest thing I'd said since Nate arrived.

"Ralphie and Errol think you'll be there," he said. "But you don't have to actually be there. You can stay home, stay safe."

"I know it might sound crazy, but I need to get back into comedy," I said. "You saw me do my stand-up at Job Talk Tuesday. This is my calling. Besides, if the ATF is there on the ready, it's not gonna be hugely risky." I was trying to convince us both.

Nate rubbed the top of his head with his hands, which messed up his hair, which made him look even cuter. "Okay," he said. "I'll call my supervisor and see what we can put together."

"It's short notice," I said.

He shrugged. "We're trained for this. It's what we do." He said it so confidently. Maybe Layna had been wrong. Maybe he would rescue me.

"Thank you. I have one more thing to tell you," I said. "It's the reason I was acting so weird after we had such awesome sex."

"You thought it was awesome?" he said, with such hope and innocence I wanted to lean across the table, grab the back of his neck, and pull him in for a kiss.

"Of course!" I said. Suddenly my mouth filled with sand. I wasn't sure I could force words out of such a Sahara. But now was the time for me to do the hardest thing I'd ever done. "It's just that when you got up to go to the bathroom, I saw you have a birthmark in the shape of Florida on your lower back," I said, my voice a dusty whisper. "And Phoebe has the exact same birthmark. In the exact same place."

He looked confused. "Okay?"

"I know this is gonna sound nuts. But birthmarks are genetic." I was talking really fast now. "You also all three have those double-jointed elbows. And the cloverleaf tongue thing." I paused. "I think you might be the twins' sperm donor."

He did not have the look of a man who'd heard joyful tidings. He looked catatonic. After what felt like the length of one of the *Dune* movies, I waved my hand in front of his face, but he didn't respond. I started to worry he was having a mini-stroke.

"Are you all right?" I said.

"I get it. You're a comedian and this is a joke. Ha. Ha." He was forcing air out of his lungs in a disturbing imitation of laughter. "Ha. Ha. Ha."

"Not a joke," I said, softly. "I have a paternity test I ordered off the internet. If you want to take it."

When he finally spoke, it was with the sort of fake cheer I'd use when convincing the twins it would be fun to go to the dentist. "Let's bust this ring of white supremacists who want to overthrow the state government—because apparently these guys think the current political situation isn't dystopian enough! Then we can figure out what to do next about . . . about this theory you have."

Feeling rebuffed, and with an aching heart, I told myself it was my turn to be patient with Nate.

I didn't have time to ruminate on the fact that Nate bolted five minutes later. I had a million things to do. Check in with Cheyenne. Warn Miley O'Riley about the situation. Find a babysitter for tomorrow. Finish my stand-up set. It'd still be rough by the time I hit the stage, but at this point I needed to focus on progress, not perfection.

But before I tackled any of that, I had an amends to make. I printed a flyer for the festival and headed over to Emmylou's. When she didn't answer my knock, I scrawled a note on the back and slipped it under her door.

*Dear Emmylou,*

*I'm so sorry I blew up at you. You're a light in our lives and we miss you. Hopefully I can apologize to you IRL soon. If you want to see me perform at the Winter Will Never End Festival, please stop by. I'll be doing a comedy set about pole dancing tomorrow, Saturday* 😌. *If it weren't for you, I'd never have material for a "comeback." Thank you.*

*Lots of love,*

*Tilly*

# FORTY-SIX

*Saturday*

The day of the Winter Will Never End Festival dawned cloudless and springlike. For the first time in almost four months, the cap of gray clouds over the Treasure Valley had disappeared to reveal a deep dazzling sky. I should've been elated. But after so much bleakness for so long, the bright blue above disoriented me. By two o'clock it was warm enough for shorts, and even though I wished I knew where Connor's body had disappeared to, for now I was just relieved it wasn't thawing out in my yard.

In the park in front of the domed Idaho State Capitol, ice sculptures of yetis and pine trees dripped dramatically. A hydraulic pump pulled snowboarders and skiers at lightning speed so they could launch off a rapidly melting snow ramp. In the Kids' Tent, volunteers put their face-painting skills to work turning sweaty children into snow leopards and ice crystals. It was a small town doing its best to celebrate big.

When I'd called Layna the night before for babysitter ideas, she'd hooked me up with a pal's daughter. Alma was a senior at Boise State who was more than fine with being paid with a gift card to Ruby Lou boutique I'd bought for my mom but hadn't had the chance to give her. She'd shown up ten minutes early with tiaras from the Dollar Store. For the twins, it was love at first sight. The three of them told me not to hurry home.

At the northwest corner of the park, I met up with Nate, Agent Mozzarella (who'd gotten an ill-advised spray tan and now looked more like Agent Cheddar), and several of their colleagues in SWAT vests and

ATF T-shirts. I told myself my impending set—not Nate's proximity—was the cause of my rapid heartbeat.

He glanced at me shyly. "I guess we're really doing this?"

"I'm not wearing velour pole shorts under my jeans for nothing," I said.

"Should I ask what pole shorts are?"

"You'll see," I said with a smile.

Agent Mozzarella formally introduced himself (real name: Agent Lanagan) and told me he'd be providing my security. A combination of Boise PD, capitol police, FBI, and ATF would monitor the area near the stage during my performance. If Ralphie or Errol appeared or tried to nab me, they'd be arrested on the spot.

Nate's gentle hand on my forearm made my scalp and toes tingle. "Good luck," he said. As if realizing he sounded worried, he added, "Oh, and break a leg!"

"In the shoes I'll be wearing, I just might."

With Agent Lanagan trailing behind me, I made my way toward the stage. A giant banner with a drawing of a rhinestone-encrusted platform shoe and the words *Cheyenne's Sentient Strippers* hung from the front. No way would the City of Boise have approved that thing, but I figured Cheyenne preferred to beg forgiveness.

Layna, Zhang Xiu, and Gucci were waiting for me backstage.

"You are going to be so great!" Layna said. "I'll be right here, hyping you! I even brought an air horn." She waved the obnoxious courtside accoutrement enthusiastically.

"Thanks," I said. It was so sweet I didn't have the heart to tell her no comedian wants that kind of distraction during her set.

A gorgeous monochrome drag queen in a ruby-red corset and tiered ruffled tulle skirt sashayed up to us. Between her platform heels and feathered headdress, she was easily over seven feet tall.

"Shade!" I yelled. "You look amazing!"

"Shade?" the towering queen said. "Who's Shade? I'm Ida Hoe,

Idaho's Most Daring Diva. Despite the state legislature's fears that nothing is more dangerous to toxic masculinity than a drag queen, I am ready to crush this! These lips don't synch, baby!"

After wishing Ida Hoe good luck, I went to find Cheyenne, who was limbering up. When the raven-haired woman next to her popped up from her forward fold, I yelled: "Salma Hayek!"

"Nikita!" she said, giving me a hug.

"I had no idea you were the friend Cheyenne was bringing!"

"One thing I learned on my ayahuasca retreat was that I need to be of service to my peeps," Salma said.

"That's where you disappeared to! Why didn't you tell me?"

Salma Hayek grinned. "I wasn't sure you were cool enough. Now that you're helping Cheyenne get major exposure for her Sentient Strippers, I'm sure. My retreat was a gamechanger. I threw up, tripped balls, healed core wounds, made lifelong friends. Highly recommend."

I gave her the "must be nice" look I often leveled at child-free people when they told me about sleeping in on weekends or drinking lattes in a slow and uninterrupted manner.

"Let's huddle up and make a plan!" Cheyenne said.

The three of us talked through my set as Agent Lanagan stood nearby. Ideally we would've rehearsed. But Cheyenne was an experienced stripper and Salma Hayek was a regular contender at national pole competitions—I could trust they'd kill. It was my own set I worried about.

Once we'd locked in our plan, we stripped down to the outfits we'd perform in and strapped on pairs of Cheyenne's Sentient Stripper pole shoes. I felt so anxious I was disassociating a little—though I couldn't tell if I was more worried about walking in those shoes, being shot by Ralphie and Errol, or bombing my set.

"Okay, my lovelies!" someone yelled. "It's time. Take your places."

The Pole Virgins, Cheyenne, Salma Hayek, Agent Lanagan, and I all moved to a backstage spot with a good view as the emcee from the

Mash the Patriarchy wrestling contest took the stage. After welcoming everyone to the festival, they said, "There's no one who loves this beautiful state more than our first performer. So let's give it up for the drag queen with the most state pride, Boise's very own Ida Hoe."

Ida Hoe catwalked out to take the microphone. On-stage, she was a glittering vision of rubies and feathers and tulle. She waited for the raucous cheers to die down before saying, "I'm here to perform a little song for you by a gal named Taylor Swift. It's called 'The Man.'"

Zhang Xiu, Gucci, Cheyenne, Salma Hayek, and I hollered encouragement as Ida Hoe began to strut, swivel, and sing, giving new meaning to the campy Swiftie anthem. The crowd bellowed along to the chorus. By the time the song ended even Agent Lanagan was tapping his toes. As the other Pole Virgins rushed to hug Ida Hoe, I wiped my sweaty palms on my bare thighs and prepared to make my comeback.

"That performance was like if RuPaul and Céline Dion had a baby!" the emcee told the crowd. "Phenomenal. Let's hear it for Ida Hoe!"

The crowd cheered as if they'd seen Charli XCX perform at San Francisco Pride.

Meanwhile, Gucci, Zhang Xiu, and Layna carried the three portable poles onto the stage, setting them up in a triangle formation. Salma Hayek silently offered me a dollop of resin to keep me from slipping, and I rubbed my palms together with a smile of thanks. I was terrified. Of doing comedy again—half-naked, no less. Of being seen. Of standing out there like a target for Ralphie and Errol. But I was ready to wrap up this gloomy, infertile period of my life. Ready to get out of the fear and into the light.

"It's time to introduce a true Boise local," the emcee continued. "This gal was born and raised right here, and she's trying out new stand-up material under her stage name. Some of it might be PG-13, so now might be a good time to take your little ones to the Kids' Tent. Now let's make some noise for: Nikita!"

# FORTY-SEVEN

As a stand-up performer, I'd always wanted my clothes to be a blank canvas, a neutral palette. But now I nervously stepped onto the stage in six-inch hot-pink plastic stripper shoes, turquoise velour booty shorts, and a matching strappy push-up bra Layna had gifted me for the occasion. Luckily, the shoes were much more comfortable and stable than they looked.

Several hundred people stood out there. Layna, Zhang Xiu, and Ida Hoe had slipped around to the front row to cheer me on. A few people held their cell phones up to film. The angle would highlight my every dimple and bulge. But no woman ever got into comedy to look pretty. That's what I told myself.

"Hello, Boise!" I called.

The crowd seemed game; a few people even yelled "hello" back.

"I see some of y'all looking at me like you feel bad I'm up here in this outfit," I said. A handful of folks chuckled like: *busted.* "But seriously, I never expected to find myself in front of a crowd in this getup. See, I've been furloughed from my job."

I scanned the crowd. The faces were smiling, eager, buoyed by the warm weather and blue skies. A woman with homemade snowflakes pinned all over her stood next to a guy wearing a snowman onesie. I hoped Emmylou was out there somewhere, but I didn't see her. Or Nate. I didn't see Ralphie and Errol either. Maybe they hadn't spotted the sign in Miranda's yard. Maybe they hadn't come. But if they had, we were ready for them—capitol police officers, Boise PD, and federal agents dotted the crowd, scanning for threats.

"Three weeks without pay," I said, "and money is tight at my house. So I decided to take to the pole." I gestured to the stripper poles behind me.

I had the crowd's attention.

"I know what you're thinking," I said, "but I'm not pole dancing professionally. And I'm not saying that in a puritanical hashtag-not-a-stripper kind of a way. Strippers are amazing. I just don't have what it takes, and not just because breastfeeding twins did something scary to my boobs—don't be fooled by what this outfit is giving. This bra could make two bowls of oatmeal look like Scarlett Johansson's cleavage."

An appreciative blast sounded from Layna's air horn and everyone laughed.

"But let's not talk about my mom boobs," I said. "Let's talk about pole dancing."

The crowd let out a collective sound of excitement—Cheyenne and Salma Hayek had stepped out onto the stage behind me. I knew they were pole walking in matching silver thongs and strappy bras. But I didn't look back at them. I wanted to give the sense that Cheyenne and Salma were figments of the crowd's collective imagination.

"Imagine, it's New York City, 1988. You want to strip?" I said. "Head up to Midtown on the D train with your big bush and your ratty undies. No Brazilian wax or acrobatic talents required. The pole is just for keeping your balance."

For the first time, I grabbed onto my own pole with one hand and gazed, dull-eyed, at the crowd, undulating mildly like a bored eighties stripper. I knew behind me, Cheyenne and Salma Hayek were doing the same.

Every person out there stared up at us, mesmerized. I was a powerful comedy witch, casting my spell.

"And the strip club patrons, they were fine with that level of enthusiasm from the dancers," I continued. "They just came for the fantasy that a woman who wouldn't give them the time of day in the real world was into them. Y'all heard of Cookie Mueller?" Most of the audience members shook their heads. But a couple artsy weirdos hooted. "She starred in a bunch of John Waters films. She was also a writer and she stripped. That was part of the patchwork of how she made a living as an artist. She said she could dance her heart out onstage. High kicking, shimmying like a showgirl."

I gave an unprofessional shimmy, knowing behind me Salma and Cheyenne were kicking higher than a couple of Rockettes.

"But Cookie Mueller, she realized she'd make more money if she just lay down on the stage." At this point I lowered myself awkwardly to the floor, where I lay on my side and propped my head up with the heel of my hand. "Yep, she'd gaze deeply into a patron's eyes, and just do some leg lifts."

I gave the crowd a faux sultry look and started leg-lifting like a young Jane Fonda. Behind me, Cheyenne and Salma Hayek were doing the same, only in a sexier way. The crowd loved it.

"Cookie Mueller said when she did this, patrons would throw twenties at her like a car dealer tossing candy from a parade float," I said.

Using the pole, I fumbled to my feet as Cheyenne and Salma Hayek did sexy pop-ups. The crowd laughed joyfully at the juxtaposition between my awkwardness and their grace.

"So even though back in the seventies and eighties, strippers could rake in fat cash by lying down and giving bedroom eyes, still they were like: 'What if we made pole dancing acrobatic? What if we made it art? Let's elevate this shit!'"

Finally I looked back at Cheyenne and Salma as they began to air walk, legs running in elegant slow motion. They inverted in unison to execute a graceful series of gravity-defying moves. I applauded and the crowd joined me, polite claps swelling to genuine appreciation. When Cheyenne and Salma's feet hit the ground and they went back to languidly moving their hips, the crowd quieted.

"So in a few short decades," I continued, "strippers developed this whole new art form, this aerial sport. Just because they could. And let me tell you, it's harder than they make it look! I've taken a few pole classes, and for the record, this is the vibe when a mortal tries a beginner's pole trick." I executed my awkward version of the fireman's spin. As the crowd chortled, I staggered back to the mic stand. "You're laughing because you know if you tried it, you'd look even worse."

The audience nodded and laughed harder.

God, how I'd missed this. How had I ever thought I could give it up? I'd been born to throw my dignity on the funeral pyre and watch it transform into the phoenix of laughter.

"By the way, the three of us are all wearing pole shoes from a new line called Cheyenne's Sentient Strippers, created by Cheyenne here."

I gestured at Cheyenne, who bowed and beamed.

"They're so comfortable even a sneakerhead like me can get around in them just fine."

Some ladies in the front row let out a volley of "Woo"s.

"I see you, Woo Girls!" I said, pointing at them, and they "Woo"ed even louder. "I learned recently that if you're a straight gal 'Woo'ing in a strip club, it's poor form to tell the strippers you respect them too much to hire them for a lap dance. In a strip club, you don't show respect by being wary of transactional demonstrations of sexuality. You show respect by tipping like a coked-up stockbroker."

I spotted Nate at the edge of the crowd. He wasn't looking at me. Rationally, I knew he was scanning for dangers, but still I felt the vise grip of disappointment at having lost his attention. Then he glanced up and smiled. His adoring eyes said: *I see you up there, doing your thing.* I smiled back.

But I couldn't get distracted. Not now.

"Now I'm just a nascent pole hobbyist," I said. "But I imagine being a stripper is a lot like being a mom. You have to set boundaries a million times a day. We moms are all like: 'No, you can't have another popsicle.

No, you can't stay up past your bedtime. Please stop putting your hand down your pants.' And strippers are like: 'No, you can't touch me. No, you can't touch yourself. Please stop putting your hand down your pants.'"

One woman in the front row was crying she was laughing so hard. But on the far side of the park, some sort of commotion had started to brew. I heard shouts and saw three officers hustling toward the Kids' Tent. Could our plan be working? Could the cops be grabbing Ralphie and Errol?

In an effort to keep the crowd's attention, I pulled the mic from the stand and leaned forward as if to impart a secret. "I'm going to level with you about the actual reason I'd never be a stripper—other than the fact that I can't pole dance for shit and would need to work at a niche club catering to guys horny for Gen X pheromones."

I paused to let the laughter die down.

"The reason I could never be a stripper is I don't have the other necessary skills. Those baddies have to be excellent at sales. And most important, they have to have the ability to act like male sexuality isn't disgusting ninety-five percent of the time—and that's one talent I do not have."

The ruckus over by the Kids' Tent seemed to be escalating. A murmur rippled through the park. I had the panicky sense I was losing my audience. But underneath it lurched hope—that law enforcement had found Ralphie and Errol, that they were arresting them right now, that this nightmarish period of my life was coming to a close.

"But I don't *not* strip because I don't want to sell my body. I already do that. In return for a paycheck and bennies for me and my kids, I spend forty hours a week slinging meatloaf, refilling ketchup, and doing the schedule in the Capitol Grill cafeteria." I pointed at the capitol itself, even though the Capitol Grill was actually in the tunnels underground. "*That's* how I sell my body."

Barely half the crowd laughed. The rest had turned to see what was going on at the far side of the park, where crying children with half-painted faces came pouring out of the Kids' Tent. I heard shouts of "Fire!" and "My kids!" Streams of capitol police, Boise PD, and ATF officers sprinted toward the tent as tendrils of smoke curled into the air. Approaching sirens wailed.

Agent Lanagan appeared beside me, rudely grabbing the mic. "Please stay calm," he told the crowd. "But we need everyone in the Kids' Tent to evacuate now."

# FORTY-EIGHT

Strong arms linked with mine as Agent Lanagan continued to instruct the crowd to stay calm. Two blazer-clad men with Secret Service agent earpieces protected me on either side.

"We're federal agents," the tall one said. "Here to get you to safety." They flashed their badges at Agent Lanagan, who gave a quick nod.

Thank goodness the twins were safe at home. I gave Salma and Cheyenne a brave wink as the feds hurried me toward the backstage stairs. Once we hit the soggy ground, the agents lifted me a little to keep my stilettos from sinking into the muddy grass. We moved away from the mayhem to a familiar flight of stone stairs. At the bottom, one of the feds buzzed the door open with a key card.

We hurried along one of the grim underground tunnels I took sometimes to get to the Capitol Grill. It was funny to think I'd be back at work there soon, joking with my coworkers, checking off shipments of ground beef, pitching in on the fryer when someone was out sick. My life dribbling away doing work I wasn't passionate about. No way out.

"Are you Secret Service or FBI?" I asked.

"Not exactly," the shorter agent said as a slight woman in a neat navy overcoat stepped out from another branch of the tunnels.

Miranda's mother, Belinda Carson. When the men stopped short, their tight hold on my upper arms suddenly felt like a restraint.

"You got her! Great job, boys," Mrs. Carson said, clapping her hands like she used to when the Boise High football team scored a touchdown. "Tilly Turner." She pinned me with her disapproving gaze. Her voice, so friendly a second before, now could've turned all the melting snow in

Boise back to ice. "With those stretch marks, you'd really be better off keeping your clothes on."

"Mrs. Carson," I managed. "What are you doing here?"

"Cut the crap, Tilly," she said. "I know you saw me at Bar Gernika. I know you know."

Bar Gernika. My eye twitched. My brain had gone glitchy. "You were there for a lamb grinder," I said. But even as the words left my mouth, I realized it. Belinda Carson had been sitting alone at a two-top, looking a little frail.

But she'd been there to pick up the grenades.

Because she was the Receiver.

Which meant I was in very deep shit.

I tried to yank my arms free, twisting my head to get my first good look at the men holding me. One had a shiny pink keloid scar on his temple. The other had a unibrow worthy of a young Nicolas Cage. Given they were sporting blazers and Secret Service earpieces, their mullets turned to tight fades, I hadn't recognized them as the lumberjacks I'd spotted bellied up at Bar Gernika. I'd assumed one of them was the Receiver. But these brutes had been there to protect Mrs. Carson. To be her lookouts. To carry the grenades.

Miranda had told me her mom hired dodgy guys to help her with her counterfeit candle business. But now I knew they were doing more than hauling around boxes of candles that smelled like Concrete After Lightning and Wild Brooklyn Lavender. I thrashed and fought as if my life depended on it—which I now understood it absolutely did.

Unibrow let go of my arm and yanked me into a headlock. Still, I wrenched and flailed. Pain like I'd never felt before—not even in childbirth—exploded from my center as the other guy punched me in the stomach. Surely something inside me had ruptured. But I couldn't double over. I couldn't breathe, and for a split second I might've blacked out. Then I was retching and gasping. Unibrow yanked up on my head and I felt a knife blade pressed to my throat. My wild panicked eyes searched for security cameras. The tunnels had them. But when I spotted the nearest one, I saw a round black sticker had been placed over the lens.

Mrs. Carson moved toward me like an alley cat stalking an overfed pigeon. As she got closer, I could see her actual eyebrows had been lasered off and replaced with aggressive penciling.

"I'm not happy about this, Tilly," she said. "Miranda told me you two are all buddy-buddy these days. And this is going to make her so sad."

"Tell them to let me go," I said, my voice shrill with alarm.

"Sorry, sweetie," Mrs. Carson said. "No can do."

The knife blade bit into the skin of my neck. Unibrow pulled his forearm hard against my windpipe, cutting off my air. This guy was going to slaughter me like a hog. I would bleed out quickly and die in this grim tunnel. My kids would be all alone.

Panicked as a trapped animal, I struggled and kicked but it made no difference. I tried to speak but not even a gargled sound escaped. Mrs. Carson watched me with cold eyes as I clawed at Unibrow's forearm. She made a slight motion and the goon released the pressure on my neck enough for me to suck in a lungful of air.

"I won't tell," I croaked. A warm trickle ran down my throat. I stopped thrashing for fear Unibrow would decide to get it over with. In another part of my reptilian brain, I was terrified the other brute would punch me again.

"Oh, sweetie," Mrs. Carson said. "I don't want to do this either. I've known you since you were a pimply teen who couldn't find a prom date. I'd rather let Ralphie and Errol do the deed. But I can't trust those incompetents to pull it off." Mrs. Carson patted at her hair to assure herself every strand was in place. "I heard they'd be here today, causing a ruckus. Everyone will think one of their boys got to you." Her voice softened. "But it really does make me feel so terrible for poor Miranda. She'll be devastated. She really could use a friend. Other women are always so intimidated by her." She shook her head as if to clear it of empathy for her own daughter. "Boys, you know what to do. I just can't watch, okay?"

The edge of the knife pressed deeper as Mrs. Carson started to walk away, heels clicking sharply on the grimy concrete. I had taken too many things for granted. I would happily spend the rest of my days ringing up meatloaf plates for ill-tempered state senators working to eradicate my rights if it meant I could live to see my girls learn to do their multiplication tables.

But Belinda Carson stepped around the corner and out of sight. In one bold movement, her henchman dug the knife blade into my throat and yanked, cutting through my carotid artery and jugular, trachea, and esophagus, all the way down to my knobby vertebra. He lowered me to the ground as my dying heart pumped blood out through the gaping smile in my neck.

It hadn't happened yet. But in five seconds, it would. I had to do something, anything to bring Mrs. Carson back, to keep her talking. To live a little longer.

"Miranda told me she appreciates you!" I yelled.

Mrs. Carson halted in her tracks and spun to face me. "What was that?"

"It's true," I said. "You've always been so hard on her. But she said you were actually incredibly helpful when she was trying to have a baby."

"She said that?" Mrs. Carson's eyes glistened as she walked toward me. I could sense pain there, longing. "She really said that?" Belinda Carson wore an armor of meanness. But I could see it now. Deep down, what she wanted more than anything was for her daughter to think she was a good mother. I could relate to that, in my way. Not to the unkindness. But to the fierce hope that despite all my parental blunders, in the end, my kids would love me, think of me fondly, grow up and tell a friend about some little or big thing I'd actually done right.

Mrs. Carson was closer now. Just a couple of steps from me. But not close enough.

"She did. She really did. She said she couldn't have gotten through it without you."

"It was awful to see her like that," Mrs. Carson said. "Wanting something I couldn't give her. And I don't know why, but somehow, for once, I knew how to say the right thing."

Deep sympathy for this sad, mean, profoundly unwell woman suffused me. But it didn't matter, because right then Mrs. Carson stepped into my range. I picked up both feet and nailed her in the stomach with the stiletto ends of my pole shoes.

She teetered, arms windmilling for what felt like forever.

And then she fell.

The thug with the keloid scar rushed to help her. The knife grazed my neck as I wrenched away from a startled Unibrow, tripping on my six-inch platforms. The concrete floor roared up to meet me and I rolled into my fall, ending up on my back with the wind knocked out of me again. As Unibrow rushed at me with the bloody knife, I waved my legs in the air like a seizure-ridden octopus. He stopped short, unsettled by my Vagina Monster, my crotch pointed at him, legs flailing like the inflatable man outside a car dealership. When he lunged to grab one of my ankles, I nailed him in the nuts with the boxy platform of my other shoe.

He fell howling to the ground, the hunting knife blessedly careening across the floor, blood droplets flying. I scooted backward, back scraping concrete, ripping off first one pole shoe, then the other, and scrambling to my feet.

As the second goon lunged for me, I jogged backward and chucked a Sentient Stripper at him. He ducked it easily and kept coming. As I turned to run, he grabbed me by one arm. I whirled, the second stripper shoe gripped tightly in my free hand. A loud pop sounded as the six-inch stiletto punctured his cheek. He lurched backward, the shoe dangling from his perforated face.

I sprinted along the dim hallway, veering right down the side tunnel I knew exited up onto Eighth Street. I burst out to sunlight and that dazzling blue sky. I'd expected to emerge into a crowd, but the sidewalks lay empty. The dome of the capitol rose against the backdrop of the foothills.

Parked cars lined the street but there was no one nearby. I was vulnerable, barefoot, nearly naked, dripping blood. An easy target. Prey.

A block away, the milling crowd of festivalgoers watched as firefighters doused the Kids' Tent. EMTs checked out dazed children in the back of parked ambulances. In that throng of cop cars and flashing lights, I could find protection, safety, Nate.

When I glanced behind me, there was no sign of Mrs. Carson's bagmen.

But as I turned back around, a familiar figure had stepped out from behind a parked car.

"You didn't have to get all tarted up just for me, sweetheart," Ralphie the Lizard said.

# FORTY-NINE

When I spun away from Ralphie the Lizard, a human fireplug blocked my way. Errol. He wore an eye patch over his left eye, and had a nasty burn on his cheek and ear from his run-in with a hot pan. Bandages wrapped one of his hands. He leered at me with his right eye. "Looks like someone else likes you about as much as I do," Errol said. "But I'm glad I'll get to finish the job."

I did a panicked one-eighty, let out a Xena war cry, and feinted right. But before I could sprint toward the safety of the crowd, Errol's arms gripped me from behind like a massive clamp.

"Let me go!" I screamed, kicking impotently at the air.

"You stole my grenades and blew up our snowmobiles. I'm taking it out of your hide," Errol said, licking my ear. "Can't have you running your mouth about us either."

"Gross!" I screamed, and then, "Fire!"

No one came to my rescue as Errol carried me, kicking and screeching and bleeding from the gash on my neck, to a parked sedan.

When he tried to shove me into the passenger side backseat, I fought like a cocker spaniel on trucker speed.

"Let go of me, you redneck piece of shit!" I managed, before Errol yanked me back and spun me around, snarling, his face so close I could see the tobacco stains on his teeth. He gave me a hard shove. The back of my head hit the edge of the doorframe as I fell into the backseat. Errol shoved my legs in, put his hands on the top of the door, and slammed it shut.

*THWACK!*

The sickening sound reached me through the car door as something sank deep into Errol's torso. A bolt had entered the left side of his rib cage. He tilted forward, face to the window, then slid slowly downward, nose pugged by the pane until he dropped out of sight. I scrambled to climb out the other side of the car and stepped onto the pavement, gasping.

Across Eighth Street, a silver-haired goddess lowered her crossbow. Emmylou! My savior!

But before I could run, Ralphie appeared from the rear of the car. He grabbed my arm, wrenching it behind my back, and I felt the cold round barrel of a gun pressing into my spine.

"I'm done fucking around," he said.

He used me like a shield as he backpedaled to the trunk. Errol's legs stuck out from behind the back tire where he'd crumpled on the pavement. Across the street, Emmylou struggled to cock and reload her crossbow, a procedure that—she'd told me countless times—was a lot harder than it looked on *The Walking Dead*.

The trunk yawned, a black hole from which I'd never emerge alive. "Shut up and get in or I'll shoot you in the spine," Ralphie said.

I folded myself into the small space like an origami chicken, too terrified to make a sound.

This was it.

I was going to die.

My children orphaned.

I'd failed them.

Ralphie slid the gun into his waistband and raised his arms to slam the trunk shut, his figure blocking out the blue sky and the sun.

My last thought before darkness enveloped me was that I hoped Emmylou would raise the twins.

But the trunk didn't close. Instead, an air horn appeared alongside Ralphie's right ear.

*BWAAAAAAAAAAAAAAAAAHHHHPP!*

At the sound of the blast, Ralphie screamed like a final girl. The air horn clattered to the pavement and an arm wrapped tight around his neck, Layna's face appearing over his shoulder. He spun to shake her off, but she clung tighter, his neck trapped in the notch of her elbow, her Adidas-clad feet lifting with the centrifugal force of a carnival swing ride.

As I pushed myself upright, Layna went flying. But before Ralphie could reach for his gun, a seven-foot-tall red blur streaked past. Ida Hoe's flouncy skirt flapped like a sail as she took a flying leap, sacking Ralphie in an NFL-worthy tackle.

"Be careful, Shade! He has a gun!" I shouted.

Ralphie's head and most of his torso had disappeared beneath cascading skirt ruffles. It was a lewd but effective wrestling hold. Ralphie kicked impotently, his screams muffled below layers of tulle.

"Get him! Crush that bastard," Zhang Xiu yelled as ATF agents with guns drawn surrounded Ida Hoe and Ralphie.

"Don't you dare shoot that drag queen!" I screamed.

Nate pinned one of Ralphie's wrists while Agent Lanagan grabbed the other. With Ralphie secured, Ida Hoe popped back up, agile on six-inch heels. Nate rolled Ralphie onto his stomach, pulled his gun from his waistband, and handcuffed his arms behind his back as Agent Lanagan read him his Miranda rights. Two other agents monitored Errol, who was bleeding like an angry hemorrhoid, but very much alive. Another helped Layna to her feet.

Emmylou had vanished.

Only when Nate ran toward me and put both hands on my shoulders, leaning in to inspect the bleeding gash on my neck, did I realize I was still sitting in the trunk of Ralphie's car. I'd never seen Nate so rattled before. "You're bleeding, are you okay?" he asked. "What happened?"

"I don't know," I said, surprised to see the cascade of blood down my front. Still, when Nate offered me his hand, I climbed out. My stomach still hurt from where I'd been punched, but it no longer felt like my spleen had burst. "I think . . . I think I might actually be fine. Or mostly fine?"

"Okay, okay. Let's get you to the paramedics first. We need to get you checked out."

But I was still shocky and marveling. "Ida Hoe," I said. "That was—"

"Incredible," Nate said, sounding more like himself. "Not gonna lie. I wish I'd been the one to take that guy down. But I've never had a drag queen sack one of our Most Wanted offenders before. Never the same day twice at this job."

Joyful chaos erupted as Ida Hoe, Gucci, Zhang Xiu, and Layna rallied around me, jostling and cheering and shrieking about the blood and asking if I was all right.

"You saved me," I said.

"Pole Virgins, through thick or thin," Zhang Xiu said, slapping her ass on the word *thick*.

"Pole virgins for life," Gucci added.

"Shade, you've got some tackle," Layna said.

"I *liked* being a college linebacker," he said. "But I *love* being a drag queen."

# FIFTY

Nate recused himself from my ATF interview. So after receiving butterfly stitches and a bandage for the shallow three-inch knife gash on my neck, I confessed everything to Agent Lanagan in a little interrogation room with stacks of file boxes in one corner, jagged holes picked in the soundproofing, and a recording device bolted into a wall cubby.

Well, I confessed *almost* everything.

What did I leave out?

Finding Connor's body in my trunk.

Stashing the corpse—with Layna's help—in my kids' playhouse.

The trip to Burgdorf.

My discovery that Miranda had tased Connor.

Gucci's liver-sorbet extraction was on a need-to-know basis and in my humble opinion, the ATF didn't need to know.

In fact, it was fine with me if they never discovered why Connor disappeared.

As long as his body never turned up, I was in the clear.

So what did I tell Agent Lanagan? I stuck close to the story I'd given Nate about talking to Connor at Huckleberry's, where Connor had drunkenly confessed his plans for Day of the Rope. He must've told Ralphie and Errol what I knew and they'd been after me ever since. Ralphie and Errol said they'd chopped the finger off a woman named Baylee who lived in Valley County. I said I believed she might need help.

My kidnapping and near murder—ordered by Mrs. Carson, to be carried out by her henchmen—was of great interest to the ATF. I told Agent Lanagan I'd known Mrs. Carson since I was in high school.

She'd never liked me and—after seeing me at Bar Gernika—had come up with the deluded idea that I'd figured out she was an illegal arms dealer. Mrs. Carson, Unibrow, and the other bagman had been arrested for trespassing and attempted kidnapping as they came out of the underground capitol tunnels on Jefferson Street. (Agent Lanagan told me it was suspected Mrs. Carson had lifted capitol key cards from a member of her book club who was also chief of staff to a state senator.)

I tried to imagine talking to Miranda Carson about all this. But I couldn't. Not today. It was too awful, and surreal, and sad. But Belinda Carson being so truly terrible really did explain a lot about the historical deficits in Miranda's personality.

When Agent Lanagan asked if I'd spotted the person who'd shot Errol through the chest with a crossbow, I swore I hadn't seen a thing.

He reported that a couple of Ralphie and Errol's IDIOT brethren had set fire to the Kids' Tent. They'd been arrested. Ralphie and Errol were being charged with attempted kidnapping and countless illegal arms-trafficking crimes. Ralphie was being held in the Ada County Jail, while Errol was in the ICU at St. Luke's in critical but stable condition and flanked by armed deputies. Agent Lanagan said he didn't know for sure, but he'd bet his ski cabin in McCall at least one of the IDIOTs would turn federal witness and Day of the Rope would be successfully quashed.

Meanwhile, I was free to go. Agent Lanagan thanked me for all my help and turned off the recording device. I kind of expected him to apologize for how badly he'd botched my security detail. But he didn't. Maybe for the sake of liability and the ATF's reputation, he couldn't admit to his mistake. And I was so relieved to no longer be on the wrong side of the law that I didn't bring it up. But I felt it unspoken in the air between us when he said, "Good luck with your comedy and your titty dancing and everything."

"We don't actually call it 'titty dancing' anymore, Agent Lanagan," I said.

"Then what the hell am I supposed to call it?" But he was smiling at me in a way I interpreted as fondly.

"Just call it 'pole,'" I said.

"Will do," he said. I had my hand on the door when he called, "And Ms. Turner?"

"Yes?"

"In the future, try to keep the phones of missing federal informants from pinging at your house, how 'bout it?"

"Copy that," I said.

With the interview concluded, I fled to the women's restroom. Knees shaking, I collapsed onto the toilet in the farthest stall. I'd barely started to pee when the bathroom door swung open and two people entered.

"Did you hear about those meth heads up in Spokane?" a woman said. She had a high, breathy voice. Think Kristin Chenoweth on the tiniest sip of helium.

"No, ma'am. Spill the tea," the second replied.

"They killed some random civilian deader than disco—then broke into the crematorium to incinerate his body. Would've been the perfect crime if the dipshits hadn't triggered the alarm."

My scalp tingled with a Hercule Poirot–level flash of insight—I still didn't know how Connor had ended up full of Botox, but I suddenly knew what'd happened to his body.

# FIFTY-ONE

My kids finally asleep, I knocked on Emmylou's door, heart in my throat, bouquet of orange Gerbera daisies in one hand, baby monitor in the other. She opened it, her hair up in her cotton after-shower hair turban. The mellow sounds of Khruangbin filled the duplex (which must have been Oat Willimena's Texas influence, since Emmylou's playlist usually ranged from Linda Ronstadt to ABBA). Through the doorway to the kitchen, I spotted Oat Willimena herself, grating purple cabbage. Instead of one of her usual embroidered huipiles, she wore a Santana T-shirt.

"I'm sorry to interrupt," I began, feeling awkward.

"Oh, come in," Emmylou said, clearly not willing to stand on formality.

Before I could think twice, I threw my arms around her.

"Thank you for saving my life," I said. I'd believed she couldn't be trusted with a secret. I'd treated her like she hadn't earned the right to give me input into my life, to speak hard truths to me when no one else would. It felt humbling and good to understand how wrong I'd been.

She rubbed my back, soothing me like a magical bonus auntie. "Anytime, toots. When those guys hustled you off-stage, I went and grabbed my crossbow out of my trunk."

"You just happened to have it in there?" I asked.

Emmylou ignored my question. "Are you okay? You were bleeding so bad. It scared me."

"I only needed butterfly stitches," I said. "I'm fine."

"Your set was so funny, *mija*!" Oat Willimena called.

"Agreed!" Emmylou said. "Physical comedy, my favorite!"

I followed her into the kitchen where Oat Willimena was packing great handfuls of juicy shredded cabbage, ginger, apples, and carrots into a large ceramic crock. "Don't mind me," she said. "I'm just embarking on a little kitchen witchery. What I loved about your set was the light excavation of our cultural obsession with strippers, along with a dollop of righteous glorification."

"Thank you!" I beamed, feeling seen.

"A real shame those assholes interrupted you by setting fire to the face-painting tent," Emmylou said.

"I'm just glad no kids were hurt." I paused, apprehensive about what I needed to say next. I forced myself to ask the rather awkward question that might clear up the mystery of how Connor's body disappeared. "It wasn't a raccoon in the kiln, was it?"

Emmylou and Oat Willimena looked at each other. Oat Willimena gave a little nod, then began mashing the contents of her crock with a wooden sauerkraut tamper.

"What else did you expect us to do with the stiff in your playhouse?" Emmylou said.

I dropped into a chair, stunned my suspicions were true. If Emmylou and Oat Willimena incinerated Connor, that meant his body was ash, could never be recuperated or found, or tied to me in any way. I tried to let all that meant for me and for Miranda to sink in. No more waiting for the other shoe to drop. When I could finally speak, I said, "You two did that for me?"

But Emmylou wasn't ready to get sentimental. Instead she'd started unwrapping the clear cellophane from the stems of the Gerbera daisies. "Let me get settled," she said, "and I'll tell you all about it."

She put the flowers into a pink conical vase and poured us each a cup of tea that smelled like lavender soap. Then she began. That fateful

Tuesday, she'd been babysitting my kids when she heard a ruckus in the backyard. She'd snuck a peek out my back window to see me and Layna shoving something large into the playhouse. She'd waited until we'd left for Barbarian Brewing to investigate, knowing the fresh snow would cover her tracks.

"I wanted to help but couldn't figure out how," Emmylou said. "The kiln was Oat Willimena's ingenious idea."

"I can't believe you told Oat Willimena!" I said. "No offense to you, Oat Dub. But Emmylou barely knew you!"

Oat Willimena held up juice-stained palms. "I'd never narc. Besides, when I saw the stiff's white-power neck tattoo, I was happy to help."

My instinct was to say I'd had things under control all along, that I didn't need their help. But it wasn't true. I hadn't had anything under control. Not for a long time.

"Thank you," I said.

"Besides, it's not spilling a secret if you tell your significant other," Emmylou said. "I just put it in the couple's vault!"

"Significant other! Couple's vault! How many dates have you two even been on?" I said.

"When you're seventy-four years old and finally find someone who knows how to give you a cervical orgasm, you aren't afraid to move fast," Emmylou said.

"TMI!" I yelled, plugging my ears. "Happy for you, but don't need the details."

"Fine!" Emmylou said, pretending to zip her lips and toss the key.

"The burnt raccoon penis bone?" I asked.

"I scorched it over the gas stove burner myself," Oat Willimena said, waving her wooden tamper over an imaginary flame. "For authenticity."

"A genius criminal mind with an impressive attention to detail," Emmylou said, gazing adoringly at Oat Willimena. It was great to see her looking so happy. "Is it safe to say those guys trying to kidnap you were the stiff's colleagues?"

"Pretty much," I said. "You were amazing, by the way. What a shot!"

"Pshaw!" she said. "I couldn't even get my bow reloaded."

"Are you kidding? You literally saved me from being brutally murdered," I said.

"Well, I stashed the crossbow in my trunk, just in case there was trouble at the festival. I've been worried about you ever since I discovered the stiff." Emmylou paused. "The guy I shot. Is he . . . ?"

"Alive?" I said. "Yeah, he's alive."

Emmylou hooted with relief.

"Also, just so you know, I didn't tell the ATF I saw you."

"Thanks, toots," Emmylou said. "I bet nobody else saw me either. This gray hair is my cloak of invisibility. Now can you tell us how you ended up with a stiff in the first place?"

"It would involve incriminating friends," I said. "But he was up to the sort of thing you might imagine."

"The kind of thing Susan Sarandon shot that guy for," Oat Willimena said.

Emmylou and I looked at her blankly.

"You know, in *Thelma & Louise*," Oat Willimena said.

"Oh," I replied. "Yes. Well, not exactly. But close enough."

"That's the kind of story I like," Emmylou said. "Man gets exactly what he had coming."

I would rather get a bikini wax than have a hard conversation with a friend. But I took a deep breath and forced myself to speak. "Emmylou, I'm sorry I blew up at you," I said. "You were right. My mom wouldn't want me to give up on my dreams."

"It's okay, kiddo."

"She'd be grateful to you for looking out for me," I said, choking up at the realization it was true.

"I'm sorry if I came on too strong," Emmylou said. "Instead of making you go shake it on a pole, I should've told you it was okay to be sad. I should have asked if you'd grieved enough."

“I know you’re grieving too.” I suddenly understood it was true. And I also knew how to show Emmylou how incredibly grateful I was that she’d not only saved my life, but had also literally made the skeleton in my closet disappear forever. “Would you consider being the twins’ godmother?”

Emmylou beamed. “I’d love to, toots.”

# FIFTY-TWO

There is nothing like walking into a bar at eleven at night and seeing a gorgeous man rise to his feet because he's been watching the door, waiting for you to arrive. Nate wore jeans and a flannel, his smile warm, his dark hair a little messy. Even as I smiled at him, I could feel the paternity test in my purse, pulsing and glowing, radioactive. I still had no idea how he felt about the fact he might be my kids' bio dad.

"You look so alive," Nate said. "And great! I mean, I'm glad you're alive. And you look great."

It was good to know he was nervous too. And that he'd noticed I'd put on a date outfit—a cotton sweater and jean skirt with platform sneakers. It was so warm out my legs were bare. The bandage on my neck made me look like someone had recently tried to slit my throat, but there was nothing to be done about that. "It's good to see you. And to be alive," I said, realizing how true it was.

Once we'd jostled our way to the bar and were waiting to order, Nate swallowed hard and said, "I'm not supposed to say this, for liability reasons. But my team completely screwed the pooch today. Agent Lanagan let you . . ." He paused. "*We* let you get kidnapped. Kidnapped! Classic interagency fuckup. So many cooks in the kitchen no one can even tell who's actually an arms dealer in a chef's hat." He hung his head in a way that reminded me of Phoebe when she was stuck on a math problem.

I patted his back. "It's okay," I said. "I'm all right."

"No! Keeping you safe was our number one priority." His eyes filled with tears and his voice hitched as he said, "I wanted to be your security detail myself, but my superiors wouldn't okay it. Said I was too 'emotionally involved.' But you could've been . . ." He shuddered.

I felt bad for him, so I said, "I mean, we already know in this country a couple white guys in suits can basically get away with anything. Add fake FBI badges and their authority is hard to question."

"Thanks for being understanding," Nate said. "Still, I'm mortified."

*Hopefully you'll be as understanding if you ever find out all the illegal things I've done over the last two weeks*, I thought. But what I said was: "Sure."

"How's your neck?"

"Aside from the fact that I look like an extra in a slasher movie, it's gonna be fine," I said, though it actually hurt like hell. "I was lucky." Wanting to change the subject, I said, "But you saw my set? At least the part I got to do?"

His face lit up. "I didn't think anything could beat your stand-up for the lower elementary crowd. But your adult material is even better."

As I gave an awkward little curtsy, my phone dinged. I glanced down to see if it was Emmylou, who'd come over to my side of the duplex in case the twins woke up while I was gone. But it was only Layna. As a single mom, turning my phone off was a "never" event. But this one time I decided to take the risk.

Once we'd gotten our beers and settled in on bar stools, Nate and I clinked pint classes to celebrate the fact that Ralphie and Errol had been arrested and the ATF would be able to put the kibosh on Day of the Rope. We'd swiveled on our stools to face each other. Even though the denim of his jeans kept our skin from actually touching, I was again acutely aware of the place where our knees pressed against each other.

"You were so brave today," Nate said. The adoration in his eyes felt so good, it was literally painful. There was no way he'd look at me like that if he knew about all the lies, all the things I hadn't told him.

I shrugged.

"You know, I'm ready to take that test," he said. He moved his hand and for a moment I thought he'd put it on top of mine, but then at the last second he retracted it. He couldn't even bring himself to touch me—or even say the word "paternity."

"Maybe you'll be off the hook." I sounded salty, but I couldn't help it. I'd been on my own for so long. I couldn't let myself be an idiot, couldn't yearn for a fairy-tale happy ending.

"I don't know what *you* want," he said. "But *I* don't *want* to be off the hook. I told my sister I'm afraid I want it too much—you know, to be the twins' donor."

My breath caught. It'd been years since I'd hoped to find a worthy guy. And I never once thought my kids would have a shot at a great dad. Still, it was hard to trust this wouldn't all turn into a tangle of complications. Hard to believe I could start a real relationship on a foundation of lies. But I wanted to try. "My woo-woo friends don't believe in coincidences."

"What do they believe in?" he asked. We were so close now I could see his individual eyelashes. I couldn't let myself kiss him until we knew for sure if he was the girls' bio dad. Otherwise things felt too muddled.

"They think coincidences are actually signposts from the Universe that you're on the right track," I said. This might not be the right track at all. This could be a disaster in so many ways. But inside my chest, hope, that most dangerous of emotions, fluttered and preened and stretched its fragile wings. I pulled the paternity test from my purse and slid it to him across the bar. "I already swabbed Alice's cheek so you just have to do your swab and drop it in the mail," I said. He looked at me and nodded, eyes solemn. My heart—straining with guilt and yearning—felt ready to burst. I couldn't stay. There was too much uncertainty, too much at stake (and also the cut on my neck really did hurt like a bitch). I stood up, leaned in to kiss him on the cheek, and hurried toward the door.

It wasn't until I'd parked the Impala behind my house that I remembered to turn my phone back on. Text messages buzzed and dinged. For a second, terror that something had happened to the twins seized me, followed by the certainty Miranda was blowing up my phone about her mom. But the messages weren't from Emmylou or Miranda.

My friend Patzi, who worked at House of Intuition in West Hollywood, had texted: *Damn, girl! You did it! Headed toward viral.*

**Miley O'Riley:** T&A and great jokes! Perfection!!!!

**Layna:** That outfit I gave you looks hawt xo

As my agitated mind tried to make sense of the digital onslaught, a link Layna had sent burst open. A fifteen-second clip of me onstage at the Winter Will Never End Festival, talking about how being a mom and being a stripper both involve telling someone else not to put their hand down their pants.

The Winter Will Never End Festival had seven thousand followers on Instagram. But the video already had 75,000 likes. It took some digging to figure out Patzi had posted it on her grid. All the hot LA influencers hire Patzi to do their birth charts and tarot readings. Some of them had reposted the reel, which was what was giving it so much traction.

Another clip, of me lying on the ground doing leg lifts while joking about the genius Cookie Mueller, already had 50K likes. I was too overwhelmed to go down the rabbit hole of who had posted it and why.

On *America's Got Talent*, when a contestant performs with such undeniable genius that one of the judges hits the Golden Buzzer, the contestant always bursts into tears as the golden tickets rain down. Sometimes she collapses onto the floor of the stage, so overwhelming is the sense of finally being seen and recognized for her talents.

I'd always thought if this moment ever came, that's how it'd be for me. But instead, I had a feeling like when you're at a party and you get stuck in the bathroom. You can't unlock the door, and right when you really start to panic, the lock unlocks and the door swings open, and you step back out into your real life. That was the feeling: a profound and nearly cellular relief.

I hadn't found my audience because I'd gotten the backing of a powerful but sexually deviant comic or a fickle manager at a fancy agency. Not even because some network executive had reached down from on high and anointed me a Queen of Comedy. I'd done it because a high school pal I'd long neglected had offered me a humble slot at a dinky festival.

And, despite threats to my person and my dignity, I'd taken a risk.

# FIFTY-THREE

*Two Weeks Later*

Miranda and I sat at my kitchen table drinking hibiscus tea and eating from a big bowl of watermelon. Even though I was back at work at the Capitol Grill and busy as a cat at a laser show, I'd been easing off my cookie, chip, and coffee diet and feeling better for it. Miranda wore Tater in what I now thought of as her dog sling, the baby girl snuffling and snoozing against her chest. The twins were in the backyard giving Little Sister a tour of the playhouse, which they were interested in again now that it was warming up.

"It's insane, Tilly!" Miranda said. "Insane. I mean, I knew my mom had crazy political ideas and that she was counterfeiting D.S. & Durga. But I had no idea she was involved in arms trafficking. And the fact that she was going to have those thugs literally slit your throat. It's insane!"

I shuddered as one hand rose to touch the gash on my neck that had finally scabbed over. "Don't remind me."

"I mean, I know some people would think that outfit you were wearing was a capital offense, but still."

"Ouch!" I said. "Holy MGM!"

MGM stood for Mean Girl Miranda. She'd asked me to call her out when she reverted to her old ways.

"Oops!" she said, digging a dollar out of her purse and tossing it into the Therapy Jar, which was for me these days. Because I'd started seeing a grief counselor about losing my mom. "I mean," she continued, "can you believe my mom wanted to actually blow up the state capitol?"

I'd heard this rant a few times already, but I was committed to listening to Miranda vent for as long as she needed. She had a lot to process. When the ATF had raided Belinda Carson's property, they'd found a monster cache of explosives and firearms along with her counterfeit candle supplies. Mrs. Carson was still in police custody, her bail set at some astronomical figure. She'd been charged with illegal possession of explosives, attempted kidnapping, and plotting an attack on the capitol. D.S. & Durga was filing a civil suit for copyright infringement too.

Miranda inhaled and let out a shaky breath. "And it makes me realize how I ended up mean—because that's how my mom taught me to be. And now that I'm a mom too . . ." She trailed off. "I really realize that my mom didn't mother me the way I needed. I mean, I kind of got it before. But now I really get it. So I'm going to do that for myself."

"If anyone could totally figure out how to reparent themselves, it's you," I said.

The rooster doorbell crowed and Emmylou and Oat Willimena blew in with a flurry of hugs and red lipstick kisses and oohs and aahs over Tater and declarations that Miranda was the most natural mother they'd ever seen. Miranda perked up visibly under the floodlights of their Big Loving Maternal Energy. We all need mothering, I realized. But it would be a mistake to think we can only get that from our own actual mothers. Mothers are, by nature, flawed. Mothers are, by nature, mortal. But the world brims with loving people willing to give us a dollop of Mother Love, if only we remain open to the gifts on offer.

The rooster doorbell crowed again. This time Layna breezed in rocking waist-length sky-blue extensions and a white cowboy hat. "Attention! Attention, please! I have big news. I'm going to beauty school!"

"Really?" I asked.

Layna said she'd realized her true calling wasn't to become an investigator. Clearly she didn't have the stomach for it. (Even learning that the ATF had located Baylee in an apartment in McCall—down a pinkie finger and ready to turn federal witness against Errol and Ralphie—hadn't revived Layna's interest in detective work.) Her new goal wasn't even to become a man-eater. At least not yet. Despite her breezy affect about her divorce, she needed time to heal. To get to know herself. Her true calling, she'd decided, was to make women feel gorgeous.

"And that isn't even my biggest news!" Layna said once we were all done congratulating her. "Salma Hayek convinced me to sign up for the beginner division of a pole sport competition in Tampa!"

While Salma Hayek would be queering Beyoncé's "Jolene" in the advanced division, Layna planned to perform to "Chim Chim Cher-ee" from *Mary Poppins*. "I'll be in a sexy chimney sweep uniform," she said. She did a body roll on the edge of the kitchen doorframe to celebrate. It was equal parts awkward and cute. Layna would literally attack a gun-wielding criminal for me. And I knew I'd do the same for her.

"I really did like pole class," Miranda said wistfully.

"If you want to go to Pole Kisses with Tilly and Layna, we'll watch that adorable little nugget," Oat Willimena said.

"Ooh, yes!" Emmylou chimed in. "You'd be a dream on the pole."

Miranda's eyes lit up at the encouraging words.

"Salma Hayek is letting us into the studio an hour early tonight so Layna can film me for some funny social media reels," I said. "I have a new Vagina Monster bit I want to debut." I'd used construction paper to make a big toothy open mouth and googly eyes. The mouth would go on my crotch, the googly eyes on the soles of my feet so that when I did the Vagina Monster I'd really *look* like a monster.

"Ooh! Spicy!" Oat Willimena said.

"I have big news too," I said. "I turned in my two weeks' notice at the Capitol Grill." Jaws dropped around the room and I rushed to explain. "My new Substack, *Make It Funny*, is up to five thousand paid subscribers. Each one of those people is shelling out two bucks a month."

Miranda clapped her hand over her mouth. Layna shrieked: "Way to bury the lede!" Oat Willimena whooped, and Emmylou said, "I like that math."

"I've decided to say 'Eff you' to the comedy gatekeepers," I said. "'No manager, no gigs, no problem' is my new artistic philosophy. I'm funny as hell and I've got something to say. So watch out, world!" My old manager had been calling and emailing, but I wasn't taking those calls. Not ever again.

"Glad you figured out how to monetize the millions of views those festival videos racked up," Layna said. "What do you have, like a hundred thousand Insta followers now? It must help. I mean, your jokes will never again be going out into a void."

"On all my platforms combined, I'm up to 250K," I said. "And yes, it absolutely does help."

# FIFTY-FOUR

*Three Days Later*

There is no worse sensation than taking a step to reach for the laundry detergent and feeling your bare toes sink into a fresh pile of dog shit.

"Little Sister!" I yelled. Coming home from the Capitol Grill on my break to do a couple quick chores, I'd made the mistake of kicking off my shoes and socks at the door.

Now as I hopped around on one foot, cursing, my phone began to ring. A midday phone call had a fifty-fifty chance of being spam or the school nurse. A Los Angeles area code. Spam. Still, I was done sending every call to voicemail. I picked up.

"Hello?" I said, jumping toward the sliding glass kitchen door on my one unsullied foot.

"Lauren McClain's office calling for Tilly Turner," a young woman said in the bored tone all viciously competitive assistants in the entertainment industry employ.

I put my dookie-smeared foot down on the back porch to steady myself. "Is it April Fool's?" I said. "Tell me it's not April Fool's."

"It's still March," the bored-sounding assistant said. "Can you hold while I get Lauren on the line?"

"Okay," I managed. I hobbled to the hose, turned the water on full blast, and sprayed the bottom of my foot. Irrationally, I believed that I could not, should not, speak to one of the most legendary comedy producers in the world with dog poop between my toes.

"Hello?" a calm voice said.

"Lauren?" I said. "It's Tilly Turner."

"Are you in the shower?" she asked. "No, don't tell me. You've hiked to the base of a Montana waterfall." Thanks to the *Yellowstone* TV franchise, people in LA thought the only thing between Utah and Canada was Montana.

Suddenly I understood that if I was going to do this, I needed to be one hundred percent authentically myself at every second. I was not going to pretend to be anything but a mother of twins with a not-quite-house-trained dog living in a state that rang no Hollywood bells. "I'm in my backyard in Idaho hosing dogshit off my bare foot," I admitted.

Lauren McClain let out a belly laugh. "Did you get a puppy? When I got my labradoodle, I had the puppy blues for a goddamn year."

"How could I not have the blues when this thing has chewed up all my power cords?"

"Did you have to go to the Apple Store to replace them?" Lauren said.

"The Apple Store is a soul crusher," I said. At the exact same time she said, "The Apple Store is hell on earth."

We both laughed. There was an awkward silence while I waited to see if she'd keep chatting as if she was an old friend or if she planned to actually explain why she was calling.

"So usually I'd reach out to your manager or agent, but my assistant said she couldn't tell if you have one," Lauren said.

"I haven't had representation since my manager at Circle of Circles dropped me like a hot potato after Mickey Larynx was outed as a creep," I said.

"That tracks," Lauren McClain said. "Tilly, I've been a big fan of your work since way back."

I made a small choking sound. This was news to me.

"Seriously," she said. "I was in the audience at Westside Comedy Theater when you were trying out your set about coconut oil."

"The only vagina-friendly lube you can use to cook stir-fry," I said.

"Or to take off your eye makeup," we said at the same time and both chortled.

"After that set, I kept an eye on you," Lauren said. "This is a brutal business. The women who speak out against powerful perps can lose their careers. But so can the women who don't speak out. When I have the opportunity, I try to make things right. At least in my corner of the universe. That's why I was asking about representation."

"I don't have an agent or manager," I said. "But I do have a great entertainment attorney."

This was true, though something I hadn't thought of once in the last year. Nelson Keeling had a calm demeanor, silvery-blonde hair, and ears so pointed I'd secretly nicknamed him the King of the Elves. He somehow had not one ounce of skeeve.

"Good," Lauren McClain said. "Because I'm calling to see if you'd be interested in doing an hour-long comedy special for HBO."

My legs turned rubbery and I sank to the wet paving stones. From where I sat on the ground, my perspective was surprisingly different. A slat in the fence had come loose. Pollen dusted the pavers. Lauren McClain was still talking.

"Your set that went viral was cut short. But what I saw of it was hilarious, innovative. A really revolutionary blend of physical and intellectual comedy. And I've been loving your Insta reels. The Vagina Monster—" She actually started laughing.

Who knew the Vagina Monster would be the gift that kept on giving? Hose water poured out all around me, soaking my jeans. Above me, the bare branches of the maple tree showed its first green leaves. Beyond that, the sky was a deep impossible blue. The cold dark season was ending. Spring was almost here. California had its endless summer. But there was a good feeling to having survived the longest winter of my life.

"Hello? Tilly? Tilly? Is that something you might be interested in?"

Is Chappell Roan gonna keep on dancing at the Pink Pony Club? Yes! Yes! A thousand times, yes! "I'm interested," I managed. "Very interested. But I have terms that'll need to be discussed. I've got seven-year-old twins with expensive taste in Barbie clothes."

"Understood."

"And if we include backup pole dancers, I'd like professional strippers and I'd want them paid—lavishly. Without strippers, there would be no pole, and thus no jokes about pole. They should be compensated accordingly."

In a tone that implied her game respected my game, Lauren said, "It sounds like there will be a lot for our people to discuss."

# FIFTY-FIVE

As we stood shoulder to shoulder at my kitchen counter, Nate and I stared at the unopened envelope like a bomb squad studying a nuclear device with a countdown clock hurtling toward detonation zero.

I could imagine a future where Nate and I happily debated whether or not the twins really needed braces or a geometry tutor. But I could also imagine bitterness might spring up between us if he decided he loved the twins but not me. It was all so terrifying.

Nate spoke first. "I understand you're the parent. I just spent ten minutes looking at a *Playboy* in a doctor's office bathroom when I was eighteen. So no matter what the contents of this envelope say, if I'm ever going to be any kind of father I will have to earn it with real-life action. I know all that should go without saying, but still I want to say it. You have done a *most excellent* job growing, birthing, and raising your girls."

"Thank you," I managed, thinking he sounded a little like Bill and Ted in *Bill & Ted's Excellent Adventure.* Which didn't make it any less sweet.

"You open it," he said, his voice husky. He slid the envelope so that it sat squarely before me. I wanted him to be the girls' bio dad. I did not want him to be the girls' bio dad. An ocean roared in my head as I opened the envelope and unfolded the piece of paper inside.

LabCorp
Tilly Turner
501 W. Franklin
Boise Idaho, 83702

Paternity Test Certificate

We were requested to perform a paternity test. The following individuals were examined:

| Sample NR | Role | Name |
|---|---|---|
| HID 123946_001 | Alleged Father | Nathan Duran |
| HID123946_002 | Child | Alice Turner |

**Results:**
In all analyzed PCR systems, Nathan Duran does not show the genetic markers which have to be present for the biological father of the child Alice Turner. The biostatistical analysis of the PCR systems was performed according to the method of Essen-Möller. The probability of Nathan Duran being the biological father of Alice Turner is < 0.0000001%.

**Conclusion:**
Based on our analysis, it is practically proven that Nathan Duran is NOT the biological father of the child Alice Turner.

I couldn't bear to look at Nate. But when I finally turned to him, his face was mournful as a silent film star who's found out her true love has died on the Western Front.

A sudden fit of church giggles seized me.

Nate stared at me, baffled and hurt. Extravagant tears rolled down his cheeks.

"I'm sorry," I finally managed. "I'm laughing because . . . because I must have watched *The Parent Trap* too many times. I started thinking ridiculous coincidences could really happen and then I cooked up this . . . this whole idea." And then I wasn't just laughing. I was sobbing too. "I really wanted it."

"I guess we both did," he said, wrapping his arms around me.

I understood now. I'd wanted it so very badly I'd fabricated this whole crazy scenario. And not only because it would've given meaning to every terrible thing I'd been through, but because it would've given my girls something I'd never let myself hope they'd have. A bigger family.

Nate was rubbing small soothing circles on my back. I kept crying there, in that safe refuge. I may have even wiped my snotty nose on his T-shirt. "Be excellent to each other," I mumbled into his chest, for some stupid reason I didn't understand, except that it was always sound advice.

"Are you quoting *Bill & Ted's*?" he said.

I shrugged. "Just because you said 'most excellent.'"

"Fair, I did say that," he said. "So maybe I'll never be the kids' biological father. So what? You're right. We can still all be most excellent to each other. Have I ever told you about my stepdad?"

I shook my head into his chest.

"He raised me and Lucia from the time I was eight and she was ten. He's the best bonus dad. Not to be presumptuous. But it's possible." He pushed me away but only far enough so he could look down into my eyes. "Each one of us gets to decide who and what our family is, that's all I'm saying."

I could raise my kids on my own. I knew I could. I'd been doing a pretty damn good job of it for over seven years. But this whole fantasy I'd concocted was forcing me to confront the idea that maybe, deep down, I wanted to be open to the possibility of a worthy partner raising them with me. I pushed down my annoying worry that it might not be a great idea to start a relationship with countless lies of omission. And for one last time, I wished I knew who actually killed Connor. But it was time to accept there were some things that would always remain a mystery. It needed to be enough to know—definitively—that it hadn't been me.

"Agreed," I said. "So we can start slow and maybe date and you can hang with me and the kids sometimes and we can see where it goes."

"But it doesn't have to be *that* slow, right?" he asked, raising an eyebrow.

"Like maybe we could start slow and get faster and faster and faster?" I said.

Nate laughed. And because there is no sexier sound than a man busting up at one of my jokes, I grabbed him by the hand and pulled him toward my bedroom.

# EPILOGUE

*A Saturday in Early June*

With my first check from HBO and my steady stream of Substack cash, I finally had more than enough money to move back to LA. Instead, I'd paid off my credit cards and two of the mortgages on my mom's duplex, which felt like an amends to her. My one splurge was on an outdoor projector and speakers so we could host outdoor movie nights in our backyard.

Now the twins were begging me to help them spread blankets and set up camping chairs. Nate was pinning a sheet to the side of the shed to use as a projector screen. He looked adorable in the three-quarter-length pants he'd bought for wearing to the climbing gym, where he was taking classes with Phoebe and Alice.

As magic hour suffused the sky with a purple glow, our found family began to arrive. Oat Willimena and Emmylou appeared through Emmylou's sliding glass back door carrying giant bowls of homemade popcorn. Miranda came next, looking happy and peaceful, Tater Tot swaddled against her chest, Chauncey in tow. She was asking me for advice on signing up for classes at Pole Kisses again when Tina, the principal's assistant, blew in with her eight-year-old granddaughter and a Tupperware full of baked goodies. Miranda, Tina, and I were chomping rainbow brownies and talking baby sleep hacks (lightly stroke the baby's eyebrows, play the original *White Lotus* theme music on a loop, et cetera) when Miley O'Riley showed up with her daughter, Bam-Bam.

"Have you made your list?" Miley asked as Bam-Bam scampered off to join the other children. Miley had invited me to headline a fall festival she was putting on, and wanted me to create a lineup of up-and-coming comedians to open for me.

"I've been working on it!" I said. "Let's have a playground date tomorrow so I can show you some reels and see what you think." Then I had to run off to say hi to Principal Cruz and Maricela, who'd made a big entrance with inflatable beach balls for the twins—which I predicted Little Sister would pop within the hour.

Johnica, her mom, and both of her mom's sister wives appeared right before Layna sailed through the gate holding hands with a muscular hottie. With his tight fade and dimples he looked very, very good for his age, which I figured to be old-but-not-grandpa-old. I recognized him instantly.

"Retired astronaut Kendrick B. Johnson!" I said. "Not a catfish!"

He smiled a little warily.

"Tilly thought you were catfishing me," Layna explained. "She said you for sure were not DMing me from outer space."

"Well, she was right," he said. "I absolutely was not DMing you from outer space. I haven't been since 1998."

"That's exactly what your Wikipedia page said!" I cried.

"If I'd met you, I would've known you were teasing," Layna protested. "But how was I supposed to understand your sense of humor?" She gave Kendrick a playful swat and they beamed. It looked like Layna's time to heal was going to turn out to be a sexual healing after all.

Kendrick volunteered to help Nate set up the projector. All the Pole Kisses gang had arrived—except for Zhang Xiu—and we clustered together to share good news. Gucci had a fantastic new grad school advisor now that Professor Bidelspach had been forced to resign. Shade had been tapped to emcee Drag Night at the Balcony Club. Cheyenne held hands with Salma Hayek as she told us Cheyenne's Sentient Strippers were on back order all over the country. "That would never have happened if those clips of your comedy set hadn't gone viral," she said.

"I wouldn't've had material for my set if badass women like you hadn't developed pole into a high art for some and a very funny hobby for others," I said.

I was chatting with Layna about her first week at beauty school when Zhang Xiu came through the back gate with a slender woman in a flowered sundress. The young woman shared Zhang Xiu's straight black hair, flawless skin, and bowed upper lip.

"You must be Zhang Xiu's daughter!" I said. "Wait, is it weird when I call your mom that?"

"My mom has always needed an alter ego. She's never really seemed like an Ingrid," she said. "I'm Peony. Nice to meet you."

"Zhang Xiu! Your name is Ingrid?"

Zhang Xiu shrugged. "Spiritually? Not really. But legally? Sure is."

I hadn't forgotten what Zhang Xiu had told me that night at Barbarian Brewing, about how some degen had assaulted her daughter in the parking lot of a bar three years ago. And here was Peony, looking at ease in her strong, willowy body. It made my chest ache to think of what she must've had to overcome, of how much strength it takes sometimes just to survive.

"Zhang Xiu told us you work for . . ." I wracked my brain, trying to remember.

"Allergan Aesthetics," Peony said. Off my blank look she added, "It's a drug company."

My head clanged between cartoon cymbals. Every Los Angeleno worth her salt knows of Allergan's most famous product.

"B-Botox," I stammered. "Allergan makes Botox."

Gucci stared at me, eyes as big as manholes.

"God bless Allergan," Layna said, gesturing at her forehead. I'd eventually told her Connor had been stuffed to the gills with Botox. Still, she wasn't catching on.

"Botox is what we're known for," Peony said. "But we also manufacture Juvederm, Kybella, CoolSculpting. Everything a modern gal needs to be flawless." She said it with an ironic twinkle in her eyes.

"Isn't CoolSculpting where you use paddles to freeze someone's saddlebags off?" Layna said. "You can have mine. Just please don't freeze my juicy butt off!"

"Zhang Xiu, can you help me in the kitchen real quick?" I said. "Sorry, Peony, I'll bring her back."

Before Zhang Xiu could protest, I dragged her inside, Gucci on our heels. The kitchen was blessedly empty; still, I pulled Zhang Xiu all the way into my bedroom. Gucci shut the door behind us. But before I could speak, Layna burst in. She wasn't clueless at all. Just a better actor than I'd given her credit for.

I turned to Zhang Xiu. "It was you, wasn't it!" I asked.

Zhang looked panicked. "Tilly, what are you talking about?"

"I can't believe I didn't figure it out before," I said. "You have a dragon tattoo! I mean, you're *literally* the girl with the dragon tattoo. You got revenge against a sexual predator who more than deserved it. Only he didn't hurt you. He hurt your daughter."

All color drained from Zhang Xiu's face and her knees buckled. I helped her to my mom's old Eames chair dupe.

Zhang Xiu stared at me. "Is Connor—is he . . . all right?"

"If by 'all right,' you mean 'dead,'" I said, "then yes."

Zhang Xiu let out a strangled noise. "I just wanted him to be violently ill. For a minute. To be afraid. To suffer a little. He deserved that, at least. I didn't mean to—"

I wanted to judge her. But when I thought of my own daughters, I couldn't.

"We won't tell," Gucci said. "But I have to know how you did it."

Zhang Xiu covered her face with her hands, then brushed them back through her hair. "Like I told you, before my daughter got sober, she met this guy at a bar. The Dutch Goose. He said he wanted to walk her to her car. But instead he—" She choked up. "He'd drugged her."

"Oh, Zhang," I said, sinking down to the edge of my bed. Gucci was already cross-legged on the floor and Layna joined her there.

"She didn't call me until two days later," Zhang Xiu said, speaking as if in a trance. "The police said there was nothing they could do. She'd spent hours in the shower by then. But she knew his name. I looked him up. I'll never forget that face. That was three years ago. Tilly, the instant I saw you fighting with him in Huckleberry's, I knew. Knew it was him."

I barely dared to breathe in case it broke the spell.

"I was driving Peony's car that night, since my Kawasaki was in the shop," Zhang Xiu said. "She always has drug samples in her trunk. Swag hypodermics that say *Allergan* too. To give to doctors. While you all were having another round, I went out front. He was still out there, staggering around, holding his head, ranting about Salma hitting him with a beer bottle. I was like, 'I remember you! We had fun that night? Do you still like to party?' I could see him thinking he didn't remember me, that I was too old. But I convinced him to meet me in the alley. I grabbed Botox out of Peony's trunk, peeled off the label. I told him it was morphine and I watched him inject himself. He shot it right into the big blood-draw vein."

Miranda would be so relieved to know for sure what happened. That she truly hadn't been responsible for Connor's death. This was a secret just for Pole Virgins, but Miranda (aka Pumpkin Spice) might be joining us in classes soon enough.

"How'd you know how much to give him?" Gucci said.

"One time I was joking with Peony about Botox being a toxin. She said it'd take a couple bottles of the stuff to kill someone. She said it in passing. But I remembered. She must've been wrong, though."

"Then how'd you get away from him?" Layna said.

"I pretended I'd eaten a bad fish taco."

"Bad fish taco!" I said. "The holy grail of excuses!"

"After that night, I got so anxious," Zhang Xiu said, rubbing her hands on her thighs. "But I read the *Idaho Statesman* every day. The front page. The obituaries. There was no mention of him." She paused as if groping for a shot of denial. "I told myself he was fine."

"Yeah, not fine," Layna said.

"Like he went home and maybe slept it off," she pressed.

*An eternal sleep*, I wanted to say. Instead I gently covered her hands with my own. "I know it'd be more evolved to say that there are better ways to heal, to move forward. But if some scumbag did that to one of my daughters, I'd chop off his dick and make him eat it like a Vienna sausage."

"Amen," Layna said.

Zhang Xiu squared her shoulders. "Then at Pole Kisses, when you asked if anyone had seen anything weird out back at Huckleberry's, it made me nervous again. Real nervous. But I put everything that happened in one little box and buried it in the back of my mind." She hesitated. "I can't believe I killed him."

"You didn't," Gucci said.

Zhang Xiu, Layna, and I all looked at her as if she'd said our Salma Hayek was the real Salma Hayek's long-lost daughter.

"The corpse had near-lethal levels of botulinum toxin," Gucci said.

"Exactly!" I said.

"Near lethal!" Gucci said again. "Near lethal is not lethal. My new grad-school mentor warned me civilians never hear what the experts are saying when it comes to cause of death. And she's right!"

"Then what killed him?" Zhang Xiu asked.

"He had heroin in his system. But not lethal amounts. Then he grabbed Salma Hayek's ass, so she hit him over the head with a bottle of Dos Equis. Again, the blow wouldn't've killed him on its own. Zhang, you encouraged him to shoot up with Botox in revenge for the evil shit he did to your daughter. Which normally would've only made him very, very sick."

I interrupted, excited. "Then someone else stabbed him twice with a pair of scissors and tased him because he assaulted *her* in the alley behind Huckleberry's."

"Not one of those things would've done him in *by itself*," Gucci said. "But all together? Lethal as fuck."

"Death by a thousand counts of being an asshole!" Layna cried.

"Not an official forensic finding, but that's basically it," Gucci said.

"And by the way, Zhang," I said. "You don't have to worry about Connor's body coming back to haunt you. It's gone. Like ashes-to-ashes gone."

"Thank god," Zhang Xiu breathed. "Thank god. Thank god."

I grabbed one of Zhang Xiu's hands and one of Layna's. Gucci closed the circle.

"You promise you won't tell?" Zhang Xiu insisted.

"Pole Virgins promise," I said and Gucci and Layna echoed the same. Our entwined fingers were unbreakable as a pinkie swear. We all startled when the bedroom door swung open.

"Y'all closing out a private AA meeting in here?" Shade said.

"Jesus, Shade!" I said. "You scared us."

"Tilly, your hunka-hunka-burning-love says he can't start the movie without you. And why are y'all having a moment without me?"

We motioned for Shade to join us. For a moment the five of us stood there, holding hands. "Before we go back out there," Shade said, "I have a million-dollar question."

"Shoot," I said.

"Now that we're done being Pole Virgins," he said, "should we do the Pole Kittens series together?"

When we all stepped back outside, darkness had fallen. Smiling groups of people I loved chatted under the twinkle lights. The air was clear and not too chilly. Trees arched green and graceful overhead, sheltering us from the vast night sky.

Boise was showing off.

A strong arm slid around my shoulders. Nate smiled down at me, his eyes warm. "Do you think it's time to start *The Parent Trap*?" he asked.

"How about in five?" I said. I wanted to enjoy the moment a little longer.

Beach balls floated overhead, bouncing between the twins and their friends—Maricela, Bam-Bam, Johnica, Tina's granddaughter. Little Sister leapt and twirled in the middle of their circle, wild to catch the floating orbs. For a moment, I could hear my mother's voice in my head, kind and familiar, saying, "Now those are some very happy girls."

She would've meant Phoebe and Alice.

But she also would've meant me.

# ACKNOWLEDGMENTS

Thank you to my beloved agent, Allison Hunter, for helping me to stay open to the book that would bring the most fun and for knowing on instinct that Tilly's perfect home would be with William Morrow. You are a wonder! And special thanks to the rest of the Trellis team, especially Natalie Edwards, Alyssa Morris, and Michelle Brower.

Thank you to my brilliant editor, Danielle Dieterich, for helping me figure out the puzzle of this novel and make it the best it could be. I am so grateful for everything! Thanks to Grace Vainisi for editorial support and for being such a bright light. Special thanks to this novel's fairy godmother, the amazing Emily Krump. Your editorial feedback and matchmaking are beyond appreciated. Thanks to Liate Stehlik for making my dreams come true! Boundless thanks to the entire William Morrow team, including: David Palmer, Robin Barletta, Lindsey Kennedy, Liz Psaltis, Jen Hart, and Kaitlin Harri. Special thanks to Paul Miele-Herndon and Mira Lou for a book cover that truly captures the spirit of the novel!

Thanks to Andrea Robinson for developmental edits and for every joke in the margins. Thanks to Brittani Hilles at Lavender PR for all of your hard work and genius!

My idea for this novel (and much of my research) came from taking pole dancing classes at Ophidia Studio in Boise. Big thanks to the Ophidia community for giving me a deeper understanding of the ways pole dancing as a hobby has branched directly from the tree of stripper pole dancing. It's all pole! Thanks as well to Ascension Pole and Dance, where I dropped in for further research. And many thanks to allllllll the pole dancers who talked to me about everything from working in strip clubs to pole competitions to Pleasers.

While I read many books and essays about pole dancing, the excellent *Whorephobia: Strippers on Art, Work, and Life*, edited by the great Lizzie Borden, provided essential insights, especially the essay "Go-Going—New York & New Jersey, 1978–79" by Cookie Mueller, which informed Tilly's stand-up set.

In this novel, the ATF and their comedic missteps are entirely fictional and do not reflect the actual Boise ATF. The real-life ATF agents I've met are the total opposite of Agent Mozzarella.

Thanks to Natanya Biskar for bringing big French-era energy, and for always saying YES! to research adventures like pole dancing and snowmobile rides. Thank you to Christine Pride. You are a friend from a dream! Thank you, Rufi Thorpe, my beloved and role model. You show me how to be happy when things aren't going my way and happy when they are.

Thanks to Lou Miller, my brother-in-law, for providing vet tech expertise. For forensics expertise, I consulted Dr. Douglas P. Lyle, MD, and crime fiction author. Thank you for your generosity, Lou and Dr. Lyle!

For insights into seven-year-old identical twin girls (and dogs!), I sought guidance from Riley, Peyton, Page, Nicki, and Jameson Payne; and Nathan, Celeste, Zoe, and Emma Holbrook. Thanks to my dear Ann Outlaw for insights into being pregnant with twins!

Thanks to Brady Udall, for line edits and for being an incredible teacher, mentor, friend. Kate Udall, you are the funniest woman in Boise!

Jackie Polzin came up with the brilliant observation that "friendship begins when one person overshares and the other responds in kind." Jackie, I thank the great goddess every day that one of us took the risk and overshared.

Many thanks to the Writer-In-Residence at the Hemingway

House program for gifting me time to write in the house where Ernest Hemingway lived and died. Special thanks to Jenny Emery Davidson, Martha Williams, Nicole Zoe Lichtenberg, and Mary Tyson.

Endless thanks to: Emily Lavelle and Lauren Lavelle (so many PR pep talks!), Nicole Cullen, Bethany Maile, Molly Nota, Maya Nash, Natalie Disney, EJ Pettinger (funniest man alive!), Richard St. Ofle, Tim Griffith, Jacqui Reiko Teruya, Mitch Wieland, Tracy Firsching, Allie Gallion, Mackenzie Huffman, Sarah Bancroft, Brian Birzer, David Moorman, Daisy Rosenstock, Zach Small, Ariel Delgado Dixon (first years forever!), Kimberly Garza, Christine Kandic Torres, Elizabeth Gonzalez James, Danielle Roderick, Jennifer Romolini, Sadie Fox Curtis, Julia Claiborne Johnson, Melissa Mazmanian, Hilary Clausing, Jenny Hassibi, Kimberly Cole, Dawn Hertrich, Alisha Medlock, Joy Williams, Stephen Harrigan, Cindy Lee Johnson, Erin McReynolds, Carrie Torrisi, Morgan Pager, Steph Hockersmith, Jen Jack, Bryan Jack, and the London Writers Salon.

Many thanks to the healers. I needed you all on this journey: Lesley Jane Sullivan, Christina Sabella, Jessica Hixson, Heather Dunnam, Carolyn Pennypacker Riggs, Beth Pickens, Dr. Gary Arthur, Dr. Raheem Mahbubbi, Pieter Kroon, Swapnali Chaudhary, Brian Carroll 1306, Deacon Millett and Ted, Leah and Bruce Kalish, Dr. Michele Gerard, and Rachel Mooers.

Thanks to the librarians and booksellers. Every day you radiate the light we need in this world. I owe a special debt of gratitude to the bookstagrammers who have helped promote my work and who give so much time and energy to lift up authors and books.

Thanks to my incredibly talented media rights team, Jason Richman and Addison Duffy at UTA. Thanks to Peter Sample, the best entertainment attorney in the land. Thanks to Kerry Kletter, for unexpected generosity.

To my ancestors, spirits, and guides, especially Grandmommy, Ralph Millett Senior, Mimi, Aunt Lynne, DJ (Doce Pasos forever!), and Venus. Thank you, Eric, for late night Raisin Bran etc. I know you'd be pleased.

Special thanks to my wonderful dad, Pete Lowry, who always rooted for my writing and encouraged my wildest endeavors. Thanks to my mom, Candy Becker, who showed me what dedication to creativity looks like.

Thanks to my wonderful family: Marymom, my amazing in-laws, my bonus siblings and brothers-in-law, Aunt Chica, Uncle Jack and Aunt Staley, magical cousins, nephews, and nieces. Thanks especially to my sister, Margaret, who listens every damn day! You are my life raft.

Most of all, thanks to George. Thank you for being there for every good writing day and every bad writing day and for all the fun. Every day I get to spend with you is the best day.

And to every single reader: I am doing a dance of gratitude and joy! I hope this novel made you laugh. I hope it was a salve that eased your pain and made your sky a little bluer. My appreciation for you is infinite.